THE WAY OF THE
BRAVE

Books by Susan May Warren

MONTANA RESCUE

Wild Montana Skies

Rescue Me

A Matter of Trust

Troubled Waters

Storm Front

Wait for Me

GLOBAL SEARCH AND RESCUE

The Way of the Brave

THE WAY OF THE
BRAVE

SUSAN MAY WARREN

Revell

a division of Baker Publishing Group
Grand Rapids, Michigan

© 2020 by Susan May Warren

Published by Revell
a division of Baker Publishing Group
PO Box 6287, Grand Rapids, MI 49516-6287
www.revellbooks.com

Printed in the United States of America

Library of Congress Cataloging-in-Publication Data
Names: Warren, Susan May, 1966– author.
Title: The way of the brave / Susan May Warren.
Description: Grand Rapids, MI : Revell, [2019] | Series: Global Search and Rescue ; 1
Identifiers: LCCN 2019014910 | ISBN 9780800735845 (pbk.)
Subjects: | GSAFD: Suspense fiction.
Classification: LCC PS3623.A865 W39 2019 | DDC 813/.6—dc23
LC record available at https://lccn.loc.gov/2019014910

20 21 22 23 24 25 26   7 6 5 4 3 2 1

It is not the mountain we conquer, but ourselves.

Edmund Hillary, who together with Sherpa Tenzing
Norgay, was first to climb to the summit of Mount
Everest, the tallest mountain in the world

CHAPTER ONE

HE SHOULD HAVE never left Alaska.

Sure, in Alaska Orion woke to his breath in a hover of mist over his face, his fireplace having simmered to a low flame, the room lit in gray, the sun denting the eternal night. But he belonged in all that cold and darkness, under the shadow of unforgiving Denali, buried under a numbing layer of ice and snow.

There, his anger couldn't break through, couldn't ignite with the injustice of the daily news.

Couldn't consume him with helplessness.

It was better to be cold.

The vast aloneness of Alaska allowed him to breathe, despite the stinging cold in his lungs. Allowed him to scream without anyone knowing.

"I hate New York City," Orion muttered now, just below his breath, but loud enough for Ham to hear as they boarded the 4 train.

"You just need coffee," Ham said.

"Vats of it." Orion tried to ignore the man who knocked into him, bumping him into the subway pole.

Orion wanted to blame his dark mood on the ache in his bum

7

knee, the fact that his body should still be sleeping, the static in his brain evidence of his jet lag. Maybe he should attribute his general sour attitude about humanity at large on the fact that his buddy Ham had insisted they route through Memorial Park to spend a few moments staring into the acre-wide footprint of the North Tower.

Orion had fisted his hands into his canvas jacket, the wind bullying him, the sun glaring off the glass of One World Trade Center, and watched as the waterfalls stirred up a mist into the brisk April air.

He couldn't escape the thud in his chest.

The start of the War on Terror, right here—a war that still hadn't been won, despite the casualties, the sacrifices, the personal losses.

All of it put Orion into a humdinger of a stormy mood.

Then he spotted the punk kid with the look of a thug slide through the closing doors of the subway car.

He didn't know why, but all the hackles rose on the back of his neck.

White, midtwenties, rail thin, the young man wore a grimy Knicks jersey, a pair of ripped jeans, and the fuzz of a few nights on his chin. He radiated an odor that suggested a night or two spent in the same clothing.

Maybe the guy was homeless—Orion shouldn't be so quick to judge. Clearly he'd watched one too many episodes of *Law & Order* during his months in rehab. Orion had probably looked the same way when he arrived at LaGuardia, freshly out of hibernation at his homestead under the loom of Denali.

Orion dismissed the kid and hung on to the bar overhead as the train pulled away from Fulton station. "We could have walked to Foley Square," he muttered to Ham, who leaned his shoulder against the pole, clearly used to the jerk and roll of the New York metro.

Ham's gaze was tracking Knicks as he moved halfway down the car.

So Orion wasn't the only one whose instincts fired.

"You're limping," Ham said, not looking at him. He sounded as grumpy as Orion. "And we're late. The rally has already started."

"I'm not an invalid. My knee just doesn't like eight hours on a plane." He watched as the guy nudged up behind what looked like a college student—brown hair, fuzz on his chin, clean-cut, a black backpack with a purple NYU logo on the flap hanging over his shoulder. "I hope White has answers."

"If anyone can track down Royal, it's Senator White. He's on the Armed Services Committee."

Orion glanced away, toward the other side of the car. A couple women sat with their bags clutched on their laps. Another woman stood, her bag over her shoulder, scrolling through her phone. A man in a suit coat holding a satchel was reading the paper folded in half in his grip.

Behind them a young man wearing a black hoodie, earbuds affixed, bobbed his head to music. He caught Orion's eye, then looked away.

"You should have told me that you went to rescue Royal and Thorne," Orion said, looking at Ham.

Ham met him with a frown. "It wasn't my information to give."

Orion's mouth tightened. "I wasn't thrilled when Logan Thorne landed on my doorstep last summer, very alive and packing a conspiracy theory."

Ham turned to face him, as if ready to share answers as to why a former Navy SEAL who'd been taken by the Taliban in Afghanistan some three years ago had appeared alive, although shot, and in the backwoods of Alaska. Thorne surfaced with stories of an off-the-books rescue mission, a CIA cover-up, and the desperate fear that someone was still out to get him.

Thorne's story sat in Orion's gut and chewed at him until, some five months later, he finally contacted former SEAL Hamilton Jones.

Ham invited him to NYC to tell his story to Senator Isaac White, who served on the Senate Armed Services Committee and had ties to the CIA. If anyone could find Royal, it was the people who'd been behind his disappearance. Besides, they owed Orion answers about a number of things. So yes, he'd emerged from the woods for a face to face with White.

Ham had been bugging him anyway to join his private international SAR team, Jones, Inc.

Hello, *no*. The last thing Orion wanted was to dive back into the world of spec ops and medical tragedies. He'd barely survived the last go-round.

Had left behind buddies, pieces of himself, and a broken heart.

"Listen, that rescue mission blew up in everyone's faces and got a good man killed, so no, my first thought wasn't to call you," Ham said. "Besides, if I remember correctly, you were still in Germany—"

"Knock it off."

The sharp voice turned both Ham and Orion. Knicks had jostled NYU enough to get a rise out of the college kid. "Step back."

Knicks, however, came up on him, gave the student a push. "What? You got a problem with me?"

Ham stiffened.

NYU moved away, hands up. "I don't want any trouble."

What he said. Orion's jaw tightened. *Please don't let the kid be armed.*

The car swayed as it screamed through the tunnels. Orion glanced at the next stop on the map above the door—Brooklyn Bridge–City Hall station, still three minutes away.

A couple people pulled out their phones.

A ripple of fear silenced the subway as Knicks took another step toward NYU. Then he got in his face with a string of expletives that even Orion hadn't heard before. And he'd been to spec ops boot camp, a special kind of H-E-double-hockey-sticks.

Yikes.

Orion's code of honor made him glance, almost in apology, at the women standing in the back of the car and—wait, *what?*

Knicks and the man in the hoodie might be working in tandem because hoodie slipped past one of the women with what looked like her wallet disappearing into his front pocket.

Aw, shoot. The last thing Orion wanted was to get tangled up in other people's trouble.

On the other side of the car, the altercation erupted. Knicks cornered the pale, yet angry NYU student, who was trying to bump past him.

When Knicks shoved the kid against the door, Ham moved.

Orion should have expected it. Ham wasn't the sit-around type—even when they were serving at their base in Asadabad, Ham got to know the locals, as well as everyone on base. The man was the base party coordinator—he'd fashioned a basketball hoop and nailed it to a pole, even dragged in music.

He'd also started a prayer meeting, but that was Ham, the rescuer of lost souls.

Probably why the man wouldn't stop hounding Orion about leaving the woods and joining the living.

No, thank you. Mostly because Orion had nothing left to give, the rescuer inside him all tapped out.

11

Truth was, he just wanted to mind his own business.

Not with Ham around. The former SEAL took four steps and didn't break stride as he slammed into Knicks. At six foot three, Ham could be imposing when he wanted to, and part of the PR for his small empire of GoSports gyms meant a regular workout.

Knicks hadn't a prayer.

In a second, Ham had his arm around Knicks's neck, pressing into his carotid artery and jugular vein, cutting off the air.

G'night, pal.

Knicks clawed at Ham's arm, stumbled back, and Ham brought him down gently, letting him go when the man slumped into unconsciousness.

For a second, no one moved.

Then, clapping erupted through the car, even as Ham stood up and put a foot on the man's chest. "Stay down," he said, not raising his voice as the kid rose to consciousness.

The train started to slow.

Orion glanced at Hoodie. He'd moved toward the door, his head down. The only one, it seemed, not watching the debacle at the front of the train.

Aw, shoot.

Because Orion really didn't come here to make trouble, find trouble, or even insert himself into the middle of trouble.

And yet . . .

He couldn't live with himself. No way Hoodie was getting away.

Orion stepped up in front of him, blocking the door as the train pulled into the station.

Hoodie looked up. Dark eyes, a hint of dark whiskers, and his eyes narrowed.

"Give it up," Orion said and held out his hand.

Hoodie frowned.

"The wallet." He didn't take his eyes off the man. "You're not getting off without returning it."

"Get out of my way," Hoodie said as the car rolled to a stop. The doors opened.

Sure, Orion could have moved. Could have given in to the life mantra that he'd embraced with two hands, clutching it to his chest after the tragedy in Afghanistan—it wasn't his problem.

But he was tired of evil winning, or at least winning the battle, and maybe God had put him right here to save one hardworking woman from having to spend the day fighting identity theft.

Not that he actually believed God intervened anymore, but apparently Ham still did, so— "I don't think so, buddy."

Hoodie tried to move around him, but Orion grabbed his shirt and slammed him back against the pole. Glanced at the woman from whom Hoodie had lifted the wallet. "Check your bag, ma'am."

She stared at Orion in horror, then searched her bag.

Hoodie grabbed his wrist, but Orion jerked his hand, turning it, and in a second, he had the thief turned around in a submission hold.

"It's gone."

Yep. He knew it. "Give it up and I'll let you go," Orion said to Hoodie.

"Ry, what's happening?" Ham came over, dragging Knicks by the shirt.

"Meet the dynamic duo," Orion said. "The old sleight-of-hand trick."

Hoodie was struggling, swearing, kicking out at Orion.

Sheesh, he didn't have time for this. With everything inside him, he just wanted to put the guy on the floor, put his knee in his back.

Okay, and maybe school the jerk about old-fashioned right and wrong.

But he was trying not to be that guy, despite the stir of anger in his chest, so Orion reached around him and grabbed the wallet from the pouch in his sweatshirt.

He released his hold just enough for Hoodie to turn.

The kid slammed his foot into Orion's knee.

Pain spiked up his leg as his leg buckled.

Just like that, Orion landed on the deck, his hand gripping the wallet. Hoodie took off running.

Orion bit back a word.

Knicks shouted, and Ham must have let him go because he nearly stepped on Orion in his scramble away from the car.

"Are you okay?" The woman knelt next to him. He felt like a fool, trying to gulp back a whimper.

But, holy cannoli, he wanted to let out a scream. "Yeah," he said, his voice strangled. He handed her the wallet.

"You're a hero," she said. "Thank you."

He wanted to respond, to shrug her words away, but it was all he could do to catch his breath.

Ham was helping him up, and heaven help him, Orion let him do it, trying desperately to fix a smile on his face.

"No problem," he finally managed. His voice sounded like a fist had closed around his lungs, and it felt like it, too, as he limped out, the doors closing behind him.

He leaned against the wall.

Ham stood behind him. "Well, that was fun."

"I need that coffee," Orion said. He ground his teeth, pushing up, finding his balance.

Ham hesitated. "Or, maybe you need one more second?"

Orion sucked in a breath. "I thought you said we were late." He limped out, trying not to wince and failing.

They took the escalator up to freedom—not a hint of Knicks

and Hoodie. He did see their victim, NYU, however. The kid's pack hung over his shoulder, his head down as he all but fled the station.

Poor kid. It never felt good to have to be rescued. Humiliating, really.

Orion worked out the pain in his knee as he climbed the stairs to Centre Street into the heart of New York's court district. Protesters stood on the steps of the New York State Supreme Court building. The scent of hot dogs and gyros seasoned the air, and his gut growled. "I'm stopping in the Starbucks," he said to Ham. "I'll meet you at the rally."

Orion glanced over to the plaza crammed with spectators. From a distance he could see White standing on a platform, half hidden by campaign signs. Orion knew the man by reputation only—apparently, Ham had served with him during his early days as a SEAL. Conservative, not easily ruffled, the man was rising quickly out of the stew of political contenders.

He didn't care what stump speech Senator White delivered—if he got on to the presidential ballot, Orion would vote for him.

"Text me. I'll find you," Ham said and headed toward the crowd.

Orion crossed the street and entered the Starbucks, painfully aware that his knee burned deep with every step. As he stood in line, he eased the weight off it. It had started to swell.

Next time he had the bright idea to get on a plane, he needed a good bang over the head. A reminder of the fact that his family had set down roots and stayed in Alaska for a reason. He didn't know why the need to find Royal ground a hole through him, but he couldn't pry it out of his mind. Answers—that's all he needed, maybe. Answers to the question of how he and his other Pararescue Jumpers—PJs—had been ambushed on that mountain, in the back hills of Afghanistan. And not just the cosmic, survivor's-guilt kind of questions, but the specific one—namely who in the CIA had pulled the trigger, armed with lousy intel that had sent two SEALS and two PJs to their graves.

Left two to be captured and tortured by the Taliban.

That question burned him awake in the long nights of the Alaskan winter, fueled an anger that he couldn't seem to douse.

Maybe if he could find Royal, bring him home . . .

Orion ordered a venti Americano and by the time he stepped back out into the brisk air, he felt almost human, the caffeine sloughing off the adrenaline, along with the dark edge of frustration. Across the street at the rally, a band played—a country music group that roused something home-grown and patriotic inside him. And from deep in the well of his memory stirred a voice, soft, light. *"How do I live without you? I want to know . . ."*

A simple song sung by the girl he couldn't forget on a base deep in the Kunar province. For a dangerous second, he let the memory light the darkness inside and stepped out onto the street.

Honking jerked him back. A taxi nearly sideswiped him.

Yeah, he hated the city.

The taxi driver flipped him off.

And people, really.

Orion waited until the light changed, then crossed over into the concrete park, searching for Ham. The crowd was still packed, the supporters not quite ready to give up the day, and Orion stood at the edge, scanning the crowd. His gaze landed on a familiar backpack—NYU. The college student he'd seen on the subway stood next to an abstract black granite sculpture. As Orion watched, NYU took off his pack and sat on the edge of the circular fountain, wearing a stripped, pale expression, a line of sweat streaking down his cheek.

The kid might be going into shock. The former trauma medic in Orion gave him a nudge.

Fine. He took a sip of his coffee and ambled over to the kid.

NYU abruptly got up, drew in a breath, and walked away.

Clearly, the kid was rattled because he'd left his backpack behind. Orion limped up to it and lifted it. "Hey, kid! NYU! You forgot your backpack."

The student turned, glanced back, eyes wide. Stopped.

Orion tossed it toward him.

NYU's mouth opened, and he grabbed the pack, clutching it to himself. If possible, his face had gone even paler. "Thanks," he shouted.

Orion had the strangest urge to follow him, put his hand on his shoulder, make him sit down, breathe.

He knew what it felt like to barely escape with your life, and sure, the kid hadn't exactly been in mortal danger on the subway, but maybe his heartbeat hadn't figured that out yet.

Poor kid should take the day off. Go back to his dorm.

Hide in Alaska . . .

As if reading his mind, NYU turned, walking away fast.

Orion let him go.

Turned back to the crowd.

His phone vibrated in his pocket and he pulled it out. Ham.

Meet me behind the stage, at the tour bus.

Orion texted back and moved around the crowd, working his way toward the large bus with Isaac White's handsome mug plastered along the side.

Ham stood, hot cocoa in hand, talking with a couple security guys in suits who guarded a roped-off area. Wind raked his dark blond hair, lifted the collar of his leather jacket. He blew on his cocoa and nodded toward Orion when he spotted him.

One of the security guys walked over and let him in. Shook his hand. "Ham says you had a little scuffle on the subway."

Orion shrugged. "No big deal. A couple thugs. We didn't save the world or anything."

The man laughed and Orion smiled as he walked over to Ham. Okay, it felt good to pull out the old warrior, dust him off. *"You're a hero."*

Not really. Not anymore.

The tour bus door opened, and a man walked down the stairs.

Orion had watched a few news clips of Isaac White but hadn't expected the immediate charisma that radiated off the former SEAL. Graying hair, blue eyes, he took Orion's outstretched hand with a two-handed grip. The man possessed the kind of smile that made Orion feel like he was in the presence of a movie star.

George Clooney, maybe.

"Senator," Orion said, wishing he'd cleaned up a little better than his canvas jacket and a pair of jeans.

"Ham said you needed my assistance." White angled Orion over to where Ham stood.

Orion's mouth went weirdly dry. His anger had suddenly abandoned him in the face of White's seeming willingness to help.

Ham must have seen his stripped expression. "We're looking for a teammate who went missing in the debacle in Afghanistan," he said. "Operator Royal Benjamin. He was one of the two SEALS captured in the attack. And one of the two—"

"Who were rescued in your rogue op." White looked at Ham. "I know."

"Then you know that something isn't right," Orion said, finally finding his voice, a little more oomph in it than he probably needed. But the anger was returning. "The other SEAL, Logan Thorne, showed up on my doorstep last summer. He told me a story about the CIA trying to cover up what happened in Afghanistan—and, trying to kill him."

White held up his hand, lowered his voice. "Not here, not now—"

Orion's mouth closed, and the heat stirred in his chest. He should have known—

"Mistakes were made, for sure," White said. "And the CIA knows it. But before you start throwing accusations around, let me do some digging."

"C'mon, Senator—"

Ham shot Orion a shut-up look, but White talked over him.

"I'm not sure where your friend is, or if he's even alive, but if you want me to find out, I'll need some time." He clamped a hand on Orion's shoulder. "And patience."

Orion wanted to believe him and his smile, but—

"Sir, we need you to come with us right now." One of the security agents stepped into the conversation. "There's been a bomb found in the square." He pushed White away from them, toward a waiting SUV. Ham jogged after him, Orion limping quickly behind them.

He caught up to the second agent. "What kind of bomb?"

The agent looked at him. "I don't know. We found a backpack near the fountain. The bomb squad is on their way, and the police are evacuating the square. It could be the same kind of bomb that took out the San Antonio rodeo arena a couple weeks ago."

San Antonio arena? Orion hadn't a clue what he might be referring to.

That's what he got for living off the grid.

Still, a fist had grabbed his gut, squeezed. "What kind of backpack?"

The man flashed his cell phone toward him.

Black, with a purple NYU stitched on the back pocket.

Orion slowed, stopped, watching as the agent climbed into the front seat.

Ham hung back and joined Orion.

"What?"

"That kid with the backpack."

"Seriously?"

Orion finished his coffee and tossed the cup into a nearby trash can. "I'm going back to Alaska where I can stay out of trouble."

■ ■ ■

The secret to not dying was simple.

Don't look down.

Shouts from sixty feet below bounced against the domed ceiling of the GoSports indoor ice climbing complex. Jenny Calhoun blocked them out and released a long, slow breath.

Relax. Assess.

Tensing up on a climb only led to mistakes. Which led to crashes.

On a mountain, that could mean landing in a crevasse or at the base of an icefall—or worse, buried under an avalanche of snow.

She hung ten feet from the top, with two more quick clips ahead of her, but the hardest move still loomed above her—the overhang.

This didn't have to be hard. She could almost hear North, her instructor, in her head as she tightened her grip on her ice axes. *"It's called a figure four. Swing your right leg over your right arm. Use that to leverage yourself up and land a new left-hand hold."*

She ticked off the move in her head, seeing her next move, the one that would position her under the overhang. *"Wind your right leg over your left arm. Release your right hand. Now you can move your axe under the overhang, wedging it against the face of the wall."*

She could then use the handle of the axe like a lever to help her push herself over the hanging ledge.

Sweat dripped down her back despite the twenty-eight-degree air. The climbing wall was essentially a vertical skating rink with multiple grades and a plywood-grafted overhang, along with a few man-made holds.

The route setter had created a grade-six climb for tonight's amateur competition.

She released her left hand and shook out the lactic acid pooling in her forearm. Her entire body shook, and her grip had nearly slipped on the last set, despite the golf gloves she wore. But Aria and Sasha stood below, next to her belayer, and she'd let her mouth make promises she prayed her body could keep.

If she expected them to trust her to lead them up Denali in a little over two months, then she needed to nail tonight's ice-climbing event.

She gripped the handle, took a breath, and leveraged herself up, slamming her axe in hard to the blue ice. Then, she unwound herself from her right-hand hold in one swift ballet move, wrapping her right leg over her left arm, just like she'd practiced.

Leaning back, she drove her left crampon into the icy wall and kept her heel down as she set her undercling.

"Nice move, Jen!"

She didn't know who'd shouted from the crowd below—maybe North, watching her apply his lessons. She liked the former SEAL, one of the many former military guys who helped run GoSports.

She eyed the next hold, a man-made jug four feet from her position.

To her right.

Which meant she had to bring her left axe next to her right.

"C'mon, Jen! Make it happen!"

Aria, her best friend and roomie.

Boston played on the speakers—"More Than a Feeling"—but she tuned it out, unwound herself, set her right foot, and unhinged her left-hand grip. She set the left in an undercling beside the right.

It freed her right hand as her feet scrambled to a better hold.

She took a breath and pushed hard, scrambling up the underside of the overhang and lunging for the jug with her right axe.

The axe embedded in the dry hold and she hung one-handed, swinging in the air, the left having unlatched with the move.

Don't stop moving. Because slowing down meant the burn could catch up.

And the goal was always to keep ahead of the pain.

She swung her left hand over the plywood overhang and stuck the axe into another man-made jug. Swinging free, and with sheer arm strength, she lunged for purchase up the face of the sheer wall crusting the upper layer of the platform.

The crowd screamed, sixty feet below.

Hanging from one arm, she tucked her left axe over her shoulder, pitched a foot into the overhang, and reached for her rope to quick-clip it into the belay biner.

One pitch left.

She glanced at the clock. Forty-five seconds.

But this was it—the final hold always eluded her. Just out of her arm-stretch to the right, the hold was artificial, a thick dry tool hold she could never quite set.

And it was a one-shot deal, because the minute she swung, the leverage on her left axe would twist, unlatch.

Every. Single. Time.

She dreamed about this move, sweating into her sheets in her tiny one-bedroom apartment in Minneapolis. Analyzed it over lunch breaks and sessions in her office at Ascend Therapy and Wellness.

Watched Skeet McKenna and North—both lead climbers at GoSports—land the move over and over.

And she'd come up with a plan. The trifecta of climbing: Leverage. Technique. Guts.

Now, she added the left axe to her hold, twisted her hand into a backhand position, her fist upside down. Then she wrapped her left leg around the hold.

This went wrong, and she just might rip her arm from its socket. Or, she'd land it.

Relax.

Please.

She released her right axe. Took a breath.

She pushed with her legs, arm and core, practicallly flying through the air toward the hold.

She landed her axe hard into the resin of the dry hold.

She cut her feet loose from the ice and hung free, swinging for a second before she slammed them back into the ice. Sticking her left axe in her mouth, she gripped the other with both hands.

Her body simmered, the adrenaline shunting the trembling in her core. But she spidered up the wall, grabbed her rope, and quick-clipped it into the final biner, three feet higher.

Her feet were already slipping.

But it didn't matter. She grabbed her axe from her mouth and swung it hard over the top of the overhang. Ice shards chipped and fell into her face, bouncing off her helmet as she dangled from the final hold.

She freed her right axe, joined it with the other, then scrambled to the top.

The buzzer sounded and finally, finally, she looked down.

Seventy feet to the crowd at the bottom—Aria, Sasha, Skeet, and North, not to mention twenty or so other competitors and fellow ice climbers.

Inside, she was fist-pumping. She wasn't going to fall. Wasn't going to crash hard and find herself in rubble at the bottom of some icy wall.

Wasn't going to let the mountain win.

Aria was losing it, her dark hair streaming out of her climbing helmet as she waved. Next to her, Sasha was shaking her head, wearing a grin, the sleek entrepreneur redhead probably evaluating her own climbing techniques.

Don't worry, Sash. I won't let you die.

Frankly, this moment was for all three of them. Because if Jenny hoped to summit Denali and get them back down, they needed to trust her.

And she needed to trust herself.

She glanced at Skeet, holding her on belay, and he gave her a nod, so she hooked her axes over her shoulder and sprung out from the wall.

For a second, she flew, no wings needed. Just her and her future. Just freedom.

Then the belay caught and Skeet lowered her down.

She hit the padding, her legs shaking, and braced herself against the wall.

Aria ran up and flung her arms around her neck. "You beat North's best time."

She glanced at the man, who was tall, rangy, and dark. He'd served in special forces with the owner of GoSports, Hamilton Jones—something she tried hard to forget. She didn't know what drew her, out of all the climbing shops in Minneapolis, to Jones's outfit. Self-punishment, maybe. But neither North nor Ham had recognized her—and why should they? She'd changed her entire life since those days in Afghanistan. Kept moving forward.

North high-fived her before helping unlatch her rope system.

She unhooked her toe clamps, grabbed them up, and fielded the fist bumps as she headed toward the locker rooms.

Outside the cold room, the regular climbing walls were quiet tonight, but in the weight room next door, a number of athletes worked off their daily stress.

Sasha caught up to her. "Lucas texted and he wants to meet us for late-night appies at Sammy's in St. Paul. You in?"

Sasha's husband was still trying to make peace with his wife's climbing hobby. Probably wanted to grill Jenny again on the specifics and precautions for their upcoming trip. "Sammy's? The hockey place?" Jenny asked.

"Apparently, they have amazing wings," Sasha said.

She headed into the locker room, Sasha and then Aria on her tail. The steam hit her cold bones with a sharp bite.

"Not everyone can sleep until ten, Sash," she said, peeling off her gloves.

Sasha unhooked her helmet. "I am up before six and you know it. Just because I run my own business doesn't mean I get to set my own schedule."

"Yeah, and she can't write off her gym membership as work-related," Aria said, opening her locker.

"Exercise is part of a healthy heart and mind," Jenny said, stripping off her workout shirt, soggy with sweat. "And I need to at least test my theories before recommending them to clients."

"And dragging your friends out for life-threatening adventures," Sasha said, grabbing a towel. "Lucas still hasn't signed off on our girls' weekend."

"It's more like a girls' *month*," Aria said. "I'm not sure I can leave my practice that long. What if I get an emergency call? It's not like I can call in a chopper and get a ride off the Wickersham Wall."

Jenny also grabbed her towel, slammed her locker. "I see you've been reading your homework."

"You might consider assigning a novel where everyone *lives* at the end if you hope to recruit people on your epic, life-changing adventures," Sasha said as she followed them into the private shower area. "I'm just glad we're not climbing Everest."

"Everyone is going to live," Jenny said. "I'm going to take you to the top of the world. And, I plan to be up and back down in under three weeks, so you can tell Lucas—and your nursing staff, Aria—to take a breath. It'll be life-changing, I promise."

She showered, then thirty minutes later, her blonde hair tied back into a braid and still drying, she followed Aria and Sasha into the brisk April Minnesota air. Overhead, the stars were sprinkled against a dark velvet sky.

It didn't have a prayer of competing with the skyscape when you stood on top of the world. Where everywhere you looked, jagged, snow-capped mountains fell under your feet, where the heavens felt so close you could reach out to touch them.

Gannett Peak, Mount Hood, the fourteeners in Colorado—she was slowly chipping away at her peak-bagging list. But Denali had been calling her name since . . .

She drew in a breath. This wasn't about Orion Starr.

Wasn't about the terrible mistakes she'd made.

Wasn't about the man she nearly killed.

At least not entirely.

"Meet you there!" she shouted to Sasha as the woman climbed into her BMW X2. She and Aria slid into her Renegade.

"Lucas is worried," Aria said, dragging up her phone. "I saw him at the hospital, and he wanted to know who our guide is going to be."

"Besides me?" Jenny said, pulling out of the lot. The GoSports complex was lit up like a beacon. Open 24-7 year-round, the franchise had exploded, with GoSports centers around the nation. She'd even seen a Super Bowl ad a couple months ago.

Hamilton Jones, SEAL to the core, landing on his feet.

Some of them hadn't gotten up quite so fast.

Some were still trying to find their feet.

No, no, she refused to let Orion haunt her.

Especially since she seriously doubted that he gave one remnant thought to her.

Street lights splashed pools of brilliance on the dark pavement as she merged onto the highway.

"No, really, Jenny. You're good, but Denali?"

Jenny looked over at her. "Fear not. I found a professional Denali guide."

Aria raised an eyebrow. "Wait—you didn't hire that Starr guy, did you? That PJ you had the wicked crush on in Afghanistan? Still have a crush on? Because it's about time—"

"No." And she tried not to bite her words off, but hello, Aria should know better.

And it wasn't just a crush. At least, for her.

Stop.

"The last person I'd hire to guide us up the mountain is Orion Starr. First—I'm not even sure . . . well, he nearly had his leg blown off, so my guess is he isn't climbing. But even more, the last person he'd want to see is me."

Aria frowned.

Jenny glanced at her, cocked an eyebrow.

"But it wasn't your fault—"

Jenny cut her off again, this time with a tight shake of her head.

"Fine," Aria said. "But for the record, I'm not the only one who needs counseling. What is that adage—physician, heal thyself?"

"I don't need healing. I wasn't hurt." Wasn't killed. Didn't have her life destroyed because of a bad decision.

No, those were men like Orion, and Ham. And four SEALS and two PJs, especially Royal Benjamin and Logan Thorne, the two men left behind.

Tortured.

"No. That's right. Don't look back. Or down. Just keep moving forward." Aria drew in a breath. "That isn't going to work forever, sis."

They weren't exactly biological sisters, but what they had felt like it, so Jenny let her words pass without comment.

Because her method worked, thank you. Keep moving. Stay ahead of the thundering roar of guilt.

She didn't have to let the past find her, pull her down. Make her crash and burn.

And this year, when the anniversary of the worst mistake of her life rolled around, she planned to be 20,310 feet above the earth.

They drove in silence until they pulled into the parking lot next to Sammy's. She liked the place. Located on University in St. Paul, just a few blocks from the Xcel Center, the pub and grill had once been a shipping warehouse, now turned vintage sports bar with wooden floors and brick walls. It hosted the largest collection of Minnesota Blue Ox memorabilia in Minneapolis—courtesy of the two owners, a former defenseman named Sammy, and his recent partner, former enforcer and assistant coach Jace J-Hammer Jackobsen.

Signed pictures, goalie equipment, and framed team jerseys decorated the walls amidst flat screens tucked over the bar and into every cranny of the joint.

The place smelled of the tangy, legendary BBQ sauce, peanut-oil French fries, and craft beer. She noticed one flat screen played the news, the others reran games on mute.

And, to her dismay, at a mic at the front a woman was singing—really? Karaoke?

Jenny shot a look at Aria, who grinned and grabbed her arm, dragging her behind Sasha.

Sasha's physician husband slid out of a booth and met his wife. The man looked more like a mercenary than a trauma doc, but he'd been a Navy surgeon, so maybe that's where he got his demeanor. He had brown hair with threads of gold and a thin beard, and he wore a black pullover, pushed up to reveal strong forearms as he pulled his wife into his arms.

For a second the Navy bio flickered and took hold of Jenny. He knew about her past, of course, but did Lucas know about her connection to Hamilton?

No. How could he? She was simply one of the best PTSD psychologists in the state. He wouldn't link her CIA past to Ham's former SEAL team.

No need to panic.

"My wife said you set some sort of ice-climbing record tonight," Lucas said as he slipped into the booth beside Sasha.

"No. Just . . . well—"

"She's being modest," Aria said. "She killed it. Faster time than North."

"North Gunderson?" Lucas said, taking a sip of his water. "I served with him—well, sorta—I was stationed at a flight hospital in Italy for a while, and he came through once with his team after a mission in Eastern Europe. I didn't realize he was back in Minneapolis."

"He's an instructor at GoSports," Sasha said. She settled into the story of Jenny's climb while Jenny and Aria perused the menus.

At the front of the room, the song ended and a man got up from a table of rowdies. Of course, Bon Jovi piped into the speakers. She winced at his awful rendition of "Livin' on a Prayer."

The words—and the rowdy table singing along—stirred up a memory. A too-handsome-for-his-own-good, brown-haired PJ and his buddies singing at the top of their lungs.

No. She breathed the ghost away and turned her attention to the television screen. They were running more footage from the San Antonio, Texas, arena where a bomber had set off an explosion after a bull-riding event a couple weeks ago. Apparently, they'd caught the man, but it didn't stop the pundits from speculating on his reasons—something about being out of a job, angry . . .

Yeah, well, anger made people do stupid things. Costly things. That's why you couldn't dwell on the past.

The waitress came up just as the song changed and another woman got up, spinning a LeAnn Rimes favorite.

Fate was merciless tonight.

"You want anything?"

She drew in a breath. And then, suddenly, the crisp wind filtered in off the thick cedar forest of the Hindu Kush mountains and caught up the scent of shishkebabs grilling on an open fire. Male laughter lifted from behind her as a group of men fought for a basketball, dribbling it against a dirt court, bouncing it off a pallet-made backboard, a naked hoop. Someone's iPod plugged into a speaker, blasted country music.

"How do I live without you . . ."

Her chest tightened, her throat thickening.

"Ma'am?"

Jenny stared at the waitress, her mind blank.

"I want to know. . ."

30

"I . . ." She closed her mouth, shook her head. Pushed out of the booth. "I'm sorry. I'm not feeling well."

Lucas frowned.

"Jenny?" Aria said.

"Sorry, Aria. I need to go home. Can you . . . are you—"

Aria's eyes widened, then, "Let's go." She looked at Lucas and Sasha. "Next time."

Jenny headed for the door. Tried not to turn into a fish as she hit the cool air, but—

"You're having a panic attack."

"I'm fine."

"Give me the keys before I need to resuscitate you," Aria said, coming up beside her to circle her arm around her waist.

Jenny looked at her and Aria gave her a small smile. "I guess some mountains you just can't quite climb high enough to conquer."

She slid into the passenger seat. Leaned her head back. Closed her eyes.

Aria's hand found hers. "Someday we'll both climb our mountains and come down healed."

"Yeah," she said.

But as Aria drove her home, back to their shared apartment complex, Jenny fell hard into the dark, brutal truth.

There was no mountain high enough to overcome her mistakes.

CHAPTER TWO

ORION WAS HOLDING his breath.

A month into the Denali climbing season, and so far, no one had died on the mountain. A few rescues—pulmonary edema, frostbitten fingers and toes, a couple falls that resulted in broken bones—but no major avalanches, no socked-in storms that buried climbers, and especially, no crevasse falls to swallow climbers whole.

And, so far, all the emergencies had been handled by the National Park Service rangers camped at Basin Camp, just past Windy Corner, on a large plateau at 14,200 feet.

Good thing, because Orion's rescue days were over.

Especially on Denali.

"Have you started to thaw yet?"

The question came from Ham, who wore a red North Face jacket, the collar up, his dark blond hair rucked up by the wind. He stood beside Orion in the middle of the street in the town of Copper Mountain, located just south of the Denali State Park line. Population 800, the town swelled into the thousands during the summer, as the sun hung high above the mountainscape to the north. Although small, the town knew how to host a party.

When the ice thawed and the snow retreated, the locals emerged from hibernation and greeted the arriving tourists with an annual country music festival the last weekend of May.

Arts and crafts vendors from Anchorage and Fairbanks set up along the tiny main street, and twangy music from bands as far away as Seattle played nonstop on the stage in the parking lot of the Midnight Sun Saloon and Grill, the one decent eatery in town.

This year, a three-ride carnival had come to town and set up a merry-go-round, a tiny Ferris wheel, and a kiddie coaster. The smell of kettle corn mixed with the smoke from the long grill set up outside the saloon. Patrons ate ribs out of paper baskets, either milling around the crowd or seated at the picnic tables set outside the saloon.

"You'll be surprised to know it can get into the high seventies in July," Orion said, in response to Ham's question.

"Get out the bikinis." Ham handed him a lemonade from the Midnight Sun. "They tapped a keg, but—"

"I don't drink before I climb," Orion said. "And Mount Huntington might be only a twelver, but it's a harder technical climb than Denali." He took a sip of the lemonade. "You sure you want to tackle French's wall on the descent?"

"I'm sure Jake and I need the rappelling practice. I thought we could do some crevasse rescue training. It's been a while since I did anything with numb fingers."

"And toes. It can drop to thirty below, and the wind is worse on Huntington. But it is gorgeous."

"How many times have you climbed it?"

"Twice. Scared myself silly on Idiot's Wall." Orion turned to Ham. "By the way, you're not fooling anyone. I know you climbed K2, and Jake's no stranger to climbing, so how about you tell me why you decided to disturb my beauty sleep."

"Sometimes you just gotta climb a mountain to figure out what is important," Ham said, his mouth tugging up.

"I was happy. Reading a Tom Clancy novel. Watching the ice go out on the lake behind my house. And most importantly . . . *staying out of trouble.*"

"You thrive on trouble," Ham said. "Otherwise you wouldn't have become a PJ."

Once upon a time, yes, it gave Orion a sense of purpose that balmed the wounds. Now, the memory of who he'd been only kept them open, bleeding. "I did that to drag people *away* from trouble. People like you. And now I'm starting to get a bad feeling about our upcoming excursion."

"Speaking of trouble." Ham's gaze scanned over to Jake Silver, who had made friends with a trio of women.

Jake wore a pair of jeans, hiking boots, and a sweatshirt and had a blue bandanna over his shaggy blond hair, which curled out as if trying to flee. He too drank a lemonade.

Orion knew Jake by reputation only—Jake hadn't been in the mess in Afghanistan that had brought Orion and Ham together. But he'd been an operator on Team Three, and a good one until he'd had to shoot a kid and it screwed up his head. Or at least that was the rumor.

That and the fact that Jake never lacked for female attention. Even now he made the brunette laugh. Next to him, a petite redhead looked away, although she smirked.

Beside the brunette, a blonde, her hair in long waves under a blue knit cap, stood with her back to them. She shook her head, probably in response to something he said.

So clearly not every woman was susceptible to Jake's charms, and it made Orion's gaze linger on her for a second. Maybe five six, fit, and wearing Gore-Tex climbing pants and a pair of boots, she looked like a climber, or at the very least, an athlete. She swayed a little to the music from the band.

The movement stirred up a snapshot in his brain.

Oh, he had a problem when every blonde he met reminded him of Jacie. Three years and he still couldn't dislodge her from his brain, the memory of her hands twined with his, the way she'd looked at him the night before his entire life exploded.

Maybe that's why he thought of her—because, in honesty, she was his last good memory. And his deepest wound, maybe. Because she'd walked out of his life without looking back.

Why couldn't his memories do the same?

He turned away from the blonde.

"I think you know why I'm really here," Ham said. "I need a guy with your skills on Jones, Inc. We have other climbers—North Gunderson, and of course Jake and Fraser have skills, but none of them were PJs. None of them know how to save a life on a mountain."

"I don't think—"

"You're up to it, Orion."

That's not what he was going to say. More along the lines of, by the time guys like him were called in, it was often too late to save a life. But maybe that wouldn't jive with Ham's international rescue team motto—to bring others back when no one else could.

"I know. My knee is fine. I'm practically bionic."

Ham smirked. "Right. But what I meant was that, well, you've got a handle on your trauma. I saw it in New York City. And it's time to rejoin your team."

His team had died on a mountain in Afghanistan, thank you. But he knew what Ham meant—the larger team of like-minded people who couldn't just stand on the sidelines. Orion could admit to a tug inside to say yes, to step outside his quiet, often lonely world and join a team again.

But he wasn't so sure about Ham's belief that he had a fist over his trauma or the anger that had erupted too easily in those early days. In fact, most of the time, the anger simmered just beneath his skin, burning a hole deeper every day. He'd simply put himself into a world where it didn't ignite.

Truth was, some days he didn't want to let it go. Mostly because he feared all the emotions waiting behind it. Betrayal. Hurt.

Grief.

Better to keep the anger tucked away where no one got hurt.

"I don't have the rescuer in me anymore, Ham. That life is over."

"You'll always have a rescuer inside you. It's in your blood and I have three weeks to prove it to you." Ham took a sip of his lemonade, nodded toward the stage. "Jake scored a dance."

Indeed, the man had somehow convinced the brunette to dance with him. She was cute—a little petite and shorter than Jake. To Orion's surprise, Jake cut up the dirt with a decent two-step. Even caught her when she stepped on his feet and nearly fell.

"I'm going to get some ribs," Orion said and headed toward the barbecue. Vic, the beefy blonde woman who ran the Midnight Sun, manned the grill.

"Hey, Vic." Orion held out a paper basket.

"So you came out of hibernation." She filled his basket. "Are you guiding this summer? Because rumor has it that Phil McPherson just dropped his trip." She nodded toward a group of wannabe climbers gathered at a picnic table. Plastic cups of Vic's craft beer stood half full, with a few empties scattered on the table. The wind toyed with the cups, the temperature still hovering in the midfifties. Overhead, the sky arched clear and bright, an illusive seduction to the danger of the mountain.

All men at the table, they wore sullen expressions, clearly stewing.

"Who are they?" Orion grabbed a packet of wet wipes.

"A group out of Seattle. Arrived a couple days ago and stayed in the motel next door. Apparently Phil is sick and Denali Mountaineering is booked up. They have a permit but no guide. From the sound of it, they're considering going it alone." She raised an eyebrow, invitation in the gesture.

"No thanks. The last thing I want to do is spend a month on the mountain with a bunch of know-it-all, loud-talking, white-collar yuppies."

"Now tell me how you really feel."

He grinned. "Besides, I'm going up Huntington with a couple of friends."

Her expression sobered. "Stay alive."

"Thanks." He glanced at the men as he returned to Ham. Well outfitted in Canada Goose jackets and wool toques, they groused about their lost climb.

"C'mon, Dixon, you've been up Denali. You know the climb. You could lead us."

Orion slowed. The statement came from a dark-haired fellow, midtwenties, lean, wearing an Oregon Ducks sweatshirt under his jacket and persuasion in his expression. His prey was a bigger guy, dark skinned, with pensive amber eyes, who seemed to be chewing on his words.

"No." The word erupted out of Orion's mouth before he could pull it back. And then more. "Have you lost your ever-lovin' minds? Denali has a 60 percent success rate, even *with* guides."

He had stopped in front of the table, but his words carried over the group. And maybe he was channeling his father, but he couldn't seem to stop himself. "Because of its height and latitude, Denali is one of the coldest mountains on the earth. Worse, the long winter season doesn't allow for the snowpack to melt and consolidate, which means higher avalanche danger. And now let's talk about the weather. Whether it's the storm fronts that pass over the mountain, or the weather on the mountain itself, you can get socked in for days, even weeks up there if you don't plan for enough equipment and time. There are easily 50 mph winds on any given summit day—in some areas they're higher and can blow you right off a peak—not to mention crevasses that are *three hundred* feet deep. You think anyone is going to climb down and get you, even if you survive that fall? Your guide might . . . if he can find you. But you'll probably freeze to death first. And that's all for people who aren't dying from acute mountain sickness, or worse, high-altitude cerebral edema. Or how about pulmonary edema?" He turned to Oregon Ducks. "Do you carry Diamox? Or Decadron? Because your guide will, and might save you from suffocating in your own fluids—"

"Ry—"

Ham's voice cut through his words, but Orion only stopped long enough to take a breath. "And we haven't even talked about the descent—the most dangerous part of climbing. You made the summit—great. But your camera is frozen, or worse, your fingers are frostbitten, so you stay too long to take pictures, or maybe while you're up there, the weather closes in and suddenly you have to get back down. *In a snowstorm.* You're frozen and exhausted and can't breathe and who do you think is going to get you down?" He looked at Dixon. "Not your fraternity buddy."

A hand came down on his shoulder. "Orion. I think you made your point."

He glanced at Ham, realizing he'd drawn a crowd. Including the redhead and the blonde, who stared at him through dark aviator glasses.

Her mouth had opened, as if horrified by his words.

He felt a little like a jerk, deflating her big expedition plans, but— "No one belongs on that mountain who doesn't know what they're getting into." He looked at Ham. "Because then it'll be you or me going up there to save their sorry backsides and risking our lives."

"We won't need rescuing," Ducks said. "We know what we're doing."

Orion wanted to take the man's beer and throw it across the parking lot.

"They can go with me."

He followed the female voice.

Oh no. Kit Murdock stood at the other end of the table. A little older than himself, Kit wore an Alaska Adventures sweatshirt, her black hair parted into two long braids, a bandanna around her head.

"Kit—"

She dropped a pair of thin gloves on the table. "Rian, stop. I'm already taking a crew of women up. They can join us."

"Kit—"

"I'm ready. We'll be fine." She gave him a thin smile.

So clearly she didn't want to talk about her own personal tragedy on the mountain, and he didn't have a right to bring it up . . .

Aw. Maybe he *should* have offered. But he wasn't connected to any mountaineering services anymore, didn't have a Denali permit, and . . .

But these dingbats could be trouble. And that was the last thing Kit needed—a group of men who needed rescuing.

He opened his mouth to say so but she shook her head.

Fine. "Take them up West Buttress. It's the easiest—"

"Of course."

39

Okay, then. He turned away. But not without spotting the blonde and the way her gaze followed him.

He stilled.

Abruptly, she turned her back to him.

Wait.

No . . .

She walked away, standing alone, her gaze half-turned to Kit, who had started grilling the men on their background, their preparation, and their plans.

Jake was still on the dance floor with the brunette, and . . .

Orion couldn't shake it. The way the sun had bronzed her face. The shape of her lips. The blonde hair, the curve of her body, lean and strong and—

He was seeing ghosts.

More, the woman looked completely rattled. So, even if it wasn't—well, he'd probably completely freaked her out about her upcoming climb.

He took a breath, glanced at Ham, who was finishing off his ribs, and walked over to her.

"Sorry about that."

She turned, and if he thought she might be freaked out before, the blood virtually drained from her face. Her mouth opened.

She was pretty, in a fierce, no-games kind of way. No makeup, her blonde hair long and wavy, in wisps around her face of gold and white.

He could see her eyes through her glasses, and they widened.

The name just spilled out, a whisper of crazy, irrational, forbidden hope. "Jacie?"

For a second, time stopped. She seemed to hold her breath, frozen. Just like that last night he'd seen her, the sky spilling stars across the mountainscape, falling into her eyes. The sweet smell of her skin swept over him, and he could nearly taste the whisper of her lips against his neck.

The urge to kiss her today might be even more powerful than it had been three years ago. "Jacie, where—"

"I'm sorry. I think you have me confused with someone else." Her voice was tight, almost stilted.

No, he didn't. Because as soon as she spoke, he knew the truth. He'd never forget that voice. It had dragged demons out of him, healed him, set him free.

"Jacie," he practically growled. "It's me, Rian."

She swallowed, then shook her head. "I . . . I'm sorry. I think—"

"Are you kidding me? What game are you playing here?" He didn't mean to raise his voice—maybe his tone was just left over from the diatribe at the table.

Still, she drew in a breath and recoiled.

Her reaction nearly knocked him to his knees. Made him take a breath.

She was afraid of him.

Yeah, that brought him to his senses.

"I'm sorry," he said softly, his gaze reaching out to her. *Jacie, what's going on?* "You . . . you look like someone . . ." *I once loved.* No, still loved, despite his best efforts to forget her. "Someone I once knew."

A beat pulsed between them, and for a second he thought she might surrender. *Yeah, it's me, Rian. I'm sorry I completely abandoned you, left your heart in shreds.*

Instead, she took a step away from him. "I'm sorry. I'm not who you're looking for. My name is Jenny. But can I ask—" Her gaze flicked behind him, at Kit, then back. "Is there something wrong with my guide?"

Really, it wasn't his story to tell, but he doubted that Kit would bring it up. And sure Kit looked strong. Healed. But he knew about the faces people wore to hide their demons, so, "Kit lost her husband on the mountain two years ago."

Jacie's doppelganger Jenny frowned. "How? Avalanche? Pulmonary edema?"

He shook his head. "No. Literally lost. They were climbing down from the peak with a group of climbers, co-guiding the group. A whiteout blew in, and when they got to Denali Pass he just . . . vanished." He'd kept his voice low, not wanting Kit to hear, but the music drowned him out—probably.

"That's terrible."

Yeah, it was. *Because losing the person you love, having them vanish from your life, leaves a hole you can never fill.* He wanted to say that, but along with it would come the shards of anger, and hurt, and . . .

He tucked it back inside. No one wanted that mess.

"They think he unroped to help someone. No one really knows. Kit got her group back to summit camp, but they got socked in for three days by weather, and by then . . . well, there was no hope. And the men she was with needed help getting down, so . . ."

He looked at Kit, who had sat down with the frat boys, outlining the route. "I don't think she's been up the mountain since then."

He didn't blame her, really. Once the mountain betrayed you, there was no going back.

"Oh." Jacie/Jenny stuck her hands into her pockets, looked at Kit, back to Orion. "Do you think—"

"She's one of the best. Just . . ."

"What?"

"You'll be fine." And then, because he knew in his heart that the woman he couldn't survive without was about to walk right back out of his life, and because he still couldn't bear having anything happen to her, he added, "Just don't rope in with any of those guys, okay? If they fall, they'll drag you all the way down the mountain."

She frowned, gave a tiny nod. "Thank you." She started to turn away.

He clenched his jaw. But he still couldn't stop the words, "Jacie—"

She stilled. "Jenny." But her beautiful profile, the tight jaw told him differently.

Okay. Fine. "Be safe." *Jacie*.

Then she walked away, and Orion hoped with everything inside him that he wouldn't be called in to drag the frozen body of the woman he still loved off the summit of Denali.

▨ ▨ ▨

"Please tell me that we're not going to die on that mountain." Aria sat on one of the double beds, on top of a homemade red-and-green log cabin quilt, running the charm of her necklace along the chain. Okay, so the woman was nervous. Jenny got that.

As if to add emphasis to her question, Sasha came in from the adjoining room and leaned on the door frame.

Sunlight, despite the lateness of the hour, gilded the wooden flooring of their suite in the Copper Mountain Chalet. Rustic but charming, the chalet was a quick walk through town into a secluded boreal and birch forest. The scent of pine seeped in through the windows, or maybe from the planked walls.

An arched stuffed salmon hung between the two beds. In Sasha's room, a watercolor of a couple bear cubs climbing a tree hung over the bed.

High luxury here at the hem of the park. Jenny had picked the chalet off the internet, wanting something rustic, yet cozy before they embarked on the mountain.

Judging by Sasha's expression, they might have just found base camp.

"We'll be fine," Jenny said. She set her pack up and unsnapped it. "Kit is coming over to look at our gear so let's get it unpacked and approved."

"You've already checked it twice—" Aria started.

"I've never climbed Denali!" She looked up and realized she'd silenced the room. "Sorry."

Aria held up a hand. "Listen, I'm not a fan of this idea of climbing with strangers either."

"What are you talking about? You were dancing with a random stranger," Sasha said.

"A hot random stranger that I'll never see again. Who, by the way, knows how to two-step. And has amazing hair. But there's a difference between a three-minute dance and three weeks on a mountain with men we don't know."

"We won't rope up with them," Jenny said, not sure why.

Or yes, maybe she did. Because Orion sat in her head, lodged there, his voice low and refusing to budge out of her brain, despite what she did to shake it away.

She'd destroyed him, again.

Why hadn't she just admitted it? Taken off her glasses, thrown herself in his arms?

"Are you kidding me? What game are you playing here?"

Not a game. Self-preservation, for both of them. Because if he found out why she'd left—

But yes, she'd wanted, with everything inside her, to turn around. To . . .

No. She pressed her hand to her gut, trying to get it to stop churning.

She pulled out a pair of gaiters and slapped them on the bed.

"Why shouldn't we rope up with them?" Sasha asked. "They're men. Wouldn't that be safer? A better chance to arrest us on a fall?"

Jenny pulled out a pair of nylon overboots. "And heavier when they fall and you have to self-arrest to save you both." She found her mittens and added them to the pile on the bed. "And the way they were drinking . . ." She climbed to her feet, holding her face mask. "They could pull you right down the mountain."

Sasha's eyes went wide.

"But that's not going to happen." She threw the mask onto the bed. "Because you'll be roped up between me and Aria. And we all know how to self-arrest, how to climb ice, we've been training for a year, and we have your back."

Sasha wrapped her arms around herself. "Yeah. I know. I'm just . . ." She blew out a breath. "It's just that—listening to that guy talk about the mountain, and—"

Jenny took two steps and put her hands on Sasha's shoulders. Met her eyes. "We're going to be fine. We've trained for this trip for a year. And Kit is a good guide."

At least she dearly hoped so. She'd talked to Kit twice on the phone over the past year, and Kit had sounded so calm, so sure of herself . . .

Maybe Jenny's instincts weren't firing right. She'd thought that she, a trained psychologist, could detect a lie when fed to her. But even she knew how to play the "I'm all right" game, so . . .

"We'll be fine."

"But we're not even going up the same route we planned." This from Aria, who was also pulling out her gear, neatly placing it on the bed. The fastidious habits of a heart surgeon. "I thought we were entering at Muldrow Glacier. Wasn't that why we were doing all this ice-climbing training? To eventually climb the Harper ice-flow?"

"Yes. I know. It would give us three more days to acclimate, and it's not as busy at West Butt, but they're technically the same. They meet at Denali Pass, and we'd take the same route to the summit, so it'll be fine." She glanced back at Sasha. "Probably better."

Then she saw it—the shadow of doubt on Sasha's face. She squeezed her shoulders again. "Listen, this trip is about conquering our fears. About going beyond who we think we are. About setting our faces like flint on the summit and reminding ourselves that our past doesn't need to keep us from flying."

Sasha pulled in a breath. Nodded. "Yes. Right. I just wish Lucas was here."

"It's a girls' trip," Jenny said.

"Not anymore." Aria finished unloading her pack. "And frankly, I wouldn't mind a few of those muscles to get our gear up the mountain." She had pulled her dark hair back, wore a flannel shirt over her T-shirt.

"Who are you? Back in Minnesota you won't let a man open the car door for you. And here, you'll let him schlep your gear up a mountain?"

"Listen to yourself and it'll make perfect sense. Besides, my car is a Corvette Stingray. Any guy who wants to open my door isn't looking at me."

Laughter, and Jenny's chest opened up a little, let her pull in a full breath. She released Sasha and headed over to their equipment box. Along with her personal gear, including boots, gaiters, mittens, hats, a parka, overpants, and long underwear, they also carried group gear—radios, tents, snow saws, snow shovels, stoves, aluminum pots, cups, and climbing gear. The one-hundred-pound gear would be divided between their backpacks and sleds.

Maybe having another group with them wasn't a terrible idea.

As long as she didn't have to make any decision that cost people their lives. But that's why she hired Kit.

I'm ready, Ry. We'll be fine.

Admittedly, his Wikipedia breakdown of the mountain had her rattled. When Kit walked up and made her offer, Jenny had been locked in place, staring at the man, trying to decide if fate could be this cruel.

Yes. Because Orion Starr was still painfully, darkly handsome—dark brown hair the color of rich coffee, mountain-green eyes that held a well of memories, and devastatingly well built with the kind of burly shoulders that suggested a lot of outdoor wood chopping, shoveling, and yes, probably some mountain rescue work.

She should have guessed that maybe she'd run into Orion in the tiny town of Copper Mountain, but . . .

Of course she would run into him. Because God wouldn't just let her slink away, lick her wounds, maybe let them heal.

Worse, the guy still had *Fear not, I'll save you* written all over him, just like when she'd met him. When she'd fallen for him, practically at first sight.

But this version, the guy who dressed down the frat boys, was also wounded, broken, all the laughter swept from his expression.

No longer the guy who shot hoops with his buddies. No longer the man who'd traced the constellations, his knowledge of the stars nearly endless. No longer the man who'd told her survival stories of his life in Alaska, shared with her the darkest parts of his heart, flirted with her as she sang along to LeAnn Rimes.

Oh. Ry. I'm so sorry.

She could almost see him across the flames of their campfire, the music twining out from an iPod, his face lit by the firelight, grinning at her. *"How do I live without you? I want to know . . ."*

The man had charmed her into giving him her heart. And she'd never gotten it back.

"What did that guy say to you?"

Sasha's question turned her around.

"What guy?"

"Really?" Aria was shaking her head. "Please. In the fifteen years I've known you, I've never seen you tongue-tied. You stared at the guy as if you'd forgotten your name."

For a second, she had. Because she hadn't been Jenny when she knew Orion.

She'd been Jacie, working undercover as a reporter, stationed on base to gather local intel.

He had no idea she'd been part of the CIA operation who pulled the trigger on their mission. On the ambush that had cost him so much.

She hadn't been completely sure of that until today, when she looked in his eyes and saw nothing of accusation. When she'd heard pleading, *not* anger, *not* blame in his words.

He really didn't know.

She planned on keeping it that way. She just couldn't destroy his life all over again.

But Sasha deserved to know. After all, secrets led to lies, and she was done with lies.

Mostly.

"Okay, here's the thing," Jenny said. "I knew him, back when I served in Afghanistan." She set down the altimeter and leaned against the desk.

Aria stopped her unpacking and slid onto the bed. "Oh my . . ."

"Yes. That was Orion Starr."

Aria's mouth opened. "Suddenly everything makes complete

sense. Now I understand why you can't forget a guy you 'just had a crush on.'" She finger-quoted her words. "Whatever."

"We were just friends. Nothing happened. We didn't even kiss."

"But you wish you had."

Jenny gave her a face.

"C'mon, Jen. It's not just the way you talk about him, but that guy was definitely kissable."

"Yeah, well, he didn't feel that way about me. He had a job to do, and so did I. We just . . . just found each other during a time when we both needed a friend."

Sasha sat on Jenny's bed. "You served with him? Did he recognize you?"

And how.

Jacie? It's me, Rian.

"He . . . yeah. But I denied it." She blew out a breath. "Aw, shoot." She looked at Aria. "I don't know why, I just . . . I panicked, I guess. I didn't want to face him, and . . . maybe he believed me. I did look different back then. I wore my hair shorter, and mostly in a hijab—it was part of my job as a reporter."

"Aren't you a psychologist?" Sasha asked.

She sighed, glanced at Aria, who lifted a shoulder. Fine. No secrets.

"No—yes—but, no, back then I was a profiler, working for the CIA."

And she just let that hang out there, let it hit Sasha, who drew her lips down, nodding. "I'm suddenly impressed."

"Yeah, well, don't be. I made a terrible mistake that cost men their lives."

Sasha frowned.

"Yeah. And that guy at the festival? He was one of the survivors. One of the pararescue jumpers who went in to save the men I sent to their deaths. He was seriously injured. Had to have his knee replaced and learn to walk again."

Outside, the sun had started to slide behind the mountains, sending a haunting orange over the sky.

"What happened?" Sasha said. "Or is it classified?"

"Yes, but . . . well, I don't know if it is anymore. Basically, my team was working with a couple local informants. One of them was the son whose father had Taliban connections—used to deliver supplies to them in the mountains. He was ten and loved to play soccer with our guys. One of our guys was teaching him English. He wanted to move to America. I thought he was a trustworthy source, so when we finally pried the location of the Taliban stronghold out of him, I vetted it as good and passed it on to command."

She was oversimplifying and she knew it, but . . . what could she say? That the kid played them all? That she knew something wasn't right, but she'd let her head overrule her heart? That she'd thought it was simply her feelings for Orion that made her afraid?

Yeah, so many mistakes, and mostly because she'd broken her life motto—*Don't fall in love. Because that's exactly when it will turn on you.*

"Command confirmed the intel with drone flyovers and a Ranger group and decided to send in a group of SEALs to root them out before winter set in."

For a second she was standing in HQ at their FOB, staring at the drone screen as Master Chief McCord communicated with Echo team. Listening to the radio chatter, her stomach a fist in her gut as they crept up on the stronghold.

"It was an ambush. Azzumi betrayed us by warning his father, who warned the Taliban." She shook her head. "Of the eight-man SEAL team, two were killed. The six who survived radioed in for help—they'd evacuated to a cave in the mountain. That's when Orion and his PJ team went in."

She got up and pulled out the repair kit, opening it, looking over the bolts, washers, baling wire, snowshoe eyelets. "Their chopper was shot out of the sky. Two PJs died. Orion and another PJ, along with the SEALs, managed to get into the tunnels and they were fighting their way through to the other side." She pulled out the Leatherman and tested it. "Except there was an explosion and half the tunnel collapsed. Two SEALs were caught on the other side."

She closed the Leatherman and put it back in the pack. "They were captured."

Sasha had drawn up her legs, wrapping her arms around them.

Aria had heard the story before, but she looked away, her eyes blinking hard.

"I never found out what happened to them."

Sasha frowned.

Jenny tossed the repair kit onto the desk, next to the altimeter. She refrained from the next words, although they built inside. Because no one wanted a psychologist who had suffered a nervous breakdown. Instead, she met Sasha's eyes. "I was unprepared for the guilt, the fact that my mistake had caused the death and injury of so many men. And not just any men—heroes. SEALs and PJs." Men she cared about. A man she loved.

No. *Not* loved.

Cared for.

Okay, arguing with herself wouldn't help. "I left the CIA, moved to Minneapolis, started my PTSD practice, and never looked back."

"Until today," Aria said.

Until today. She nodded.

"No wonder you looked like you'd been punched."

"I did not."

"Uh, yeah, you did," Sasha said. "Did you know he'd be here?"

She kept her voice even. "Orion used to talk about Denali, and I knew he grew up around here, and maybe I got the idea from him, but . . ."

Okay, it had crossed her mind that he might be here, more than once.

Her head betraying her heart again. Because seeing him standing there, the wind in his hair, wearing his canvas jacket and gray Gore-Tex pants, had knocked her sideways.

Stirred up the heat she'd tried to forget, to run from.

"You said that Orion was one of the PJs? Does he know . . . well, what you did?" Sasha asked, bringing up exactly why she should Stop. Thinking. About. Him.

"I don't think so, but I'm not going to stick around and find out." Jenny stood up and pulled out her cell phone to call Kit. "That's why I want to make sure we don't screw this up and get stuck on the mountain with a bunch of unprepared climbing wannabes. The last thing I want is for Orion to have to climb a mountain to rescue me."

She looked at Sasha. "We're our own team. And I am going to get you up that mountain, and back. No matter what happens."

CHAPTER THREE

THEY SHOULD GET OFF the mountain before it killed them. Although maybe that was just the doom and gloom that had burrowed inside Orion after two-plus weeks of being trapped inside a snow cave on the side of a glacier while the world turned to white around him.

It only made it worse that this was the second blizzard to sock them in.

Of course, the second blizzard, a nine-day stretch of white, gave him plenty of time to consider their mistakes on their failed attempt up Mount Huntington the first time around.

Why Ham had picked the almost-insurmountable north face, Orion couldn't guess. And they couldn't climb it expedition style, with fixed ropes connecting to forward camps. No, they had to attack the mountain alpine style, with belay ropes. A fast-moving yet dangerous approach that required them to camp somewhere on the face once they started the 5,700-foot ascent from the base of the glacier.

The fact they could fly in and park on the Ruth Glacier at the base of the mountain seemed like a reasonable trade-off—at least they didn't have to hike the sixty miles of tundra to get to their base camp.

Barry Kingston, their ride from KingAir, had managed to land his Cessna skis on the massive west arm of the glacier. They'd unpacked, set up camp, took a good gander at the mountain, and that night, the first storm rolled in.

Terrifying, freezing, and relentlessly mind-numbing, the blizzard trapped them in a tiny three-man wind-blown tent. Orion, Ham, or Jake climbed out every few hours to clear snow from around the domed dwelling. Between the noise of the blizzard and the crashes and explosions of seracs—icy fingers jutting from the mountain—loosening from peaks above and booming into the glacier fields around them, Orion slept fitfully.

Ham called it the voice of the mountain.

If so, it felt like it might be warning them off, practically waving semaphores.

The first storm had finally blown out after five days, and the next morning, Orion had awoken to such a deep silence he thought the world had inhaled, holding its breath, waiting for disaster.

But the sky arched blue, crisp, and glorious, and staring at the peak looming above them, even Orion felt the stirring of adrenaline. A guy couldn't live in the shadow of these mountains and not be spurred by the desire to stand at the top and reach for the heavens. "The mountains are calling, and I must go."

Orion's words made Ham turn, frown.

"John Muir, the father of our national parks, once said that. My own father liked to quote him. He was a ranger and worked the 1967 mega-storm disaster. Twelve men went up the mountain, only five made it back down. My father worked on the recovery team. It gave me a healthy respect for the mountain."

"Let's get up there," Jake said, stirring up eggs on the propane cook stove.

They'd packed their gear and took time to assess their route up the massive, jagged tooth of the north face called the Rooster Comb.

At the top, a hanging glacier formed a sort of roof, buttressed with a line of ruthless seracs, like a parapet along the ridge. They'd have to come up under it and climb to the left of the ridge.

The sight of the icy cornice put a fist in Orion's gut, and he'd thrown out a friendly "Who thought this was a good idea?"

Ham, of course, had to turn it into a spiritual moment. "I lift up my eyes to the mountains—where does my help come from? My help comes from the Lord, the Maker of heaven and earth."

Jake, standing nearby, propped his pack onto a snowbank, about to strap on. The mountain reflected in the glare of his Vuarnets. "Yeah, well, I hope he's on our side, because—"

A shotgun crack shook the mountain. Orion froze as a section of the parapet broke from the line. Boulders of ice and a devastating cloud of debris avalanched directly down the face of their climbing route.

Jake sat hard on the snowbank.

Ham stood, staring dumbly.

"I think God just said no," Orion said.

It took the wind out of Ham's sails, for sure. They'd spent the night re-tasking the climb.

The next day, weather rolled in again.

Orion endured two more days listening to the wind rattle the nylon tent like machine-gun fire until he finally decided to shovel out a snow cave. The first day it housed only him, but after a week, he'd tunneled deep enough to create Hotel Starr, with separate sleeping rooms and a central kitchen.

The cave was warmer than a tent, too, the only problem being having to clear out the entrance regularly to keep from being snowed in and suffocating.

That, and the fact that Ham and Jake were starting to drive him bat crazy—Ham with his snoring, and Jake with his not-so-clever cooking. Orion had never considered Spam a food group.

Spam and Ramen noodles.

Spam and eggs.

Spam and macaroni, with peas.

Spam fried rice.

He should have maybe raised his hand when they loaded the blue cargo box of Spam onto the Cessna. The supply had even raised an eyebrow from Ham, but as long as they didn't have to trek it up the mountain along with the climbing gear, Orion didn't care.

After two weeks at base camp, he'd started to care.

Hunger, and listening to the wind trying to rip them off the mountain, had driven Jacie back into Orion's brain.

Not that she'd ever left.

But he knew without a doubt that those blue eyes had belonged to Jacie, the girl he'd loved in Afghanistan.

By the way she'd looked at him, an almost haunted look, she recognized him, too.

He couldn't pry himself away from the fact that she was on Denali, right now, maybe holed up by the same storm.

He'd let his worry out of the bag one night to Ham and Jake, more in a mutter than actual conversation. "I hope Kit is smart and followed my advice to go up West Butt. Which meant that the group probably made it up Heartbreak Hill from Base Camp, went around Mount Francis, and might have camped at Ski Hill for the storm."

Jake had put down his journal. "If they're climbing expedition style, they probably have sleds and snowshoes."

Orion hadn't taken the guy for a journaler, but perhaps being trapped in a smelly, freezing tent brought out a creative desperation.

"If they pressed hard, they might have even passed Kahiltna Glacier," Orion added.

He hoped Jacie had listened to him about not roping up with the men. The glacier was riddled with crevasses that widened with the summer thaw. "If they pressed through the whiteout, they could have even gotten past Kahiltna Pass all the way to Motorcycle Hill at eleven thousand."

"Isn't that where the Basin Camp is?" Jake said.

"No. That's past Windy Corner, on a large plateau at fourteen-two," said Ham, who turned the pages of a Don Mann SEAL Team Six paperback. "Doesn't the NPS have a camp there staffed with rangers during the climbing season?"

"Yes. I worked it a couple summers as a volunteer rescuer before I joined the military," Orion said. "It's a good place for climbers to take a few days to acclimate and get ready for the next push."

"Kit and her crew had a head start on us, so, given the window of weather, they might have reached Basin Camp," Jake said.

"If no one has taken a header off Windy Corner in the 100-mph winds, or fallen down Kahiltna Pass, or gotten lost in a whiteout." Ham picked up his book again.

"That makes me feel all warm and fuzzy. Where's the radio? I want a ride home," Jake said. He wore a stocking cap, his hair twining out from the back and a blond beard thick on his face.

"Calm down. We're not going to get lost or fall, Silver. Stop your crybabying," Ham said.

Orion lay on his back. "Kit is pretty savvy. She'll probably have them run supply caches up from Basin Camp along the Headwall to the High Camp before she bids for the summit."

No one said anything, all of them probably thinking of their own failed bid for the summit.

"Why are you so worried about them?" Ham finally asked, quietly.

Oops, the jig was up.

"I know that was Jacie I saw in Copper Mountain."

"Jacie?" He put down his book. "That journalist from Afghanistan?"

Orion sat up. "Yeah. Didn't that blonde woman look familiar to you?"

"What blonde?"

Right. "At the Midnight Sun. She's climbing Denali with that group of frat guys?"

Ham lifted a shoulder. "Sorry, bro."

"I saw her," Jake said, looking up from his notebook again. "I danced with her friend, Aria. They're both docs in Minnesota."

Orion had spent too much desperate time thinking about Jacie.

"I don't know, Ry. Jacie had short hair, and she was a journalist, not a climber," Ham said.

No, not a climber. But she had enough guts to be one, considering she'd embedded a special ops group.

Maybe that's why he noticed her around camp. She was there when he arrived with his PJ crew, but she kept to herself, mostly.

Still, he couldn't *not* notice her. She'd caught his attention shortly after he arrived, when she walked into the mess hall, her hijab pulled off her face, her blonde hair short, her face tan. Then she sat down and started reading a book. She closed it with a bookmark when she'd added herself to the line for food, and he took that moment to walk by casually and glance at the cover.

Stephen Ambrose. *Undaunted Courage.* The Lewis and Clark epic journey.

He didn't know why that made him like her, but he thought

about that, a woman who filled her time trying to understand the motivations and fears of the brave.

He'd searched for her after that, on base, and caught glimpses of her as he worked out, coming in from runs. Asked a few people about her.

Journalist. With the AP wire. Serious. A seeker of truth. He liked that about her.

That, and the way she seemed unafraid amidst a world of chaos. And she had a decent jump shot.

"C'mon, Starr, you afraid of a little one-on-one with a girl?"

She'd walked by the campfire that night—just a regular night, he and the guys unwinding. He blamed the allure of the bonfire, the fact that he had wanted to break free of the knot of tension, his endless review of the wins and losses of the last mission.

She was on her way, probably, back to her tent where the other journalists bunked under the protection of the military. She wore a pair of black pants and a white T-shirt, the clothes she'd wear under her abaya, and she carried her hijab.

Whatever reporting she did, it meant going out of the FOB into the populace of the nearby city.

Laramie Nickles had called her over. "Hey there, AP, wanna join us?"

She'd looked at Nickles, then over at Orion, and a smile tweaked her lips. As if he might be the reason she'd say yes.

He'd lost his heart right then.

"What kind of trouble are you guys into?" She came into the circle where the team guys and other PJs sat on boxes, camp chairs, and wooden planks. Some of the guys were just finishing a pickup game on their makeshift basketball court.

"Just licking our wounds," Laramie said and handed her a cold beer from the beat-up cooler. Orion noticed that she barely touched it. And that she crossed the fire and sat down next to him.

"Hopefully nothing serious?"

Orion had finished a lemonade and now tossed it into a nearby box of recyclables. "Not today. Everybody lived."

"That's a good day, then," she said and met his eyes.

He drew in a breath. Not only at the measure of her words, but at her blue eyes, intense, catching his, as if she might be evaluating him.

He nodded, his heart oddly, suddenly wakening.

Maybe that's what made him pick up the abandoned basketball. Toss it in her direction.

Calm down, Rian. She's not into you.

To his surprise, she grabbed it and met him on the court.

"Try and keep up, PJ," she said, waggling her eyebrows.

He made to bat the ball away, but she turned and sent a perfect, arching shot into the netless basket.

"Lucky," he'd said, catching the rebound.

"Skill," she shot back.

He turned to face her. She stood in the flicker of the nearby bonfire, her eyes shiny, her face tanned, smiling at him, the stars winking in approval overhead.

No, *lucky*. So much so that right then he started to believe in happy endings. Crazy thought, but maybe . . .

Orion's mind traveled over to Denali, wondering if she'd been socked in by the same storm.

Wondering if she might be thinking of him too.

Maybe not. After all, theirs had been a quick, one-month, barely there romance. He hadn't even kissed her.

And in the end, she'd run from him.

Still, for a time, she was a safe, calming pocket inside all the chaos of the base. He told her things. And he gave away big pieces of his heart he'd never gotten back.

It left him hollow, with her in his head waiting for the storm to die.

This morning, Orion had practically lit a fire under Ham when the storm broke, the skies clear and blue, the peak singing their names.

They bagged the peak today, or never.

He'd filled up with the last of the powdered eggs, coffee, and a leftover blueberry cobbler—a climber's breakfast—and they'd left just as dawn, or what resembled it, arched over the eastern horizon.

"Climbing!" came Ham's voice from below Orion's perch.

Now, Orion sat, his crampons dug into the snow, his harness anchored into an icy slab that jutted out from a granite wall. The belay rope ran through his mittened hands, the silence of their climbing broken only by the creak of snow some fifty feet below as Ham chipped his ice axe and crampons into the crusty wall.

The view could steal Orion's breath with its glory. Below them, the glacial wall dropped in a series of ice-falls into a football field of rubble. He could make out their tiny blue-domed tent some two thousand feet below, still bright in the high sun.

They'd been climbing for six hours, and the day was young.

In the horizon, as far as he could see, the Denali massif rose, imposing, a jagged spine of granite and ice, the peak spearing through the haze and into the blue. The grandeur of the mountainscape filled Orion's bones with an awe that turned him a little weak. The crisp air bit at his nose, but sweat ran down his spine, coated his skin with the rising temperature.

The heat of the day set a rock in his gut as they climbed the lower, neighboring peak. Perfect avalanche weather. The melting snowpack could loosen and shudder down around them, take out

Ham, picking his way up the face on the route Orion had set. Unseat Jake, clipped into an anchor below.

But at least they were climbing.

Not stuck on a glacier in a blizzard.

They'd started the climb up a wide wall to the right of the debris field toward a coulee—a riverfall of ice and snow between pillars of snow. Ten pitches up and they'd cleared the wall, approaching the massive bergschrund at the top edge of the hanging glacier.

Orion had stopped at the edge of the schrund, a wall of ice that had separated from the granite. The fall inside could extend three thousand feet down.

The snow had begun to spindrift off the buttress overhead, and he'd climbed in the lead, diagonally, passing a coulee before finally climbing up to the rocky ledge that he wished were bigger.

Then Orion had screwed in his ice anchor and set himself to belay.

A few more pitches and they could stop for lunch. Or elevenses. Or whatever to call a meal during this endless day.

He hadn't gotten a real straight answer from Ham as to why this trip, now. *"Sometimes you just gotta climb a mountain to figure out what is important."*

He knew what was important—staying alive. The truth was, he'd never really been able to say no to Hamilton Jones. Maybe that's why Jake was stuck on the side of the mountain turning to ice too.

The wind lifted the collar on Orion's jacket and he shivered, the sweat on his back cooling.

Snow slides dribbled down the coulee. He wanted to look down, to see if he could spot Ham, but he couldn't sacrifice his position. Instead, Orion slipped his shoulder under the overhang for protection. Overhead, the sky was turning hazy and gray.

"Ham, hurry up!"

He spotted him now, his black hat and red jacket fifteen feet below the ledge.

"Took you long enough."

Ham looked up at him, his glasses reflecting the mountain, snow covering his nose flap, his reddish-blond beard. "What, you have somewhere else to be?"

A crack sounded above, and Ham's grin vanished.

"Watch out!" Orion stiffened and braced himself.

Ham slammed the picks of his ice axes in hard with two mighty wallops, pinioned his crampons, and ducked his head.

The mountain thundered down over him.

"Hang on!"

The world turned white. Orion hunkered down to hold his belay. The rope yanked hard, nearly unseating him. "Ham!"

But his shout was drowned by a deluge of snow. The snow pummeled Ham, unseen, below—Orion felt it through the rope.

Then, suddenly, the snow dropped away, leaving tiny wisps hanging in the air. Orion spotted Ham, blanketed in snow, unmoving and hanging by his wrist loops, his feet dangling free of the wall.

"Ham!"

A heartbeat. Another. Orion started to track through his options.

Finally, Ham raised his head, blowing out hard.

"You okay?"

He came back to himself fast, slamming his crampons into the snow, re-grabbing his ice axes. His weight eased off Orion as he reset himself onto the side of the mountain.

Then Ham turned, looking down to Jake's position. "Jake!"

Orion tried to lean forward, but Jake was fifty feet down perched on a ledge—

"He's gone," Ham said. "I'm going down."

Acid pooled in Orion's chest as he belayed Ham down. Ham attacked the wall with terrifying ferocity, and when he shouted up for Orion to join him, Orion rappelled, leaving his anchor screwed in.

Because Jake wasn't on the ledge. His anchor had been ripped out. Orion imagined him hurtling down the icy wall two thousand feet into the debris field.

"Jake!"

Oh, please—

"In here, mate!"

The voice echoed up from the darkness of the crevasse of the bergschrund.

"Belay me," Ham said.

Orion set his anchor, then hunkered down as Ham worked his way down the wall to the gap the ice formed between the granite and the snowfield. He worked his way in and vanished.

"Ry! Get down here!"

Orion dropped him the rope, then worked his way on belay down to the crevasse.

Leaned inside.

His heart nearly slipped from his body. Jake sat on a wide ledge, maybe eight feet deep, six feet down from the lip of the crevasse. "You okay?" He climbed down next to him.

"I thought I was going to die, and then, whoop, I fell in here, like the hand of God opening up to grab me."

Ham sat down, breathing hard.

Orion met his eyes. "I think the mountain wins."

Ham's mouth tightened. But he nodded. "Let's set up to rap down."

Orion glanced up into the swirl of snow, the storm-clouded sky. "We'd better hurry, or we'll be socked in."

As he climbed out of the crevasse, setting up his anchors to rappel down, he couldn't help but stop and watch the clouds as they churned toward Denali.

And of course, Jacie walked back into his head, just for a second.

Be safe, Jacie.

■ ■ ■

Jenny climbed mountains because being at the top of the world—with the wind whipping against her face, the cold seeping into her pores, and the gut-clenching drop-offs—kept her laser-focused on her next step.

On either side of her, the world slid away as she picked her way along the summit ridge, a final two-foot-wide quarter-mile-long trek to the highest point in North America.

To the right rose the eight-thousand-foot south face, with a view of Cassin Ridge and South Buttress Ridge. And, at her feet, the six-hundred-foot drop fell to the plateau below. On the left, the world fell two miles, down Harper Glacier, across the Muldrow Icefall and glacier right to the foot of Ruth Glacier, from which rose the craggy granite spire of Mount Huntington.

The rest of the Denali massif poked up their ragged heads between wispy, low-hanging clouds, the sky to the east a brilliant blue.

It could take her breath from her chest. But climbing was the opposite of adrenaline. Exhilarating, but it required her not to run, not to panic, but to *think*. To take her fear and shove it into a hard ball and keep moving forward.

Her breath razored in her chest as she moved her feet, the crunch of snow the only sound besides her gasps.

Wind scraped snow in a wave off the top. Up here, everything was simple.

One careful foot in front of the next, all the way to the top. A person couldn't turn around. Not without falling.

Ahead. Up. Focus.

Get to the top.

Then get back down.

"You can do it, Sasha." Jenny didn't want to turn around to face Sasha, roped up between her and Aria, but she threw the words over her shoulder.

Sasha had stopped talking shortly after their early morning ascent through a relatively flat section called the Autobahn. They'd stopped for water and a power bar at Denali Pass.

Sasha had met her eyes with enough fear in them that Jenny had to hunker down with her, grab her hood, meet her eyes. "We are stronger than we think we are, right?"

Sasha nodded, breathing hard. But they *all* were breathing hard.

"I can do this," Sasha had said.

"Yes." Jenny stood up, pulling Sasha with her.

Sasha picked up her ice axe and waited as Jenny trekked out ahead of her.

Aria turned to face the mountain, her expression like flint. "This is for Kia," she said. Tears streaked down her face.

Jenny too felt a little like crying after seventeen days climbing through driving snow, not thick enough to trap them in their tents, but brutal enough to make hauling gear up the mountain between camps, up and back, miserable. Fourteen days of adjusting to the diminishing oxygen, fighting insomnia, nausea, and cold, and two rather brutal nights in High Camp enduring a storm that came off the mountains to the south. She'd spent her time watching the wind pummel her tent, worrying that they'd run out of food before they made the summit.

Most of all, she'd spent the last seventeen days trying to forget the man who'd told her to be safe.

She'd almost managed to put Orion behind her, scrape from her mind the way he stood there, looking healthy and solid, unbroken. A lie—she knew it. But it stirred up memories that only wandered her dreams.

She blamed the altitude for the way his laughter rode the wind at night. The eternal sun kept her from full sleep, twining her instead into the memory of fighting him for the basketball, watching the way his body leaned out in his jump shot, his form toned and capable.

She'd even found herself leaning into the rich, dark moment when he'd walked her back to her tent that last night, one of many glorious, amazing, soul-nourishing evenings with Orion Starr. His hand finding hers, a soft squeeze, his gaze lingering.

Wow, she'd loved him.

One more memory she had to put behind her.

They crossed the ridge, and an hour later she was breathing hard, the air searing her lungs through her face mask, her body working against a sweat despite the -30 chill.

"Jenny!"

The voice rose from ahead of her, and she looked up to see that one of the men—Dixon, the handsome Samoan frat boy—was waving at them from the peak.

She liked the men's group—what little she knew of them. She'd joined them occasionally during a break, and they sometimes ate dinner together. A group of friends from the University of Oregon, they'd played football together years ago and now got together once a year to climb.

Only one of them hadn't made it to the summit day, a guy named Mike who was developing what Kit thought might be altitude sickness. He'd woken up with a headache, nausea, and slurred speech.

She had asked one of the coleaders she brought in, a twenty-one-year-old college student named Chris, to hike with him down the mountain. That left her other coleader, a seasoned climber who went by Boyd, to rope in with the guys. He wore his hair in dreadlocks, sported a long scraggly beard, and looked like he lived on the mountain full-time along with the rangers at Basin Camp.

Jenny waved back to Dixon. He was pointing and she looked over to see a puff of snow rise from the base of Huntington. Another spectacular avalanche. She'd been listening to the mountains heave and groan around her for two weeks, seracs and buttresses plummeting down ice fields into the valley below. Now, seeing the cloud rise from Huntington made her realize . . . God had been watching out for them on this trip.

No one was going to die.

Maybe, in fact, he'd even forgiven her.

Not that she expected him to—she hadn't even asked. It felt too great a request, really.

She wasn't the only one to blame, but good men had died.

And those who came home bore horrible wounds, in their bodies and souls.

No, she didn't deserve forgiveness.

She just wanted, for a fraction of a moment, to be free.

To breathe in the great breath of grace.

Jenny dug her spike into the snow, following Kit's footsteps, every breath fire in her lungs as she fought for the final three hundred feet. Kit stood at the top, along with the four frat brothers, grinning at her.

When she arrived, Kit high-fived her. Then, Jenny turned to greet Sasha.

She was openly weeping, the tears freezing on her cheeks.

Aria joined them, collapsing into a heap. They fell together, laughing. The top wasn't remarkably wide, so they huddled up and Kit took their picture. Then they joined the guys and took another photo.

Jenny sat at the top a long while, surveying the 360-degree view—Mount Hunter and Mount Huntington to the south, Mount Foraker to the west, and all of the Alaskan Range spread out in jagged, rugged brilliance, snowcapped, the sheer granite walls rising to meet the horizon.

If only she could stay here forever.

"We need to get moving," Kit said.

Yes. Clouds had gathered below the peak, the sky above turning leaden, and as she got up, the sweat drying on her body, a shiver whipped through her at the brutal lash of the wind. She noticed the peak of Huntington had disappeared into a layer of dense clouds. And over Foraker, a lenticular cloud had formed.

She'd taken bare supplies on her summit push—a stove pot, a sleeping bag, a tent, shovel, and food—just in case they had to brave a night on the peak, but that was the last thing she wanted. And, the ice climber in her had added a couple quick additions she probably wouldn't need—a long piece of webbing with tech—a number of carabiners, ice screws, an ascender, a figure eight rappeler and a couple snow pros, pickets that could anchor her into the ice.

The guys had already started down. Kit roped up with the women and they started down the ridge. "Most accidents happen on the way down, so watch your footing, and anchor in to the fixed line when we get to the pass."

The wind started to lift off snow from Pig Hill, sweeping it down into a plateau called the Football Field. Overhead, the clouds moved in to shroud the peak.

Jenny had purposely chosen an ice axe instead of a ski pole in case she'd had to self-arrest, but now she wished for the balance of the ski pole as she tried to slow her steps, keep from moving too quickly. Kit had placed pickets along the path on ascent, and now Jenny could barely make out the orange flag attached to the wands, the white whipping over her goggles. What she would give for some chemical hand warmers.

One foot ahead of the other, keep looking forward.

The temperature dropped as they crossed the Football Field, and save for the line connecting them, she would have lost Kit. A tug behind her slowed her down and she turned, the snow blinding her. "Sasha!"

The wind cut off her words.

Jenny tugged on her rope to stop Kit and headed back to Sasha.

Sasha had fallen into the snow and was bending over, breathing hard. Aria stood next to her, shouting as Jenny came up to her.

"I think she's getting altitude sickness!"

Right about then, Sasha threw up.

Jenny knelt next to her, fighting the rise of panic.

If she was getting AMS, then it wouldn't be long before she developed pulmonary edema or even cerebral edema.

But she'd be better as soon as they got to a lower altitude.

Sasha leaned up. "I'm fine," she said, not caring that spittle froze into her face mask. "I'm just tired."

Kit came up and leaned over them. "If we can get her back to High Camp, we can send her down the NPS's rescue line in Rescue Gully."

"She'll be fine," Jenny said, not sure of her words. *Please.* "Can you walk, Sasha?"

She nodded and Jenny and Aria helped her up. Hooked their hands around her arms.

"You need to stay apart from each other, in case you fall," Kit said.

"She needs help!" Aria said, and clearly wasn't moving away from Sasha.

Kit's mouth tightened. "I won't have time to arrest if you fall. We need to keep a longer running length."

"I'll take the coil," Jenny said. Kit considered her a moment. "I can do it," Jenny said.

Kit unclipped and handed her the coil of rope. Jenny slid it over her shoulder in a kiwi coil, tied it off, and clipped it into her locking biner on her harness.

Kit gave her work a glance, then nodded. "Watch your steps." Kit moved out ahead of them.

They fought their way across the Football Field, one agonizing step at a time, finally reaching the notch at Denali Pass. Kit waited for them, clipping into the NPS fixed rope that led down the pass.

"Just take it one step at a time!" she shouted over the wind. "The sun isn't going to set. We just need—"

A crack shuddered the air, but Jenny couldn't see anything in the whiteout. She took a step toward Kit.

Then, suddenly, Kit vanished. Just dropped away, into the white.

Jenny screamed, but in a second, the rope behind her yanked her off her feet. She landed on her back, head first, moving fast backward off the mountain along the twenty-degree pitch. But with the falling snow, she hadn't a clue how soon the mountain dropped off.

Stop!

Snow jammed into her mouth, shoved away her goggles. Blinded her.

Self-arrest.

She could feel herself careening, picking up speed—in seconds she might fly right off the mountain.

No—*no*—

Her ice axe dragged on the snow, attached to her arm by the loop. She managed to grab it with her free hand. Her body rolled, but she kicked, twisted. Turned herself around.

She jammed the axe into the snow.

It dragged, hardly slowing. But she couldn't reset it, so she hung on with both hands, angling her crampons into the snow. Sticking her backside up, she flung her other hand over the axe, climbing up on it.

The axe dug in, stopped.

"Sasha, dig in!"

She gulped a breath as the rope locked into her harness caught up. She dug down hard, bracing herself, and let out a scream.

The yank of the rope jerked her hold free, dragging her again down the slope. By some miracle, the axe stayed lodged in the snow, the pick pinging ice and snow into her face. She held on to her axe and the descent slowed.

The harness pressure burned into her bones, bruising.

She screamed again—or maybe hadn't stopped, but it helped to find her core. Dig down.

Almost abruptly, they stopped.

Snow lifted in a cloud around her, then settled over her, burying her into the side of the mountain.

Only her heart still moved, pounding its way out of her body. That, and the snow and ice crashing, echoing into the expanse as it fell two thousand feet below.

Her screams finally died in the gray expanse of the great Alaskan Range.

CHAPTER FOUR

SOMEHOW, JENNY AND SASHA AND ARIA hadn't plummeted en masse over the edge of a cliff or into a crevasse, hadn't broken ribs, hadn't slammed into a bone-crushing boulder.

Jenny's legs shook with the effort of arresting their fall, her body a fist over her ice axe. The tension on the rope clipped into her harness had lessened.

Which meant that maybe Sasha had self-arrested also.

Now they—well, *she*—clung to the side of a mountain by three very thin points.

In a whiteout.

With the temperatures dropping fast.

Jenny could barely see beyond her face, the wind howling in her ears. She knew Denali weather changed quickly, but the wind shear that had toppled them off the mountain had come out of nowhere, like the breath of God.

"Sasha!" She glanced over her shoulder, careful not to ease up on her hold, and barely made out Sasha's red climbing helmet six feet away.

She hadn't a clue where Aria might have landed, her rope nearly forty feet long between her and Sasha.

She could be dangling over a crevasse, for all Jenny knew.

"Sasha!"

The red helmet moved. "I'm okay!"

Jenny wanted to weep with the rush of emotion. But she didn't have time to let the what-ifs turn her weak. "Dig in, I'm going to set an anchor."

Step one, arrest.

Step two, set the anchor, secure the team to the wall.

Step three, make sure Aria was still alive.

Step four, find a place to bivouac until the storm died.

Then, get down the mountain and don't look back.

Jenny pivoted back on the pins of her crampons, testing them. Then, feeling secure, she unseated her axe and chopped away the loose, junk layer of snow and ice to the blue two feet down. Taking an ice picket off her pack, she worked it into the mountain and clipped on her quickdraw—two carabiners connected by a nylon cord. She clipped it into the rope, then, leaning on her ice axe, slowly transferred the load onto the ice screw.

It held.

She let out a shuddered breath. Now to get down to Sash.

She added a Prusik—an external rope knotted onto the main rope that acted as a brake—onto the rope below the connection and transferred herself to the Prusik. "How you doin', Sasha?"

"Hurry up!"

She wasn't unaware that Sasha held all of Aria's hanging weight, if Aria hadn't self-arrested. "Just going to set up another anchor!"

She uncoiled the rope to give herself room, then chopped out another hole not far from the first ice picket and pounded in her second picket. She attached the rope to it. Now the weight was on two anchors.

"I'm coming down to you!" She used her Prusik on the line to self-belay down to Sasha, digging her axe and crampons into the snow.

Sasha was crying, her face in the snow.

"I'll anchor you in, just hold on."

Jenny dug out and screwed in another anchor, then she clipped Sasha into the anchor with a quickdraw. Finally, she screwed in another trio of anchors, moved the rope to the anchors, and freed Sasha.

Jenny was trembling by the time she finished, the wind abating some but still stinging her face with snow and ice.

"I need to check on Aria," Jenny said. Sasha had stopped crying, and now looked at her, clearly trying to be brave.

"Stay here." She maneuvered down the main rope, chopping into the snowy layer.

Her exertion dampened her face mask, just her breathing and the crunch of the snow evidence of life.

Don't look back, keep going.

She followed the rope until the mountain seemed to flatten out, and as she saw Aria's position, her heart nearly stopped. Aria had slid over an icy overhang the length and width of a bus. The rope cut right down the middle.

Jenny probed the area with the shaft of her ice axe, then crawled over to the side.

Aria hung upside down, her pack pulling her down. She'd forgotten to clip her chest harness to the rope. And she wasn't moving.

"Aria!"

Nothing.

The wind had lifted enough for Jenny to study their predicament, and she nearly went weak with relief.

Aria hung off the serac, over a lesser grade of frothy snow. Maybe, if she lowered her down, they could take refuge under the serac—and this felt like a terrible idea, but what choice did she have?

She worked off her heavy pack and dropped it into the snow, digging it into a hole to anchor it. Crawling to the edge, she leaned over again. "Aria!"

No movement.

She blew out a breath, debating.

But Aria might be suffocating, the pack cutting off her air supply, or maybe worse, suffering from a broken back or internal bleeding. Jenny had to get down to her.

She pulled her last picket from her pack and secured it into the snow, then she unlooped her kiwi coils, threw in a double figure eight, and attached the knot to the anchor with her last biner. From her utility harness, she unclipped her self-braking descender, attached the descender to the rope, then clipped herself in.

"I'm going down to Aria!" she shouted to Sasha, before testing the edge.

She leaned back, letting the rope bear most of her weight, stabilizing herself with her crampons against the ice as she lowered herself beside Aria.

Her friend hung, arms over her head, her ice axe dangling from her wrist, the pack clipped on at her waist.

"Aria." She grabbed her by the pack harness, bringing her closer. Drew her face next to hers.

Breath, but barely. And then a groan.

"Hang on." She reached over and grabbed the pack's haul loop, then unclipped the pack's waist harness, holding on as the pack dropped away. She managed to not let it jerk, but lowered it by its tether to dangle off Aria's harness.

"Aria." She took off her mitten, tucked it into her jacket, and reached over to wiggle her hand into the collar of Aria's jacket. She found Aria's neck and pressed against her carotid artery.

A steady beat there. So maybe Aria was just woozy from so much blood to her head.

She needed to hurry and get her down.

She secured Aria's harness to her rope so she could create a lowering system. Then she grabbed Aria's axe, removing it from her wrist. "I'll be back as soon as I can."

She climbed back up, breathing hard.

Sasha shouted something, but she couldn't make it out.

Besides, she was too out of breath to answer.

The snow had turned blinding again, and she had to wipe out her goggles before she headed back up to Sasha.

Her friend was shivering. Maybe going into shock. "Breathe, Sasha. Just stay calm. We're going to be okay. Aria is alive. She's hanging upside down, and I'm not sure how hurt she is." She didn't suggest anything beyond that.

"We'll lower her to the snowpack below, and then we'll hunker down and ride this out."

Sasha's eyes were huge in hers, and she nodded.

Yes, they were going to be okay. Jenny would set up their tent, dig in, make some soup, get everyone warm . . .

Maybe pray, although this sort of felt like some divine retribution.

Apparently, a woman with her mistakes didn't get to feel free.

"Good girl. I'll be right back."

Since the load line was clipped to Sasha's anchor, she climbed up to unhook her line, retrieved her ice screws, and returned to Sasha.

"I'll belay you down to the serac, and then I want you to clip into the anchor and wait for me. Do you think you can do that?"

Sasha nodded.

She hooked Sasha back into the main line with the descender, then anchored herself to the ice pros and set herself into the snow, seating her crampons and herself into the snowpack. Then she secured Sasha on belay with the final length of the rope. "On belay. Descend when ready."

"Descending," Sasha said, her voice thin. But she bravely chipped her way down to the head of the serac and clipped into the anchor.

Using her Prusik to self-belay, Jenny worked her way down to Sasha.

Her breath had created an icy layer in her mask and she needed to rest, her heartbeat dangerously high. She blamed the lack of oxygen and the fact that she wasn't sure just how terrible her idea was.

What if the serac collapsed and dragged them down the mountain?

Not now. That was thinking too far ahead, maybe. She just needed to figure out right now.

"I'm going to lower you down so you can catch Aria, okay?" Sasha nodded.

"But I need to set the lip." She worked her way down to the edge of the serac, then set Aria's ice axe in horizontally over the edge. "When you go over the edge, let the rope drag over the axe handle. Set an anchor with your axe at the bottom and clip the rope in." That would at least keep her and Aria from screaming down the mountain if one of her anchors budged.

She returned to her anchor and reset the descender onto the free line to lower Sasha down. "Ready?"

"Ready," Sasha said.

"Lowering," Jenny said, and Sasha stepped backward as Jenny took the descender off auto-stop. The rope slipped through her mittened hands, held to friction by the descender as Sasha worked her way over the edge.

The weights pulled against her—her harness, uphill, and Sasha's body, downhill. Her legs began to shake.

Please, help us get off this mountain. A chill had sunk into her bones despite her exertion. But it wasn't long before she felt the slack in the rope. Sasha, at the bottom. Hopefully she anchored in separately with her ice axe.

Now to lower Aria.

She added more anchors, reworked the ropes, and created a lowering system, finally clipping Aria's line into it.

"Ready?" Jenny shouted.

"Lower her!" Sasha said.

Please don't let her drop Aria on her head.

"I got her," Sasha finally yelled.

Jenny wanted to weep. But she unclipped the ropes, tied herself back in to the main rope, coiled the excess back into a kiwi loop, and retrieved her anchors. She hoisted her pack back on, retrieved Aria's axe, then took the long way around the serac.

Sasha had unclipped the pack from Aria, and it sat not far away, an orange beacon in the whiteout.

Aria lay in Sasha's arms under the unlikely protection of the serac. Some of her dark hair had escaped her hat, turning to ice against her face. Jenny dropped to her knees beside her. "Aria. Wake up."

Aria's eyes were already starting to flutter. She woke hard, with a start and a scream.

Jenny put her hand on Aria's chest. "Shh. Stop. We're okay." But Aria was starting to hyperventilate, her eyes wide.

"Listen, we got blown off the mountain. But we're okay. We're going to be okay."

Except now Jenny was shaking hard—needing her words as much as Aria did.

She didn't want to consider the truth.

They'd tumbled into a whiteout, and for all everyone else knew, they'd fallen to their crumpled, frozen deaths. She didn't want to think about Kit and what had happened to her, but she had a feeling that perhaps the icy cap had broken away, just as it did on Everest so many years ago. Who knew if High Camp had even survived the inevitable avalanche?

Everyone else could be dead.

No—no. She couldn't go there.

"I need to get the tent up."

She took off her pack, reevaluating her crazy thought about camping under the serac. But it gave them protection from driving snow, and with the falling temperatures, it wouldn't be in danger of melting, breaking off, and careening downhill.

In theory.

Besides, it wasn't a gnarled-toothed overhang, but more of a jutting, almost-protective shelf.

Okay, her gut said never camp under a serac, but she couldn't even *see* the rest of the mountain. They could be ten feet from a sheer drop-off.

And Aria just might be going into shock.

Jenny pulled out her shovel and dug out a well, building up walls in a circle and packing the sides against the wind as high as she guesstimated the tent to be.

Then she pulled out the tent and pitched it in a few quick moves. Sasha helped, holding it down as Jenny assembled the rods and secured the metal stakes into the ice and snow.

She would have liked a snow saw to build actual bricks, but she didn't have time.

"Let's get inside," she said. She helped Sasha bring Aria into the tent, pulling off her crampons. Sasha did the same. Jenny retrieved their sleeping bags and pulled the packs under the tent's vestibule.

The wind was howling now, a whine in the sky that burned into her ears and bulleted her face. She was so cold her teeth rattled, her toes were numb, her bones brittle.

As she took off her crampons and shoved her ice axe next to the door, she stood for a moment, her mind snapshotting onto the moment before her world turned deadly.

Staring at Kit, her eyes in hers, offering her hope.

Except hope was deadly. Just when you reached for it, it slipped out of your hands.

Jenny climbed into the flimsy, shaking tent.

Sasha had gotten Aria into a sleeping bag and tucked herself into her own.

"I'll get tea going," Jenny said through her teeth.

"No. I will in a minute. Let's get warm." Sasha had unfurled her sleeping bag. "Get in, now."

Jenny acquiesced, climbing in fully clothed. Then she turned onto her side, wanting, really, to curl into the fetal position.

Aria too lay on her side, looking at her, breathing easier. "You okay?"

"I think I broke my ankle trying to self-arrest. And I wrenched my shoulder pretty good."

Jenny nodded but closed her eyes, her body still shaking. "They'll find us. We still have our avalanche beacons."

Aria lifted her gloved hand and put it on Jenny's cheek. "This isn't your fault."

Jenny drew in a hiccupped breath.

Then Sasha nudged up behind her in her sleeping bag and set her head against her neck. "We're stronger than we think we are."

Maybe. Maybe not.

Because right now, all Jenny could hear were her own screams, still dying in the howl of the wind.

▓ ▓ ▓

After eighteen hours clinging to the side of a cliff, working his way down the most harrowing wall of jagged ice in a near-whiteout, the winds fighting to tear him from his scrabbled perch, Orion just wanted to sleep like the dead.

But the dead refused to leave him alone. Oh no, they shouted at him from across the expanse of his nightmares, Nickles and Dirk, fellow PJs, and SEAL operator Royal Benjamin. Except Royal had been captured along with Logan Thorne, and according to Thorne, rescued. Still, his buddies showed up with their sunburned faces, their wide grins, and called his name from where they shot hoops.

He blamed Jacie. Or at least the woman he'd met three weeks ago. She dragged up the ghosts to prowl his sleep. It had to be the wind, the howling he heard behind the tenor of their laughter, but it left a hole in the center of his gut.

Or maybe it was all from the Spam soup Jake had made when they returned to camp. Whatever the case, Orion woke up nauseated, his head pounding, and just barely made it out of the snow cave before his supper dumped onto the snow.

He wore his long johns, his snow booties, and a thermal shirt, and had the unfortunate timing of landing on his knees just as a beautiful white Cessna buzzed over them.

He leaned back, grabbing a mouthful of snow, then spit it back out.

"You okay, Ry?" Ham sat on one of their gear boxes, holding a radio.

"Sure. I'm just in serious need of real meat." He pressed his hand to his gut. Or maybe he should leave it empty, because given the way the wind scurried over the glacier, it would be a bumpy ride back to Copper Mountain.

"And a shower." Ham made a face. But he was one to talk. The man wore a haze of amber and gold whiskers on his chin and looked like he'd walked out of the woods of some horror flick, his face sunburned, his lips chapped. Under his wool hat, his hair was surely matted.

Probably, Orion looked the same—he felt like it.

"Get packed up. Larke Kingston is heading in to pick us up."

Larke, Barry Kingston's daughter. Former army medic and wilderness doc. He knew her three brothers, now deployed in three different branches across the world.

The wind scurried through his thermals. Orion judged the temps to be in the low teens, the sky overhead somber and gray. But the blizzard had died to mere wisps, the snow no longer pelting him. He could even spot the faintest outline of Denali in the distance, although the peak was still shrouded in a layer of haze. He had no doubt everyone at High Camp, and maybe even below, had hunkered down in their tents—although sometimes the storms that hit the lower mountains like Huntington and Hunter bypassed the High One.

And sometimes the lower mountains received a glancing blow of what hurtled itself against the great peak.

The drone of the returning Cessna alerted him, and he scooted into the cave.

Jake was packing the kitchen. He wore his shell pants and suspenders over a thermal shirt. "I have some leftover Spam—"

"Stay away from me," Orion said. He pulled on his shell, leaving his thicker pants off for the ride home, and stuffed his sleeping bag into a compression sack. He'd already packed most of his gear—

his harness, ropes, crampons, ice axes—and now he grabbed his jacket and hat, his gaiters, mittens, and gloves, and rolled up his sleeping pad.

By the time he dragged his pack outside, Jake and Ham were already loading up the plane with the kitchen and camp gear. "Sorry, guys," he said, not meaning to leave all the work to them. "I guess I overslept."

"You were shouting in your sleep last night. We didn't want to go near that," Jake said. "Thought you might punch me if I woke you up."

"I might anyway," Orion said.

Larke was grinning, her blonde hair in braids under her wool hat. "Hey, Ry."

"How's that boyfriend of yours?" He'd met Riley McCord during a big fire a couple summers back.

"He just earned his trident and is waiting to get assigned to a team."

"Your boyfriend is a SEAL?" Ham asked as he climbed out of the back of the Cessna.

"Fiancé. He proposed on the beach in Pensacola." She was walking around her plane, giving it a quick assessment. "As soon as he gets his assignment, I'll join him."

"What does your dad say about that?" Orion loaded his pack into the back. Ham added his and closed the door.

"Dodge's tour of duty is over next summer, and he says he's coming home, so he can slog you mountain rats around." She had landed in a perfect swath, throttling around so that her skis faced back along the track she'd made landing. Now she opened up her door.

Orion got in on the passenger side, with Ham and Jake climbing in the back.

He stared out the window, back at the snow shelter that he'd made into a strange palace. Then his gaze slid back up the grizzled edge of the mountain, with its gnarly granite walls, thick seracs like dollops of frosting rising hundreds of feet, the layers of cream sliding down the sides, the skim of snow swirling off the top.

The mountains are calling and I must go.

Not today.

Funny, in his youth he would have made promises to himself to return.

Now, he just strapped himself into the plane and held on as Larke throttled up and moved off the glacier, dropping into the pocket then rising fast above the tundra.

The world of ice and snow dropped away as she flew over ice floes and glaciers and finally the muddy bogs and greening alps that littered the mountain.

The world turned green and lush, the boreal forest adding color—purple and gold, orange along an aquiline blue lake. Outside the mire of the mountains, the sky turned a deep blue, tufted with thick clouds.

Orion had donned headphones and now glanced at Larke. "Is your dad flying the chopper?"

Her father also ran a chopper service, sometimes bringing in supplies to Denali Base Camp. He even rigged it as a water bomber during fire season.

"Yeah. There was an accident on Denali last night. High winds on the pass and apparently an entire roped team fell. They think they're in Peters Glacier, but they're still looking for them. Dad brought in an NPS team from Anchorage to help."

Orion had stilled on her words, spoken with sadness, but with the cool-edged solemnity of a seasoned Alaskan.

"What team? Do you know if it was Kit's group?"

She glanced at him. "I don't know."

He drew in a breath and glanced at the range. He'd experienced those high winds, had barely hung on to the mountain, and he'd been anchored in. So much of the time roped teams didn't carry the gear to the summit they needed for self-rescue—ice screws, descenders, belay systems—preferring a light run up the mountain to preparing for the worst.

Kit, however, wasn't that kind of guide. She would have made her crew at least take provisions to spend the night trapped in weather.

Or, looked at the skies and not gone at all.

He settled back in his seat. That's what the NPS rescue team was for—it wasn't his problem.

He pressed his hands over his gurgling stomach.

Larke set them down at the Copper Mountain FBO where Ham had left his rental car. They unloaded the gear into Orion's Ford Ranger, also parked in the lot.

"I'm headed to the motel to shower up. How about I pick up a couple steaks and we meet at your place?" Ham said to Orion. Jake lingered by the rental car.

"Still not finished trying to convince me to join your little SAR group?" Orion tossed his keys in his hands.

"C'mon, Ry. That thing inside you that you can't keep dodging, that pull to do something more with your life? You think it's about Royal, but it's not. It's about the fact that God isn't finished with you yet. He's calling you to something—I know it, and so do you. And I think it's Jones, Inc. Join me, Ry. Let's do good things together. Help people. Bring the lost home."

Orion glanced out toward the hazy, gray peaks to the north. "God doesn't want a bitter, angry guy like me, Ham." He looked at him. "And neither do you."

"Yes, I do. And yeah, you're right about God—he doesn't want the darkness inside you to win. But maybe helping others is the first step to letting it go. To healing."

Orion shook his head. "It's not something I can let go. I'm not even sure I want to." And maybe it was because he'd nearly died with the guy, but Orion let the truth spiral out, even as he looked away, across the tarmac, watching Larke tie down her plane.

"Thing is, right now I'm like this guy holding on to a tree in the middle of a tsunami. There's dark, lethal water all around me, and at least as long as I hold on to the tree, as desperate as that is, I'm safe." He squeezed his keys in his palm, letting them bite. "I let go into that mess of betrayal and grief and who knows where I'll end up." He opened his car door. "Trust me, this is safer for everyone. Me, alone with my darkness."

Ham's mouth tightened. "Warm up the grill. I'll be over with the steaks."

Orion lifted a hand to Jake and climbed into his truck. He took the highway north, back toward the park where his family had homesteaded over a hundred acres of pristine pine forest, running dogsleds and snowmobiles as his father worked the park.

His father had rescued so many people off Denali, it was practically in Orion's gene mix to think about where the climbers might have gotten lost. Maybe an avalanche had ripped out the fixed ropes to the pass, taken them all down. Or, like Larke had said, maybe they'd all blown off, careening into Peters Glacier.

He turned onto the dirt road that led back to his place, built on the edge of their property. Originally a hand-crafted two-room cabin, the house had been upgraded by two generations of Starrs to include timber framing, a grand wraparound porch, and a two-story great room that faced the park.

Denali, of course.

He got out and headed inside, toeing off his boots by the door before he went upstairs to the lofted bedroom—once his parents', now his—and right into the shower.

He took off a layer of grime so thick he thought he might be de-scaling. But when he emerged, he felt human again, his smell no longer offensive. He shaved too, just because, and changed into a pair of jeans and a flannel shirt before he padded barefoot down the stairs.

The timber framing and the shadow of the looming pines that surrounded the property sent a chill into the house. He built a fire in the soaring rock fireplace, let it crackle its warmth into the house, and went into the kitchen to scrounge up some food.

He hoped Ham would keep his word, because he had nothing but an old piece of cheese and some spoiled milk in the fridge.

Orion scrounged up a half bag of stale chips from the pantry and walked out to the picture window. Stared at Denali, at the gray hood that hovered over the peak.

Be safe, Jacie.

His words found him, and he drew a breath, but not fast enough to press Ham out of his head, too. *"That thing inside you that you can't keep dodging, that pull to do something more with your life? God isn't finished with you yet. He's calling you to something—"*

A knock came at the door and he turned, seeing Ham pulling open the screen to step inside. He was carrying a paper bag in one hand, his cell phone in the other.

Jake was on his tail, holding a six-pack of dark bottles. Maybe craft root beer, because he knew Jake didn't drink alcohol.

He set the bottles on the counter. They'd both showered and shaved, dressed in clean clothes.

Ham put the paper bag—groceries, Orion hoped—on the

rough-hewn table in the kitchen. Then he put his phone down and looked at Orion.

"Okay, what's going on?" Orion asked.

"It's time to join the team, bro," Jake said.

"We need you," Ham added. He walked over to the picture window. "I just got off the phone with my buddy Lucas McGuire." He pointed to the mountain. "His wife went to the summit yesterday. And she didn't come back down."

Orion looked at him.

"Her guide had access to a sat phone and was supposed to call him from High Camp after their ascent. And when she didn't, he started to worry."

Orion's gut was grinding again. "Don't tell me—"

"Sorry, but she was on that team of all women. Jenny Calhoun and Aria Sinclair. They're all three missing."

Orion turned back to the window, to the gray cap hovering over Denali.

"We're going back on the mountain," Ham said softly as Jake came to stand beside them.

Orion nodded, his appetite gone. "We're going back on the mountain."

CHAPTER FIVE

JENNY HEARD GEESE.
    Which of course couldn't be right.

Geese, and the smell of fresh-cut grass, and the taste of the ocean on her lips, salty and dry. So dry. She swallowed, and her saliva stuck like lard in the back of her throat.

She couldn't speak, her voice a common casualty in her dreams, but the world opened and for a moment she recognized the memory. Mount Rainier poking its glorious white dome up from a layer of clouds, the deep blue of Puget Sound rippling out along a rocky shoreline. The occasional breaching of a whale.

Silence and safety, and she sank into it, still hearing the geese.

In her dream, she sat on a bench and wore a blanket, her feet cold in the grass. She shivered against the wind.

"I'll find you."

She drew a breath at the voice, deep and husky, and like dreams go, she found herself suddenly in the dirt-packed compound of the FOB in Kunar, the sky overhead a deep indigo, a million lights dusting the night. And beside her, solid and emanating an earthy masculinity, Orion Starr.

More memory than dream now as they lay on their backs on a

table, their shoulders against each other, the strength of him radiating through her even as he folded his hands on his taut stomach.

She'd made a comment about the dark Afghani sky, the way the stars fell so close to the earth.

"If you want to see stars that feel so close you can pull them from the sky, you need to come to Alaska. Better yet, if you're real brave, climb Denali. It's . . . well, there's nothing like sitting on the highest peak in North America, in arm's reach of the universe. Although you have to climb it in summer, when the sun never sets, so it's hard to see the stars. But they're still there."

"Denali?"

"Mount McKinley. My father was a park guide his entire life on the mountain, and I worked rescue on the mountain for two summers before I joined the Air Force. We lived on a homestead on the southern edge of the park."

"I'll have to visit sometime. I'd like to meet your father."

He'd drawn in a breath then, stiffening beside her.

She'd gone too far. Taken their friendship past right now, this place, this snapshot of time.

What was she thinking? That the man she'd been watching since he arrived on base, the quiet one who seemed to be always thinking, would want more than just a friend? This relationship had all the staying power of a shooting star, blazing hard, but dying out fast the moment she was transferred.

She got herself in trouble when she let her heart do the thinking. "Sorry, I—"

"No. I'm sorry. It's just . . . my dad died a couple years ago."

Oh. Great, Jacie. "I'm so sorry. Was it an accident?"

"Sorta. Yes. A climbing accident on Denali. He unroped when one of his clients fell, and when he went down to help him, he just . . . slid off the mountain."

91

She couldn't breathe. Silence fell between them.

"Ry . . ."

He rolled over to his side then, looking down at her. His green eyes could stop her world, reach down inside her and make her heart beat.

She was falling for this man, hard.

And it wasn't just because he listened to her. Talked to her about her love of history, as if it mattered to him.

Wasn't because he could name every star in the sky, as if he might be Galileo. *"My parents named me after the constellation because it was the brightest one in the sky. But I like to think it was because Orion was a hunter."*

And it wasn't because he had this uncanny way of making her feel like she was the only one in his universe. Or the crazy stories he told her of Alaska, stirring up a world she wanted to see. Or even that he had this amazing ability to compartmentalize his world, to tuck all the danger and fear into a neat pocket and remain calm.

It was the fact that when he looked at her like he was now, everything she'd been running from dropped away, and for a moment, she could catch her breath.

Orion Starr was safe.

No. He was the brightest star in her world. The one she wanted to run to. She'd heard stories about the spec ops guys—thought these men were arrogant and unapproachable. Hard-edged, honed by the demands of their job.

Then Orion had invited her into his world, let her see beyond the body armor, and she felt like she'd discovered a hidden treasure.

Wow, she could love him. If only they'd met at a different place, a different time.

He traced her face with his gaze. She wanted to kiss him. Lose herself in his touch. Nearly looped her arms around his neck and pulled him to herself.

Except, what then? If she got too close?

He might discover the truth about her true reason for being here. And frankly, she had rules.

His breath hovered over her face, the scent of the night, the campfire, the hard-work smell on his body twining through her to awaken every cell in her body.

She bit her lip and turned away.

He must have taken the hint because he rolled onto his back. "We should probably turn in. The SEALs have an op tomorrow and we are spinning up to support them."

She knew that, of course. But she said nothing as she got up. He walked her back to her Quonset in silence, and she had the craziest feeling that he was trying to unlock something from inside and not quite winning.

Yes, well, maybe he shouldn't.

Maybe some things should stay locked up.

His hand had knocked against hers, hot, his skin rough and calloused. Work worn.

He twined a pinky through hers, testing.

Oh. She shouldn't, but she let it linger, a moment of connection that suggested hope. Tomorrows. Even in the dream it seared through her, touched her heart, turned it to fire.

A sudden squeeze in her chest made her gasp, probably the dream combining with her semiconscious mind, and for a moment she tightened her hold on him.

Don't go.

He didn't notice her panic, of course, because now the memory made him weave his fingers through hers. "If there's trouble—"

"Yeah." She cut him off, nodding. "I know."

He drew in a breath.

Even in her dream, the pressure to speak the truth built inside her. "I know what you do, PJ."

And what do you do, Jacie?

He hadn't asked her, but she felt the question, and swallowed through the thickening of her throat.

He tugged on her then, stopped her and she turned. He met her eyes. "I'll find you when I get back."

He wore the finest hint of a beard, his eyes so green she couldn't breathe, lost in them. "What if I'm gone?" She'd been kidding, but he didn't smile.

"Then I'll still find you."

"What, should I send up smoke signals?" She gave a pitiful laugh.

Her heart caught when he reached up and touched her face. "Whatever it takes, I'll find you, Jacie."

"I'll find you."

She gasped, still caught in the dream, in his eyes, in the husky smell of him.

Kiss me.

Oh—

And the geese were honking. Louder and louder and suddenly she was back at the sound, surrounded by the birds, black and white and louder and louder and—

"Sasha, breathe. Long, deep breaths—"

She woke to Aria's voice. Blinked to sort through her surroundings.

Bright orange walls, shivering under the wind still pummeling their shelter. She lay, clothed in her thermal underwear, her booties, and a hat, and was still nearly sweating in her sleeping bag. Her last clear memory was drinking chicken broth that Sasha had heated.

Now, Aria was out of her bag, crawling over her, the wind whipping inside as Aria unzipped the door.

Jenny rolled over onto her back.

Sasha was climbing out of the door, dressed in her thermals, her jacket, and a hat. She collapsed just beyond the vestibule, still packed with their tents, staked down by their harnesses into the snow.

Then, she began to throw up.

Aria had also shed her outer clothing. Now, she pulled on her jacket as she slid out beside Sasha.

Snow billowed into the open doorway as Sasha's body wracked.

"What's going on?" Jenny said.

"She's been hyperventilating. And then suddenly, she had to heave."

Jenny scrambled out of her sleeping bag just as Sasha scooted back inside. She wiped her face. "I'm okay. I'm just nauseated." She crawled over to her sleeping bag and lay down. "And dizzy." Her auburn hair fell over her face and she didn't even bother to wipe it away.

Aria leaned over her, pressed her fingers to her carotid artery.

"I'm so tired," Sasha said.

"You were talking in your sleep," Aria said, glancing at Jenny. "Making funny noises, too."

"I heard geese," Jenny said, not sure why.

"Maybe you heard Sasha hyperventilating."

"I'm fine," Sasha said. "I just have a headache."

"Let's get some fluids in you." Jenny pulled on her jacket. She unzipped the tent and climbed out. The wind gusted against the vestibule as she took out the camp stove. She wedged it into the snow and lit it, then scooted out of the vestibule to fill the coffeepot with snow for tea.

The tent door unzipped, and Aria stuck her head out. "Hey. So, in my professional medical opinion, I think Sasha is coming down with acute mountain sickness. Her heartbeat is fast, and she's not breathing well."

Jenny set the pot on to boil. "How are you doing?"

Aria made a face. "I packed my ankle and I think the swelling is going down, but it still hurts. It might be broken."

"Oh no." Wow. Where had she been? "I slept through all that?"

"You were pretty out of it. I was worried—we've been in the tent for a good fourteen, maybe eighteen hours."

She blinked at her.

Sat back, the chill from the vestibule finding her bones.

Eighteen hours. And no one had found them yet. She let that sit for a second.

The avalanche beacon hadn't worked. Maybe the signal was blocked by the mountains. Or maybe they were just too far away for anyone to find them.

And perhaps because he'd already wandered around in her dreams, Orion's tirade before their climb flooded back to her.

"You think anyone is going to climb down and get you, even if you survive that fall? Your guide might . . . if he can find you. But you'll probably freeze to death first."

Oh. She swallowed again, and the lard filled the back of her throat. She had to go for help.

She tried to keep her hands from shaking as she dug out the tea bags. While she was at it, she checked their food cache.

A bag of nuts, dried fruit, a couple MRE packets, tea, and four energy bars. She had a protein bar in her bag, some electrolyte mix, and another MRE.

The water began to boil and she took it off. Set in the tea bags to steep, turned off the stove, and climbed back into the tent.

Sasha lay with her eyes closed.

"Sash?"

She moaned.

What had she done? Dragging Sasha out of her safe, ordered life onto a mountain that could kill her. And Aria, her best friend. She was a world-renowned pediatric cardiothoracic surgeon, and Jenny had convinced her to give up a month of her life.

Maybe her entire life.

All because she believed that . . . what? That somehow climbing a mountain might make them stronger?

She couldn't breathe.

"See if you can get some tea into Sash." Jenny grabbed her parka and headed back outside.

The wind against the tent's vestibule turned into a jackhammer, so loud she wanted to press her hands over her ears. But she zipped up her parka, pulled on her mittens, her goggles, and her face mask. Laced up her boots, minus her gaiters. She just needed air, something to keep at bay the scream that threatened to break free. But she took the time to attach her crampons and grab her axe.

Then she unzipped the vestibule and stepped out into the white.

The wind gave the blizzard a false bravado. It scraped off the layers of snow, gusted them into a maelstrom of icy brutality, but beyond that, the sky seemed to be clearing, at least enough for her to get her bearings.

Or not, because nothing looked familiar. She planted her axe and looked up, gaging the distance they might have fallen. She couldn't see the top from her position and hiked out beyond the serac to get a better angle.

The ragged spire of Denali's peak rose and disappeared into the clouds, but the angle . . .

She drew in a breath. No . . .

She turned, trying to make out the peaks in the distance through the haze.

The gray spire that looked like a ragged granite tooth might be Mount Huntington. And the flatter humpback next to it . . . Mount Hunter.

Her legs gave out under her, and she sat, hard, her heart a fist slamming into her chest.

She closed her eyes, trying to get a handle on her breathing.

No . . . *no.*

How could they have fallen northeast—off the backside of the mountain, down the lethal glacier fields of Harper's icefall?

Her thoughts channeled back to that terrible moment when Kit had vanished.

Except, maybe Kit *hadn't* been the one who'd fallen. Maybe the top layer of Harper Glacier on the backside of Denali's Pass had given way, loosening the footing on the pass.

From her best guess, they'd fallen into the coulee between the north and south peaks and were stuck at nineteen thousand feet.

No wonder Sasha couldn't breathe. At nineteen thousand feet, they'd all develop AMS, and maybe worse if she didn't get them down.

And it *was* up to her. Because while they had a chance of being found on Denali's West Buttress, they hadn't a hope of being discovered on Harper Glacier.

"I'll find you."

Orion's voice from her stupid dream. It razed under her skin and slid into her brittle bones.

Right.

She drew up her knees, put her head onto them, and for the first time wished his words might come true.

■ ■ ■

He didn't like the look of the mountain. Orion stood in the snow at seven thousand two hundred and stared up at the hazy clouds that stirred snow off the face.

Cold. Unforgiving. Brutal.

And somewhere up there, a group of climbers could be freezing to death.

Larke had flown them to the 7,200-foot Base Camp, fighting the wind as she landed on the snowy runway. Orion was never able to shrug off the deep sense of awe that always found his bones whenever he landed on the wide glacial ice pack that sat in a gully between the imposing Alaskan Range. Along the runway, twenty or more tents of every color grouped in huddles of expedition teams. To protect them from the prevailing winds, climbers had cut out ice blocks like igloos to create castle walls. It reminded him of the small Afghani villages that created their own base camps in the Kunar mountains.

No, he'd never forget those.

"We need to get up there," he said now, to no one, to everyone. To anyone.

God.

Because maybe Ham was right. God had something more for him, and today it might be pulling three women off the mountain.

One of them he couldn't seem to forget—especially now that he knew she was in trouble.

What was it about Jenny that he couldn't get her out of his mind?

"Bringing back memories?"

The question from Ham rocked Orion for a moment, and he looked over at him.

Ham had come out of the Base Camp Quonset to join him and Jake as they loaded up their sleds with gear. Just in case Clancy Hermon, the private chopper pilot tasked with rescues off the mountain, came back with bad news.

Orion wasn't sitting around to wait for the grim news of Jenny's death.

Which was exactly how he felt when he'd heard about the ambush of the SEAL team so many years ago. With every tick of the clock, people could be dying.

So, the answer to Ham's questions was apparently *yes*. The entire operation—gearing up to fly up the mountain to then trek out to find the lost team—dragged up plenty of memories.

"Except I'm eating snow, not dirt. And, hopefully we won't have anyone shooting at us." He glanced at Ham, and meant it as a joke, but it came out flat and not funny at all and Ham's mouth flattened. He nodded.

None of them were in a joking mood. Not after being briefed at the Talkeetna Ranger station.

Not one, but two teams were missing. And yes, they were both Kit's teams—one of them the male team. The other, Jenny's team.

Apparently, the women had taken his advice and not roped up with the men. Which saved them from careening off the Autobahn, the slope just below the pass that led back down to High Camp, when an avalanche hit the fixed rope and ripped the team from the mountain.

The entire group of men, plus their assistant guide, a seasoned climber named Boyd, had fallen and were now lost on the mountain. Only Kit had made it back, arresting herself as she slid down blue ice on the wall back to High Camp at seventeen. She'd made it to High Camp seven hours after her fall, frostbitten and traumatized.

A ranger team had been dispatched to find the men.

No one knew where the women might be. According to the ranger, last time Kit had seen them, they'd been helping Sasha get to the fixed ropes. Orion dearly wanted to know why Kit hadn't been roped in with them—a question he would ask her the minute he caught up with her. But she'd opted to stay on the mountain and help with the search, and he could give her points for that.

"We'd like to do a flyover—they could be stuck on the Football Field, just above the pass, but the winds are too strong to get a chopper up there," Clancy said when they met for a powwow shortly after they arrived, lugging their gear—freshly repacked from Mount Huntington.

In fact, back at Orion's house, Ham had thrown the steaks on the grill while Orion and Jake checked the climbing gear, packed fresh clothing and sleeping bags, and added more rations. With the sun still high, they headed back to town.

Now, around midnight, a blood-red glow lit the gully that housed Base Camp, the sun shadowed by the High One. Higher up, a cloud blanketed the mountain.

"Can you get us to Basin Camp?" Ham had asked Clancy.

Clancy, a lean man with short dark hair, tall and all business, had stared at the mountain and given Ham a dark look.

That's when Orion stalked out, commandeered a park-issued sled, and began to pack his gear.

He'd climbed three thousand feet in a day. More, even. He could be at Basin Camp in twenty-four hours.

"They are freezing to death up there," he said now to Ham.

Ham wore dark, ultraviolet glasses as he stared up on the mountain.

Then, abruptly, he went back into the Quonset.

"He has that look," Jake said, standing up from where he'd been fixing his snowshoes to his pack. "We had a twelve-year-old

101

girl go missing this winter at a ski hill in northern Minnesota, and he refused to give up long after the ski patrol had quit. Finally found her off trail by a mile. She'd found shelter at an unused rental house. He'd skied her trail and followed her into the woods."

Orion glanced at Jake. "You do that a lot? Look for lost kids?"

"Usually it's someone who has gone missing, yes. Too many of them are kids."

"And how often do you find them?"

"Depends on how soon we get involved." Jake wore his wool cap and, like Orion, had made the mistake of shaving. He ducked his chin into his jacket farther as a gust of wind rolled down the gully and rippled the walls of the nearby tents. "I hate the ones with the kids, though." He shook his head and looked away.

Orion didn't have time to follow his comment because Ham emerged.

"Let's go."

Orion frowned but shouldered his pack and pulled the sled over to the chopper where Ham waited.

"I told him we didn't need to be babied. Just get us near the drop site and we're good to go," Ham said.

Orion raised an eyebrow but okay, yeah.

He and Ham lifted the sled and shoved it into the belly of the chopper, a Eurocopter AS-350 B3. A little lighter than the Chinooks and Paves Orion was used to flying in, but at least it was a ride. He climbed into the back seat, and Jake joined him.

Ham took the front.

Clancy climbed in, wearing his snow jacket, a baseball hat, and a grim set to his mouth. "We have a tightening window, and this might not be pretty, but I'll get you up there."

He strapped in, and Orion looked out the window as the rotors started to spin. In a moment, they lifted off, the world dropping away.

For a second he was flying over the snowy Kunar Valley, the muddy Kunar River flowing through the barren fields, sometimes populated with goat herds.

That others might live. The PJ mantra filtered through his brain. The rumble of the machine, the roar against the wind as it slipped through the valley, ascending, it all stirred up—

They stood in the cool morning of the FOB, right outside the cinder-block hospital. In the back of the building was the TOC—Tactical Operations Center.

He was still buzzing from his late night stargazing with Jacie. Walking her home, winding his fingers through hers. The smell of her as he stopped outside her Quonset.

With everything inside him, he'd wanted to kiss her. Let his gaze roam her face, drop to her lips. *"I'll find you when I get back."*

He wanted to weave his fingers through her short, blonde bob. "What if I'm gone?"

For some reason, her question hit him squarely in the chest. He swallowed, the strangest rush of panic filling his throat. "Then I'll still find you."

He spoke his words softly, with more commitment and husky desire in them than he wanted her to know, but they lingered in the night, the stars overhead blinking as if in surprise.

"What, should I send up smoke signals?" Her voice quavered a little.

He touched her face then. "Whatever it takes, I'll find you, Jacie."

"I'll find you." The last thing he'd said to her before he took off, before his life exploded.

And just like she'd suggested, she wasn't around when he returned.

Well, he hadn't actually returned, but she'd certainly taken a hike out of his life.

Her absence had hit him in the gut. Clearly he hadn't thought about the fact that someday their wartime friendship might end. She'd burrowed into his life so fast it felt like she always belonged there, lodged inside. Maybe because she listened, acted like she cared about him. Cared about his life in Alaska, or even his endless list of useless facts.

"I'll have to visit sometime. I'd like to meet your father."

He watched now as the mountain rose before him.

"He just . . . slid off the mountain."

Their conversation now felt painfully prophetic. The thought of her huddled against the wind, injured, maybe even becoming hypothermic put a fist in his gut.

Maybe he'd given away his heart too quickly to a woman who'd made him no promises. But he'd definitely given it away.

I'll find you, Jenny.

The wind buffeted the chopper, bouncing as snow gusted off the peaks. Snow dusted the gray-blue granite spires that rose around them, the nose of the chopper forcing its way higher. Mount Frances seemed so close he could reach out and touch it, and the surface of the main Kahiltna Glacier was so smooth, it resembled a thick layer of frosting he'd like to drag a finger through.

Orion's stomach dropped as Clancy used the high wall of Motorcycle Hill to protect them as they rose to eleven thousand.

"Hang on!" The wind off West Buttress's plateau nearly sent them spiraling back into a snowy wall, but Clancy fought it and they cleared Windy Corner.

Orion looked down upon the creamy snow, a pristine, lethal landscape that hid crevasses and fissures in the ice.

Suddenly, Basin Camp appeared. The most populated site on

the mountain. He spotted a clutter of tents, rippling and waving in the winds, some protected by a wall of ice blocks. Others simply staked down.

They sneaked in just below a ring of clouds. Orion located the large orange tent inhabited by the NPS rangers protected in a wide, snow-berthed area. Beyond Basin Camp, the Headwall rose two thousand feet to an icy ridge that led them to High Camp.

A climber would be crazy to attempt the Headwall in this wind, but for a second, he found himself wondering.

If they started now, by midnight they'd be at High Camp.

Or, of course, flung from the mountain by the ruthless wind.

Orion held his breath as Clancy hovered over the snowpack, not eager to land in the soft, blowing snow. "Get out!"

Ham opened his door and tossed his pack out, some ten feet down. It landed in the snow, half-buried.

This would be fun.

Orion opened the door, and he and Jake pushed the sled out onto the snow. It sank into frosting. His pack followed, and then he pushed himself onto the skid, closed the door, and leapt.

The snow was deep, soft, and an easy landing. He worked up a sweat climbing out, however, found his pack, and by the time he'd strapped on his skis, Ham was skiing up with the sled.

The chopper had peeled off, leaving them on the plateau. But the sound of it shook the mountain and Orion listened for avalanches.

Nothing boomed in the distance.

Ham stood in the snow, watching the chopper vanish beyond the peak.

Then, all went quiet, save for the train rumble of the wind.

Jake came up. Looked toward the camp, then the peak. Shivered. "I'm already cold."

Orion stared at the gusts of snow, the foreboding peak, and wished the mountain would stop calling him.

⬛ ⬛ ⬛

There was crazy, and then there was *crazy*.

Jake had always been game for living on the edge, soaring above the jagged peaks, staring down at life from above, and fighting fate to survive. It was how he'd learned to live with himself. Seeking the adrenaline. Living above the clutter of his life, his mistakes. His wounds.

Tempting fate, really.

But even he could recognize *crazy*.

"How high is this thing?" He shouted the question into the wind, but it carried his voice away into the rest of the blowing snow. The temperature had dropped into the negative thirties, his fingers were starting to numb, and, save for the exertion of climbing up a fifty-degree pitched ice wall, he might be shivering so hard his teeth could rattle out of his head.

Staring up at the mountain from the safety of Basin Camp, Jake put their chances of reaching High Camp in the negative. The snow was drifting off the ridge of the West Buttress, down along the icy Headwall, and through the plateau that made up Basin Camp—the sky bullet gray, clouds obscuring the peak.

"Two thousand feet to the next camp!" Orion yelled. So apparently Orion, in the lead, had heard him, despite the howl of the wind and Orion's being some thirty feet above him. And that was only because the wind had died enough, the skies clearing enough for them to see each other.

Orion and Ham had huddled inside the orange FOB tent at Basin Camp for over an hour, trying to get a fix on what had happened to the climbers.

It wasn't hard to figure out.

Given the booms still sounding in the distance, the way the mountain seemed to tremble, the two teams had been swept away in a massive avalanche that dislodged the snowcap on either side of Denali Pass.

The searchers needed a chopper, something like a Pave to search the backside of the mountain. But no one was going any higher with these winds, which meant they'd have to wait.

Or go it on foot.

That's where the crazy came in.

Ham and Orion had emerged from the tent, Orion's expression set. Jake didn't know the guy well, but Ham said he'd been a Pararescue Jumper. Which meant he charged into battle, tracers flying, to save the already injured.

He wasn't going to be stopped by a little wind.

Besides, Jake had seen Orion's skills on Mount Huntington. If anyone knew his way around snow and ice, it was Orion Starr.

Ham, too, looked annoyed enough to take on *crazy*, but then again Ham took rescues personally. That's what happened when you lost the woman you loved during a rescue op. And he'd had a kid sister who'd been seriously injured when he was serving overseas. It had taken him ten agonizing days to get to her.

Ham and Orion had *rescue* in their DNA.

Jake possessed enough crazy to want to follow them.

Except, well, he really *did* understand their grim expressions. He wasn't the only one who couldn't get the idea out of his head that three women they knew could be freezing to death on the mountain.

Which was why he'd helped unload the sled, divided the gear between them, and clipped his ascender onto the fixed rope.

"We're going up to High Camp," Orion said, just as Jake

expected, as they started their hike to the Headwall. "I have the GPS. I've been up the mountain a dozen times. Stay on my tail."

So yes, it was crazy, but he was all in. Because try as he might, he couldn't get Aria out of his head. Couldn't peel from his memory the sound of her laughter as he spun her on the packed-earth dance floor under the midnight sun. Maybe it was the long solitude of sitting in their snowy ice hotel on Mount Huntington, trying to think of anything but his next Spam recipe, but he'd let their short conversation play out in his memory way too much.

"So, you're off to climb the mountain?" He gestured at Denali, off in the distance.

He'd seen her from a distance and had chased her red Solo cup down when the wind took it off a nearby table. He'd returned it to her with a "You dropped this."

She'd smiled at him, and the first thing he noticed was her dark brown eyes, the color of rich black coffee, something stirring in them. Curiosity, maybe.

It only sparked in him the same.

"That little bump?" She winked and lifted her shoulder. "No, we really just showed up for the ribs." She finished wiping her fingers with a wet wipe, wadded the wipe up, picked up the basket, and threw it away. "Totally worth the six-hour flight, two-hour drive, and five bucks."

"Let's not forget the music." The band was playing a new song, although he couldn't place it.

"Love me some Tim McGraw."

He didn't know if she might be telling the truth, but just in case—"Wanna dance?"

He knew it was bold—he didn't even know her. But he lived by the motto of *Live now, or you might miss it,* so he gave her his best Jake Silver smile and held out his hand.

She took it. "Why not?"

She fit so easily, so smoothly into his arms, sliding into his embrace like she knew him, and they fell into step as if they'd been dancing together all his life.

It sort of rocked him back and he tripped. Which caused her to step on his foot.

She laughed. "Should I lead?"

"I got this," he said, not sure why she rattled him. He knew how to dance. Had learned from his cousins down in Nashville.

Apparently, women liked to dance.

And he liked the women in his life to be happy—all five of his sisters, his mother, and even his sweet grandma Lou. So, yeah, he'd learned to dance.

He dipped her at the end of the song, and she hung onto his neck as he brought her back up.

"You're a charmer, aren't you, Cowboy?" she said, letting him go. Her brown hair had fallen out of her bun, and he resisted the urge to tuck it back behind her ear as the music changed. "What's your name?"

"Jake. Silver. You?"

"Aria Sinclair."

The music slowed, and he raised an eyebrow, held out his hands.

She grinned. "I see you like to live dangerously, huh, Cowboy Jake?"

He wanted to frown at that, but in truth, yes, maybe he did.

Unfortunately, because of it, people around him tended to get hurt, caught in the line of fire, or lost.

Which was why he kept things short term, without commitment. Fun.

And this was fun.

They fell into the slower song, something easier to talk through.

We said goodbye on a night like this
Stars shining down, I was waitin' for a kiss

"Are you climbing Denali also?" she asked.

"Nope. Mount Huntington. It's only a twelver, but highly technical, so my boss thinks it would be good practice."

"For what?"

"He runs a private search-and-rescue group—mostly international, but we do all sorts of things, so he wants us to be prepared." He leaned closer to her. "Actually, we're on a recruiting trip. He's trying to talk one of his old military buddies into joining us."

"Military, huh? Did you serve?"

And this was where it got tricky. Because although he wanted to pull out his SEAL creds, invariably it was followed by questions. Half answers. Or, if he got truthful, probably the night would end right here, right now.

He liked her enough to want another dance, so, "Yeah, I was in the Navy. Got out a year ago and started working for Ham."

Her eyebrow raised then. "Ham? You don't mean Hamilton Jones, do you?" She glanced over his shoulder. "Wow, that's a small world."

He frowned.

"We train at GoSports fitness. I think he owns it, right? I wondered why he looked so familiar—I've seen his picture. He did an ad during last year's Super Bowl with Adam Thielen, a wide receiver with the Vikings."

Huh. Yes, small world. "Yeah. They're good friends. I'm a Go-Sports coach. Mostly swimming, scuba diving, and parasailing."

"Are you from Minnesota?"

He nodded. "You?"

"Minnesota Viking, to the core."

He had a mental picture of her wearing purple, shouting "*skol!*"

"What do you do now?"

"I'm a doctor. So is Jenny, although she has a doctorate in psychology. Sasha is our resident entrepreneur. Runs an essential oils and soap company. Her husband, Lucas, works with me."

"So what brought you to the mountain?"

He twirled her out, the chorus thrumming inside him.

> Turn around, listen to your heart
> I need you so much, don't tear me apart
> Even if I knew you'd be the one that got away
> I'd still go back and get you.

She came back into his arms. The sun was behind him, shining in her eyes, and touched her face with a tan. "You know—work hard, play hard, right? Jenny and I climb a mountain every year just because we can. It makes us feel alive." Then she grinned at him.

And in that moment, *he* felt alive, something stirring inside him, loosening.

Alive.

He'd sort of forgotten what that felt like.

Unfortunately, that was when she glanced past him and frowned. "Uh-oh."

He followed her look and spied Orion standing at a table, dressing down a group of climbers. The music drowned out his words, so Jake didn't catch it, but it clearly had Aria's blonde friend upset. She wore an expression Jake might call horror.

Maybe Orion was spinning one of his catastrophic tales of demise on the mountain. He did that—told stories of his father's career as a park ranger on the mountain. Apparently Orion had worked as a mountain rescue volunteer for a couple years before he joined the Air Force.

Maybe Orion read the woman, because he walked over to her and said something as the song ended.

"I'd better go find out what's going on," Aria said.

Then she looked up at him, smiled, and left her memory lodged in his heart because she gave him a peck on the cheek. "Try to stay alive, Jake Silver."

"Try to stay alive."

The words thrummed inside him like a heartbeat as he kicked his crampon into the mountain. The snow was wind-bitten, a crust layering the top, and he broke through, using his ice axe to grip with one hand, the fixed rope sliding through the other.

Orion had nearly reached the top of the eight-hundred-foot Headwall and was waiting for them before they continued up the ridge. The ridge with snow casting off the top, causing a near whiteout. The ridge that dropped a thousand feet on either side.

Below him, Ham was nearly a polar bear with the snow caking his face guard, hat, and hood. Jake searched for a foothold in the snow—but the wind had erased Orion's steps.

He kicked in another step, aware of his breathing. And the slightest hint of nausea. He needed food.

Sleep.

Heat.

And most of all, maybe just enough crazy luck to not get blown off the mountain.

Stay alive, Jake Silver.

CHAPTER SIX

THEY HAD TO GET DOWN the mountain.

Today.

While the sun shone, the wind died, and most importantly . . . before Sasha got any worse.

"C'mon, Sasha. Time to get up," Jenny said. "We need to get your boots on."

Sasha leaned up in her sleeping bag, grimacing as Aria worked her foot into her boot. After eight more hours in the tent, the storm had finally cleared enough to leave blue skies, a slight wisping of snow, and the reality that no one was coming for them.

Or, if they were, they'd have to rescue them from lower heights. No chopper was going to be able to pluck them off the mountain at nineteen thousand.

More critical, they had to get Sasha down to lower elevation to slow down her advance toward pulmonary edema. Already she was coughing hard, her bones were aching, and she was unable to keep food down. Jenny feared waiting any longer for help would bring them to a point of no return.

The wind buffeted the tent as Jenny stuffed the bags into a compression sack, then into the packs just outside the door. She'd already secured the stove, the food bag, and the rest of their gear, repacking it into mostly her pack.

Aria seemed to think she could walk on her own swollen ankle, but she could move it so maybe it wasn't broken.

Still, she let out a pained gasp as she pulled on her boot.

Leaned over, blowing out breaths.

Jenny crouched at the edge of the tent, looking at Sasha and Aria. They both seemed exhausted, their eyes edged with pain and not a little fear. Sasha had to be weak, dehydrated, and dizzy, so she planned on short roping her and Aria together.

She'd go out ahead, breaking trail. That way, if they fell, well, maybe she could slow their fall before catastrophe happened.

Not only did they have to cross the glacier, but the snow was thick and slick, the slope ripe for an avalanche. But, once they traversed the glacier, they could camp at Parker Pass and tackle Karstens Ridge tomorrow.

She didn't want to think about the technical work of Karstens Ridge, the steepness, the fact that she'd need to lower Sasha—and probably Aria—down in pitches.

Breathe.

They just had to get low enough for Sasha's body to stop working against her. Then maybe Jenny could go for help.

"Listen, we take it slow going down Harper Glacier. We need to traverse carefully, as it's riddled with crevasses and icefalls, and we need to watch out for snow bridges—flimsy arches over crevasses that are made by the wind. But set your feet, use your ice axe, and follow my trail."

Please, please let her not be making the biggest mistake of her life.

Okay, another biggest mistake of her life.

It seemed she couldn't escape threatening the lives of people she loved.

She helped Sasha out of the tent, then clipped her with a butter-fly knot onto the line in the middle. Aria attached her figure eight onto the end of the line.

Meanwhile, Jenny took down the tent and stuffed it into her pack. Aria carried a lighter pack, as did Sasha. She tied into the line at the front, the rope coiled around her.

The sky had cleared to a light, wispy blue, the temperature in the minus twenties, but nothing of danger settled in the air.

Last night, she'd talked through their descent with Aria and Sasha.

She'd plotted their line down the glacier, a reverse from the ascent she'd planned for months. She knew the Muldrow Glacier route. At least on paper.

Once, she'd watched a video of someone skiing down Denali, through the West Buttress route. It had turned her hands clammy, her stomach twisting. Now, as she stared down the mountain, the rise of the Alaskan Range towering around her, her stomach twisted again.

Please, God, don't let us fall.

Maybe she should have been praying a little more over the past two days, but frankly, she wasn't sure God was even listening to her anymore.

Maybe she'd do better on her own, instead of reminding him of her vast mistakes.

Why she didn't really deserve help. Again.

Her crampons kicked into the snow, windblown and stiff from three days of assault. Tiny dribbles of snow trickled down the slope.

The wind hummed in her ears, skimmed up snow, but it wasn't so much as to knock her over. She looked back and spotted Aria and Sasha working their way behind her, traversing the hill, eight feet of rope separating them.

Aria leaned hard on her axe, but she seemed to be moving okay.

Maybe Jenny should be behind them, in case they fell, but so far Sasha was muscling through. And Jenny wasn't sure she could trust them to spot a crevasse.

Pressing the handle of her axe into the snow, she tested each step before her foot crunched down. Riddled with seracs and icefalls, the field hid a thousand endless crevasses. Her thighs burned as she kicked into each step. She refused to look down at the sheer drop of nearly a thousand feet into the frosted glacial field below.

She glanced back when they reached the pitch through the first icefall. They'd traversed the ridge, leaving behind their serac and the view of the Denali summit. Sinking down into the snow, she waited for Aria and Sasha to catch up, surveying the route.

As if God had emptied his ice-cube tray onto the hillside, the route was riddled with enormous snow-covered boulders, ridges, gigantic seracs, and drifts.

Sasha sank down beside her, drew up her knees, and leaned back with the weight of her pack.

"How are you?"

"I'm not going to tell you," she said.

Jenny gave her a smile, reached out and touched her mitten. *We're stronger than we think we are.* She wanted to say the words but held them back as Aria came up.

"The good news is that I'm so cold, I can't feel my ankle to know if it hurts." She didn't sit down. "But I vote that next year, instead of climbing a mountain, we go to Cancun. That feels like something Kia would have wanted me to do."

Jenny had pulled out her water bottle and now she nearly spit out the water. "Yeah. Or Hawaii. There's always Diamond Head."

"You know what's wrong with our epic trips?" Sasha said.

Jenny gave her the bottle, but she passed it on to Aria.

116

"There are no men," Sasha said. "I vote next time we bring men to carry the heavy things."

Jenny stared at her. "That's the point. We don't need men to carry heavy things."

"Not *need*," Aria said. "Want. I agree with Sash. I want a man to carry heavy things."

"Oh my—sexist much?"

"Mmmhmm," Aria said, wiping her mouth. "What can I say? I like strong men."

"Like that guy you were dancing with in Copper Mountain?" Sasha asked, now accepting the water.

"Yeah, like Jake." Aria was grinning then. "I wouldn't be sad if he showed up right now and said, 'Aria, let me carry your pack. No—Aria, let me carry *you* down the mountain.'" She turned to look at the icefall. "Yep. Men. I vote yes to men."

Jenny shook her head. But okay, she wasn't horrified by the idea. Maybe by the idea of *one* man showing up. "When we were in Afghanistan, Orion told me that he'd find me."

"What?" Sasha handed her the bottle back. "I thought you barely knew him."

"If you call *barely* calling out for him in her sleep," Aria said.

"I did not—"

"Please. I was your roommate. I know your sounds."

"It wasn't anything serious. We never even kissed." Jenny capped the bottle and put it back into her pack. "Although, I sometimes dream that we did."

"Maybe he's looking for you right now," Sasha said.

"How could he be? If I remember, he was going to climb Mount Huntington." She gestured to the razor-sharp peak below them. "Nope, if we want to get off this mountain, we have to do it by ourselves, ladies."

She forced herself to her feet, grunting with the weight of her pack.

"You shouldn't have lightened ours," Aria said.

"I'm fine. Really. Let's get past this icefall and have some lunch."

"Or supper?" Aria said.

"Who knows?" Jenny said as she considered the terrain below her. Like pie meringue. Creamy, ridged, and beautiful, especially with the sky still bright and blue, the tiniest edging of red along the horizon.

"Let's rope up farther apart," she said to Sasha and moved her butterfly knot, clipping her thirty feet from Aria. "Stay alert."

Jenny had already worked up a sweat by the time she hit the ice field. She worked her way through thick snow, testing her route, moving around buttresses as big as three-story buildings, through passes the width of a bus, and around lumps and ridges in the snow. The sky had turned blood red by the time they landed on the next smooth ridge of glacier.

So, it might take them longer than she'd hoped to get to their camping spot for tonight. But so far, no one had fallen.

"Let's heat up some soup," she said.

"I need to get warm," Aria said. "And probably Sasha does too."

Jenny nodded. The wind wasn't so gusty that they couldn't set up the tent, so she pulled it up and, as Aria held the wickets, erected it in moments. She didn't bother staking it down—they wouldn't be using it long.

Pulling out the stove, she handed it to Aria along with the water bottle. "Add some of the water to the snow to get it melting." She grabbed the pot and filled it with water. "I'll find the soup."

Aria had taken off her crampons, but moved fully clothed into the tent, carrying the stove with her. Sasha did the same.

Jenny walked over to get a better view of the next icefall. She could almost see the path—a gully that wound around boulders and seracs all the way down to the bottom of the glacier. Then they could camp at the base of Browne Tower before tackling Karstens Ridge tomorrow.

They just might make it.

A scream erupted behind her and she jerked, fearing an avalanche.

She turned—

The tent was in flames. Caught by the wind, the entire thing flashed over in a whoosh.

"Aria!" She leaped toward the tent.

Aria had already fled, dragging Sasha with her. They scrambled back in the snow, Sasha kicking snow onto the inferno, but the thing was gone in a second, the nylon coughing up black.

Jenny fell beside Aria, still pulling her away.

Sasha pressed her hand over her mouth. "It's my fault. I accidentally kicked the stove."

"It fell against the side of the tent—"

"Why did you light it inside the tent! That's what the vestibule is for—" Jenny slapped her hand over her mouth. "I'm sorry. I'm— I'm really sorry."

Sasha grabbed her hands. "No, I'm sorry. I didn't mean—I was just going to lay down."

"I was cold," Aria said, shaking. "I know better . . ."

No tent. The stove blackened, possibly unusable. Jenny fisted her hands into their parkas, drew them close, mostly to stop her shaking.

Think. Just— "Okay, okay. We're okay. We'll just . . . we'll just build a snow cave." She met their eyes. "Here's the good news. We still have our shovel. And our packs. And . . ."

"If the stove is toast, we can't melt snow," Sasha said. "No tea. No soup . . ."

"We have the lighter," Aria said and pulled it out from her pocket. Gave Jenny such a desperate look Jenny couldn't help but nod.

"We have the lighter," Jenny said.

"And each other," Sasha said.

"Yeah. Who needs men?" Aria gave a wan smile.

Sasha's eyes teared up.

Jenny nodded, hating the joke, but needing it. "Yeah, who needs men?"

■ ■ ■

It was a summit kind of day. The kind of day where the air felt buoyant, crisp, and light, the sunshine hot, the snow sturdy.

Except the rising sun could heat the snowpack that hung over the High Camp like a roof, let loose, and take out climbers in a lethal run of snow and ice.

"Let's get moving."

Jake was finishing off a bowl of oatmeal, boiled eggs, and a muffin that had turned to crumbs in his pack. He just glanced up at Orion, then back at his meal. He'd already downed a cup of coffee, maybe two.

"Don't tell me you're missing Spam."

"I'm missing my bed," Jake growled.

Ham, too, was wolfing down breakfast, lines etched into his windburned face.

Okay, yes, Orion could feel every bone in his body after their climbing stint yesterday and their scant sleep. He probably needed something more fortifying than a power bar if he expected to have enough energy to climb the two thousand feet to Denali Pass. But he felt like he might be able to scale the mountain on adrenaline alone.

Especially after his sit-down with Kit. He and his team had climbed the Headwall in record time. It was the narrow ridge along West Buttress that had slowed them down, the wind turning personal and nasty as it tried to knock them off the mountain. They scrabbled over the icy rocks and finally reached High Camp as the sun was faux-setting on the mountain, pouring blood red into the valley.

While Ham and Jake set up the tent, digging in against the high winds, Orion had tracked down the guide.

She sat alone in her tent, her frostbitten fingers bandaged, heating up soup. He'd knocked, climbed in, and got the lowdown, in quiet, somber tones.

Kit knew, too well, what it felt like to lose someone she cared about on the mountain.

And even if Jenny Calhoun wasn't Jacie, he was still worried.

Aw, who was he kidding? He was going a little crazy with the idea that Jacie—and Orion knew mostly, *definitely* it was Jacie— might be frozen at the bottom of Peters Glacier.

Kit poured him a sierra cup of soup. He practically inhaled it, not realizing how famished he'd been. "Boyd roped up with the guys—one of their team got AMS and we sent him down the mountain with another team."

"Why weren't you roped up with the girls' team?" He tried to keep his voice easy, but her head came up and her eyes sparked.

"Because Sasha was getting AMS and Aria insisted on linking arms with her to help her down the mountain. It's a great way to get everyone killed."

And he got it. Her husband had been helping one of their clients when he vanished right off the mountain.

"There isn't enough time to arrest a fall when you're walking that close," she said softly, looking away. A beat pulsed between them and she finally looked up. "We were at the fixed ropes at the pass when the mountain just . . . it just *shook*. A wind came out of the south and tore off the snowpack at the top."

He remembered that wind too well. Had wondered how it would hit Denali. "Maybe it was a troposphere wind. It nearly knocked us off Huntington, too."

"I dropped about a hundred feet before I stopped myself. I was still hooked to the fixed line at the top, which might have saved my life because it kept me from careening off the mountain. But I'd lost my bearings and it took me hours to get back to High Camp. That's when I realized the guys were missing. They must have been lower down, on the fixed rope, and were taken away with the avalanche." She finished her soup and put her bowl down, filling it with hot water and a cocoa packet. "We still haven't found them."

"What about the women?"

"I don't know. Maybe they're just stuck up on the pass. Without the fixed ropes, the pass is intimidating. But the wind has been too high for us to ascend."

"Did they have gear?"

She gave him a look. "Of course. A tent, food, and I made sure they had belay and climbing equipment. Their leader, Jenny, seemed pretty capable."

He hoped so.

She reached out and caught his parka as he got up to leave. "Find them." Her eyes wore a haunted expression. "They can't simply go missing on the mountain. It's not . . ." She sighed. "Everyone needs an end to their story."

He squeezed her hand and headed back to the tent. While Ham and Jake slept like the dead, he dreamed of Jenny huddled in her tent on Denali Pass, trying to stay warm.

"I'll find you."

He didn't know why those words had lodged inside him, found a place right under his skin, but they buzzed him awake shortly after the sun peeled back the shadows over the peaks to the east. By the time Ham and Jake rose, he'd made breakfast, packed his gear, and was antsy to go.

The wind had cleared and with it the whiteout. High Camp was populated with a handful of groups waiting to bag the summit, and he wanted to push out before they got started. The last thing he wanted was to wait on a fixed line for a bunch of timid rookies to find their inner climber.

Kit was up, too, and on the radio, her black braids falling from her hat, her red hood pulled up.

He came over to her, and she gave him a sitrep. "A ranger spotted the guys an hour ago. They're below us, clinging to a spur on West Buttress. We just sent down a ranger team, and I'm calling Clancy to see if he can fly in a basket."

"How many survivors?"

Her mouth made a tight line. "I don't know."

He drew in a breath. "I need a radio. Probably two."

"Yes. And by the way, all the women were wearing avalanche locaters." She pulled out hers from her outside pocket. "I changed mine to receive, but . . ."

Maybe they were out of range.

"Hopefully they're hunkered down in the Football Field above the pass," he said as he retrieved two radios. He checked the batteries, then tucked one into his jacket. He gave Ham the other one.

Ham checked it. "We're going to find them, Ry."

Orion nodded and looked up the mountain. First, they'd have to climb up to Denali Pass and this time of day, the route was shadowed in dim sunlight. Worse, the pass grew steeper with each step. But Orion could trek it with his eyes closed.

No, the climb up wasn't why his stomach was knotted, his chest tight. "Yeah, sure."

Ham didn't move. "Dude. I feel it in my gut. Every time I pray, it's like God is saying he'll help us find them."

Orion looked at him. "And now you're just ticking me off. God doesn't make promises like that—and if he does that makes me even madder, so let's just go, okay?"

Ham grabbed his shoulder as he made to push past him. "Ry. What's going on?"

Orion stopped, blew out a breath. "I don't know. Just . . . something about . . ."

"Jenny Calhoun?"

He looked at Ham. "No. Yes. Just . . . everything."

Ham looked at him. "Wait—is this about your dad? The fact that no one found him?"

"They found him. Broken at the bottom of Peters Glacier. No . . . I just don't want to hear about any of God's promises, okay?"

But Ham's gaze didn't leave Orion.

"What?"

"I was thinking about your question about Jenny—if she looked familiar."

Orion stared at him. "From two weeks ago?"

"Lots of thinking. Jenny. Calhoun. J. C."

Orion's breath caught. "Aw, I'm an idiot. I can't believe—" He turned. "I knew it. I *knew* it."

"She was a reporter, not a climber. And she looked different, right?"

He'd never forget those eyes. That smile.

"Maybe she didn't recognize me. Maybe . . . do I look that much different?"

Ham lifted a shoulder. "Guess you didn't make an impact."

Orion stared at him.

Ham smiled.

"Let's get up the mountain, find her, and then you can ask her."
Ham picked up his ice axe and headed toward Jake. He roped in
behind Jake and left Orion to clip in ahead.

Didn't make an impact?

Orion nearly sprinted up the Denali Pass, digging his feet in
with relentless momentum, sweat beading his back. He looked
back once, saw his footprints in the snow, Jake trudging behind
him, the camp below. He couldn't see West Buttress from here but
hoped the rangers had found someone alive.

He refused to believe that thirty-six hours on the top of the
mountain meant the worst.

"Keep moving," Jake shouted, seeing him stop. "If I stop, I'll
never start again."

Right. Orion kept moving up to the pass, where it turned rocky,
and he waited as Jake and Ham caught up.

The shelf on the pass had given way, at least a little, because it
revealed more rock than he remembered. But the snowpack on the
Football Field, which led up to the final ridge climb, was crystalline
white, unblemished.

His breath came hard while he tried not to let his disappoint-
ment bite at him.

"Do you see them?" Jake asked as he scrabbled up the rocky
outcropping toward him.

He said nothing.

Ham joined them, and they stood a long time before Ham
moved ahead of him. "Let's keep going."

The wind up here still buffeted him, burning his ears, but he
couldn't move. If they weren't camped on the Football Field then . . .

He couldn't take his gaze off the drop-off into Harper Glacier.

Beyond, in the valley below, Mount Huntington and Mount Hunter rose like old friends to greet him. But between them lay the Muldrow Glacier.

The first ascent up Denali had been made across the glacier, then up Karstens Ridge, and finally Harper Glacier.

Some people still climbed the High One via the Muldrow Glacier route.

But not Kit. And not Jenny—she wouldn't have the first clue how to descend the backside of Denali.

He couldn't get Kit's words out of his head. *"Their leader, Jenny, seemed pretty capable."*

Orion was standing there, staring out into the ragged mountainscape, when Jake said, "What do you make of that?"

He pointed to a wisp of black smoke, rising, dissipating into the blue sky. As if someone had made a campfire. And for a second, Jacie was in his head, her voice quavering, as if unsure. *What, should I send up smoke signals?*

Yes. Yes, you should.

"We're going down Harper Glacier," Orion said.

Ham had come back, frowning. "What?"

Orion turned to him. "Listen, I don't know why, but . . . I think they're down there."

"You think they fell off?" Jake said, his jaw tight.

"No. Maybe. I don't know. But . . . they're not here, so . . . ."

He looked at Ham, then Jake. "We're going down the glacier."

"Seriously."

"And . . . we're glissading down."

"That's what I'm talking about," Jake said, unhooking.

Orion turned to Ham. "It's safer. Lower center of gravity. And—"

"Fun." Ham grinned. Okay, he hadn't expected that, but Orion wasn't going to argue.

Ham unclipped too, and Orion wound up the line over his shoulder in a kiwi coil, then tacked it down with an overhand on a bight into his locking biner.

Glissading. Sliding down on his backside, the axe driven into the snow to slow him down, guide him.

It might be a little steep.

He walked over to the edge of the glacier and looked down. The Harper Glacier fell like a white river between the north and south peaks, gliding through Karstens Ridge and the Taylor Spur. At around twelve thousand feet, it cut between Karpe Ridge and Pioneer Ridge, spilled out into the Great Icefall, then cascaded to the lower icefall until it merged into Muldrow Glacier.

Nineteen thousand feet of blue ice, powder, ice chunks, and lethal crevasses.

He spied the final trickle of black smoke and pointed it out to Jake and Ham. "There's our target."

He estimated maybe three thousand feet down.

He sat on the icy slope and took off his crampons. Then he clipped them onto his pack.

"Remember, don't dig in too much with your heels or you'll launch yourself right over. Lean back into your axe."

"Sheesh, Starr, you think we'd never seen snow before," Jake said, sitting down beside him, crampons off.

"Yeah, well, maybe you've never slid on your backside down a mountain—"

Jake took off. He held his feet out, the snow shearing up in front of him, leaning back into his axe, riding it as he careened down the glacier.

Not too fast!

But Jake seemed to know his technique, and in a second, Ham also pushed off.

Which left Orion to catch up. He leaned back, letting gravity carry him. After nearly three days of wind, the snowpack was slick and icy and he fought to keep his heels dug in, his axe planted enough to keep him from careening down the mountain.

In front of him, he spotted Jake roll over, grab his axe, and slow himself down.

"You okay?" he asked as he skidded by him.

"Nearly supermanned!" Jake said, stopped now and looking over at Orion.

Okay, so the guy would be fine.

Ham had slowed too, the snow flying over his head.

Orion dug in, veering around a wide serac. He skimmed past that and slowed, suddenly spotting a worked trail.

He dug in and came to a stop at the trail.

Ham shot past him, then rolled and self-arrested.

"Is that a trail?" he shouted.

Jake sprayed him with an arc of snow as he stopped, also self-arresting. Orion was climbing to his feet as Jake said, "Hey, is that a depression under that serac?"

Under a serac? Who would be—

Except, yes. Orion followed Jake's point and made out what looked like a camp under the shadow of the shelf-like serac.

Huh. He turned, scoping the mountain, trying to find the black smoke. It had vanished under the fall of the ice field.

But somewhere down there, Jacie was alive. He felt it in his gut, just like Ham said.

"No matter what it takes, I'll find you, Jacie."

■ ■ ■

Aria needed to stop letting her heart make decisions her body couldn't deliver. Like buying a motorcycle, taking lessons, and then letting the sleek Honda Rebel 300 gather dust in her storage unit. Or finishing the online scuba diving course only to avoid taking her underwater test.

The only reason she actually made it onto a mountain was because of Jenny, really. Because Jenny didn't give up. And because Aria had made herself promises.

But really, she blamed Kia for the impulse inside her that looked at a mountain and heard, "Climb me."

Yeah. No. Next time the words *Just Do It* pulsed inside her, Aria was going to turn on *Vertical Limit* and remind herself just why freezing to death on a high peak might be a bad idea.

Mostly because, aside from dying, she really needed her fingers. All of them.

It was hard to operate on tiny hearts without fingers.

Now, she flexed her fingers inside her liners, inside her gloves, hoping the fingertips weren't as badly frostbitten as they felt. Which was—not at all.

That had the surgeon inside her concerned, if not edging toward panic.

Numb fingers, numb toes, and in truth, a numb heart—frozen over with dread as she followed Sasha and Jenny through the icefall, pressing her axe into the snow with every step. They went before her, and she stepped directly into their footsteps, but Aria couldn't help but notice the fissures in the ice, the blue-white glacial walls that fell thousands of feet. She took every step deliberately, waiting until Sasha finished her own deliberate steps across snow bridges and thick ridges, until Sasha had anchored in and waited for her to cross.

Just maybe, they wouldn't die on the mountain.

Except, she'd burned down the tent. The black smudge they'd left in the snow a thousand feet up made her want to scream. It hadn't been exactly her fault—Sasha had kicked the stove—but she knew better than to light it inside the tent.

Fingers. She'd just wanted to warm her fingers.

She'd wanted to suggest they stop for the day and dig in, right there, maybe figure out how to resurrect the stove. But probably it was toast, and besides, the doctor in her knew they had to get Sasha to a lower elevation. At least her friend had stopped throwing up.

"We'll camp at the bottom of this icefall," Jenny had said during their last huddle, right before they entered the chaos of ice debris the size of small buildings.

The wind whipped up into Aria's face mask and crusted her goggles with sleet.

Cancun. Yes. She'd only been half kidding when she suggested it.

She may or may not have been kidding about the men showing up to carry the heavy things.

Yes, indeed, men like Jake. *I wouldn't be sad if he showed up right now.*

Now that had been Kia talking. Frankly, it had been her inner Kia who'd even said yes to Jake's invitation to dance in the first place.

Kia was always getting her into messes.

Except, for a moment, Aria had let herself enjoy the idea of dancing with a stranger, of seeing the curiosity in his eyes as she flirted—yes, *flirted*—with him.

Okay, that had been all Kia too, because Aria didn't possess a flirting cell in her entire body.

"You're a charmer, aren't you, Cowboy?"

Oh brother.

In front of her, Sasha was trudging up a tiny rise. The late-afternoon sun crested down, bathing the mountain valley in deep pink, the sky blue, snow scurrying off the icy boulders around her.

I have to go where I feel most alive. Do the things that ignite my soul.

Good grief. Her sister had a way of climbing into her head at the most inopportune times. *Yes, yes, of course. We all want to live wild and dangerously, Kia.*

But there was danger, and then there was *insanity*. And then there was sitting on the sofa, under a blanket, *watching* the insanity on television.

Definitely Cancun next year.

A crack and boom and Aria stilled, her foot pressed into the snow. Except, it wasn't a fissure under her boot that opened up, but in the distance, off Karstens Ridge, a glacier head cracked and spilled into the bowl of Muldrow Glacier below them. A poof of white billowed up.

"Careful!" Jenny yelled. "The snow's melting!" She stood on top of a serac, probably to check on Aria's progress.

Funny. Back home, it was Aria keeping an eye on Jenny. Making sure she rested, didn't drive herself too hard, didn't get in over her head with life, with work. Because, like her, Jenny didn't have anyone else. Aria didn't have to be a psychologist to figure out why she loved Jenny like a sister.

Like she'd loved Kia.

Aria patted her head, giving Jenny all-okay.

Please, let them be near the end of the icefall. Her legs burned, her feet were frozen, and she kept flexing her fingers.

And stay where, Aria? You burned up the tent.

Okay, enough of that. She pressed her axe into the snow, testing, then followed with a step, the soft crunch of snow. *"I vote next time we bring men to carry the heavy things."*

So maybe that was a little bit sexist. *A lot* sexist.

Even if Jake decided to show up, she hadn't a clue what she'd say to him. She hadn't exactly spent a lot of time in med school dating, or even talking to men on a social basis.

Then again, she'd been twenty, the youngest in her class, and fixated on getting her specialty.

Besides, Jake Silver was miles over her head. Dark blond hair that twined out under his wool cap, the hint of golden-brown whiskers, pale blue eyes, thick shoulders, and a grin that did dangerous things to her heart.

Or Kia's heart, technically.

And maybe it was Kia he liked, because Aria could hardly believe her own words when she said, *"I see you like to live dangerously, huh, Cowboy Jake?"*

Apparently, *she* was the one living dangerously.

A man like Jake Silver wouldn't seriously like her. Especially when he discovered that she wasn't anything like the woman she'd let her mouth betray her as.

She cleared the tiny valley and stepped onto the cornice that Sasha had been standing on earlier. Sasha had descended to the bridge below, and Aria set her ice axe in. Didn't hurt to be careful.

So she'd flirted a little with Jake. She liked his smile, his laughter, and even the way he'd led on the dance floor, like she could trust him.

But she'd never see him again, so probably she should stop fantasizing about him showing up. Carrying her backpack.

Carrying her.

She grinned. Okay, sometimes she and Kia could agree. Jake was a fine-looking man and she wasn't sad she danced with him.

Sasha cleared the bridge and climbed up the opposite side. Jenny was out in front, a good thirty feet, descending into another bowl, hopefully near the end of the ice field.

Aria took a step across the cornice, following Sasha's indentations.

The ice gave not even a hint of warning, not a crack to bite the air so she could throw herself against the ice with her axe. Not even time to alert Jenny and Sasha with a "Falling!"

The cornice simply gave way, dissolving from under her.

She dropped into nothingness.

Debris clogged her mouth, cutting off her screams, ice buffeted her face, her arms windmilling.

Oh God, help—

A jerk around her waist and shoulders wrenched her to a stop. Her breath ripped out of her. Pain rippled through her shoulders, and she dropped her ice axe, flailing in the air.

"Aria!"

She heard Sasha yelling, but she couldn't respond, still fighting for breath.

More snow fell above her. She grabbed the rope, holding on, realizing that Sasha's and probably Jenny's self-arrests were the only thing keeping her from plunging to an icy death.

Stop struggling.

The voice—crisp, demanding—slammed through her.

Calm down.

She obeyed and got a breath into her lungs. She must have crashed through the snow bridge. The cascade of snow slowed to a trickle. The air cleared, the only sound was her hard breathing hitting her mask.

Overhead, snow gusted off the cornice that had just given way. She hung horizontally, the line clipped into her waist and chest biners. The harness burned into her thighs, and the waist belt bruised her hip bones. She didn't think she'd broken any ribs, and she didn't want to think about internal injuries.

She couldn't look down.

"We got you!" Jenny's voice hovered from the top and Aria tried to grab the words, hold on.

To not let the truth take her heart.

No, she wasn't dangling from the soft edge of a glacier.

Okay, she was, but no, she shouldn't think about it.

She guessed herself to be about ten feet down, which meant that Sasha had self-arrested fast. Probably she'd set her anchor on the far side before Aria took her fatal step.

Which meant that Jenny could set an anchor, maybe build a snow bollard, and Aria could use her Prusik line as a foothold to climb up.

The fissure wasn't that wide—she fixed her crampons to the wall to keep from spinning.

Then, she simply hung from the rope, staring at the blue sky, trying not to panic.

And wishing that her too-brave-for-her-own-good deceased twin sister might get her out of messes as easily as she got her into them.

CHAPTER SEVEN

JENNY SHOULD HAVE LOOKED BACK. Should have checked on Aria, in the anchor position on the line, picking her way through the route she'd cut.

Shouldn't have assumed that just because Jenny had trodden that route that Sasha and Aria were safe.

She'd been caught by the brilliance of the Muldrow Glacier flowing out before her, bathed in an eerie, deep blush, the low-hanging clouds gathered above almost bruised, in shades of lavender and rose. They might not have a tent, but she'd already worked out how to build a cave, and next on her list was melting snow for water.

Always looking ahead.

Which was why she didn't see Aria fall, just heard the scream, then Sasha leaping on her already planted ice axe—good girl. Jenny hit her knees, dug in her crampons, and fell on her axe.

Aria reaching the end of her rope had yanked Jenny backward and she knew the force must have also ripped Sasha from her hold. She glanced over her shoulder and Sasha was digging in again, dangerously close to the edge of the crevasse.

Jenny hunkered down and held her breath, her body shaking. Please.

The line stopped moving.

"Sash!"

"I got her!" Sasha said. She hadn't gotten worse as they trekked down the glacier, but given the way she'd struggled to keep anything down, she had nothing but sheer will holding Aria to the mountain.

"I'm going to put in an anchor!" Jenny said.

"I can't hold her myself."

Right. She shoved her axe all the way into the snow, braced herself around it, then clipped her quick clip between the wrist strap and her line. Please—she leaned off the anchor, ready to grab it should it inch out.

It stayed in the snow.

She clipped out of the line, leaving it attached to the axe anchor, dropped her pack, and went to help Sasha. She clipped Sasha's quick-clip line to her ice axe strap. "Stay there, I'm going to check on Aria."

She walked over to the edge. Leaned over.

Aria hung over a drop of two hundred feet, maybe five feet wide, but brutal with its icy blue depths. This time, the pack hadn't ripped her upside down, but it hung from her shoulders and hips as she lay horizontal.

"You okay?"

"Just hanging out."

"That's not funny." She didn't know how Aria did that—figured out how to lean into the chaos of life without panicking. She seemed to thrive on challenges, from her medical prowess to the adventures that added an edge to life.

Or maybe that was only her living to the beat of her sister's heart in her chest.

Whatever it was, it made Aria the perfect climbing partner.

"Good. Then pull yourself up, and anchor yourself into the wall."

"I'll try."

"Then release your pack and let it hang from the pony leash."

She returned to Sasha, swallowing back the acid in her chest. How had she let this happen twice?

Sasha was groaning. "I don't feel well."

The sudden rush of adrenaline hadn't helped her AMS. Jenny knelt next to her. "Okay, let's build an anchor—"

A scream echoed from the crevasse and a shock rattled through the line. It ripped Sasha's anchored axe from the snow, dragging it over.

"No!" Jenny leaped on the axe, on Sasha, now being raked through the snow.

She'd forgotten to unhook Sasha from the line. She grabbed the axe, piniponing her feet in hard next to Sasha, fighting the pull of the axe.

"What happened to the other anchor?" Sasha said, breathing hard.

She searched for it. The jerk on the line, and their scramble, had ripped Jenny's axe free.

"Aria!"

"I dropped the pack! It jerked me out of the wall!"

Right. Jenny couldn't move, her face in the snow, her feet planted, her hands gripping the axe.

If she moved, Sasha and Aria would go right over the cliff.

But she couldn't set another anchor without moving.

Next to her, Sasha started to hyperventilate.

"Sash. Can you unclip your rope?"

"Not and hold on to the axe."

"I got the axe."

A pause, then, "If it rips out, and you can't hold it, Aria dies."

Jenny closed her eyes, her body shaking.

And shaking.

She couldn't breathe, her throat tightening, her arms burning with the effort of holding in the axe.

They were going to die out here. All of them. Because she wasn't going to let Aria and Sasha go over the cliff, but yeah, she couldn't hold the axe.

Not on her own.

"I know!" She pressed her goggles into the snow, gritted her teeth. "I know. I just need a minute to think. To work it out—" She drew in a breath. "Just give me a minute."

But she didn't have a minute. Because the longer they hung here, the more the snow would give way, the more the mountain would eat their strength.

And sooner, rather than later, they'd all fall into the crevasse.

Why had she insisted on this stupid trip? *We're stronger than we think we are?*

No, no they weren't. Or she wasn't.

"We're going to die out here, aren't we?"

Oh, Sash. Jenny couldn't answer her.

"Don't let go!"

The male voice trumpeted through her.

"We got you—just stay put."

Then someone stepped over her, his knees on either side of her, his chest against her back, strong arms enveloping her as he pushed his weight onto the axe. "Don't move. It's going to be okay."

She lifted her head and was just barely able to make out the sight of a man, a climber, dressed in a red jacket, black climbing pants, and a snow-crusted hat pounding in her ice axe and taking an arrest position. The pressure on the rope eased.

But the presence above her didn't move. "Not yet," he said.

In moments, a man in a blue jacket pounded in two snow pickets. Then he ran webbing through the two pickets, attached a Prusik to their rope line, and clipped the line into the new anchor.

Around her, her rescuer's coat crinkled, the snow squeaked beneath his legs, and his breath moved in and out against his face mask as he quietly saved their lives.

How—?

"Okay, you can let go."

She eased up on her hold just as he too eased up. Leaned back. The anchors held.

She reached over and unclipped Sasha from the line.

Sasha rolled over on her back, breathing hard.

Jenny wanted to cry. Instead, she turned and found a mittened hand outstretched to help her up.

She took it and stood up.

Her hero wore an orange jacket, goggles, and a lime-green wool hat. His face mask was crusted with snow, his dark goggles pulled down to protect his eyes.

"We'll haul you up!" Beside her, the man in blue was setting another anchor and clipping himself in. The man in the red jacket joined him, also hooking in.

They added an ascender to the line to use as a hauling tool, then together they began to drag Aria to the lip.

Jenny leaned over the cliff and spotted Aria walking up the edge, her crampons digging in to keep her from being crushed by the lip.

They pulled her up and over the edge.

Aria dropped to her hands and knees, breathing hard. One of

her rescuers leaned over and pulled up her pack, still attached to the leash.

Then they both backed away from the edge.

Jenny wanted to collapse, painfully near tears. Aria sat back, her hands shaking.

"You okay?"

She nodded. "Except, I think I'm going to throw up."

Jenny too. She leaned over, grabbing her knees, just trying not to hyperventilate.

It's going to be okay.

She leaned into the voice, let it find her bones, soothe her.

"Thank you," she said softly and turned to look at her rescuer.

The man in orange had crouched in front of her, staring at her, concern in his eyes gleaming through the dark frame of his goggles.

She knew those eyes . . . oh . . .

"Where did you guys come from?" Sasha said.

"The top of the mountain," said the one with the blue jacket, gray snowpants. "We saw smoke."

"The tent," Aria said. "It caught fire."

But Jenny couldn't take her eyes off . . . "Ry?"

He smiled.

The jig was up. She wanted to clamp her hand over her mouth, to yank the name back, but it was out there, forced free by relief and not a small amount of shock.

He took off his goggles and unleashed the full power of his gaze, and suddenly, her throat thickened, heat filling her entire chest.

She saw it all, right there in his gaze. Their past, the grief she'd caused him, even that way he had of calming her entire world.

And behind it all, the burning fire that was Orion Starr.

"Hey there, Jacie."

She didn't know what to do with the crazy flux of emotions—

run, cry, throw her arms around him—so she just sat there, as if
frozen, as he said, "It looks like I found you."

■ ■ ■

She'd just stared at him.

Clearly Orion had made much, much more out of their epic-
in-his-head relationship three years ago than she had because the
woman just blinked. Nodded. Emitted a soft, "Thank you."

Okay, so not the dramatic meeting he'd pictured as he'd glis-
saded down the glacier.

In fact, if he read her right, he hadn't meant anything to Jenny—
J. C.—Calhoun.

But, she *did* know him, hello, because he hadn't dreamed up her
utterance of his name. "Ry?" Nor the little catch of her breath.

Yeah, honey, it's me.

Although maybe that catch had been the wind because she said
nothing, just crawled over to Aria.

Which left him baffled, and not a little irked.

He probably needed to let it go, stop letting the fact she seemed
unfazed by their unlikely reunion eat into him as he built a wind
wall around the two tents they'd erected. Good thing Jake had
added the cook tent into their supplies because the women could
take shelter inside.

After a dinner of Spam and noodles.

Yum.

The tents blew against the wind, which was starting to pick up
as the night settled in around them. Not dark enough for him to
need a light, but the mountain did shed long shadows into their
enclave. And, if he judged the temperature correctly, it might have
dropped another ten degrees.

He barely felt it. Fact was, he might still be running on pure adrenaline, ignited the moment he'd spotted the burned shell of their tent. Even Jake looked a little sick, dropping to his knees to fish through the remains.

An overturned, blackened pot, and a metal water canister.

But no sleeping bag, no packs, so at least the ladies had their gear. They'd left tracks traversing the glacier and down through the icefall, which meant no one was seriously injured.

The *scream*, however . . .

It had sent a fire through him and he'd practically abandoned his better sense as he took off in a run, nearly dragging Jake and Ham with him through the glacier rubble. He'd spotted the team from a distance by their red and yellow jackets as they scrabbled against the face of the ice to save their friend.

He'd nearly been too late. He'd seen Jenny digging in, trying to keep her friend from plunging to her death, and did the only thing he could think of.

He'd leaped on top of her. Full force, his body pinning her down.

Then held her in his embrace as he kept the axe anchor from moving.

"It's going to be okay."

So maybe he'd been a little presumptuous there. He'd reverted to his PJ days, arriving like the hero on the scene.

However, maybe they would be okay, because after they'd shaken off the near fall, they'd managed to climb down below the second icefall without incident. Jake had carried Aria's pack after he noticed she was limping. They roped Aria between Jake and Ham, while he roped in front of Sasha, Jenny at the back.

He'd been down this route only a couple times, but he remembered a place to camp, just before Karstens Ridge.

Now, the women were huddled in their tent warming up, and according to Ham, who'd checked on them, assessing Sasha's AMS.

Orion didn't want to think about what might have happened to them if he hadn't seen that smoke. Hadn't listened to his gut.

Ham's words had been hanging around in his head.

"Every time I pray, it's like God is saying he'll help us find them."

Maybe. Or maybe they just got lucky.

He placed another brick on the wall that circled their tent camp. Jake was cooking outside, in the enclave kitchen he'd built. Now, Orion planted the shovel and came over to the pot. Tiny diced Spam chunks rose to the surface of what should have been chicken soup.

"I have a treat for you tonight, Ry-man," Jake said.

"Someday I think we can be friends, Silver, but only if you stop serving me Spam."

Jake grinned from beneath a two-day growth of golden-blond whiskers. "Someday you're going to thank me for Spam."

Ham was in the tent when Orion retrieved his sleeping bag from his pack and tossed it in. He sat in his overpants and fleece, wore his polar socks. "I've been trying to get ahold of Kit, but the mountain seems to be cutting us off."

"I'm not surprised. Try it tomorrow, when we're on Karstens Ridge."

Ham put down the radio. "So that's the plan? Hike down the ridge and out through Muldrow Glacier?"

"I don't see another way."

"Did you take a look at Aria's ankle? She says it isn't broken but I'm not sure. And Sasha still hasn't kept anything down. It won't be long before she's dizzy, and that's a bad recipe for Karstens. It's knife sharp, a thousand feet down on either side . . . I don't know, Ry."

Orion blew out a breath. "I suppose we could hunker down here and try and pull them off the mountain by chopper."

"If we can get ahold of camp."

Orion sighed. "At least we found them."

"So, that is Jacie, right?"

"Yeah."

"From Afghanistan. The reporter. Who played basketball. What happened between you two?"

"Nothing. We just . . . we were friends."

"Not even. You talked about her when we were trapped in the cave, if I remember correctly."

He'd said a lot of stupid things in that cave. Even a prayer.

He hoped Ham didn't remember that.

"Maybe that's why God was calling you to the mountain. Because you and Jacie aren't done yet."

Orion stared at him. "You know, God isn't in charge of everything that happens."

"Uh, yes he is."

Orion sighed. "And now you're only making me mad again."

Ham frowned.

"Really? Should we talk about Nickles and Dirk? Thorne and Royal? How about your man McCord? Or you—you lost your career. If God was in charge of all that, then maybe I'm angry at the wrong people."

"See, that's the thing. We get angry with God when he doesn't do things our way. But I know God had a new season for me."

"Says the man who spent twelve years on the Teams, who was headed for Master Chief."

Ham reached for his hat. "It's all about your perspective. I can choose to be angry about the way the Navy treated me, or I can see it all from a bigger place. It's like this mountain. We're down here, on the face. We can't see the routes, the crevasses, even the avalanches that might take us out. But God can, and we can trust him."

"Like the CIA trusted the informant who blew our lives up?"

"Not even close."

"Yeah, well, here's the deal. I'll be willing to trust God if he sends me answers. If he lets me find Royal. And if he brings a little justice to the men who killed my brothers. When he does that, then we'll talk about trusting God." He made for the door.

"That's not what you prayed in the cave."

He stilled, turned back to Ham. Frowned.

"'God, please help us find a way out.'"

"I was pretty focused on the moment."

"And so is God. But he also sees the big picture. That's why we have to live by faith, not just by sight. Because he is always working on our behalf, in the moment, even if we can't see it."

"Yeah, like I really needed a new knee. So glad God took care of that for me."

Ham's mouth tightened. "I took my troubles to the Lord, I cried out to him and he answered my prayer."

"I couldn't walk!"

"And now you can."

Orion shook his head.

"I'm just saying that God is on our side. And we can trust him for the big—and small—details."

"Okay, great. Maybe God could help me figure out why it bugs me so much that Jenny Calhoun didn't remember me."

"Oh, she remembered you. The bigger question is, why did she deny it?"

Ham's question brought Orion up. He stared at him.

Unzipped the tent.

Jake stood at the stove, ladling out the soup into sierra cups. He took two and went over to the ladies' tent. Unzipped it and climbed inside.

Orion stood there, not sure what to do. The smell of the soup—rehydrated peas, carrots, chicken broth, and of course Spam—stirred the air. His stomach clenched with hunger.

Until the ladies' tent unzipped.

Jenny crawled out. For a moment, she just stood there, dressed in her jacket, a wool hat, her blonde hair loose, wearing her over-pants and down booties. She stuck her hands into her pockets, bit her bottom lip.

"Hi," he said, feeling stupid.

And then, yes, a little angry. Because *of course* she recognized him in Copper Mountain. He hadn't grown his hair out, turned into someone completely other than who he'd been three years ago.

"Hi," she said, shuffling over.

"Want some soup?" he said, trying to unlatch the other words from where they felt gummed up inside. *Why did you lie?*

She came closer. "What is that floating on top?"

"Spam. I apologize."

She looked at him. "At least it's not C-rations. It could be ham and lima bean stroganoff."

So she was going there.

Okay. He nodded. "And how about cold spaghetti mush?"

"See, this is practically gourmet." She reached for a sierra cup and he poured some soup into it. She took a spork from her pocket. "Thanks." She walked over to the edge of their tent area and sat down in the snow, staring out at the mountainscape.

Not a terrible dinner view. He helped himself to soup and walked over to her. "So . . . can we talk?"

She nodded.

He sat down.

They ate in silence for a moment while he gathered his words. Her too, because—

"Okay, fine. I'm sorry I acted like I didn't know you back in Copper Mountain." She held up her cup and drank out of it.

Yes. *Yes.* He knew it, but probably a fist pump wasn't appropriate so he just nodded.

"Why did you act like you didn't recognize me?"

"I . . . I guess I thought maybe that was then, and this is now." Her mouth tightened around the edges.

Now. As in, not Afghanistan. Not the war. "You know I was shot, right?"

She nodded.

"I thought you might—well, call it crazy, but I thought you might be in Germany when I woke up."

And he looked away, wincing that he'd let himself admit that.

"I . . . yeah. I'm sorry, I was . . ." She shook her head.

And it was the expression on her face that sent a fist into his chest. Embarrassment.

Oh. He must be some kind of self-absorbed fool to believe that he'd meant to her what she'd meant to him. That she'd spent the past three years pining for him. Waiting for him to show up and find her.

Wow, Orion, get a grip.

"Wounded."

Her word brought him up, stilled him. "What? How? Were you shot?" He set down his bowl, now empty.

"No. Nothing like that. I . . ." She blew out a breath. "I . . . I had a nervous breakdown."

He had nothing. Living on an active base, surrounded by the threat of Taliban invasion—it had to be stressful. He'd always wondered why the AP had embedded her with his group.

But a *nervous breakdown*?

"I heard about what happened to your team, to the SEALs and

. . . anyway, I wasn't in a good place for a while. They sent me to a hospital in Seattle. That's where I climbed my first mountain—Rainier. Part of my rehabilitation."

"I'm sorry." Except, how had she heard about the ambush on the mountain? He thought that was classified. Only how could it be when she lived and worked on the FOB? Probably word had filtered through the base. She probably didn't know details, but certainly the media would have been briefed.

She looked at him, then at his leg. "Your knee, right?"

"I had a knee replacement."

"I'm sorry."

"At least I lived. We lost—"

"Two PJs and four SEALs."

He nodded. "Two SEALs. Two were captured."

Her mouth made a tight line. "Yes, right."

The wind kicked up snow, dusted it across their feet.

"I thought of you." He didn't know why he said that.

She looked over at him. Swallowed. "I thought of you too." A smile tugged up her mouth. "You found me."

"You sent up a smoke signal."

Her mouth opened.

Then, she laughed. Full and robust and it filled his bones, chasing away the last remnant of ire. "I did—I mean, I didn't—that was Aria and Sash, but—" She looked at him, and it wasn't the first time he wanted to fall into her beautiful blue eyes, but right here, right now, brought back that last night. The smell of her as he drew her close. The feel of her hair between his fingers.

"What are you doing here?" he said softly.

"I fell off Denali Pass in a high wind. Got caught on a glacier. Nearly died and this guy showed up like he might be a hero or something."

He cocked his head. "Yeah, but what are you doing *here*? Again. In my radar?"

She wrinkled her nose. "Oh. Well. This other guy I knew talked about Denali. And how it had the most amazing views."

"Amazing views," he said softly, unable to stop himself.

She smiled, looked away. "Okay, PJ, stop. Let's talk about how we're going to get off this mountain."

He was about to point out Karstens Peak when the tent behind them unzipped.

Jake stuck his head out. "Ry. Get in here. We have a problem. I think Sasha is in trouble."

Orion scooped up his sierra cup, then grabbed Jenny's and headed back to camp. The stove was off and Ham was pouring soup into insulated bottles for him and Jake. He took the cups from Orion, and he headed to the tent.

Jenny was already inside.

Sasha was sitting up, but her face and hands looked swollen. She was trying to shed her clothing.

"You need to leave that on," Jenny said as Aria held her hands.

"I'm hot—"

"It's thirty below, Sash," Aria said. "Try and eat something."

Her bowl sat untouched.

Orion picked it up and moved it away. "How's her breathing?" He moved over to her, pulled off his gloves, and pressed his fingers against her carotid artery. "Her heartbeat is rapid. And her skin is pretty pale."

He looked at Jake. "I think we need to consider leaving her here and hiking down. I don't have any dex, or we could give that to her."

Sasha leaned over, coughing.

Jenny looked stricken as she cast her gaze to Orion.

149

Okay, that was it. "I'm staying here tonight, with Sasha."

"Me too," Jenny said.

"I'm the doctor here," Aria said.

"And I've spent more time on the mountain than all of you combined," Orion said. "I've seen AMS more times than you want to know."

Aria's mouth tightened into a thin line.

"Be honest, Aria. You're not in much better shape. You took a wicked fall today."

"And two days ago," Jenny said. "She's injured. She just won't admit it."

"Thanks for throwing me under the bus."

"Just out of the tent," Jenny said. "You need a good night's sleep. Go into the other tent, with Ham and Jake."

She looked at Jenny as if she'd asked her to run naked through camp.

Jake looked away, as if embarrassed.

"Aria. This isn't church camp. We're all grown-ups here," Jenny said. "Go—get some rest."

"No," Jake said. "Listen, don't make her do something that makes her feel uncomfortable—"

"We're camped on the side of a mountain, for Pete's sake!" Jenny said. "We're all uncomfortable."

"Still," Orion said. "He's right—"

"It's no big deal," Aria said. "And yes, Jenny's right. It's just . . . I'm the doctor here. I should stay."

"There's nothing you can do," Orion said. "But most importantly, you're injured too. And that leads to its own dangers."

"We need to get you all down the mountain, alive," Jake said quietly.

Aria wore a strange expression as she looked at him. Then,

"Okay." She grabbed her sleeping bag and Jake followed her out of the tent, picking up her pack as he went.

Orion turned to Jenny. "We need to heat up some tea, or at least get some warm water in her."

Jenny nodded. Turned toward the door. Paused. Sighed.

Then she turned back to him and touched his arm. "I'm really glad you found me, PJ." Then she headed out the door.

Hooah. Now that's what he was talking about.

■ ■ ■

He hadn't been that scared in years. Sure—Jake had experienced worse moments in his life, but watching Aria dangle above a sheer drop while her two friends struggled to keep from sliding into the abyss . . .

Jake still didn't have an appetite.

He might be getting a little tired of Spam, too, but mostly the raw clench in his gut came from the scream that still echoed deep in the chambers of his mind. Heart. Soul.

Whatever. It embedded there, stirring up a terror he couldn't shake even hours later.

Seeing Sasha deteriorate with the clear effects of AMS didn't help either. But mostly, he was worried about Aria.

And her limp.

And the way she eased herself onto the sleeping bag, hiding a grimace, as if she might have broken ribs.

The way she kept clenching her fists and wiggling her fingers, trying to get the blood circulating.

"Okay, that's it. Make up your mind."

She looked up at him, frowning.

"First, you drag me up a mountain to rescue you, and now you're coming up with reasons not to dance with me."

Her eyes widened. "Dance with you—what—?"

"Let me see that ankle." Ham had gone outside to help Jenny heat up tea, so Jake sat on his sleeping bag. "I promise I'll be gentle."

She narrowed her eyes at him. "I'm fine. And I don't want to dance with you again."

"Sure you do. You've been thinking about me since you left the dance floor. Now stop your crybabying and lean back and let me look at your ankle."

She gave him a look of annoyance.

He matched it, hoping the pulse in his neck didn't give him away, but he'd met women like her—strong, independent. In fact, he had five sisters she'd get along with very well. But masking her hurt wasn't going to get them off the mountain in one piece. "Give it up, Grey's Anatomy, and show me your ankle."

"Oh brother." But she leaned back and let him lift her foot to his lap.

No, this wasn't going to work. He couldn't get a good look at her leg with her overpants in the way. "Um, let's take these . . . uh . . ." And this felt weird . . .

"Seriously. Now you get shy?" She pulled off her jacket and wadded it behind her. Then she unhooked her overpants, leaned back, and wiggled them over her hips. She wore a thick pair of fleece leggings under them.

He pulled the overpants off and handed them to her. She wadded those up too, creating a pillow, and lay back. "It's not broken, it's just . . . well, take a look."

He took a breath, not wanting to hurt her. She closed her eyes, her dark hair splayed on the pillow, her hands fisted on her stomach.

"I haven't been thinking about you, by the way."

He smiled as he pulled the thick wool sock down her leg. She grimaced, especially as he got to her heel. "Sure you have. You were thinking . . . It would sure be nice if that charming guy I met in Copper Mountain showed up to save my backside from becoming crushed ice—"

"I did not."

He pulled the sock over her heel.

She made a noise that took out a piece of his soul, then glared at him.

"Sorry." He swallowed hard. "Okay, so tell me how this all happened. You're standing at the top of Denali, and suddenly you decide to take the scenic route?" He was probing her foot, running his thumb down the bones of her ankle, watching her face.

Oh, she had a pretty face. Dark eyebrows, a hint of a sunburn on her aquiline nose, high cheekbones, and long, dark lashes.

"Yeah. That's exactly what we were thinking." She'd closed her eyes again. "I mean, descending the usual route, down the Denali wall with 50-mph winds? Boring. Let's take a header down a glacier instead, maybe really get our hearts racing and slide about a hundred feet. And then I decided to add an extra element to the fun and launch myself right off a ledge, hoping my girlfriends could stop me going thirty miles an hour."

She raised her eyebrows but didn't open her eyes, and nodded. "I think we got one of the highest technical scores, but our artistic numbers weren't great."

He chuckled, hopefully something light and convincing because her words had grabbed him up and wrapped an icy hand around his heart. He'd known about the avalanche, the fall, but to hear her say it, to know she'd lived it—he couldn't breathe. "Did you break any ribs?"

He didn't mean for his voice to sound so concerned and wished

153

he'd said something like, "So, did you crush all your ribs in the fall, or just the two bottom ones?"

Her eyes opened at his tone. "No, Doc. I'm fine." Her mouth pinched into a dark line. Then she closed her eyes again. "And don't think I'm falling for your attempt to look up my shirt."

He wanted to smile. Wow, she was brave. And okay, funny. But yes, he wanted a look at her injuries. Internal bleeding changed the game entirely. "You're a lousy patient, Grey's."

She opened one eye. "Flash me some creds, there, Cowboy, and I'll be glad to show you some skin."

"I was a Navy SEAL, does that count?" He didn't know why he let that emerge, but, okay, maybe he wanted her to admire him a little, too.

It worked. She opened the other eye. "Really?"

He steadied her leg with one hand, and wrapped his other around her foot, ready to move it, to test it. "Mmmhmm. And I was the one with the most medical experience on our team, so—"

"Wait!" She leaned up fast and grabbed his wrist, no kidding in her widened eyes. "That's enough."

He cocked his head. "Methinks someone's been lying about her injury."

She moved his hand away from her foot. "Not lying. Just . . . okay, listen. I packed it with snow, and the swelling went down. It's just aggravated from today's hike is all." She pulled her foot away. "It just needs ice."

He studied her, and all his joking died. "How hurt are you?" He reached for her shirt tucked into her fleece pants.

She caught his wrist. She had strong hands, which he'd guessed, but he didn't expect the way her touch might ignite something under his skin.

"Hold up, there, pal. Not on the first date."

Now he felt creepy. "Listen. I need to know what we're dealing with. Are we hiking down tomorrow, or am I going for help?"

She considered him. "Fine. Why aren't you a SEAL anymore?"

The question knocked him back. "What?"

"Well, it feels like you're asking to completely invade my privacy, and I don't get anything back."

"I'm not—"

"Playing doctor?"

He made a face.

She raised an eyebrow.

"Fine. What do you want to know?"

"Were you hurt?"

"No . . . I just . . . it was time to be done."

"How long were you in?"

"Twelve years. I got out a year ago."

"With what team?"

"Who are you, Katie Couric?"

"You're not getting a peep until you tell me something personal."

"Fine. I have five nosy younger sisters. And I know all the games you women play, so if you think you can crack me, welcome to Fort Knox."

Her mouth made a tight line. "I want a secret."

"What is this, a stare down?"

"You said you have sisters. Who do you think will win?"

"Listen, sweetheart, I know you're just trying to delay me discovering the truth."

She didn't move.

A secret. "Fine. Okay." He swallowed. "I might have been thinking about you, too."

She blinked at him, her mouth opening.

"Of course, I probably wouldn't have gone to the great lengths of tumbling off a mountain and burning my tent down to get your attention, but some of us are more needy—"

She reached for the hem of her shirt as if to untuck it.

"Now you have my attention."

She glared at him.

"I'm kidding. Sheesh. I showed you mine. You show me yours."

"Really? Are we in high school?" But she tugged on her shirt. "Make it snappy. I don't want to get cold."

He hid a smile, shaking his head, and lifted her shirt just enough to see her ribs, where the waist belt might have gripped.

A little bruising, but nothing deep red, purple, or black. He turned her, checking her back. No bleeding in her kidneys. He rolled her back to her sleeping bag.

"Satisfied, Hawkeye?"

He looked at her. "*M*A*S*H*?"

"My parents' favorite show. They watched it on TV Land every night."

"And who are you, Hot Lips Houlihan?"

"In your wildest dreams."

And for a second, yes, he had a fleeting thought of what it might be like to shut her up with a kiss, just for a second. To taste the smile that now slid up her face.

"You really have five sisters?"

Normally the question wouldn't dig in, wouldn't rake open the wounds, but for some reason, it hit like a gut punch.

His smile faded.

She frowned.

But he couldn't go there. Not tonight.

Probably not ever, so, "Yeah. Five beautiful, smart, independent, nosy sisters who would think you are pretty brave."

Her expression turned suddenly stricken. Her breath spiraled out, as if he'd somehow landed a blow, too. "I'm not brave. I was scared to death hanging over that edge today. And if you hadn't shown up . . ." Her voice shuddered. She looked away.

"Hey." He found her hand, took it. "But we did show up. And you're okay. And I'm going to get you down this mountain, even if I have to carry you."

Her gaze returned to him then, her expression unreadable.

Then her eyes sparked, her expression so warm and real that it reached right in and took ahold of his heart.

Completely erasing the scream inside.

"Good. Because I need a strong man to carry my pack. And I think you'll do."

CHAPTER EIGHT

THE FIRST TIME SHE'D SEEN ORION, he'd been climbing off a Chinook helicopter, dirty and tired, carrying the IV of a man on a stretcher. Geared up in desert camo, wearing a helmet, his weapon off his shoulder, Orion had carried the man to the FOB hospital, then actually stuck around and gave blood.

Despite being grimy, whiskered, and battle worn, something in his expression told her that he loved his job.

Loved saving people.

Maybe all the PJs loved what they did, but he had a focused energy that intrigued her. He was usually reading, occasionally playing basketball with his guys or working out. All of it, combined with his quiet presence, conspired to put him on her radar.

It didn't hurt that he was easy on the eyes. Brown hair, green eyes with flecks of blue and gold, a solid body, and commanding a rare smile that could stop her cold in the street.

Sort of like he did that night across the campfire.

He might not have seen her before, but she might have been in love with Orion Starr before he even opened his mouth.

Now, she recognized the man she'd lost her heart to, at least a little, in the way he took care of Sasha. He held her up with one strong arm as he tried to ladle tea into her. Sips at a time, waiting between each one as she struggled to hold the tea down.

"It's a good thing you kept moving down the mountain," he said, looking up, meeting Jenny's gaze. "Two thousand feet makes a big difference."

She sat in her sleeping bag, having shed her outer clothing, and finally felt her toes, her body warm, her muscles thawing.

Hurting, if she were honest, from the tension of the day. She might have pulled a muscle bearing down on her crampons to keep Aria's weight from pulling them to their deaths.

If Orion and his guys hadn't shown up . . .

"How did you know we were lost on the mountain?" He'd alluded to the smoke signal, but really, "How did you even know where to look?"

He lowered Sasha back and zipped her up into her bag. Then he ladled the rest of her tea into a thermos and tucked it in beside her.

"We heard about the guys getting blown off the mountain—"

"The guys?" And Kit! "Are they alive?"

"I don't know. Kit was on the search team. A team of rangers found them after the storm lifted but we left before the chopper picked them up."

"Is Kit okay? The last thing I saw was her disappearing in the whiteout. I thought an avalanche had taken her out."

"It did—or at least it tried to. She was able to self-arrest and I think most of it fell below her. She was frostbitten, but otherwise okay."

She drew up her knees. Wrapped her arms around them. "We had a glorious summit day. I don't know what happened. We were on our way down, and suddenly it hit. First a whiteout, then this terrible gust—maybe a hundred miles an hour. It hit the cap, and then we were falling. I just remember trying to roll over, get my axe into the mountain."

"Kit said you were short-roped."

"Not really. Aria and Sash were walking arm in arm. Sasha wasn't feeling well, and Aria wanted to walk with her. I kept a longer length."

"You probably saved you all."

"We worked together." She didn't want to talk about those harrowing hours on the mountain. "But I'm pretty sure this is the last mountain Aria is going to climb with me."

He too had shed his outer jacket, and now even pulled his fleece over his head, shoving it into the bottom of his bag, leaving only a blue thermal shirt that stretched over his physique like a second skin. He climbed into his bag.

It felt a little intimate to be sharing the tent with him, even with Sasha asleep between them. Especially with his hair ruffled, the layer of dark whiskers on his chin, and the sudden memory of his body camped over hers, saving their lives.

"You do this a lot? Climb mountains?" He settled back and lifted his arms behind him to pillow his head. Looked at her with those hostage-taking eyes.

"Every year. It's . . . well, it's a way to remind us that we're stronger than we think we are." Only now the words felt flimsy and stupid. She made a face, looked away.

"Hey. It was a fluke accident. Denali is famous for crazy weather and accidents, so . . . actually, I think you've got some serious climbing chops."

Sweet, but . . . "No. This was my idea. Aria wanted to go to Cancun. And Sasha . . . well, she's climbed with us before—Gannett Peak and Rainier, but she wasn't so sure about Denali."

"Her husband called us," Orion said. "He was the one who asked us to go look for you."

"He called *you*?" Her breath caught. Because Lucas was one of the few who knew that she'd been in the CIA. Knew her connection to the event in Afghanistan.

"Lucas called Ham."

Oh. But her throat had thickened.

How much did Orion know about what . . . well, who she'd been? And, what she'd done? He'd seemed surprised about her nervous breakdown. Even sympathetic. And in Copper Mountain, she'd been convinced that he knew nothing.

But, if Lucas told Ham she'd been in the CIA, he could have told Orion and . . .

"So, it's an annual thing? This addiction to touching the sky?" Orion rolled over, propped one hand on his head. "Why?"

It might be a test. She met his eyes. "Because every time I summit, my past falls away, and I feel free."

He said nothing, just stared at her. But nothing of accusation, nothing of malice entered his gaze. Then, inexplicably, he nodded. "I get it. I push myself to go higher, and I forget . . ." He shook his head. "It makes me forget what I lost."

She stilled. Swallowed. "I'm sorry about that."

"Someday I'm going to have answers. And until then . . ." He lifted a shoulder. "Maybe I'll just keep climbing."

Silence fell between them. Orion sat up and pressed his fingers to Sasha's neck.

"Her heartbeat has slowed," he said. "That's a good sign."

"Do you think she'll be able to climb in the morning?"

"I don't know."

"What if you still can't get ahold of the chopper?"

"We'll find a way." He offered a smile. "So, Jacie Calhoun, where do you live now?"

"Minnesota. I'm a psychologist at a clinic in Minneapolis. And, it's Jenny."

He raised an eyebrow. "Okay, Jenny. Is climbing mountains part of your therapy?"

"I might reconsider. Go to Cancun instead."

He laughed. "You never mentioned you were a climber when we met."

"I wasn't at the time. I was . . ."

"A reporter. I remember."

Mmmhmm.

"And yet, now you're a psychologist?"

She'd told him too much. She lifted a shoulder, trying to deflect.

"So, how does a woman go from journalist embedded with the military to a psychologist?"

Oh. "Well, a good investigative reporter has to read her subject, right? I was a psychology major in college. Just sort of fell into journalism."

Her words turned her stomach. Because she was done with lies.

She didn't even know how to start that conversation. *You know that ambush? The one based on intel some embedded CIA specialist dug up? The one that destroyed your life?*

She very much wanted them all off this mountain alive. And maybe revealing that she was the one who had the answers might not be what he needed. Right now.

Later, yes.

Orion deserved the truth. Especially since . . . since . . .

Since he'd kept his promise and found her.

She wanted to cry with the injustice. "What did you do after Afghanistan?

"Mostly, I came back to Alaska."

"So you could be a ranger, like your dad?"

"You remember that, huh?"

"'If you want to see stars that feel so close you can pull them from the sky, you need to come to Alaska. Better yet, if you're real brave, climb Denali.'" She looked at him. "Am I brave enough yet?"

His smile was slow, and warm. "You've always been brave enough, Jacie."

She caught her breath. Oh. No.

She couldn't bear letting her heart fall for him again.

Maybe he sensed her panic, even her sudden urge to flee, because he added, "Nothing like sitting on the highest peak in North America, in arm's reach of the universe."

"Yeah." She paused. "I'll bet your family was glad to have you back."

His smile vanished. "Actually, it was just my grandfather waiting for me. He lives in Anchorage now, in senior living. My mother and brother were killed in a snowmobile accident when I was fifteen."

She couldn't move. "Orion. I'm so sorry."

"It's okay. I never told you. I had my grandparents. They raised me."

"How—I'm sorry. It's none of my business."

He shook his head, then cupped his hand over Sasha's mouth, testing her breathing.

"It was an accident over ice. We were crossing a river during the thaw—Dad and me on one machine, my mother and brother on the other. They went through the ice. Dad tried to get to them and he nearly went in, too. I had to help pull him out."

She stared at him, suddenly seeing a fifteen-year-old boy standing at the edge of a river, watching his family drown.

And then she'd gone and killed his band of brothers.

Her breath shuddered out.

"Aw, that's why I never told you," Orion said.

Her eyes had filled and she blinked hard, looked away. "No, it's
. . . Thanks for telling me."

Silence. Finally, "I ran away from Alaska for a long time, trying
to leave the grief in the past."

Ran. Yes, she got that.

"But, and I don't know why, the mountain keeps calling me
back." One side of his mouth lifted up. "At least that's what Ham
keeps saying." He lay back, pulling the edge of his sleeping bag up.
"Actually, that's why Ham's here. He's trying to recruit me for his
international SAR team. But I don't think . . ." He made a face.
"Sometimes I think I've never left the mountain."

"Which means you're here when someone needs you."

He didn't move. Finally, his mouth tightened. He looked at her,
something soft in his eyes. "I like your hair long."

Oh.

Then he rolled over, facing Sasha. "I'm a light sleeper," he said.
"I'll keep an eye on her. Get some sleep, Jace—Jenny." He closed
his eyes.

She lay on her side, too, tracing the outline of his face under
the brightness of the midnight sun, and let her heart break for all
she'd cost him.

■ ■ ■

He'd given away too much of himself.

What was he thinking telling her the story of his parents? And
then he added even more sap to the table with his pitiful *sometimes
I think I've never left the mountain.* What was *that* about?

Orion just wanted to get up and take his sleeping bag outside,
away from the sense that he'd sounded like a crybaby.

So what? His life had imploded.

At least he'd come home.

Other people had problems, too. *"Every time I summit, my past falls away and I feel free."*

He didn't know what she'd meant, but the fact was, he understood feeling imprisoned. By anger. By unanswered questions.

Someday I'm going to find answers.

He'd been driven by that dark, singular thought for a long, long time. The anger and frustration that brewed deep in his veins.

In order to live with it, he'd sealed it all off, retreated into the woods, and he'd been doing a pretty good job of keeping it all tucked away until Ham had to go and drag him out of the woods and onto the mountain.

A mountain that, indeed, he couldn't seem to escape.

Orion stared at the tent walls rippling, listened to the wind moaning in his ears. Beside him, Sasha was breathing steadily. He rolled over and again found her pulse on her carotid artery.

Still steady, and she seemed to have fallen into a deep sleep.

It might be fatigue, or it could be the beginnings of cerebral edema.

He needed dexamethasone. He hadn't even thought about bringing it on his fourteener climb and had forgotten to shove some into his bag when he headed out for Denali.

Reacting, rather than thinking.

Kit probably had some, but he'd been so focused on getting to the top of the mountain . . .

That's what happened when he led with his emotions. He forgot the essentials.

Forgot, even, to care about others.

"I had a nervous breakdown."

Oh, Jacie.

No. *Jenny.*

He cast his gaze to her and watched her sleep in the dim glow of the sun. He guessed the hour to be past midnight, and the tent was starting to lighten. She still wore her wool cap, but her hair fell across her face.

"I like your hair long."

He didn't know why he'd said that, either. Maybe *he* was getting a little altitude sickness.

Sasha moaned, as if she might be waking. Maybe he should get up and fix her some more herbal tea. He reached for his overpants, his jacket, and a hat and left the women to sleep as he slipped out of the tent.

To his surprise, Ham sat in the early light, the stove going, the blue flames humming around a pot of melting snow. Perhaps Ham didn't hear him, because his head was bowed.

Oh. Right. Praying.

He'd caught Ham more than once praying over the years. In Afghanistan, it gave him a sense of hope that maybe God might be looking out for them all.

Until he didn't, of course.

But if Ham wanted to believe that God cared, well, maybe Orion shouldn't let it irk him quite so much. His parents had believed, too, so maybe it would make his mother a little happy to think that he'd made a friend who prayed for him.

He let that thought sink in as he sat down next to Ham on a block of snow. Across the plateau of ice, the sun was coming alive, bathing Mount Huntington and the southern Alaskan Range in shades of gold and yellow. A harsh beauty.

Ham looked over at him. "Trying to figure out how to get everyone off the mountain?"

Oh sure, yes. Not at all about the woman in the tent, and what could have caused her to have a nervous breakdown.

Or how he'd turned into a weakling in front of her.

"Yep."

"Any ideas?"

Orion opened the lid of the pot to check the snow. It had nearly melted, tiny bubbles forming around the edges. "I think Sasha is coming down with HACE."

"There's no way she's going to make it down Karstens Ridge," Ham said.

"She'll barely be able to walk."

"And Jake thinks Aria's ankle is sprained pretty badly."

"They need to stay," Orion said. "And we need to get help. My guess is that we should be able to get radio reception from the top of Karstens Ridge."

"Maybe."

The lid began to rattle on the pot. Ham lifted the pot with his mittened hand and poured water into a thermos. "You need some tea?"

Orion pulled out a bag of peppermint tea from the food cache and dropped it into Sasha's thermos. Ham poured the water in.

Orion let it steep as he stared out at the golden early morning.

"Did you ever hear about anything happening to Jacie after I left? A trauma of some sort?"

Ham shook his head. "We were all pretty consumed with getting Thorne and Royal back. Actually, I don't even remember her being around. Why?"

It wasn't his story to tell. "I have reason to think that something happened that felt too big for her to handle."

Ham looked at him. "Really? She looks pretty put together to me. Even yesterday, fighting to save Aria's life. She didn't seem the kind to go down without a fight."

He frowned. Nodded.

"But I suppose we all run up against a fight that takes us out." Ham filled the pot with more snow, added some water, and put it on the flame to melt. He looked at Orion.

"Ambushes you," Orion said.

"Which is where we step in, Ry. Rescue those who are in over their heads."

Orion shook his head. "Still recruiting."

"Until you say yes."

He let himself smile. "Ham, you are a stubborn son of a gun."

"I just know a good man when I see one, Orion. You nearly gave your life for those women today. If that axe had given way, you could have gone over with them. Brave."

Orion's smile fell. "Naw. Stupid. Impulsive." Sort of like he'd been tonight with Jenny.

"Keen instincts."

"Listen, Ham. I'm just trying to stay alive. Get down the mountain. If it will let me go."

"'The weapons to conquer the mountain exist inside you, inside your soul.'" Ham looked at him. "Walter Bonatti, solo climber of the Matterhorn."

"I thought you only quoted the Bible."

"Okay. 'I took my troubles to the Lord; I cried out to him, and he answered my prayer.' Psalm 120:1."

Crazy, but Ham's words made him feel a little better. Orion wasn't sure why.

Maybe they *would* get off this mountain.

"You know what your problem is, Ry?" The lid was starting to rattle on the pot.

"I can't wait."

"You're mad because God didn't answer your prayer back in the cave the way you wanted him to. You asked him to rescue us—but you meant without any wounds."

"Of course I did."

"But you might consider that God uses our wounds to heal us. Make us stronger. And give us compassion for those who are also wounded."

"I'm not wounded anymore. I'm fine."

Ham raised an eyebrow.

"See. This is why I can't work for you. You'll have me on my knees and praying before every mission."

"And during, and after, I hope." Ham picked up the pot and poured the hot water into another thermos.

"I'm not wounded." But he *was* angry. Except, maybe not so much right now. In fact, talking with Jenny had felt oddly freeing.

Although a little breezy. As if he'd opened his chest, his emotions hanging out there in the wind. *"Sometimes I think I've never left the mountain."*

Oh for Pete's—

"Which means you're here when someone needs you."

Okay, maybe. Like yesterday, when he'd crouched over her body, when he'd added his strength to hers. He could nearly taste the old adrenaline. Fast roping down into a war zone, or pulling someone out of a freezing ocean.

So that others might live.

Ham was grinning at him. "I'm really going to like having you on my team."

"Don't start embroidering shirts yet." Orion fished out the tea bag and dropped it into the carry-out bag. He tested the tea, then added snow to cool it. Capped the thermos. "Another couple hours and then we'll move out."

He was turning away when the screaming erupted from inside his tent.

"What the—" Ham said, but Orion was already to the door, on his knees, fearing the worst.

Fearing Sasha in the throes of delirium, her high-altitude cerebral edema already taking hold. Already pressing so hard against her brain, it had turned her mad.

But it wasn't Sasha. Jenny thrashed in her sleeping bag. He couldn't make out her words, jumbled together, but something had ahold of her.

It happened often that the lack of oxygen produced such vivid dreams, they felt real.

And terrifying.

He scrambled inside, dropped the thermos, and climbed over her, his knees straddling her, his hands on her shoulders. "Jenny! Jenny, wake up!"

Her head thrashed, and she struggled against him.

"Jenny, it's Orion. Wake. Up. You're safe. I promise you're *safe*!"

Her eyes opened, but they stared at him, unseeing. Widening.

"Shh." He didn't know what else to do so he leaned over and pressed his forehead against hers, hoping some human contact might—

Her arms snaked up around his neck and suddenly she was pulling herself against him, into his arms.

Sobbing.

What—?

But he closed his arms around her, pulling her up, holding her. "Shh. It's okay, it's just a dream." He smoothed her hair, her cap having fallen off her head.

He was right—it was silky and smooth even days without a shower and shoot, he shouldn't be thinking about her hair right now, but it was either that or the feel of her body against his, shaking, holding so tight to him he really hoped she was awake and not dreaming.

"Jenny, wake up, please."

"I'm awake." She loosened her hold, just slightly, and nestled her head against his shoulder. "Sorry."

He didn't let her go. "It's all right."

She reached up and wiped her face with her hand. Leaned back. Tears still glistened on her other cheek and he used his thumb to wipe them away. Offered a tentative smile. "That was a doozy of an altitude dream."

She nodded. "I was . . . I was in Afghanistan."

Oh. And he didn't want to ask, but maybe . . . well, maybe he'd find out what had happened that had made her—

"And I was watching you fly away. You were sitting on the deck, your weapon across your knees . . ." Her breath hiccupped. "And then suddenly you fell out, and you were just falling, and falling . . ." She shook her head. "It was just a dream."

But, about *him*. He stared at her. "You dreamed I fell?"

She nodded. "You don't think, I mean, it's not . . ."

"A sign? That I'm going to fall? No, it was probably just seeing me, the shock of it, and then the altitude, you know?"

She looked back at him, caught his gaze a long, long time. Then, finally, she nodded. "Probably."

"Probably."

He knew it was wrong—an emotion wrought from the stress of the past few days, the coziness of their tent, and the very warm proximity of her body, but his gaze roamed her face, down to her mouth. Back to her eyes.

Which had widened.

She swallowed.

His hand touched her cheek. "Jenny?"

She caught her lower lip in her teeth. Drew in her breath.

Next to them, Sasha moaned.

Jenny looked over at her. Back at Orion. "I was screaming pretty loudly, wasn't I?"

Huh? "Um, yeah."

"And she didn't even wake up."

Oh. He looked at Sasha. No. "We need to wake her up. Get some fluids in her."

Jenny pushed herself away. "Or she could go into a coma."

He helped Jenny prop up Sasha, uncapped the thermos, and brought it to Sasha's mouth. "C'mon, Sasha, work with me."

And for the first time in years he wanted to pray.

God, we take our troubles to you . . .

■ ■ ■

Aria had lied to Jake on so many levels. And not just about her pain.

She'd wanted to scream when he took her ankle and probed it, his hands gentle, but heat spiking up her leg until she knew, if he moved it, she would cry out.

He'd figure out that maybe it wasn't just a sprain.

It was possible that sheer will had gotten her down the mountain yesterday, because every movement of her ankle sent fire up her leg.

Then there was her body—she might not be bleeding internally, but everything ached from the violence of her falls.

She just wanted to curl into the fetal position and stay in her warm down bag. She'd only been slightly kidding when she told Jake that she needed a strong man to carry her pack.

She'd let Aria speak the truth when she told him that she wasn't brave. Was scared to death as she hung over that crevasse.

For a moment, when he'd taken her hand, when he told her she was okay, that he was going to get her off the mountain, something pulsed between them. Something honest and raw and . . .

It scared her nearly as much as hanging over a cliff. Because Aria could see herself falling for Jake Silver, cowboy dancer and all-around hero, with his sweet *I will rescue you* demeanor, the concern in his pale blue eyes.

Hello, trouble.

Her inner Kia came to the rescue. Fast-talking, witty, flirty—her sister had emerged again and saved her from turning into a blubbering mess. Because who was she kidding—he knew how to talk to women. Knew how to make them feel strong and beautiful. Knew how to flirt. *"Five beautiful, smart, independent, nosy sisters who would think you are pretty brave."* He was probably just giving her a pep talk, something to keep her from quitting.

Please, let her quit.

She lay on her side, watching Jake sleep, trying to tell herself that she wasn't being creepy, but he had a delicious softness in sleep, long dark lashes, the laugh lines around his mouth eased, his dark blond hair tousled. He lay with one muscled arm up, under his head, and his words landed, found room in her heart. *"I was a Navy SEAL."*

Maybe she shouldn't have asked why he wasn't in the Navy anymore—it had been a deeply personal question. But she'd been trying to stall, afraid really, at the thought of what bruising he might find.

She so didn't want to die on this mountain.

The scream broke through the night. High. Terrified.

Aria jerked, but her body protested movement.

Jake sat straight up. In a flash she saw him orient himself, calculate the situation.

He looked at her first, then scrambled toward the door and unzipped it. He still wore his polar booties but grabbed his jacket, and in a second he was out the door.

The screaming had stopped, leaving behind only the residue of Aria's thundering heartbeat. Sash—

She tried to push up to a sitting position, but her body had hardened to stone.

God, please—

The zipper moved and Jake appeared, crawling back inside. "Jenny. She's fine. Apparently it was a nightmare." But he sat on his sleeping bag and pulled on his overpants.

"What's going on?"

"Your friend Sasha isn't well. I'll be right back."

He met her eyes then, and offered a small, steadying smile.

Then, he took a piece of her heart with him as he climbed back out.

She closed her eyes and in walked Kia.

You know you like him.

And yes, she knew she was arguing with herself, but sometimes she just missed her sister, so . . .

I do, but that doesn't matter. What happens after we get off the mountain?

You think too much—be spontaneous. Follow your heart.

You mean your *heart.*

She shook away the argument. How screwed up was she that she still let her dead sister tie her into an emotional knot?

Aria rolled over, despite the ache, and finally pushed herself into a sitting position. Then she untangled her overpants from the wadding she'd used for a pillow and shook them out.

Now to get her foot into the pants.

She unzipped her bag and worked her feet out.

Her ankle had ballooned to three times its size. Probably part altitude, part stress, but there wasn't a hope of her jamming that foot into her boot today.

Maybe tomorrow.

But Sasha didn't have tomorrow.

Raised voices outside caught her attention. "Asking her to climb down Karstens Ridge on that ankle is a recipe for disaster. And we can't move Sasha, Ham." Jake's low, husky voice. The concern in it was dangerous to her heart.

"We have to move Sasha—she needs to get to a lower elevation." Ham, solid, rational, in charge.

"Or we get some dex—one of us could climb back up to High Camp. We'll radio down to the Basin guys and have the doc bring us some." She recognized Orion's voice in the mix.

"That'll take a day, maybe more—" Ham's voice.

"Then we go down." Orion. "*I'll* go down, get into radio range, and call Clancy.*"

"Can a chopper get this high?" Jake.

"What else do you suggest? We can't carry her." Orion again.

Silence.

Jake's words filtered back to her. *"I'm going to get you down this mountain, even if I have to carry you."*

No. He *didn't* have to carry her. She'd gotten herself into this mess—she'd figure out a way to get herself out. She grabbed her overpants, bunched up one leg, then leaned over and pulled it over her foot.

She didn't mean to let out a whimper as she jarred her ankle, it just burst out of her. But she had the pants leg over her foot. She lay back, breathing hard, sweat prickling her forehead.

She could do this.

Really? Because you aren't the brave one, Aria.

She blew out a breath and leaned up again, grabbing her pants and moving her other leg into them.

Yes. Yes. She lay back and worked the pants over her body and around her waist. Buttoned them.

Now, boots.

No, wait. Socks. She'd slept all night with just the polar boots but that wouldn't be enough to keep her toes from freezing.

She found her wool socks at the bottom of her bag and sat up, shaking them out.

Looked at the balloon of her ankle. This was going to hurt.

Just give up already, sis.

"No!"

Now she was really going crazy. But she clenched her teeth, worked her thumbs into the sock to bunch it up, and, holding her breath, eased it over her toes.

"Oh!"

She gulped back her cry, then closed her eyes as she pulled the sock up, feeling it compress her bones with its weight.

She let out her breath as it moved up to her heel.

Leaned back on her hands, just for a second.

C'mon, Aria, you survived worse than this. Her own voice this time, and her hand went to the scar that bisected her chest, under all her layers.

Yes, she'd survived much, much worse.

She leaned over, grabbed the edges of the sock, and pulled.

Her cry emerged without stops, brisk, sharp, and sustained. But she bit it down, containing the agony through her teeth, and pulled the sock up her leg.

Then she flopped back on her sleeping bag and just breathed.

She could do this.

The door unzipped. "What the—hey, what are you doing?"

She opened her eyes, and sure enough, Jake had heard her, was scrambling inside. He zipped the door closed behind him, then moved next to her. "What's going on?"

"I know this is a shock to you, but I'm getting dressed. I do it every day. Well, usually. I have been known to wear a bathrobe around the house on the occasional Saturday when it's snowing out and I'm watching the Hallmark Channel. But otherwise, it's all clothes, every day."

He didn't look amused. "You put your sock on?"

"All by myself. Since I was three years old." She leaned up and grabbed her other sock. "Watch, I'll do it again."

"You're not funny, Aria. You have a serious injury here."

"And my friend Sasha is dying. We need to move her down the mountain—"

"You're not going anywhere." He was watching as she put her sock on, his jaw in a hard line. "You won't make it."

"I have news for you, pal. I'm one of the youngest board-certified pediatric cardiothoracic surgeons in the nation. And—" She stared at him, sucking in her next words. *And a heart transplant survivor.*

Because no, he didn't need to know that if she hoped to convince him she was fine.

She wasn't unaware of what the altitude could do to her body.

"I'm tougher than you think."

"I think you're plenty tough there, Houlihan." His eyes glittered. "I just don't want you to fall and drag me down the mountain with you."

"Don't rope up with me." She leaned over to grab her boots, just inside the door, but he put a hand on them.

"Too late for that. I already promised to get you down the mountain."

"I absolve you—"

"Are you trying to get us both killed?"

She recoiled. Stared at him. The teasing fun from last night had vanished from his expression.

"That's not how this works, Aria. You fall, I fall." His jaw was tight, and as she stared at him, emotion ringed his eyes. He looked away. Shook his head.

Blew out a breath, as if trying to gather himself.

When he came back to her, he'd transformed into the man she'd seen at the dance. "Besides, you promised me another dance. And I'm not leaving until you pay up." Then, he winked.

She just blinked at him. Who—

Except, maybe she got it. Because it was so much easier to be Kia, the girl who just wanted to have fun, than to let Aria—fragile, serious, all-work Aria—have a voice.

No one liked Aria.

"I did not promise you a dance, Cowboy."

He let go of her hand on the boots. "But you were thinking about it."

"You really have an ego on you, don't you?"

He was opening up her sleeping bag. "No. It's just who I am, honey. A good time, a great dance, and worth the wait. Now, get back in your sleeping bag."

"Wow. That line work a lot?"

"I don't know. It might need refining." He raised an eyebrow.

She reluctantly got back in.

He zipped it up.

"What's going on with Sasha?"

He sat beside her. "Orion thinks she's developing HACE—

high-altitude cerebral edema. She's really drowsy and is starting to moan in her sleep. He's trying to get fluids in her, but Ham thinks we need to send a team down the mountain."

"You're going to get help."

He considered her, and for a second, she thought he might say something quippy, like, *It's what I do, bay-bee.* Instead, "Orion knows this peak, and Ham doesn't have the medical experience I have, so . . . it looks like you're not getting rid of me yet. They're packing up to go."

She opened her mouth, then closed it, and crazy tears heated her eyes. He wasn't leaving her. She looked away.

"Hey—wow. I thought we'd hit it off here. Sheesh, just when I was going to order out for pizza and put on the Hallmark Channel."

She laughed, then groaned. "Don't."

"What?"

"Make me laugh. I hurt everywhere."

Oh. She hadn't meant to say that.

His smile vanished. "Really?"

No, she couldn't go there. So, "Now you want to look up my shirt again, don't you?"

His eyes narrowed. He let a beat pass. "On a scale of one to five, what are my chances?"

"Zero."

He made a noncommittal sound.

"I'm just sore."

"I'll bet. You sure you didn't break anything?"

"I'm a doctor."

"Of the *heart.*"

"Please. It's a specialty. I did a general residency before I went into pediatric cardiothoracic surgery."

He wore a strange expression.

"What?"

"You just . . . you're pretty amazing."

She let out a sound. "You're still at zero."

"Aw." But he grinned. "It was worth a try. Besides, it's true. You are amazing. A doc of tiny hearts *and* a mountain climber?"

"Trust me. I'm not amazing—my sister—she was amazing. She was the real brave one in the family. I climb because of her."

She wasn't sure why she'd admitted that, but maybe she was tired of pretending. "Kia was spontaneous and adventurous and fun and . . . well, she always dreamed of climbing Denali, so here we are."

"So, this is about your sister? Why isn't . . . oh, wait . . . Is this a bucket-list thing?" He made a face. "Please don't tell me—"

"She passed away when she was seventeen. Motorcycle accident."

"Aw, I'm sorry, Doc." He made a face. "That's rough."

"She was my twin." Sheesh, maybe she did have altitude sickness, too. Next thing she knew she *would* be lifting her shirt to show him her scars. Please.

"So was being a doctor a dream of hers too?"

"No. That was all me. I was always . . . well, I was the one who studied. I graduated high school at sixteen, undergrad at eighteen, and by twenty-two, I had my medical degree. Five years of general surgery residency, and three years in the cardiothoracic program, with an emphasis on pediatric surgery. I've been board certified for three years."

"And, in between saving little lives, you climb mountains."

"It's my way of keeping Kia alive. I celebrate her birthday at the top of a mountain."

"Okay, now I'm compelled to get you off this mountain, because you might be the best person I've ever met."

His words found her bones, heated her through. Oh no. "Yeah, but I wasn't a SEAL, saving the world."

His expression fell. "I didn't save the world."

No, just me. But she didn't want to say that, not with the way he swallowed, looked away. Took a breath.

Something . . .

"Okay, I gotta get you into the other tent. We're taking this one down for Ham and Orion to take with them."

He leaned over her. Then, before she could stop him, he lifted her, sleeping bag and all, into his arms. "Put your arms around my neck and hang on."

She wanted to protest—probably Kia would have—despite her appreciation of a man with muscles, the hard curve of his body as he pulled her against himself.

But Aria, well, she was tired of being brave and witty and capable. So she obeyed, looping her arms around his neck. He smelled of the wild, his whiskers rubbing against her forehead. And she couldn't remember the last time she felt . . .

Safe.

Oh no.

"That's a good doctor," Jake said as he maneuvered them out of the tent, crawling on his knees. Once outside, he rose with her, as if she weighed nothing, and carried her across the snow.

But before he tucked her into the other tent, he stopped. "Look at that view, Aria."

The sun had glazed the far mountain glaciers in flames, turning the jagged granite peaks to a deep platinum. The wind lifted the snow in gusts, huffing and puffing a white breath into the panorama.

Jake's arms tightened around her.

"Not a bad place to spend your birthday."

She looked at him, frowned.

"If she was your twin, it's your birthday too, isn't it?"

She caught her breath. Oh . . .

He smiled. "Yeah, that's what I thought. Happy birthday, Houlihan." He pressed a kiss to her forehead.

Then he carried her into the other tent.

CHAPTER NINE

JENNY WAS BREAKING every promise to herself by leaving Sasha on the mountain.

She might even be physically ill as she knelt beside her.

Sasha's eyes were closed, her red hair splayed out on the wadding of her jacket. Her skin seemed nearly white, deathly, as Jenny ran her hand over her forehead.

"Sash. We're going to get you help. Stay with us."

A flicker of her eyes, and Jenny caught her breath as Sasha looked at her. "Jens. Tell Lucas—tell him, I'm sorry about the baby."

Jenny froze, swallowed. *Baby?* But now wasn't the time. "Okay. Yes. But you'll see him real soon, I promise." She leaned forward and brushed her lips against her forehead.

Then she looked up at Jake, seated next to Aria on her sleeping bag. He gave her a solemn nod.

"Ari—"

"We'll do everything we can." Aria was in worse shape than she'd let on, given the cry she'd emitted when Jake brought her into the tent. The man carried her as if she weighed nothing.

Solidly built, bulky shoulders, with a hint of blond whiskers that scraped across his jaw. Jake reminded her of the SEAL guys she once knew.

So maybe Sash and Aria *were* in safe hands.

She grasped Aria's hand, squeezed, and then climbed out of the tent.

Ham and Orion were waiting for her by her pack. They'd lightened the packs for the hike out, leaving half the food here. Hopefully, they'd get in radio contact with help when they reached Karstens Ridge.

Her gut didn't like it, though. First, there was the clutter in the sky, a building of cumulus traffic—thick white clouds moving slowly over Mount Huntington. Then there was the wind, dusting snow off the creamy white ridge.

Karstens Ridge might be the most dangerous section of the journey—three thousand feet along a two-foot-wide path with gusting winds and a drop-off over a thousand feet on either side.

The beauty that fell before her, however, could nearly choke out the foreboding in her gut, the one that said this was going to go terribly wrong.

Orion reached for her biner and clipped her into a butterfly knot in the center of the line. "Ham will be behind you. I'll be in front of you. And Jake has the other radio, so we'll be in touch."

She looked up at him, seeing herself reflected in his dark glasses, her image nearly unrecognizable in her face mask, hood, hat, glasses. She'd kitted up, too—carrying her webbing of ice screws, a descender, an extra cordelette. Jake had given her his snowshoes in case they ended up hiking through Muldrow Glacier. She'd shoved a couple pickets into the outside straps of her pack and refreshed her avalanche beacon, now inside her jacket pocket. Ham and Orion wore beacons also.

Orion checked her biners and made sure the rope ran through her chest harness. Ran a hand up her pack tether.

"Good kit," he said and smiled.

She wanted this day to go right. No more accidents. No falls.

But she'd had that dream—no, *nightmare*—and whether it was a premonition, a memory, or just an oxygen-deprivation-induced altitude dream, it left a residue that she couldn't shake.

That and the way Orion had looked at her, desire in his eyes, raking up all the memories she'd been trying to forget. It left a warm hum inside her that she should probably shake away.

If he knew what she'd kept from him, what she hadn't told him about the dream, he certainly wouldn't be looking at her with anything warm and cozy—or otherwise—in his thoughts.

How was she supposed to know that a ten-year-old could lie with so much authenticity in his eyes? *"Is he telling the truth? Is he reliable? What's your professional opinion, Dr. Calhoun?"*

"Ready?" Orion said.

"Are you sure we shouldn't be climbing back up?" She'd heard the argument after Jake and Ham had burst into the tent, then powwowed afterward. She should have added her opinion. If they climbed back to the summit, at least they knew they had people waiting on the other side.

The Muldrow Glacier route, while still used, was the road less traveled. If they couldn't get the signal out, they had days and days of hiking before they came to civilization. And Sasha didn't have that long.

Ham, in his red jacket, crunched over to her. It wasn't just his height or the way he carried himself, but his expression, one of confidence, of surety that gave him presence. Now, he looked at her. "Don't worry. Orion knows this route—"

"So do I. I studied it for over a year before our climb. We

were going to take this route up. It takes a little longer, but you get acclimated slower, and . . ." She closed her mouth. The *and* would have included the fact that maybe Sasha wouldn't be struggling with fluid in her brain if they'd taken longer to get to the summit.

If they hadn't taken a different route.

If she'd spoken up in Copper Mountain.

She just couldn't make a good decision, no matter what she did.

"I . . ." She looked up to the summit. "I just wish I knew where to find help the fastest."

Ham drew in a breath.

"Let's go," Orion said. "I feel a prayer headed our direction."

"Doesn't hurt to pray," Ham said. He turned to Jenny. "God will give us a discerning mind if we ask for it." He clamped his hand on her shoulder, then on Orion's.

Something about Ham's voice, confident, solid, praying to God on the top of the mountain seeded her bones with hope.

"Make our steps safe, and go before us. Finish the task you've pressed us to. Amen."

"Feel better?" Orion said to Ham.

"Always," Ham said.

Orion turned and headed toward the spine that wound up the backside of Denali.

When Jenny had picked this route—and not only for the acclimation elements—she'd been drawn into the photos of the valley below the ridge. Breathtaking.

She guessed the time might be three in the morning, the low sun turning the Muldrow Glacier at their feet a deep cerulean blue, leaving a lip of deep salmon along the jagged horizon, topped by a layer of pure golden sunlight.

The valley itself looked as if God had filled it in with layers and layers of whipped topping, with dollops and peaks and a line of pure cream down the middle.

Deceptive.

Orion walked in front of her, and she let the rope out enough so that if she fell he had time to self-arrest, and also so it wouldn't create enough of a pull to yank him off his anchor.

Admittedly, with Ham an equal length behind her, she felt just a smidgen safer. She remembered their quick work on the glacier.

She always loved the strange peace inherent in climbing. The crunch of her feet in the snow, the wind whipping in her ears. The heat working through her body despite the minus-zero temperatures. Out here, it was just her against the mountain, her against herself. Her against the power of gravity to pull her back.

"Make our steps safe, and go before us. Finish the task you've pressed us to."

She could get on board with that.

They climbed past Browne Tower, and the world opened up even wider. If she ever wanted to take a running leap and let the wind catch her, it was here, as she stared out into the valley. An endless rim of spiring peaks, the cloud shapes captured in shadow in the valley as they moved across the sky.

Orion stopped and held his hands out, the signal to stop.

Just a break, apparently, because he pulled out a thermos. Surveyed the view.

She broke out her thermos, drank some tea, capped the thermos, and replaced it.

He held his axe in the air.

Go.

She followed him across the thinning cap of the ridge, her chest thickening with each step. She didn't dare turn around to check on Ham, not wanting to risk falling.

Orion reached the edge of the ridge and was setting in an ice screw, digging down to the ice to fix it, when she caught up to him.

"We're going to belay each other down the face."

She looked over the edge and refused to give in to the flip of her stomach. The pitch felt like a straight slope to death. "Have you tried the radio yet?"

"No reception."

She turned, spotted Ham coming up behind her. The north and south peaks of the mountain rose behind her, deceiving in their closeness. "Try again."

He looked up at her and nodded. He clipped in his line to the anchor, then pulled off his mitten to grab the radio. "Clip into the anchor while I—"

His words weren't out before they heard the shout from behind. "Falling!"

Ham!

She dropped to her knees, shoved her feet into the snow, and lay on her axe, digging it in hard.

The jerk on her harness didn't come. She hunkered down with her face in the snow, the wind barreling into her ears, her breath caught in her chest.

Beside her, Orion had dropped to his knees, taking the same position, but after a moment he scampered over to her, again dropping down over the top of her to fortify her position.

Nothing. "Stay here." He reached under her and clipped her into the ice screw with his quick clip. Then he got up.

"Ham!"

The ropes remained slack.

"Don't move," Orion said.

He got up, and she guessed he was searching for Ham.

"He self-arrested," Orion said as he came back. "You're good."

She rolled over and spotted Ham just a few feet off the trail, working his way back up the ridge.

Her breath leaked out in a slow trail of relief.

Okay, so maybe she'd been wrong about their chances.

Or maybe his prayer had actually worked.

"I dropped the radio."

She looked at Orion, his words stilling her. *What—?*

He was clawing through the snow. "I can't believe I dropped the radio!" The panic in his voice raised her own.

She dug in, helping him.

Nothing but thick folds of snow.

"Where is it?" she said, her voice shaky.

No, *please*—

By the time Ham had joined them, Jenny was nearly in tears. "What's going on?"

"When you fell, I dropped the radio," Orion said, his voice dark.

"It has to be here—" Jenny said.

"Is that it?" Ham pointed to a tiny wedge of black metal in the snow.

Now Jenny really wanted to cry.

Orion scooped it up.

"Call the rescue team," she said.

Orion picked it up. Toggled the switch. "Denali rescue, come in."

Static.

"Denali rescue?"

Nothing.

"Maybe they can't pick up our words, but let me try Morse code." Ham reached for the radio.

Orion handed it to him and pulled out his GPS. Read off the coordinates.

Ham clicked them out. "I sent an SOS also."

Jenny collapsed onto the ridge, breathing hard.

Please.

"Jenny, are you okay?"

She nodded but pressed her face into her mittened hands, her shoulders shaking.

Don't fall apart. Don't—

Crunching feet. Someone sat beside her. "We're going to get help, I promise." Orion.

She looked up, studying the horizon. "If Aria and Sasha die because of my stupid idea—"

"Stop."

His sharp voice made her look at him.

Snow caked his face mask, and she couldn't see his eyes through his dark glasses, but she could almost feel his gaze, hard on her. "Your friends aren't going to die."

She drew in a breath. "Sometimes I think I'm just . . . I'm doomed." She didn't mean to let those words escape, but . . . "I try to do things right and still, terrible things happen."

He let a beat pass, or maybe he just didn't know what to say because they sat there, the wind whipping against their clothing, dusting snow into the blue sky. Then, "You're not doomed today. Today, we save lives."

Then he got up and reached out a hand.

She took it. And wow, she didn't deserve this man showing back up in her life. Not after . . .

Not after she'd killed his friends.

"Let's get down this ridge and keep moving," Orion said.

She heard Ham's voice as she let Orion rope her up and began her descent down the wall.

"Make our steps safe, and go before us. Finish the task you've pressed us to."

※ ※ ※

"Today, we save lives."

Orion's words hung in his head, embedded in his chest, and worked into his marrow as they trekked across the relatively level cirque of Muldrow Glacier, on their way to the Great Icefall. The wind had slowed, blue skies overhead. His snowshoes left impressions on the crystalline snow.

"Sometimes I think I'm just . . . I'm doomed."

Jenny's words, uttered after he'd almost lost his mind, after they'd recovered the radio, had reached in and nearly broken his heart.

Especially because he understood.

Oh, he understood.

He'd felt doomed for most of his life.

"I try to do things right and still, terrible things happen."

He wanted to shrug away her voice, broken, plaintive, as if hoping he might have answers.

None. He had nothing. Because he'd given up trying to find a reason for why terrible things happened to the people who didn't deserve them.

People like his mother. His brother.

His father.

And, frankly, every single soldier who died at the hands of evil.

"You're just mad because God didn't answer your prayer the way you wanted him to."

Yes. Yes, he was.

He deserved a little better from the Almighty. After all, he'd picked himself back up after God took his entire family, thank you. Went into the family business of saving lives.

So, yeah, he expected God to deliver him from near destruction in one piece. What good was God if, when you took your troubles to him, he didn't answer?

Worse, he had nowhere to put his anger. Because what did a guy do when he was angry at the Almighty? The God of all creation? It felt a little like spitting into the wind.

Would only come back to mess you up.

Felt safer to blame . . . *anyone* else, frankly.

Sorry, Ham. He wouldn't be dropping to his knees anytime soon to put his trust in a God who ignored him.

Even mocked his pain.

Except . . .

He glanced behind him, at Jenny. She followed his tracks, stepping into each one, fighting her way through the snow. What *was* she doing here?

That felt like a weird sort of answer to an unuttered prayer.

He could almost hear Ham's voice, thundering forth from the past.

"You okay, man?"

The cave in Afghanistan. Orion had looked over at him, making out his eyes in the darkness, lit only by a couple flashlights. He'd been trying not to retch from the pain, trying not to let the shouts, the occasional pop of gunfire shoot holes into his soul.

They weren't getting out of this.

"We're going to get out of here." Again, Ham's voice. But sitting in that cave, his knee a mess, his fellow PJs casualties in the dirt on the mountainside, trapped and out of radio contact . . .

"Maybe," Orion said. "Maybe not. But I'm thinking of all the things I wish I'd done."

Ham had knelt in front of him, leaned over to look at the dressing around Orion's knee. "Like what?"

"I should have kissed Jacie."

Ham raised an eyebrow.

"I know we haven't been hanging out long, but there's something about her. And she sort of looked at me like she wanted me to kiss her, but . . . aw, I'm just feeling the morphine."

Except, he could almost feel her lips against his, whisper soft. Could nearly taste her smile.

He very well might be in love with her.

He'd never been the kind of guy to crack open his heart and let a woman in. Sometimes he felt a little like the mountain his father loved. Cold, foreboding. Not easily conquered.

That thought caught him up now, as he trudged through the snow. Maybe he *was* tired of being alone on his mountain.

"Ry!"

He slowed, turned, not realizing he'd been walking so fast. Ham was behind him, his arms out. *Stop.* Jenny turned, too, shading her eyes.

"Stay there!"

Orion surveyed their position as Ham caught up to him. He hadn't realized they'd breached the Great Icefall, he'd been so consumed in his thoughts, but yes, it was probably a good thing to stop. Below him lay a minefield of glacial traps, crevasses, depressions, and seracs.

Ambushes.

But as long as they were careful . . .

He waited as Ham and Jenny caught up to him. Jenny leaned over, breathing hard.

"'Sup, man?" Orion asked.

Ham pulled down his face mask. "I was looking at the glacier, and it feels like maybe we need to move to the right as we go down this icefall. There's a linearity through the snow fifty feet down—see the depression?"

Ham pointed to a well that ran a hundred yards, maybe more, horizontally through the field. "I think there's a giant crack there."

"Could be the remains of the bergschrund that broke free years ago."

"We could travel in an echelon—in a V formation," Jenny said.

"But if one of us falls, there's only the other one to catch him. Or her," Orion said. "Better to stay in a line, perpendicular to the crevasse. We'll find a place to cross over it."

He ran his gaze over her kit, just to make sure she was secured. But she'd been a pro on Karstens Ridge, working with them as if she knew exactly what she was doing.

Of *course* she did. Just because they'd had an accident didn't mean she needed his help the rest of the way down the mountain.

Except, he wanted to help her.

That thought drew in his breath.

What was it about Jenny Calhoun that made him want to step into her life? And invite her back into his?

Hadn't he learned his lesson?

"I can lead for a while," Ham said.

Orion considered him. Glanced at Jenny.

Well, this way, if Jenny fell, he could be in a better position to self-arrest. "Maybe we should put on our crampons."

Ham nodded and they switched out their footwear. Then, he traded places with Ham.

The key to glacier travel wasn't just the probing and picking routes, but keeping the line taut enough to not let too much slack create a force that would knock you over in a fall. But not tight enough that you might end up face-first down a mountain.

Jenny followed Ham.

He followed Jenny.

She muscled along without complaint, keeping pace. He liked a person who looked at challenges without flinching.

Challenges like him.

"It's not the morphine. You've had your eye on her since we showed up here. And since you met her, you seem less knotted up inside. What is it about this girl?"

Ham, again, bothering him out of his pain in the cave. Thorne and Royal had taken defensive positions at the front of the cave. The other SEAL, North Gunderson, had gone to scout an escape route.

Which left Ham to figure out what to do next.

Apparently, it was to badger Orion about his love life. Or maybe he was trying to keep him alive. Whatever.

"I don't know. There's something honest about her. Brave, maybe."

"There's brave, and there's crazy. Embedded in a war zone?" Ham shook his head.

"Crazy like you and me?" Orion said as he heard shouts.

"Crazy because she's risking her life for a *story*."

A couple shots popped off. Ham stood up. Royal, calling back. More shots.

"Get down!" Ham said.

A crack, and Orion came back to himself, to the mountain and the fact that Ham was waving his arms—*danger*.

"Icefall!" Ham shouted. He backed up, rerouted, and disappeared behind a tall serac.

Another crack. This time a cornice gave way under the sun and crashed down the glacier to the left. Orion stiffened, but the avalanche careened down the mountain some quarter mile away.

Okay, so he was jumpy.

He came around the ice chunk that had hidden Ham and spotted his friend on the other side of a two-foot-wide gap. He had moved forward and was taking an anchoring position—laying on his ice axe, his feet dug in.

Orion's heart lodged into his throat when he spotted Jenny's intentions. "Wait!"

Jenny turned. "It's only two feet!"

Her voice filled his head. *"Sometimes I think I'm just . . . I'm doomed."*

Not today. "Let me anchor you in."

He too knelt and anchored himself in, leaving enough slack for her to jump. "Okay, clear."

He hunkered down, bracing himself for a fall, but none came and in a moment he looked up.

She was on the other side of the crevasse, her axe in the air. "Clear."

See, keeping terrible things from happening was all about planning ahead. Anticipating trouble. He couldn't stop every random event from taking him out, but . . .

So maybe it wasn't about stopping the random events; maybe it was about learning to live with them when life was snatched out of your control.

He leaped over the crevasse, his heart pounding. Held his axe up.

Ham waved. "Let's take a break while I try the radio!"

Jenny unhooked her pack and dropped it to the ground, and pulled off her climbing gear from around her shoulder. Ahead of them, Ham unroped and walked toward a dome of snow, probably to get higher reception.

Orion shrugged off his pack, letting the weight fall into the soft snow with a crunch. Pulled out his water bottle and took a sip of tea.

See, they weren't doomed.

And maybe it was time to stop letting the past grind through him. Let go of the anger, the frustration, the lack of closure holding him hostage.

Maybe he should just . . . come down from the mountain.

Grab on to this random second chance with Jenny.

It wasn't like God would show up and give him any answers about the past anyway.

Another crack split the air behind him, but he didn't turn, the sound echoing in the distance.

Until—

"Orion, look out!" Jenny looked past him.

Her voice froze in time. Then she picked up her ice axe and fled horizontally across the ice field.

He turned. His breath caught.

The giant serac behind him thundered down in a great torrent of white.

Avalanche.

■ ■ ■

"We're going to die up here."

Aria was sitting up on her sleeping bag, a slight sweat beaded across the brow of her wool cap, her body trembling with a bone-deep shiver.

Jake just about agreed with her. Just about gave in to the knot that had tightened in his gut for the past eight hours as he watched Sasha groan in her sleep, tried to ladle tea and Spam soup into her, tried to fortify the snow wall around their tent.

Outside, the clouds were moving, darkening, kicking up flurries. *Hurry, Ham.*

Jake closed the zipper of the tent behind him. "No, we're not.

Help get her up." He knelt next to Sasha, who lay on her side, breathing deeply. *Please be sleeping and not in a coma.* "Sasha? It's time for some dinner." Or lunch, or breakfast—it was hard to keep track with the endless sunshine. He'd followed Ham, Orion, and Jenny's progress as they trekked Karstens Ridge but had lost them down the backside. They were probably in the glacier below, but he'd yet to spot them.

"More Spam soup?" Aria said as she leaned over to Sasha, shaking her awake. Sasha stirred, groaned. "Thatta girl. I know it's not super tasty, but you have to eat something."

"What, you don't like my soup?"

Aria glanced up at him, cocked her head. Every time she settled those beautiful brown eyes on him, something forbidden moved deep inside him. "It wouldn't be my first go-to if we got off this mountain."

"When. Not *if*."

Her mouth tightened. The playful girl he'd met in Copper Mountain had vanished as the wait for help drew out. Now he recognized hints of a no-nonsense bedside manner as she continued to shake Sasha. "Wake up, Sash."

Sasha's eyes flickered open.

"We're out of Spam. This is just broth." He didn't mention it was the last of their broth. No one needed to panic here.

"Good girl," Aria said and pushed Sasha onto her back. "Time to sit up."

Sasha seemed dazed, at best, and Jake didn't want to comment on the fact that she'd turned into a zombie. People could die within twenty-four hours after full-onset HACE.

He couldn't let another person die on his watch.

Sasha's auburn hair hung in strings, her face sweaty and lined. He helped brace her and handed the soup to Aria.

Sasha's head rolled back onto his shoulder. "C'mon, Sasha. Wake up. Eat."

Aria had gotten more forceful. She took Sasha's mouth and opened it, then poured broth into her mouth, closed her mouth. Sasha's reflexes took over.

He glanced at her. "Remind me not to hunger strike around you."

"I'll keep you alive." She winked, no smile. She poured another forced spoonful of broth into Sasha's mouth.

"Did you really graduate from college at eighteen?" He'd been thinking about their conversation, her accomplishments.

And her crazy words about her sister. *"I'm not amazing—my sister—she was amazing. She was the real brave one in the family. I climb because of her."*

He knew what losing a sister did to someone, so yeah, he got it. But if he did the math, she'd graduated a year after her sister died. That was some kind of dedication.

Aria took Sasha's face mask and wiped the dribble on her chin. "I was . . . I was bedridden for a while, so I studied a lot. Online school." She didn't meet his eyes. "And, I liked school."

Bedridden? He frowned, but before he could ask, she said, "I'm such an idiot—Sasha went to Miami right before this trip. I think she might have even gone scuba diving. Maybe she didn't have enough time to acclimate to the change in altitude."

She shook her head. "I should have warned her, but she needed to get away after losing the baby."

Jake didn't move.

"She found out she was pregnant after Jenny finalized our trip, and didn't know how to tell her—and then, well, she didn't have to." Aria's face tightened, as if she might be fighting tears. "Except it was her fourth miscarriage. And probably she was in no state to climb a mountain. Lucas took her to the beach, a sort of healing trip, and I should have said something. . ." She fed Sasha another spoonful. "Good job, Sash."

"Why was this climbing trip so important?"

She lifted a shoulder. "It's a triumph trip. To show us that we're stronger than . . . well, the things that want to hold us back."

He wanted to ask her what things, but she continued.

"Sasha is so much stronger than she looks right now. She's not only amazingly smart, but she survived a home invasion and a rape. And Jenny—she survived her mother's death, and . . . well, some terrible things that happened in Afghanistan."

He couldn't stop himself. "And you?"

She paused, mid-bite. Her lips tightened. Then, "I survived a heart transplant."

He stared at her. "A . . . heart transplant?"

"Yeah. I was born with a bum heart, spent most of my childhood in bed. Studying." She looked up. "Reading about adventures."

"And now you're living them."

"I might go back to reading when we get down."

When. He'd gotten her to *when*.

"I think she's done," Aria said. "She keeps spitting it out."

"At least she's staying hydrated."

"I wish I'd brought a steroid with us. I was . . . shoot." She shook her head as Jake lowered Sasha back onto the sleeping bag, zipping her up. The wind rippled the tent. He should probably go outside and check their wind protection. The last thing they needed was for the tent to tear, or even blow away.

With them in it.

He made a mental note to check the stakes too.

She started to hand him back the soup.

"No, you finish it."

"What about you?"

"I'll make more."

She nodded and drank the soup down. "I think I prefer it with Spam."

He grinned. "Right? I realize that it's probably not the healthiest thing for everyday life, but each serving contains fifteen grams of fat and seven grams of protein. It's compact and easy to transport, and an entire can feeds six people—or three guys. And it comes in twelve flavors, including jalapeño and teriyaki."

She was looking at him, one eyebrow raised. "Your agent get you that sponsorship gig?"

He blinked at her, then grinned. "Yeah. I'm working on a little jingle."

Her entire face lit up when she smiled, and for a moment, the doc vanished, and in her place returned the flirty woman he'd met in Copper Mountain.

"In all honesty, I've considered opening up a little food cart in the Minneapolis skywalk. Spam burgers, Spam on a stick. Deep-fried Spam."

She laughed, and it fed his bones, something sweet and tasting of hope.

Maybe they would live through this.

"Sounds like state fair food."

"Right? I could have a booth right between the chocolate-covered bacon and the deep-fried Twinkies." He reached out for her empty bowl.

"You'd have a line all the way to the midway." She handed it to him. "I love the state fair. I used to go every year as a kid."

Me too. The words nearly emerged. But a hand tightened over his chest and suddenly he couldn't breathe. He'd walked right into the memory without thinking.

"You okay? Jake?"

Calm down. "Yeah." He swallowed away the voices, the sirens, and forced a smile. "Gotta love the animal barns."

"Maybe we can go when we get off the mountain."

His mouth opened.

Silence dropped between them. Uh . . .

"Sorry—I . . ." She held up her hand, looked away. "I . . ."

"I'd love to see you again after we get off this mountain, Aria." His words emerged without his permission, but once they were out, the balloon in his chest deflated.

"Yeah, well, I work a lot, and you probably do too, running that food cart." She looked away.

Huh. "Yeah, right."

"And all your parasailing classes, and—what else do you do?"

He stared at her. "Aria—"

She put her hand to her neck. "You know, it's funny that I've never seen you around GoSports. I mean, I work out there all the time—" Her hand stopped. She pressed her palm to her chest, then searched her neck. "My necklace. It's gone."

She patted her body—she wore her fleece jacket, a thermal shirt under it. "I don't have it." Her voice wavered. "Oh—please, no—" She began to pat her sleeping bag, lifting up the layers, searching.

"What necklace?" He leaned up, searching for it.

"It's just a silly little cheap gold necklace. One of those half-heart necklaces you give to a friend—oh . . ." One hand went to her mouth, her breathing quickening.

"Calm down. We'll find it. Maybe you dropped it when you were helping Sasha." He began to search around Sasha's bag, under her jacket and overpants that were bunched under her head, then peeked around Sasha's sleeping form.

202

Aria had gotten up, making tiny noises of pain as she jostled her fat ankle.

"Hey—hey. Sit down. I'll find it."

He climbed over Sasha and in a second was in front of Aria, kneeling on either side of her legs. He grabbed her shoulders. "Aria. Take a breath. We'll find it."

His voice must have arrested her because she looked at him.

Oh wow, tears glistened in her eyes. Her jaw tightened as if she were fighting all-out weeping. "I . . . I can't lose—"

"It's right here." He swept up a tangle of gold chain that lay behind her, just out of her sight. Probably, it had fallen off in her sleep. He held it out to her. "It looks like it might have gotten snagged on something. The chain is broken."

She picked it up out of his hand, pressed her other hand over it. Closed her eyes.

"What's going on?"

"It's nothing." She opened her eyes, let out a breath.

"It's something, Houlihan." He searched for her gaze. Raised an eyebrow.

"It's just a trinket my sister gave me when we were kids."

Her sister. Her *dead* sister.

"Oh. Well then, we'd better keep it safe. I've got a tin in my pack that I keep odds and ends in—it'll be safe there." He held out his hand.

She nodded and dropped it back into his safekeeping. He ran his thumb over the edges of the broken heart.

He was moving outside to put it in his pack when she stopped him, grabbing his fleece.

"Jake, are we going to get out of here?"

He turned back to her. Settled his gaze in hers. "Yes. And you know why? Because my buddy Ham is out there. And he's not just a former SEAL, he was a Senior Chief. The leader of Team Three, and the guy has 'never quit' inside him."

He dropped the necklace into his zippered jacket pocket, then knelt next to her sleeping bag. "Let's get you tucked back in."

She didn't give him a snarky comeback, which had him a little worried. "Ham and I served together for about ten years. In all that time, there was one promise he didn't keep. One mission that he didn't complete." He eased her fattened ankle in, trying to ignore the low moan she emitted. Yeah, there was no way she was walking off this mountain.

"We were, um, doing some training in an undisclosed Eastern European country about ten years ago, maybe more, and this guerrilla group took over a local aid hospital. We deployed to rescue the US workers there, and one of them was taken captive. A woman. Problem was, Ham knew her. She vanished . . . She was killed before he could rescue her."

She was listening. "With the woman."

He nodded. "Ham wasn't good for a long time after that. He wasn't a leader at that time, so he found his way back and eventually took over Team Three, but I don't think . . . I don't think it ever really left him. And it certainly put the never quit inside him." He zipped up her bag. "Ham will get us off this mountain."

She offered the tiniest of smiles, nodded. "I believe you."

And with everything inside him he wanted to lean down and press his lips to that smile.

Maybe just to help him believe his words, too.

She closed her eyes, and he swallowed away the urge. "Get some rest, Houlihan."

He climbed out of the tent, trembling a little.

After finding his pack, parked under the vestibule of their tent, he drew out an old shoe polish tin. He put her necklace next to his military identification tags and capped it. Shoved it back into his pack.

Then he drew in a deep breath as he stared out at the horizon. A lenticular cloud was forming over Mount Hunter, blue skies all around. The wind skimmed up a layer of snow, brushed it over the snowpack. He shivered—the temperature was dropping.

He didn't have to be a meteorologist to sense the stirring of a storm.

Never quit.

Please, Ham, don't let me down. Because he didn't want to have to choose which woman to carry off this mountain.

And which woman would die.

CHAPTER TEN

RUN!"

The mountain had unlatched and was rumbling down in massive ice chunks directly toward them.

Jenny had experienced avalanches before—seen them from afar, and once ran from one on Rainier, but nothing like this torrent of destruction. The slide ripped seracs off their moorings, slew ice chunks the size of Volkswagens into its path, and sent forth a cloud of ice shards and freezing snow.

Their only chance was to get out of its path. Ham was already running over the top of the dome he'd climbed to radio for help.

She ran hard to follow him as the monster roared.

Her last glimpse of Orion showed him fleeing the torrent also, ice axe in hand. "Run!"

Her breath razed hard in her throat. Please let her not get swept away, end up upside down in some icy tomb, suffocating.

"Get down! Get down!" Ham vanished behind a wall of blue ice, across a valley of unblemished snow.

She turned, searching for Orion, and spotted him just outside the cloud of snow.

The avalanche was pummeling the hillside with golf-ball-sized rocks. The ground beneath her feet began to shake.

She fell behind a thick serac the size of a backstop, hit her knees, and had the presence of mind to grab her axe and shove it in. She dug her crampons in and hunkered down, trying not to scream.

God, please, *please*—

Because probably, most likely, she'd jinxed the mountain with her stupid, fate-daring statement. *"Sometimes I think I'm just . . . I'm doomed."*

Or maybe it was Orion who jinxed them, trying to find a reply. *"You're not doomed today. Today we save lives."*

What was the poor man supposed to say? And of course, she only made it worse, because nearly everything Orion said to her reminded her of the man he'd been.

The life she'd stolen from him.

So much for escaping her past—it seemed to be plummeting toward her.

The mountain shuddered as the torrent swept past her, massive ice boulders bouncing off seracs around her, tons of ice rolling by her. She heard screaming and realized it was her.

The air turned to a whiteout, burying her in a snowy breath.

Then, deep inside the thunder, a scream lifted. Pain, or perhaps fear—

Orion!

Before she could react, her harness jerked hard, as if he'd been thrown into the flow. She dug in, but in a second the power of the slide yanked her from the mountain.

It dragged her across snow and ice, blinding her, filling her mouth.

She was falling.

The earth dropped out beneath her legs, and she had a moment of clarity before she went over a snowy jagged edge. Enough to slam her feet into an icy wall, enough to jam her axe into the lip.

Still, some invisible force dragged her down and she put her other hand on the axe. Refused to let it loose, kept her ankles down, and fought to stay affixed to the wall.

The ice and snow cascaded down around her, into her jacket, pulling her down.

She couldn't look.

Then, just like that, the terrible roar died as it hurtled its way down the mountain.

It left her shaking as she clung to the blue ice. Only her heartbeat, her heavy gasps, filled the silence.

Then a terrible roar of agony bounced up around her, filling her ears, ricocheting off the walls around her. She took a breath and wiped her snow-filled goggles on her arm.

She couldn't let go of her position. But as the air cleared, she made out her predicament.

The slide had ripped open a crevasse, perhaps with one of the icy snowballs on its way down the mountain.

And, maybe out of spite, threw the interlopers into the icy maw.

The sound of agony had died to hard, stiff breaths, an audible moaning.

"Orion?"

She willed her heartbeat to slow. At least now she could see. Through the frozen residue of the sleet on her goggles, she made out a gulf of blue ice, narrow on one end, widening on the other where the ice blocks had hit it.

Darkness swelled from the unknown depths below.

And, on a lip of ice, jutting out maybe two feet, and nearly twenty feet below, Orion clung to a nob, his axe shoved into the icy wall, one foot drilled in, the other . . .

Oh, the other.

Something terrible had happened as he fell, maybe his crampon grabbed into the wall and refused to release, but his leg was twisted into a grotesque angle, his knee clearly dislocated.

No wonder he was moaning.

"I'm coming," she said. "Hang in there."

She didn't want to look down, but she had to know how deep the crevasse went. To her left, the icy wall extended, rough hewn, with jagged edges, narrowing into a tiny, impassable vein.

Icicles hung like torpedoes above her, and over the lip above Orion.

The chill of the icy tomb found her body, and she shivered. She drew in a breath, painfully aware that they might have been wedged in forever if they'd fallen a mere twenty feet farther down the mountain.

Toward Orion's side the crevasse was connected in bridges, maybe twenty feet down.

"Ham!" She looked up, the blue sky a wide swath of rescue some ten feet above. Somehow she'd managed to stop herself from plummeting by holding on to what looked like a former ice bridge, jutting out at a forty-five-degree angle.

"Ham!" Her voice pinged off the ice, back to her.

Orion's moans had died.

Nothing from the top. Ham's rope, however, hung down from above.

Jenny listened, praying. What if Ham was knocked out? Or worse, buried? She heard Orion's quiet hum of pain and named a decision.

She'd have to climb down to Orion unbelayed. If she was clipped into the line, and she fell, not only would she pull the rope from the top but she'd drag Orion right off his perch into the darkness.

And she couldn't do that to him again.

She unclipped her biner from the knot, freeing herself.

"I'm coming down!"

Orion said nothing.

She drew in a breath. Held on to her axe.

Released one foot from the ice, stretched down, and slammed it back in.

Then moved the other.

She moved the axe next.

"What are you *doing*?" The horror in Orion's voice told her that he'd looked up.

"Climbing down to you."

"Get back on belay. Right. Now."

"If I fall, I'll rip you off the wall." She kept moving. A word that betrayed his military background ripped through the crevasse.

"C'mon, Jenny. Please. Clip in and climb up."

"I'm halfway down to you."

"Climb up!"

"You're hurt! I'm not leaving you down there. Now stop distracting me!"

He let out another word but then stopped talking.

She moved down, carefully, her heart a fist in her chest. The breath of the crevasse turned frigid the lower she climbed.

As she got closer, she saw that he'd anchored himself into the wall with an ice screw. His harness, with his anchors, still hung around his shoulders. And, when she was close enough, he grabbed her harness and hooked her into his quick clip.

"Are you okay?" she said, coming alongside him.

"Don't do that again," he growled, his voice thin.

"What? Fall into a crevasse?"

"Do something stupid to try and save me."

She looked at him, not even knowing where to start. If she could go back in time, that's exactly what she would do.

Stop Operation Bulldog, no matter what the cost.

But now, she bit back her words and assessed the situation. "Your leg—"

"I tore out my artificial knee," he said without elaboration, his words spoken behind clenched teeth.

"Can you climb up?"

He blew out a breath. Swallowed. And she had a sense of what his answer cost him when he shook his head. "I might be able to use my Prusik to climb up if we could fix a rope from the top, but . . . where's Ham?"

"He hasn't responded. Let's get you onto solid ground. There's a ledge below you that looks secure."

She helped him anchor in two more ice screws and created a triad belay system. After she secured the rope to the ice screws and attached a descender, she reached for his harness to attach him on to the rope. "You go down. I'll come after you."

He stopped her hand. "No. You first. I can't go down until I know you're safe." He unhooked his line from his biner and hooked himself to the wall with his quick-clip line.

He'd removed his goggles, securing them on his hat, and now his gaze pinned to hers.

"You're hurt—"

"And I'm not going anywhere until you're off this wall!"

She didn't know why, but his pained growl found soft soil, dug in.

"Go down the line, Jenny. Now. I'm not leaving you here by yourself."

His words pinged against the icy walls.

"Fine." She rappelled down the icy walls, landing on the ledge. It careened out eight feet, a platform perhaps six feet wide that squirreled down the side of the crevasse and into the depths. A gulf of five or more feet yawned between the ledge and another on the opposite wall, clearly a former ice bridge.

"Send the descender back up."

"You'd better not fall," she said, unclipping herself.

He pulled up the line, then he hooked into the descender.

She watched, her breath tight, as he rappelled down, his groans emitting from deep inside.

She grabbed him as he hit the ice, then helped him ease back.

"Easy . . ." He was breathing hard, trying to hold back his pain. He leaned back against the wall of the glacier as she unhooked him from the rope.

He reached out and grabbed her hand. "Thank you."

She wanted to cry. And, in that moment, didn't have the ability to do anything but lower her forehead to his gloved hand. "Please tell me we're going to be okay."

He seemed to hesitate for a moment, then suddenly tugged her against him, wrapping his arms around her.

"We're going to be—"

The ice above them cracked, a giant icicle breaking off. It careened down, hit their ice anchor, and suddenly the entire rig, rope and all, unlatched from the wall and careened into the blackness.

■ ■ ■

The pain didn't dismantle him the way it had in Afghanistan, but Orion had to breathe through and settle his heart back into his chest. Let himself relax into the ache. And the pain wasn't just from his destroyed prosthetic knee joint.

The fall had done a number on his body. The terrible cascading fall. One second he'd been running along the glacier, the thunder of the avalanche crashing down over him, the next second he had been swept up as if he might be on a wave of water. The force of it turned him over and over, burying him, crushing him.

Then, suddenly, he launched out over the edge of the crevasse. Falling. Only his crash into the icy spire had stopped his fall into oblivion. He'd slammed his axe into the wall, dug his crampons into the ice, and hung on with everything inside him.

Die. He was going to die on the mountain that had taken his father. The mountain his father had loved.

No. Worse. He was going to drag two people down with him. The worst moment was when he looked up and saw Jenny careening over the edge.

Wow, she was fast. Strong. Brave. Fighting the pull of the rope, trying to save them both.

The force of the slide had opened up the crevasse, great chunks of ice falling deep inside. The rest continued to plummet down the mountain, and he could only hold his breath and offer words that felt very much like a prayer.

Please.

Please save us.

Please let Ham be alive.

The fact that his friend hadn't appeared in the gap of the crevasse tightened the fist around his chest. *Please, Ham, don't be dead!*

"What are we going to do?" Jenny said, her body tucked next to Orion's.

He said nothing, just clung to her.

"Please tell me we're going to be okay."

He was trying to find the words. But he needed a moment to settle himself, to put his heart back into his chest. To take a deep breath and sort it all out.

Compartmentalize.

Finally, when his voice wouldn't shake, "We're fifty feet from the top. I don't think our voices would carry even if anyone was out there."

"What about the radio?"

"Ham had the radio . . ." He looked at her as she leaned away from him. She looked at him with a growing realization in her eyes.

"I saw him hunker down on the other side of the glacier. Maybe he's . . . maybe he's just . . ." She stared up into the blue, as if unable to say the rest.

He didn't want to suggest that Ham might be buried under a sea of ice and snow. The thought, however, crippled him because he lowered himself to the icy floor. Leaned his head back to look up, truly assessing their calamity.

They were surrounded on every side by jagged blue ice, an overhanging lip at the top preventing their escape. It would take a champion ice climber to get them out.

He might be able to use his Prusik and foot hitch to inch his way up but that meant someone had to send a rope down from the top.

Which meant they'd have to rescue the rope from the depths below.

"If Ham's okay, he'll find us," he said now to Jenny.

And if he wasn't . . .

As if reading his mind, she got up and walked to the edge.

"Be careful!"

She glanced at him. "I'm being careful." She looked over the edge. "I see the rope. Most of it's about eight feet down, draped over a thin ice bridge. Maybe I can go down and get it."

"Have you lost your mind?" He drew in a breath, aware that his voice echoed like gunshots.

Jenny stiffened.

"No," he said again, this time calmer. "Better to figure out how to belay ourselves up with Prusiks and ice anchors."

Jenny came back to him. "Ham is dead, isn't he?"

"We don't know that."

"He shouldn't have unclipped."

"He was trying to get to higher ground."

She was looking up. "It looks like things are getting whiter out there."

"Could be the debris from the avalanche."

"Or could be another storm coming down the mountain." She blew out a breath and shook her head. "I can't believe I jinxed us."

"Huh?"

She looked at him with what looked like pain in her expression. "It's my fault we're on this stupid mountain. And now we're going to die in a sliver of ice!"

"Hey. *Hey*. Breathe." He wanted to reach out to her, but she stood too far away. "We'll get out of here."

She shook her head and unzipped her jacket, pulling it off.

"What are you doing?"

"I'm trying to keep you from going into shock." She knelt beside him, tucking the jacket over him.

"Not on your life! Jenny—put your jacket back on!"

"I'm sweating."

"And then you'll start shivering. C'mon. Please don't make this worse for me."

She stared at him, then pulled her jacket off him, slipped it back on.

"Thank you."

"Don't think you've won the war." She looked at his leg. "This is really gross."

Yeah, it was. His leg angled out below his knee about 30 degrees.

"You probably need to straighten it. And splint it."

She knelt, her knees bracketing his legs. "Are you going to be okay with me doing this?"

"Oh, I'm thrilled with the idea."

She looked up at him.

"I don't have a choice. It's got to be moved back into place if I want to restore the blood flow. Once the shock is over, I'll be okay. It's really the mechanical joint that's out of place." Although by the pain that ebbed through his body, he guessed he probably had a broken tibia, too.

"It's not as bad as the first time around."

She looked up at him. "The first time around?"

He let out a long breath. "In Afghanistan in the cave where . . . well, you know the story, don't you?"

She gave him the strangest face. "Um, why would I know the story?"

Oh. "I thought . . . well, you were a journalist and living on base, so I just assumed you would have gotten a briefing of the ambush."

Her mouth opened. Closed. She looked back at his leg, reaching now to position her hands. "Yes. Of course, yes. I knew that your team had to go in after the SEALs." She looked up. "Ready to straighten your leg?"

He blew out a breath. "Yes."

Her eyes met his, something of pain in them, then she looked down.

"On three." She counted and moved his leg back into the socket.

He emitted a howl that lifted his own skin from his bones. It ricocheted through the ice canyon and left his body trembling.

She, too, flinched, and her jaw tightened. "I'm sorry. I'm *sorry*." Then she looked up. Her eyes glistened. "I didn't mean to hurt you." She pressed her hand to her mouth. "I really, really didn't mean to hurt you."

The pain had turned him blind, paralyzed him. But like a fist releasing, he finally caught his breath. Found his voice. Climbed out of the debris of his agony. "I know."

She got up and stepped over him, shucking off her outer jacket again.

"Jenny—"

"Just until I know you're not going to go into shock." She looked at him, something brutal in her eyes. "Please don't die on me and leave me here all alone."

The tremor in her voice silenced him. He let her tuck the jacket around him.

"I wish I had something I could splint your leg with."

"How about an icicle?"

She gave him a long, slow look, tears edging her eyes. But she blinked them back and smiled. "Brilliant."

Wow. Just seeing her carry his pain—he shouldn't have let his hurt keep him from finding her sooner.

Keep him from reaching out, moving on.

A number of icicles littered the ledge. She used her axe to free one, brought it over to him, and used a piece of webbing to wrap his leg to it.

She had removed her face guard and her mittens. Her breath formed a cloud in the air.

He leaned his head back against the rock, breathing through the pain. But he could live with it, and the cold was already beginning to numb it.

White had started to wash over the sky, which had turned pewter gray. "There's a whiteout coming," he said. He didn't want to think about Ham, out there, buried. He studied the wall. Yes, he could use the Prusik and foot loop to pull himself up, build an ice-anchor ladder system . . .

"I'll climb up."

"No." He looked at her. She'd been looking up too, clearly reading his mind in her uncanny way.

"What? You think you're the only one who knows how to ice climb? I trained for an entire year."

"And I trained my entire life, and I'm still trapped in a crevasse with a busted knee!"

She recoiled.

"Sorry. I'm just . . ." He blew out a breath. "I get mad when I'm trapped."

"Yeah, well, I can't let you die because of my stupidity."

"Stupidity? What part of this is stupidity?"

She looked at him. Blinked. Looked away. "The stupidity that thinks that climbing mountains will somehow help me figure out how to . . ." She shook her head. "Just, how to live with myself, I guess."

He let those words find roost.

The snow from the top of the crevasse had begun to drift in, falling softly upon them, dusting her hat, her fleece jacket like ash.

He couldn't stop himself, the pain of her words pressing out his own. "What happened that caused your nervous breakdown, Jenny?"

She said nothing. After a moment, she got up and went again to the edge. "I should get the rope."

What was her problem? "No. Please, no."

"We need to get out of here—"

"And what—climb up into a whiteout? Without gear?"

She looked at him. "We'll freeze to death down here."

"Not tonight we won't. Mistakes are made—people get killed—when we're tired. Please, don't let your fear cause you to make a bad decision."

Her eyes widened and she drew in a breath, seemed to consider his words. Then she sighed and returned to him. Sat down, pulling her knees up to herself. "Tell me about the ambush."

Oh.

Well.

"I'm not sure where to start."

"I saw you leave that day. Operation Bulldog."

She had? But the entire base probably knew about the mission. "The SEALs had left before dawn. We were mostly just sitting around, waiting for a nine-line call."

"I saw you guys. Kitted up. Hanging around the chopper. Two choppers."

"We were really jocked up. I remember—it was early in the morning, and it was cold out. The thing about being a PJ is that you always have to be ready, but if you get called out, then you know something bad's happened. So, it's a hard line. I wanted to go, you know, but at the same time I was hoping they didn't need us."

"But they did."

"Yeah, the flight engineer came out of the TOC and said the nine-line had come in. We were on the birds in three minutes, and the Pedros were in the air in less than five."

He looked at her, and she shivered.

"Jenny, take your coat back."

She shook her head. "The entire camp thundered with those Pave Hawks."

Oh, the woman was stubborn.

"I remember the sky that day. Weird, but as we lifted off, I looked up and saw the blue between the spinning blades. I was sitting in the door of the chopper, my back to our gunner, my weapon across my knees."

"Like my dream." Her eyes widened. "Oh . . . my . . ."

"Hey." He reached out to her, grabbed her ankle. "It was just a dream—"

"And then you fell." She pressed her hand to her mouth.

He blinked at her. Swallowed.

"And Ham—"

"There's nothing we can do for Ham." His mouth tightened. "If he's . . . crushed, or buried, then twenty minutes is all anyone can last."

Silence stretched out between them.

"Aw, shoot." He leaned back. "Ham was a great guy. He was . . ." He looked at her. "He was on the ground that day, the leader of Echo team. He popped a trail of purple smoke and we spotted him as we came through a notch in the mountains. They were stuck on the side of a mountain. Below us was the Taliban base—a grouping of dismal mud huts, a few terraced gardens etched into the mountains, and a handful of goats. I remember thinking—we have all this weaponry, this training, a tactical advantage, and still people who herd goats and live without running water are killing my friends."

He had let go of her ankle, and now made a fist. "I still don't get it, really."

She said nothing, just wrapped her arms around her legs, pulling herself into a warmer ball.

"I was looking at that village when suddenly, I saw a flash from a doorway. Then, the pop of gunfire. I was wearing ear protection with my comms, and I still felt it in my bones. Because that's when I realized they were shooting at us. I remember Nickles shouting that they were taking fire."

She didn't move.

"Then suddenly, the other Pedro exploded. Just erupted into flames. Debris from it nearly took us down. I hit the deck, and we spun away, and when we righted ourselves, the chopper and all the guys had hit the mountainside."

And then, suddenly, he was there. The smoke choking him, and he was unable to breathe past the scream clawing through his chest.

"But we had to get to the SEALs trapped on the mountain, so we came back around. I kept thinking—just get out of the chopper. The shooters in the houses were raining down fire on us. Our gunner was firing back on the 50-cal.

"I've never gotten down a rope so fast in my life. I have to give creds to my chopper pilot. She held that thing in a hover, heavy machine-gun fire and rpgs tearing at the mountain around her.

"As soon as we landed, it was Happy New Year, Talis throwing us a party of everything they had, exploding around us. I scrambled up to the position where Ham and three of his guys were entrenched. Two had been shot. I got to Hicks—young guy, maybe twenty-five. His first deployment. He'd been shot in the gut, his intestines were everywhere. I was trying to shove them back in, trying to figure out how to pack him—my only priority was getting him into the litter, getting him back to base. Do what I'd been trained to do. And then—my world exploded."

"Your knee."

"Took me out, slammed me against the mountain. For a long second, I was just paralyzed, and then suddenly, Ham was there. He dragged me back into the cave."

"Is that when you called in the danger-close air strike?"

He stared at her. She lifted her shoulder. "I heard about it."

Oh.

"Not yet. They'd found an entrance to a cave, and we hauled

ourselves inside, took up a position there. Ham was still trying to figure a way out."

He looked up. The sky was dour and white, sifting snow into the crack. "Ham left a couple operators at the entrance—Royal and Thorne—and sent another guy, Gunderson, to find a way out. I did my best to stabilize my leg—wrapped it, then helped the two injured SEALs. One of them had a thigh wound. The other was Hicks, still holding in his guts. I wrapped him up the best I could. We sat there for what seemed like days but I think it was more like two hours until Gunds came back. And by that time, the Taliban had worked their way up the mountain. Ham called in the strike, then ordered Royal and Thorne to retreat, and that's when everything . . . well, it was already the apocalypse, but then it turned into . . . I don't know. As Royal and Thorne were e-vacking to our position, the entire cave collapsed. Between them, on them, we didn't know. We just knew that a strike was on its way, and we were dead in the rubble if we didn't move.

"I helped myself to my morphine, but my leg was wasted."

He paused, his jaw tightening. Cut his voice low. "Ham had to carry me. He made a choice—me or his two buddies. Hicks died on the mountain. But I was sent to save him, so some rescuer I turned out to be."

He drew in a breath, shook his head, still hearing Ham's grunts, the dust and grit in his eyes, his ears ringing against the screaming inside.

"We climbed out into the night just as the mountain exploded with the power of two massive five-hundred-pound bombs."

He shook his head. "The other guy we went in to get also died. I ended up in Germany, and it took me six months to walk again."

A hiccup of sound made him raise his gaze and he frowned as Jenny pressed her gloved hands over her face.

She was weeping.

And not softly, either, because her entire body shook, her tears coming hard, her cries breaking through. She bent over into herself, took a breath, and her cries rattled out of her, her body wracked as if with grief.

"Jenny?" He froze, not sure what—

"I'm sorry. I'm just . . . so sorry."

Her words dissolved as she took another breath, then began to cry again, this time harder.

What the—? "Jenny, it's okay. It's . . ."

She looked up at him, her eyes reddened, her voice breaking. "I'm so sorry." She ran her hand over her face. "I'm sorry that happened to you. All those men . . ." Her breath caught. She shook her head.

Then she dissolved again, this time collapsing onto the ice.

Her words rang through his head. *"I had a nervous breakdown."*

Not on his watch. Whatever this was, he wasn't going to let her go through it alone. So he reached out and grabbed her arm and pulled her to himself, tucking her under the jacket. He wrapped his arms hard around her and held her tight. And finally gave her the words, whether he believed them or not. "We're okay. We're going to be okay."

CHAPTER ELEVEN

*G*ET UP. *Calm down. Keep moving.*

The voices in her head thrummed inside Jenny, even as she bent over, gulping back her tears, her breaths.

Stop. Freaking. Out.

Because the more she unraveled, the more every cell ached to tell Orion, well, *all of it*. And that would be the worst possible thing to do, really. Because that's the last thing they needed right now, her telling him that she was responsible for his terror, his friends dying, and of course the fact that he'd spent six months learning to walk again.

Especially since she was now tucked into Orion's arms, the very man who should probably push her off the cliff. How she longed to just stop the lies. To let him calm her world.

Help her breathe again.

No matter what, she couldn't let herself spiral out, couldn't find herself in that place where she had no hold on anything.

Couldn't go back to that moment when her world shattered before her eyes.

Because she'd been there, on the other side of the horror, listening as Orion and Ham's team fought—and ran—for their lives. Heard Ham on the radio, calling in the strike.

Wanted to scream at the desperation in his voice.

She practically ran, a full-out sprint, back to her quarters, horrified.

And had woken in Germany herself, probably in the same hospital as Orion. Apparently, someone had found her wandering the camp, disoriented, incoherent.

She had no memory of any of it.

And clearly Orion had no idea that she'd been the cause of all his nightmares.

She pulled in her breath, holding it, fighting to tuck her emotions back inside.

"Jenny, it's okay. You're just . . . tired. And scared," Orion said, still trying to soothe her.

No, she was heartbroken.

Keep moving.

Right. She couldn't stay here, let it pour over her, pin her down. Trap her.

Push through. Look forward.

Get out of the crevasse.

She made herself push away from him. He released her.

"Jenny?"

She could weep at the worry in his voice. "I'm fine. I'm just . . ." She wiped her face and climbed to her feet, putting her arms through her jacket. "Sorry. I'm just . . . yeah, a little scared, maybe. We need to get out of here."

She couldn't look at him, so she looked up. Overhead, the world had turned white. In the distance, thunder rolled, probably more avalanches releasing in the whiteout with the accumulation. The entire mountain shook and tossed down snow.

Another slide might take out their perch, if it found its way into their crevasse. Barring that, however, their crevasse was an icy blue wonderland that could protect them from the elements.

For now.

"Jenny."

"I think if I use the ice anchors, I can get down the wall to the rope. Then, I know I can climb up. I'll find Ham and radio—"

"Jenny."

"Or I could keep hiking out—"

"Jenny, sit down." He reached out and grabbed her jacket. Tugged.

She looked at him, terribly aware of the wreckage on her face.

"We're going to get out of here."

"We're trapped in a crevasse."

"We are not doomed."

She swallowed. Closed her eyes. "No, you're wrong, Orion. I've been doomed my entire life, and I . . . I just have to admit it. I make terrible decisions. And, when I do, people get hurt."

"It wasn't your fault you got blown off a mountain—"

"No!" She couldn't stop herself. "It was my fault . . ." She shook her head, finding the easier truth. "It's my fault bad things happen."

"What kinds of bad things—"

"All of them. Like—falling into a crevasse . . . and letting my mother be murdered!"

Oh. She hadn't meant for *that* to emerge. For that messy, bloody memory to spill out between them.

He stilled. "What do you mean, murdered?"

Her voice cut low. "She was beaten to death by my stepfather."

Just like she thought, he looked at her with such horror on his face, she knew she should have just kept her mouth shut. Kept moving. Away from the past, the wreckage, the pain. It did no one any good to dredge up the past.

She drew away from him, out of his reach. "I'm sorry—I'm sorry. I shouldn't have—it was a long time ago." She walked over to the edge. "I'm going after that rope."

"Jenny. Come back here and sit down."

"If I anchor in—I can belay myself from screw to screw—"

"Jenny. We're here. Right here. Right *now*. And . . . we're not going anywhere. And yeah, I get not wanting to look back at it, to be there again. Believe me, the last thing I wanted to do was climb Denali again. I swore to myself that nothing would make me set foot on the slope of the High One—not after it betrayed me. And it's still betraying me. But I did it—I did it for *you*, Jen. You can trust me."

She closed her eyes. "You went looking for me."

"I went looking for the woman I met in Afghanistan. The one who told me she wanted to touch the stars. The one who beat me in one-on-one. The girl who sang to me . . ."

"How do I live without you . . ."

She turned to face him, the memory ripe. The music over the fire one random night, the words from a LeAnn Rimes song easy to sing, emitting from her heart.

She wanted him to love the girl he met overseas. Not the wreck she'd been before. Or was becoming now. "You don't want to know—"

"I want to know it all. And I'm not going anywhere." He held out his hand. "Ham will be here. He's alive, I know it. And he'll get us."

Orion was lying to her, she knew it. But she took his hand, sat down next to him. He was shivering, and so was she, the cold settling into her bones. Overhead, a blizzard was sweeping over the ice field.

No, Ham wasn't coming for them. But she didn't say that as Orion unzipped his jacket, pulled her against himself, and settled his jacket around her. His body heat radiated right to her core, his arm tight around her.

"How old were you?"

"Thirteen."

He made a sound, deep in his chest, something of a grunt, as if her words were a punch.

"The worst part is, Billy completely deceived us. Looked me in the eye and told me that my mother and I were the most important people in the world to him. When she met him, he was leading her AA group. I thought he was trustworthy. Kind. He made us both believe in love. And . . . neither of us saw it coming."

Orion tucked her in, under his chin. Her shivering slowed.

"It was the little things. Like, after he moved in, she wasn't allowed to use the phone without his permission. He told her how to dress and what music to listen to. He cut her off from her friends— wouldn't let her go to AA anymore. Said that he could give her all the counsel she needed. And sometimes he'd lose his temper and yell at her. Throw things."

Orion made a noise, deep in his chest.

"He was so nice, though. Smiled when he told her that she had to stop trying to control everything, that he knew better than she did. Made her quit her job—not that it was a great job. She worked in a Super America as a clerk. But she liked it. And it paid the bills. And she knew people. But he said he would take care of her. Us."

She could feel his heart thumping hard inside his chest, but outside, he didn't move.

"My biological father died when I was three, and it had always been just me and my mom, so . . . so I really wanted a dad."

For a moment, she was back in the tiny two-bedroom townhouse in the middle of Brooklyn Park, lying in bed, listening to her mother laugh with her new stepfather, the Christmas lights from the tree spilling down the hallway and into her room.

Her voice dropped. "I wanted a dad so badly I was willing to keep my mouth shut about . . ."

Orion smelled unfairly good—a hint of his masculine musk on his skin. She had the strangest urge to turn her face to his neck, breathe it in.

She lifted her head. "He never touched me . . . well, beyond lingering hugs and looking at me in a way . . . but it scared me."

Orion's jaw tightened.

"I should have said something. But in between the yelling, she seemed happy. I don't know. Maybe she was miserable, but she wanted so badly to build the family she'd lost, so . . ."

"So she stayed with an emotional abuser because she didn't know what else to do," Orion said quietly.

"I know that now. Once I realized my stepfather would never love me, or my mother, I just saw her as weak. And then one day, I came home from school and there were police at my house. He'd . . ." She pressed her hand to her mouth. Shook her head. "They had a fight. It got out of control."

He kissed the top of her head.

She stilled. Looked up at him. A fierceness had entered his green eyes, and yes, just like before, the whirlwind inside her stopped. Focused. And she heard his words reaching in. *"I'll find you."*

Maybe he had found her—at least the part of her that she'd been running from.

"What happened to him?"

"He went to jail. Manslaughter. And I decided that I would . . . well, for one, that I'd never let anyone fool me again."

"It wasn't your fault, Jenny. He was a monster."

"We fell for his charm. And he betrayed us. Maybe he wouldn't have if I'd spoken up."

"You were thirteen. And scared. Who knows if she would have believed you. Abusers make their victims feel powerless and like it's their fault."

She did. But sometimes the knowledge didn't touch her heart.

"That's why you became an investigative journalist."

She wanted to retch with the lie. *I wasn't a journalist. I was with the CIA.*

He deserved to know. Especially after he'd climbed . . . wait. "Why did Denali betray you? Because your dad died on the mountain?"

"You remember that?"

She leaned back, still under his jacket. Pressed her hand to his chest. "Yeah."

A beat pulsed between them.

She had to at least tell him *something* of the truth. "I remember everything about Afghanistan. And, I wish I'd been there in Germany when you woke up."

He blinked at that. Swallowed. Looked away.

Her voice thickened. "I was . . . well, I was already in trouble, or I would have been there, Ry. Really."

"It was a long time ago."

Not long enough by the twitching on his face. His voice dropped. "You know, after I got home from Germany, I did some rehab time in Walter Reed, and then I . . . I didn't have anywhere else to go, so I came back to Alaska."

"The shadow of Denali."

He looked at her, and one side of his mouth tweaked up. "Yeah. Always there, always watching. And I did exactly what my dad did after my mother and brother died."

She frowned.

"I fell apart."

Oh. Uh—

"After their deaths, my dad just . . . he lost it. Started drinking. Lost his job on the mountain. Lost himself for a long time. And then, when I turned eighteen, I asked him to teach me to climb Denali. That changed him. We spent the summer climbing it—I actually went up three times. I went away to Anchorage, to the university, and he pulled himself together. Got a job as a guide with an expedition team. When I came back, I spent the summer on the mountain, volunteering at Basin Camp, on the Denali volunteer rescue team. He took up groups."

"Is that . . ." She drew in her breath.

"Yeah. That's the summer Denali changed him. Healed him." He drew in a breath. "And then Denali betrayed him. And me."

His jaw hardened. "I was so angry when I got back from Afghanistan. At my leg. At the mountain and what it took from me. At the CIA for sending us into an ambush—all of it. Honestly, I'm still angry most of the time. And I didn't know what to do with it until about a year ago when Logan Thorne showed up."

Logan—*wait.* "What? He was one of the two guys who went missing, right?"

He nodded. "We thought for sure no one could have lived through the bombing, but as we were being choppered out, Ham spotted a group of Taliban hiking out with Royal and Thorne."

She closed her eyes, praying she didn't betray her relief. They were *alive.*

"Yeah, I guess Ham and Chief McCord and a handful of SEALs went in and got them, later, but I was in Germany, getting a new knee, and I never knew what happened until Thorne showed up last summer, shot."

"He's alive." She opened her eyes, fighting to keep from crying again, but his words had unwrapped a fist around her heart. Alive. She hadn't killed them. But oh, the torture they must have gone through—

"How was he?"

Orion blew out a breath. "Actually, Thorne has a whopper of a story. Black ops, CIA, and a host of other players who have tried to keep Operation Bulldog and his and Royal's rescue under the hood. And, Royal's still missing, so in my gut I think his story is true. If it is then Royal could be in big trouble, on the run and in over his head."

She knew where he was going with this, and it wasn't going to be good. "You want to find Royal."

He frowned at her. "How—"

"Because I know you, Ry. You're a rescuer. You're the guy who runs *toward* the bullets to get your friends out of trouble."

His chest rose. Fell. His heart thumped hard under her hand. He met her eyes, something fierce in them.

Oh my.

"I should have kissed you that night." His voice dropped, a near whisper, and with it, his gaze, onto her lips. Back to her eyes. "In Afghanistan, before I rolled out. You were so beautiful—still are. And I wanted to kiss you." He blew out a breath. "I wish I didn't always have to think about everything. Tear it apart, analyze it. I wish I could just—react and believe and trust and know that—"

"That the mountain won't betray you with a sudden avalanche?" She didn't know why she said that, but her voice fell to a whisper and she understood. Oh, she understood.

"Or a fall into a crevasse with the woman I've been aching to find?"

Her breath caught.

"Jacie Calhoun, I've really missed you."

She swallowed. "I missed you too," she said quietly, ignoring the screaming in her head, her brain tapping hard on the door of her heart. *Run!* "I wish you'd kissed me, too."

His smile was slow, a hint of fire lit his eyes, and he grabbed her zipper at her neck, using it to tug her toward him. She let herself be moved, and he wound his hand behind her neck.

Then he kissed her. Softly at first, and her heart stopped, savoring the taste of him, salty, a little parched, his lips gentle on her mouth. He stayed there a moment, chaste, sweet, and she closed her eyes.

She pictured him unlocking yet another door inside him, walking through, or perhaps letting her in. He was holding his breath too, because he let her go, leaned his forehead to hers, and his breath shuddered out. He swallowed, licked his lips. "Not enough," he whispered.

She met those green eyes. Nodded.

Not enough. She could never, really, get enough of this amazing man.

He kissed her again. This time, in his touch emerged the man she'd seen climb aboard the chopper, the fierce warrior, the rescuer who'd scaled the mountain to find her. He kissed her with a hunger that he might have been fighting for three years, a desperation, even a beauty in it for all the pieces of his heart he was giving over.

Orion. He wrapped his other arm around her, holding her to himself and she let it all crash over her. He was an avalanche, a cascade of chaos and white, gathering speed. Deep inside she knew if she didn't slow them down, her heart might hurtle off the top never to be recovered.

But she *couldn't* stop. She grabbed the lapel of his jacket and pulled him closer, surrendering. He was strength and power and fierceness and . . .

Safety.

She wanted to weep with the strange swell of emotions he unleashed in her as he held her cocooned in his jacket, a tiny fortress of hope and courage and . . .

Oh. *No.*

She trembled even as she pushed away from him. "Orion. I—"

"Jenny, I've been wanting to do that for three years." His gaze found hers and held it fast. "I can't believe it took me this long to find you."

Oh. "Me too, PJ. Me too." She leaned in and pressed her head to his chest, needing his heartbeat.

Because as soon as they got off this mountain, she'd have to keep running.

But this time, she'd leave behind her heart.

■ ■ ■

The locomotive thunder of the wind against the tent woke Aria.

Or it could have been the coughing that wracked her body. She'd been struggling with the sense of weight in her chest for hours, holding back her coughs.

She wasn't so stupid to not recognize the early onset of AMS.

She felt the fine hairs on her neck burning as she opened her eyes. Jake sat up on his sleeping bag, one arm folded over his body, the other in a fist over his mouth, as if in thought. His gaze was pinned on Sasha, but tracked over to her as she unzipped her bag and sat up.

"Jake?"

He looked rough. His blond hair fell in tangles out of his wool cap, a thickening golden-brown beard across his chin. He still wore his fleece jacket, but he'd unzipped it at the neck, revealing his thermal shirt.

She'd never seen a man in a tighter knot of worry. "You okay?"

He nodded, sighed. "You're coughing."

"I'm fine. But you're not. You haven't slept, have you?"

Stress lined his face.

She, however, felt like she'd slept for a year. And her ankle had stopped throbbing. She tried to move it and stopped at the flash of heat. Nope, not yet.

"I'm fine," Jake growled.

"Have you eaten?"

He made a face. "We're . . . so, we're out of soup."

Oh. Uh. "What time is it?"

He raised a shoulder.

Ho-kay. Yes, his entire posture had her worried. "Jake, what's going on?"

He said nothing.

"You're scaring me."

He met her eyes then, his expression softening. "Sorry. I'm just . . . we're in another whiteout."

She shivered, realizing now the drop in temperature.

"I fortified the wind break, but . . . you know Denali. We could be here for a while. And a chopper can't get in . . ."

Hence the darkness in his expression.

She coughed.

He winced. Looked away. Clenched his fist. She had the sense that if he could, he'd hit something.

"I'm okay." She pressed her hand to her chest.

"Yeah, whatever." Jake had vanished. "Please tell me it's not your heart—"

"No. My heart's fine."

"But don't you have anti-rejection meds—"

"It was a good match, Jake. Trust me."

He stiffened at her tone. "Okay, Doc."

And right then she wanted to say it. *My heart belonged to my twin sister.* But even after a decade those words contained a crippling edge that she couldn't bear. So, "I'm fine. I just have a little edema. It'll pass as soon as we get off the mountain."

His mouth made that tight line again. The tight edge of his jaw was scaring her.

"Okay, really, what's going on?"

He blew out a breath. "I . . ." He shook his head and when his gaze met hers, a chill brushed through her. "When this whiteout passes, I think . . . I think . . ." He looked away from her. "I gotta get help. Or . . ." He met her eyes again. "Or take you down the mountain."

"Right. Okay, so we make a sled—"

"You." His gaze didn't waver.

His meaning slowly slipped into her. Turned her cold. "Jake—"

"We don't have a choice here."

"Yeah, actually, we do. We can trust Ham, like you said—"

"Ham could be dead." His tone was a knife, cutting through her.

"What?"

"There was a big slide in the ice fields. I heard it while I was packing up the kitchen. About three hours ago, before the wind came up." He looked stricken. "I don't know if they were in it, but . . . and there's been slides all over the mountain today—"

"There are slides on Denali every day, it doesn't mean anyone is dead." She didn't know why she was suddenly reaching for hope, but, well, someone had to.

Kia would.

So, she softened her voice. "Jake. Listen. We don't have to make any hard choices here." She glanced at Sasha. "No. You can't—"

"I can, and I will, Aria, if I have to. I can't reach anyone on the radio. We're in this by ourselves."

He sounded so cold, so far away, and she didn't know what to do with the grim-faced, dark soldier he'd suddenly morphed into. She shook her head.

"I've made hard choices all my life, Aria." And something behind his eyes suggested those hard choices had cost him pieces of himself.

Silence moved in, the thunder of the wind bulleting the tent. And she couldn't stop herself. "What kind of hard choices?"

He closed his eyes, a sort of wince.

Aw, Jake. All the charm was a mask. She unzipped her sleeping bag.

His eyes opened. "What are you doing?"

She didn't answer him. Because she didn't know if it was Kia or Aria inside her, but she did know this man was hurting. And she couldn't see someone in pain without wanting to fix it.

"Aria?"

She got to her knees, climbed over Sasha, and landed in front of him on his sleeping bag.

"Your ankle."

"Is fine. You're not."

Then she wrapped her arms around his neck and pulled him to herself.

He froze, his arms still at his sides. "What are you doing?"

"Oh please. You have five sisters. Certainly you can figure it out."

"You're hardly my sister." But his arms moved up around her. She let out a breath when he tugged her close against him.

Lowered his head onto her shoulder. Let his breath shudder out of him.

"Wanna talk about it?"

He just held her, his breaths matching hers.

"Okay, no problem—"

"I had to shoot a kid." His arms seemed to tighten around her as he said it, maybe to hold on to her as he delivered the news.

Maybe because he, like her, couldn't get past the knife-edged pain of his own admission.

"Jake." She didn't let go either, her voice soft. "When you were a SEAL?"

"Mmmhmm." He turned his face to her neck, his whiskers against her skin. "It was a judgment call. I thought he was a suicide bomber . . . He was running *toward* our guys, and . . ." He drew in a breath. His heart hammered against her.

She leaned away and cupped her hands on either side of his face, holding him there. "And you had no choice."

"He wasn't wired up. I shot an *innocent* kid."

Oh. She pulled him against herself again, this time tighter.

He shuddered against her.

"That's why you left the SEALs."

He nodded. "They exonerated me, but . . . yeah, I was no good after that."

She wanted to weep for him.

"Jake, listen to me. You don't have to make that choice right now. Right now, we're safe. And we're not going anywhere, and . . . please, Jake, don't do this."

He said nothing.

She leaned away from him. His jaw was tight. But he nodded.

Right then, a very large part of her wanted to love this amazing man. She wanted to blame the emotion still lingering in his eyes. Part hurt, part desperation, but it reached in and tugged at the healer inside Aria. She barely knew him, but according to Kia, life was risky, and sometimes you had to do something crazy. Something brave and impulsive if you wanted to live large—

Aria kissed him. Just pressed her mouth to his, not caring that they'd been stuck on the mountain for days or that he was rough-edged and fraying. She set aside the voices that called her back and wrapped her arms around his neck, settled over him, and kissed him.

Giving him, for the moment, her heart.

She hadn't a clue what he might be thinking when he drew in his breath, hesitating for a moment.

Then he wrapped his arms around her, drawing her body against his, and unleashed himself. A full-on, raw unwinding of the turmoil she'd seen in his eyes. He was like the mountain, unpredictable, beautiful, catching her up into its wildness. Especially when he deepened his kiss.

Her hands dropped to his shoulders, those amazing, molded shoulders, and she could feel his heart quickening against hers.

What was she *doing*? But she couldn't seem to stop. Even when he leaned back and searched her eyes, as if, finally, asking.

She met his gaze. Swallowed.

And kissed him again.

This time, he slowed them down, as if fighting to pull himself back in check. Gentled his touch. He wrapped his arms around her waist and rolled her over, laying her back into the sleeping bag, bracing her in the crook of his elbow.

The gesture—smooth, practiced—triggered something deep inside her, but she brushed it away. Hung on to his neck as he left her mouth, moved to her neck, the touch of his whiskers against her skin igniting feelings she'd never before experienced.

In fact, the entire thing felt . . . well, way over her head. Her breathing quickened, and he lifted his head. "Aria, you okay?"

She swallowed. Closed her mouth. Nodded.

He met her eyes, worry again in them. "Um . . . so. I realize that we're . . . sort of alone, but not, and . . . I'm not sure what's happening here . . ."

Her either. But she was caught in his blue eyes, too many voices in her head.

"Aria?"

Stop thinking. She grabbed the front of his jacket and tugged him back down.

He shifted, moving closer to her—

"Ah!"

"What?" He jerked back.

"You kicked my ankle." She closed her eyes, the pain spiking up her leg. Wow, she was some kind of loser. Talk about killing the moment.

Especially when Jake looked stricken and scrambled away from her. "I'm sorry. I . . ." He sat up, putting space between them. "I'm so sorry, Aria." He blew out a breath, pressed a hand to his forehead. "Probably this isn't the right time to . . . well—" He frowned, as if bereft of words.

Her heart went out to him, he looked so confused.

But maybe, yeah, she didn't quite know where to go from here, either. She hardly knew Jake, and . . .

Still, the man was unravelling with each passing minute, and if she climbed back over to her bag he might just sit up all night long watching them.

He needed sleep. And then maybe tomorrow, when the blizzard died, he'd make a sane decision. One that wouldn't cost her—or Sasha—their lives.

So, "Maybe we just keep each other warm?"

What looked like relief cascaded over him. She didn't know how to decipher it. But he nodded and lay down beside her. She turned her back to him and cradled her head against his arm. He draped his other arm over her, tucked her against him, and pulled the sleeping bag over them. "Try not to hog the covers," he said into her ear.

"As long as you don't snore."

He said nothing. But it wasn't long before his breaths lengthened out, his body relaxing.

Well done, Doc, Kia said. *Well done.*

And outside their tent, the blizzard roared.

■ ■ ■

Jenny was freezing. Her body emitted tiny trembles as she leaned against Orion, and her breathing had slowed. "Jen, wake up. Stay with me."

Overhead the sky was still white, the snow piling up around them as it swirled into their pocket in the ice. It dusted her coat, her wool hat, glistened on her nose.

He wanted to kiss it away, to warm her body by pulling it tighter to his.

No, he wanted to get them out of here and back to safety. Then maybe figure out how to stop the whirring in his head, the what-ifs and maybes that kept churning through him.

God is calling you to something, I know it, and so do you.

Ham. In his head. Keeping him alive, like he did before.

"I think Ham is dead."

Jenny's words, reading his mind again, jerked him out of his thoughts. "What?"

"He would have come for us." She raised her head. "It's been hours. We have to rescue ourselves, or we're going to freeze to death."

He wanted to kiss her again, to stop his brain from spinning out the scenarios—the worst one being their frozen bodies entombed forever in the ice. But he had other scenarios, too. Like them being rescued—Ham being alive, *not* dead—and finding them, also not dead. And getting off this mountain and back to civilization and maybe finding themselves with a fresh start.

"Let's do good things together. Help people. Bring the lost home."

Yes, maybe he would have liked to do that again.

"I know you, Ry. You're a rescuer. You're the guy who runs toward *the bullets to get your friends out of trouble."*

He'd liked himself, right then, the man he'd seen in her eyes.

Yeah, once upon a time, he'd been that guy.

"God isn't finished with you yet." "Ham's not dead. He's probably—he's hiking out, right? To get help?"

"Then why didn't he come to find us?" Her lips moved against his neck, a brush that ignited its own kind of heat through him.

"Maybe . . . it's a big crevasse, and a big mountain. Maybe he thinks—"

"We're buried." She lifted her head. "He thinks *we're* dead."

He stared at her, and his throat dried. Oh. One more scenario to add to his equations. The fact no one knew they were alive.

"We're on our own, PJ," she said quietly. "And we need to get out of here."

He heard her words, and yes, she was probably right, but strangely, he found himself shaking his head.

"What?"

"I . . . I don't know. It's something Ham kept saying. That he felt in his gut that God would help us find you. And . . ."

"You did. I don't suppose Ham's gut said anything about God getting us off this mountain?"

He had nothing.

She shook her head. "It's not that I don't believe in God. I do, actually. But . . ." She sighed. "I have reasons to think he's probably not interested in helping us."

"Except, we did find you. Miraculously." He could hardly believe he was saying this. Ham's crazy faith was rubbing off. "And yeah, ten hours ago I would have said, 'No thank you, God, I don't need your help.' But I think we do." He looked up at the whiteout. "They're not going to find us without a miracle."

Her lips tightened into a thin line.

"Listen. Here's the thing. I get it—thinking that maybe God isn't interested in helping us. Back in Afghanistan, when we were trapped in the cave, Ham prayed. And I . . . I prayed too. I prayed that God would rescue us."

"And he did."

"Yeah. And no, it wasn't the way I hoped—I was angry about my leg, and the fact that Ham had to drag my backside out. But, God *did* get me out, and as much as I want to rationalize that away, I can't."

She was listening. Just breathing in his words.

"The fact is, I'm still angry at . . . well, maybe God. So I get the idea that maybe I'm not his favorite, but, we have nothing else, Jen. We're not even at the end of our rope—literally, we have *no* rope." He tugged her close again. "I'm getting cold without you."

She lay against him for a long moment, her hand against his beating heart.

He looked up, to the sifting of the white, dropping like stars from the sky. And he couldn't help it, because yes, he was desperate—*God, if you're for us, please save us.*

"Ham might be dead." She leaned away again, her blue eyes fierce. "Or he might be alive, but I know that Jake and Aria and Sasha will be dead if we don't get out of here." She untangled herself from his arms. "You're like a freakin' furnace."

He stared at her, not sure if he should be panicking as she got up. "What are you doing?"

"You told me that today, we save lives. I'm going to get that rope."

"Jenny—"

"If we stay, we freeze to death. I'd rather die trying."

He wanted to yell. But she was probably right. He stared at her, his jaw tight. "Okay. If you're going to go down, please anchor in the entire way."

She pulled off his webbing sling and looped it over her shoulders. Along with his ice ax, she had a half-dozen anchors, two Prusik lines, and two quick clips. Then she picked up her axe. "Happy?"

"Hardly, but whatever."

"I'll be back in a jiffy."

He wanted to look away, but dread kept his gaze glued.

She walked over to the edge and drove in the first screw. She clipped her quick clip to it, leaving his to dangle, then stepped over the edge.

"I see the rope. It's about eight feet down."

He couldn't help himself—he zipped up his jacket and rolled over, crawling to the edge.

There it was, lying like a coiled snake, on an ice bridge. One of the ends dangled down, as if it might be trying to slither away.

His heart nearly left his body. "Please, Jen, be careful."

"Yeah." She drove in another screw at knee level, and clipped his line to it, then detached hers and worked her way down into the deep blue.

He followed her red cap, listened to her tiny grunts, the chipping and clank of the ice screws, her biners against the ice, as she worked her way down, using the screws like a ladder, moving her quick clip down with each one.

He couldn't breathe until she stepped out on the icy ledge. The bridge thinned as it stretched over the abyss. The edge of the rope lay just out of reach, about four feet out.

"Jenny—"

"I have to unclip."

He might throw up. "You're killing me."

She unclipped. Dug her ice axe into the root of the bridge. Reached out and snagged the end of the rope. "Got it!"

He let out his breath. But his heart didn't start thumping again until she backed up, re-clipping into the biner.

She stood on the edge and began to pull up the rope, winding it between her neck and her arm to loop it around her body.

Overhead, another rumble, and he tensed as the thunder of a faraway slide shook the mountain.

"Hurry."

Snow spilled down, careening against the ice, falling.

She looked up.

"Anchor in," he said.

"I'm secure." She resumed her coiling.

The ache in his leg had died to a deep burn, but the cold had numbed it, turned it manageable. He was a decent ice-climber. And, given her precision as she climbed down, they could make it to the top.

Into the whiteout.

"Coming up." She'd tied the rope around her, securing it. Then she unclipped her quick clip and set her ice axe, reaching for the higher screw.

"Clip in—"

But the thunder from above arrested his words and he turned. He threw his arm up as snow and ice crested down from the lip, ricocheting against the walls. "Get down!"

The wash buffeted him, chunks of ice the size of footballs slamming into the ledge, careening off, a shower of snow pouring over him. Another crack. Above him, ice rocks were bouncing off a thin ice bridge webbing the crevasse at an angle not far above him and hitting his ledge. As he watched, a monster boulder broke free.

"Watch out!" He covered his head.

She screamed. The icy boulders banged through the chamber and a terrible explosion echoed up against the icy blue walls.

It jerked his head up.

The ice bridge had collapsed.

Jenny dangled from her perch, gripping the nub of the ice screw with one mitten, her axe dug into the blue wall with another. Her quick clip dangled from her harness. But she hung out over a ledge, nothing but air beneath her, nothing for her feet to grip.

"I'm coming for you!"

"Stay there!" She looked up, breathing hard. "I got this."

But she was sweating, her eyes big, and the ice continued to fall.

No way was he going to watch her plummet to her death. He rolled over and grabbed his ice axe, looped the handle over his wrist, and extended it down. "Grab this. Let me pull you up."

She was trembling, her feet scratching for purchase, breaking free, her arms frozen to the wall. "I can't." Her voice emerged thin and raspy. "I can't—"

"*Look at me.*"

She shook her head.

"*Look at me*, Jacie."

She moved. Probably forced herself to look up, given the look of terror on her face.

"Don't look down. You're anchored in good with your ice axe. Just reach out and grab my axe."

"No! I'm just going to pull you down. I can do this."

"You're too jacked up. Breathe. Grab my axe. Let me help—"

"You'll fall!"

"Then we'll fall together!" Okay, all this emotion didn't help. Orion schooled his voice. "Grab it."

"No. You're not falling again. Not because of me!"

"This isn't your fault! Now grab the axe or I'm coming down there!"

So maybe he'd given up trying to tuck everything back in.

She glared at him. He glared back. "I'm completely serious, Jace."

"Fine." She blew out hard, then lunged for his axe. Any purchase her crampons had dislodged and suddenly she was hanging from the two axes. His entire body screamed with the weight of her, but he bit it back. Dug down, and with every ounce he had in him, hauled her up.

"Climb up with your feet!"

She slammed one foot then the other hard into the ice, working with him as he wrestled her to the top.

She lipped the side of their ledge and he grabbed her harness, dragging her the rest of the way. She sprawled on the ice next to him.

"Now breathe." His words were more for himself than her, but he rolled onto his back, his hand over his chest. *Breathe.*

"You shouldn't have done that. You could have gone over."

But he ignored her. "What's that?" He pointed to the broken ice bridge above them, where the deadly boulder had originated. And, more importantly, the frozen blue fabric revealed in the broken edge.

"What's—" She rolled over. "That's a backpack." She got up. "I think it's—a climber. A frozen . . . a dead climber." She made a face, turned away.

He had sat up and was working his way away from the edge. "Some poor guy fell down in this crevasse and couldn't get out."

She sank down next to Orion. Maybe she didn't even realize she reached out to grab his hand. But he clenched it tight.

"He died here." Her voice shook.

He jerked her, and she looked at him, her eyes wide.

"But we won't," he said, and his words found his bones, his cells. "We won't, Jenny. Because we have a rope. And ice screws. And . . . we'll have a pack. If you can get up there to get it. Whatchya say, champ?"

Her mouth lifted into a beautiful smile.

CHAPTER TWELVE

JENNY WAS GOING TO GET THEM OUT of this mess. And save Orion while she was at it.

Maybe then when she finally told him what she'd done so long ago . . . well, maybe his anger might not be quite as terrible.

Maybe he'd forgive her.

Especially after her tedious but triumphant climb up to the ice bridge. One that he made her rope in for, retrieving the one screw she'd dug into the ledge, then belaying her down to get the other ice screws. He'd belayed her again as she climbed up to the dead climber.

She didn't want to look at the corpse, frozen in time, and averted her gaze as best she could as she chipped away the pack. He was encased in ice and snow, but she anchored in and slowly he came free. She didn't know what to do with his body, so she left him embedded in the ice, used her Leatherman to cut his webbing and straps from him, then lowered the pack down to Orion.

It contained a bivouac tent, a sleeping bag, freeze-dried soup, a stove, more webbing and biners, a water bottle, tea—enough for a night or two out in the open. As if he'd been summiting and fell.

She set up the bivouac tent, used a ski pole to re-splint Orion's leg, tucked him into the sleeping bag, and made tea.

All the while, trying not to let it all sift into her heart—the fact that now God had miraculously saved them *twice*. Maybe three times, if she counted Orion finding her just as she, Aria, and Sasha were all about to tumble into a crevasse. She wanted to take back her words—*"I have reasons to think he's probably not interested in helping us."*

Maybe she was just looking at herself and assigning her own responses to God. She wouldn't rescue herself . . . but maybe God didn't base his actions—or his love—on what she thought of herself.

At least that's what Garrett Marshall, her foster dad, had told her.

Orion sat in the bivouac sack, drinking the reconstituted chicken soup. She'd staked down the sack to the ice. Overhead, the snow continued to blow. As soon as it cleared, she'd climb out and go for help.

She sat down beside Orion. He looked over at her and grinned. She hadn't a clue what time of day it might be, but the hours had added a thickness to his dark beard, turned him devastatingly rugged. He'd stripped off his jacket, but it hung around his shoulders, which looked impossibly large in his fleece jacket. He wore just his polar booties, his boots tied into an ice screw near his head.

He looked half invalid, half mountain man, and suddenly, she couldn't get that kiss out of her head.

Good thing it was only a one-man bivy sack. "What are you grinning about?"

"Nothing," he said, and continued to look at her. "Except I think my dad would have liked you. You're his kind of people."

She didn't know why that warmed her core. "I had a foster dad

that was . . . he was great. They lived in this small town in Minnesota. The Marshall family. They ran a winery, of all things, but
they were Christians. And they believed that God was for them,
even when bad things happened. The dad, Garrett, used to tell
stories at the dinner table. One of his favorites was this Bible story
about how the Israelites were escaping Egypt, and God told them
to stand aside while he saved them. Then he parted the Red Sea.
Or something like that. It was the first time I'd ever heard that
God could protect me." She finished off her tea. "I really wanted
to believe it."

Orion had also finished off his soup. She poured tea into his
empty sierra cup.

"My parents were God-fearing people," he said. "But they never
really talked about God. My grandmother, however, was a strong
believer. She and my grandpa worked at a missionary camp every
summer. She'd say things like, 'If God is for us, who can be against
us,' and 'When we are weak, he makes us strong.' She had this
song she loved . . ." He hummed it. The sound found her bones,
a deep tenor that matched his voice. "'In Christ alone, my hope is
found . . . He is my light, my strength, my song' . . . I don't know
the rest. And I guess, well, after Dad died, I didn't really want to.
I sorta felt like God betrayed me."

"And then you felt like he did again when you were ambushed."
Oh, she didn't mean to bring that up, but—

"Actually, not until I woke up alone in Germany."

Oh.

"I realized that everything I'd worked so hard for was over.
And . . . that's when the anger started to live inside me. I expected
. . . well, I guess I'd expected to not get hurt. I'm not sure *why* I
expected that—I was in a war zone. But . . ." He lifted a shoulder.

"Do you think God does that? Betrays us?"

Her words sifted between them and fell into the silence. For some reason, she needed to know, because . . .

Because she'd started to believe that maybe she could turn around and face all the wreckage behind her. That if God could forgive her . . . maybe Orion could too. And she couldn't face it if God was the kind to make her believe, only to turn on her.

"I want to think that he is on our side," he said. "But it's hard, you know? Sometimes it feels like all the evidence says that he doesn't care. That no matter what we do, we're in this alone."

Oh.

He met her eyes then, something sparking in them. "But Ham is this strong believer in God's goodness. He says that even when we can't see it, God is at work. He thinks he brought me up on this mountain because he has a plan for me. To make me deal with my anger at life . . ." He looked away. "At God, I guess, because he didn't do things my way."

"And?"

He stared at his cup. "I don't know that I'll ever be able to find peace. Not without answers."

Oh. But because she had to know, for sure, "Answers to . . ."

He met her eyes, pain in his, and shoot, she shouldn't have asked. "I guess . . . why? Why my dad had to die? Why the CIA sent us into an ambush? Why we're sitting down here in a crevasse?"

Maybe it was the psychologist in her, but she couldn't help but ask, "And what does the answer do for you? Will it make it easier to live with it? To grieve? To have peace?"

He stared at her. "I don't know."

"There's a difference between understanding and acceptance. Do you have to understand to accept?"

"I . . . I guess I don't know. Maybe not. I mean—it doesn't change anything, right?"

"No. It doesn't. I tried for a long time to understand why Billy killed my mother. He was a narcissist. Maybe even a sociopath. And in the end, it didn't change anything. But sometimes it helps to have someone to direct your anger at."

His mouth tightened. "I'm already blaming . . . everyone. The military. God." He drew in a breath. "But in truth, I guess I want to know so I can . . . argue. I can get angry and find the right people to lash out at. Figure out what went wrong. I know it won't help, but I just hate the randomness of life. That things happen that I can't control, and it leaves me . . ."

"Broken?"

He looked away. "Busted up, maybe. Helpless."

"And running away." She didn't know why she said that. But she met his gaze. Opened her mouth. Closed it. Then, because it felt so close to the mark for both of them, "Rian, I think you're scared."

He stiffened.

"I get it. Guys like you don't get scared, but anger is just a big mask for fear."

"I'm not scared. I'm—"

"Broken. Wounded. Trapped and not sure how to get out?"

"What are you, trying to psychoanalyze me?" His mouth tweaked into a smile, clearly trying to turn it into a joke.

She didn't laugh. "I am a psychologist, remember. And, I specialize in PTSD."

His smile fell. "Seriously?"

"I have my doctorate."

"Because you had a nervous breakdown?"

She drew in a breath. "No—I was a psychologist before that."

"And you used it to become an investigative reporter."

Oh. Right now. She could tell him right—

"I don't have PTSD."

"Orion—"

"Really, I'm fine. I'm just—"

"Angry all the time? Hiding out in the woods? Avoiding humanity?"

Now he *was* angry, given the thinning of his lips. "Trying to figure out why life keeps turning on me."

She swallowed. She could tell him the truth, but the fact was, it wasn't just about life turning on him, but terrible miscalls in judgment, betrayal, lies, and—

"Hey." He touched her arm. "It's okay. Right now, life is on our side."

"No—"

"Yes." He set down his cup. "C'mere."

He was sitting up, and now he unzipped the bivy bag.

"Orion, there's only room for one."

"Please. Jen. You're not exactly a hippo. Get in here. We're fully clothed. I promise, we just need to keep warm and survive the night. I'll behave myself."

That wasn't the problem. She didn't want him to know she was about to cry. But maybe he'd think it was the fact they were trapped fifty feet below an ice field, the snow accumulating above them . . . Yes, that was something to cry about.

But she was cold, and he was warm and . . . well, if they were going to die down here, maybe she'd do it in his arms. So she slipped off her boots, tied them by the laces, and clipped them to the ice screw. Then she shed her jacket.

He scooted over and she eased in next to him, facing him, trying not to bump his leg.

His arms went around her and he pulled her down to his chest, where she could settle her ear against his steady, safe heartbeat.

Yes, if they lived through tonight, then tomorrow, she would save this man's life.

■ ■ ■

Aria was getting sicker. Her last bout of coughing had subsided, but tucked this close, with her asleep in his arms, Jake heard the rasping in her chest.

He wasn't doing great, either. His bones ached and hunger was a beast in his gullet. Worse was his admission, skulking around in his head.

"I shot an innocent kid."

He winced at the very words, torn out from inside him, a letting of blood and sorrow. Aria had looked at him, so much horror on her face a second before she reached out for him.

He'd practically fled inside Aria's arms like some sort of cry-baby. Except, holding on to her had helped. Just a little.

Or maybe a lot, especially when Aria had . . . oh, wow, she'd kissed him. Grabbed his face and gave him a kiss that had nearly made him forget he was in a tent on a mountain, nearly frozen.

Maybe it was pity, he didn't know, but the way she kissed him made him feel forgiven and whole and maybe a little like the man he longed to be.

Which was why he'd backed away from her. Okay, maybe *after* he'd accidentally kicked her—smooth move, Silver. But her cry had made him slow down, find the pieces of his common sense that kissing her had scattered to the wind.

Down in Copper Mountain, on the dance floor, if she'd leaned into his ear and suggested a quick tumble he might have said yes. But here, trapped on a mountain with her, after knowing her—her literal *broken* heart, the death of her sister, her courage, and even her amazing achievements, the idea of indulging in something quick and meaningless turned his gut.

Not with Aria.

She coughed again, her body wracking, and he resisted the urge to hold her still.

Sasha, however, hadn't moved for hours.

He had to get one of them off the mountain, or he'd have two dead women on his hands.

He pushed away the acid that climbed up his empty gut, waited until Aria's body stopped trembling, then slowly peeled himself away from her, climbing over her body and pulling his warm sleeping bag over her.

He shivered as the air bit through his layers. But the wind had died, the tent no longer trembling.

He checked Sasha's breathing—yes, still alive. He took her pulse, found it weak but steady. Maybe he'd make her some tea.

Sliding on his jacket, he unzipped the tent, grabbed his boots, and slid his polar-slippered feet into them. His boots were icy and stiff, just like his body as he slid out into the vestibule, and he fought the urge to turn around, climb back in beside Aria. He pulled out his stove and brought it out into the kitchen area, a protected area, now slightly snowed under. Retrieving his shovel, he dug out his work area, sifting through the options.

He could probably put Aria on his back. Carry her to Karstens Ridge. Maybe even leave her there, bivouacked, while he went back to fetch Sasha. But the last part of Karstens Ridge was too steep to descend with either of them on his back. Maybe he could lower Sasha, with Aria guiding her down.

At least then, they'd be down another three thousand feet. But Sasha needed immediate medical help.

Or, she might be beyond help.

He patted down his work area and set up the stove. Filling the pot with snow, he returned to the tent to grab his thermos of water. Aria was coughing again as he zipped the tent shut.

She needed to get to a lower elevation, and now.

He added water to the pot, the wind licking down his open jacket as he lit the flame.

The skies had cleared, and the valley unfurled before him, the Muldrow Glacier spread out like a layer of whipped topping.

Now. If he wanted to escape the mountain, it had to be now. The voice nearly rose up, audibly inside him, and he had the craziest sense that it might be God speaking to him, a little like he did to Ham.

He envied Ham, the way he could live in peace despite the broken pieces of his past.

Despite losing the woman he loved to Chechen rebels.

Yeah, Ham possessed some sort of divine insight that sometimes made Jake jealous. Hungry for some divine insight himself.

God, I could use some help here. He stared at the melting snow, his stomach roiling.

If he left Sasha behind in the tent, maybe he could get Aria down to a lower elevation, then climb back up and . . .

He pressed against his gut, feeling like he might retch.

Behind him the tent zipper sounded. He turned just as Aria crawled out of the tent.

"What are you doing? Get back inside."

"What is this, gulag? I'm not your prisoner." She climbed to her feet, steadying herself on a nearby ice axe that she'd picked up.

"No, but you *are* sick."

"I'm fine." She limped over to him. "What are you doing?"

"Making water."

She stared at it, back at him. The wind trickled her dark hair over her face. She wiped it back. "Jake—"

257

"It's time, Aria." He couldn't look at her. "You're getting sicker, and you need to get to a lower altitude. I don't think I can carry both of you."

"You don't have to carry me! Look, I can walk." She turned away from him and took one step, leaning hard on the axe. Then another.

On the third, she slipped, and cried out.

He could have let her fall into the snow to prove his point, but he caught her, pulling her up into his arms. "Stop trying to be brave."

She pushed out of his arms. "No." She turned to him, her eyes bright with tears. "You can't leave Sasha here."

"I'll come back for her. I just need to get you to a lower level—"

"What if you can't? She'll *die*. And you can't carry her the entire way. You're weak, too. You'll fall." Her jaw tightened, as if she might be trying not to cry.

"I'm going to give Sasha some water, and then we're leaving."

The wind whipped between them, her eyes fierce in his. "I hate you."

He took her words into him, absorbed them with a nod. "Yeah, well, get in line. I hate myself."

He turned away from her, picking up a spoon to stir the melting snow.

Next to him, she coughed.

He winced. "Listen, I have a plan. We'll put her into your sleeping bag, she'll be warm, and we'll share mine, and . . ."

"Please, Jake—"

"I can't carry her and you!"

"Then take her. I'll be fine."

He rounded on her. "Please, Aria. Don't do this to me—"

"Don't make *me* live at the cost of my friend!" Her eyes turned wild. "Don't make me live while someone I love dies. I can't do it again."

He stared at her, at the tears that flushed her face. "Aria? Do *what* again?"

"I . . . I have my sister's heart."

He froze. What?

"Her heart—she died, and I got her heart. It's why I can do all the things—it was an identical match."

Oh no, please—

She covered her face with her hands, unmittened, and they must be freezing. In fact, she'd come outside without her jacket, and now he reached for her, pulling her into his open jacket.

"She died, and I lived, and I can't do that again."

He closed his eyes and just held her. Because yes, he knew what it felt like to have someone you loved die—and sure, it wasn't her *fault*, but she'd had to keep living. With her sister's heart in her body.

Yeah, that wasn't fair. "I'm sorry, Doc."

She slid her arms around his waist and held on.

His heart might be tearing apart, tiny fissures growing and ripping and widening and—

"I hear something." She lifted her head.

He heard it too, now, and let her go, cupping his hand over his eyes. She stood next to him, shivering, also scanning the horizon.

Shucking off his jacket, he draped it over her shoulders.

The whump-whump rhythm of a chopper deepened, pulsed through him—

A bird appeared over Karstens Ridge. Deep red, a dollop of life against the white peak. He waved his arms, crazily near tears.

The radio crackled in his jacket pocket. "Denali camp, come in."

A voice he didn't recognize, but he didn't care. He fished out the radio. "Denali camp, here."

"We see you. We're sending down a line."

"Let's get Sasha bundled up," he said to Aria.

She was crying.

They had Sasha tucked into two sleeping bags and out of the tent by the time the chopper had lowered an Alaskan pararescue jumper with his basket down to their camp. And with him came—

"Ham, you son of a gun."

"Sorry we took so long." Ham unhooked from his line and crunched through the snow toward Jake. "Things got a little complicated."

Ham looked windburned, sunburned, and ragged, his blond beard in snarls, his eyes a little bloodshot. "How's Sasha?"

Jake's mouth formed a thin line as he shook his head. "I dunno. Still breathing." His throat thickened with that news as Ham and the PJ secured Sasha in the basket.

The PJ attached himself to the basket and the chopper hoisted them aloft.

Jake covered his head as the wind whipped up around them, shivering their tent. "Now Aria."

She had slipped on her boots, leaving one untied, and her jacket and hat. The harness came back down on the cable and Ham grabbed it, unhooking the harness while he held the cable.

Jake turned to Aria, the wind, the roar of the chopper nearly drowning out his words. "I told you I'd get you off this mountain." He knelt before her as he held out the harness legs.

Balancing on his shoulders, she lifted her injured ankle and slid that in. Blew out a hard breath as she lowered it.

"Wait," he said. "No. I said I'd carry you if I had to." Then he stood up and swept her up into his arms. "Ham. Can you help get this harness on her?"

Sure, it was charming, but really, he just wanted to hold her one last moment, the curve of her, the warmth imprinted on him.

He didn't know what it was about Doctor Aria Sinclair, but in a strange way, when she was with him, he felt healed. At least a little.

Ham worked the harness onto her legs, then Jake reluctantly set her down and steadied her as Ham fitted it over her shoulders and snapped her in.

"Are you coming, Jake?" she asked.

"Not yet. I need his help," Ham said as he clipped her into the line. He waved to the chopper. "Orion and Jenny are missing."

Jake froze, shot him a look. Ham gave him a thin-lipped nod.

Maybe Aria didn't hear it because up top, the PJ began to hoist her up.

Jake guided her up, letting her go to swing free into the sky. He watched her all the way to the deck of the chopper.

"It'll be back for us and we'll search the mountain," Ham said. "Let's pack up."

He was still staring at the chopper, watching as the PJ secured her into safety. Then the bird veered away from the mountain, into the blue sky.

Thanks for the dance, Hot Lips.

■ ■ ■

What if they never left?

Of course, the thought was not only crazy but lethal, because if they didn't freeze to death, they'd starve. Still, as Orion held Jenny, her body warm as she rested her head on his chest, her breaths even, her blonde hair silky against his cheek, he didn't hate the idea.

He didn't know why being with her awakened a dormant hope,

a sense of peace he hadn't had since . . . well, since the last time he'd held her, the stars spilling across the sky, blinking at him. Watching.

He drew in a breath and stared at the blue swath overhead, the clear sky. *"And what does the answer do for you? Do you have to understand to accept?"*

Jenny's words had lingered in his head, digging in to find his bones, not unlike the cold of the ledge, the ache in his leg.

He did want to argue with the outcome. But it didn't change anything.

So then what? How did he live with a life that wasn't what he expected? Or wanted?

It would be easier if he didn't have to look down and see the scars every day. But maybe yes, it wasn't about understanding, but acceptance.

He still didn't know what to do with the anger, but he'd lived with it this long, maybe acceptance was the best he could hope for.

At least it might help him stop hiding. Because as Jenny sighed again and roused, the idea of climbing out of the crevasse and . . . well, Ham lived in Minnesota.

Jenny lived in Minnesota.

And if Ham wasn't dead—*please!*—then maybe he could join Ham's SAR team, answer the nudge inside him. *"I know you, Ry. You're a rescuer."*

He let those words saturate him as Jenny leaned up, cold air rushing into the space she'd occupied. Sleep lines ran through her face, her hair tangled. A line of sunburn ringed her eyes, touched her nose.

With everything inside him, he wanted to grab her jacket and pull her to himself. Taste that smile that now slid up her face. Her blue eyes met his. "How're you doing? How's the leg?"

"Ready to climb."

She arched an eyebrow, then looked up at the slice of blue. "Let's get some breakfast."

He couldn't argue with some hot tea, reconstituted oatmeal, dried fruit. He didn't want to know how old the grub was, but it still filled his belly. Although, "What I wouldn't give for a cup of dark, bracing straight-up coffee. And maybe a donut."

Jenny was quiet as she sipped her tea.

"What are you doing?"

"Trying to think through how to get us out of here."

He'd spent the better part of the night churning through the same thoughts.

"I'll belay you up to the top. You lead climb, set in the screws as you go. Then, when you get to the top, set up a fixed line and I'll use my foot strap to ascend."

Her mouth tightened into a thin line.

"What?"

"I just . . . maybe I should haul you up." She met his eyes. "And no comments about me not being strong enough. I'll use a haul system."

"There's not enough rope for a haul system. It would need to go from the top, back down, back up, and leave room for you to pull."

She seemed to be measuring his words.

"I'll be fine, Jen. We're going to make it."

The crevasse walls resembled waterfalls of frozen ice—rippled in places, with rugged overhangs and horizontal layers of snow packed tight, nobby juttings of former ice bridges, and massive hanging icicles that, if they unlatched, could spear them through.

A cruel beauty.

"I'm worried about that overhang." He pointed to the shelf over the edge.

He was also worried about Ham. Which only set a fist into his gut as he remembered Ham's prayer.

"Make our steps safe and go before us. Finish the task you've pressed us to."

He wasn't going to assign any blame, because yeah, answers didn't change anything. But for all the guys to fall on the mountain . . .

"I can climb the shelf," Jenny said. She stood up. "I'll go up this waterfall-type section—the ice is bluer here, probably more stable, then I'll set my screws on the overhang as I climb it."

He traced her route. Not unlike rock climbing with ridges, nodules, and sheer pitches. But he liked how she thought. They could do this.

She finished her tea, packed it away. Then she kitted up, pulling on her harness, her crampons, attaching the anchors, slings, and webbing with the biners onto her harness.

Meanwhile, he set up the belay system. He flaked out the cold, stiff rope, running his hand over it, checking for knots and working out the kinks. Then he knotted the free end onto the pack. "We'll haul the pack up after I get up top."

She was roping into her kit, tying a figure eight, clipping it into her biner. She looked over at him and smiled. "We'll need it for the hike down."

Any other time, any other place, and when his leg wasn't completely messed up, this might be the perfect date. A pretty girl, blue skies, a hint of adrenaline? Yeah, they were going to make it. The sense of it found his gut, pressed through to his bones. She was a smart, capable climber.

And he had been practically born to ice and snow, to climb this mountain.

It couldn't hold him hostage any longer.

"You having a good time or something?" he asked as he pushed himself up. Bit back a groan.

"Just thinking that today, I'm going to save you, PJ."

"You think so." He hobbled toward her. Grabbed her jacket. Pulled her close to him. "Maybe you already have."

Her mouth opened, as if in surprise. "I don't—"

"Jacie—Jenny. Whoever you are, seeing you, finding you, even us landing down here, alive—it's like a miracle. You're right. Getting answers isn't going to change the outcome of what happened. God's not going to answer my questions . . . and maybe he doesn't need to. Maybe it's enough that he saved us. And he's still saving us."

She closed her mouth, her gaze hard in his as she swallowed. Nodded. "I hope he's also saving Aria and Sash."

He didn't know what to say to that. "We'll get out and find help. We're going to escape down this mountain and then . . ." He lifted his mouth in a smile. "What if I followed you out of the woods and back to Minnesota?"

"Uh . . ."

He frowned. Oh no, too soon—

Then she smiled. "You sure you're ready to do that?"

Oh, honey. "I'm ready to stop hiding. And yeah, maybe I am a rescuer. Or I want to be, again. And if Ham's . . ." He took a breath. "If Ham gave his life for us, maybe Jake and I need to pick up Ham's dream."

She touched his face with her ungloved hand, pressed the warmth of it to his whiskers. Met his eyes, an emotion in them he couldn't read.

Then she kissed him, a sort of solid determination in her kiss that had him wrapping his arms around her waist and leaning back against the ice to pull her to himself.

She made a sound deep inside, a sort of hum, and he drank it in.

Yeah. He'd get off this mountain and start over. Let go of the anger and start appreciating what he still had.

Jenny. Life.

A fresh start.

She pushed away from him, her face a little flushed. "Okay. Let's get out of here."

He let her step back, then couldn't stop himself from checking her knots. He hooked the belay device into his biner at his harness, and wove the rope in.

"Ready?"

She'd taken his axe, as well as her own, and stared up at the wall. Took a breath. "On belay?"

"Belaying."

"Climbing."

"Climb on."

He stepped close to the wall, praying hard she didn't fall before setting the first screw, not sure how his leg would hold up. He bore little weight on it, but he didn't need it to arrest her fall once she clipped in. Just his leverage and good technique.

She chipped into the ice with her axes, then her feet, climbed up ten feet, and set in the first screw. He gave out slack as she clipped in the rope.

Freedom beckoned fifty feet up.

She kept climbing and he fed out the rope, working his feed hand and his brake hand in tandem, one always on the line. She clipped in another anchor twenty feet up, then climbed onto a small ledge.

"There's a lot of loose snow above me. I'm going to move to the right."

He fed out the line as she traversed the wall. Then she set another anchor and started up the icy blue waterfall.

Overhead, snow kicked up, a stirring of the wind, and he braced himself for another whiteout when they reached the surface. But they had the pack, so they could probably work their way down. He'd slide if he had to.

And, they still had their beacons, so anyone who got close enough might find them. Except, no one even knew where to look for them.

No, if they got out, they were on their own.

Or rather, maybe not. God had been on their side—

"Falling!"

He yanked down hard on his brake hand, stiffening as the jerk came. It dragged him off his feet and he sat back in his harness to brace his feet on the wall. "You okay?"

He looked up and his heart about stopped. She dangled upside down, swinging. "Jenny!"

"I'm okay! Stupid me, I let the rope get behind me." Her axes dangled from her wrist loops, her feet searching for purchase on the wall. "I was reaching for the ice screw and missed."

He wanted to go up and help her as she struggled to dig her crampons into the ice, to wrestle herself upright.

"Maybe you should come down."

"Everybody falls. I got this, Ry! And you got me, right?"

"Right." He'd checked their gear—the system was solid. But it didn't stop the clench in his gut.

As he watched, she braced her feet to the wall, then swung her right axe around, into the ice.

He could hardly believe it when she wrapped one leg around the arm gripping her axe. "I'm good. Give me slack."

He let out the rope, easing off his brake hand, and settled back on the ledge. A sweat formed under his hat.

"Climbing!"

"Climb on!"

She was some kind of acrobat as, in one smooth move, she used her leg to leverage herself up, slam her other axe into the wall. Then she wiggled out her hand from the loop, set the ice screw, grabbed the rope, and clipped it into the anchor.

Yeah, she was good at this game. Maybe even a better climber than he was. Still, Orion blew out a breath as he watched her scramble higher. Over a notch in the wall, which she used to brace herself as she put in another anchor.

"How many do you have left?"

A pause. "Three."

Three. And twenty feet left. They'd also salvaged off the pack two pieces of ice pro—long anchors they could drive into the ground at the top. That and one of her ice axes could make a triad anchor system. She could use the other ice axe to create a cushion for the rope over the cornice as he levered himself up.

Then, somehow, they'd hike down to Muldrow Glacier, and . . . well, by then, if the skies were clear, surely someone would be looking for them.

Please, please let Sasha, Jake, and Aria be alive.

"I can see the top!" Her voice echoed down.

He could barely see her. She'd curved around the cornice to climb up its side, her yellow jacket just barely visible.

"I'm setting a screw at the bottom of the cornice. Slack!"

He spooled it out for her. Saw her clip the rope in.

"Be careful!" Stupid, because of course she'd be careful. But he could see the problem in his mind's eye. She'd have to ratchet in the axes, let her legs dangle, then somehow move her axes up the lip. Problem was, they were already at her arm's length. And he didn't know how much arm strength she had left.

He stepped back from the wall, nearly to the back of the ledge, to get the angle to see her. The fist in his gut tightened when she released her feet from the wall, dangling just by one axe, on the cornice.

A fall now would slam her against the icy wall.

Maybe rip out the anchor.

He couldn't watch. Except, his gaze was pinned to her.

She looped one of her legs over her arm, and again levered herself up using her core.

Landed her left axe into the snowcap above her.

She unwound herself and moved her right axe parallel to her left.

Dangled there.

Her arms had to be on fire. She kicked out, trying for purchase with her feet on the cornice, but she wasn't yet high enough.

Her body swung with the action.

"You're almost there!"

She tried again, her feet scrabbling against the underside of the overhang, and for a moment, she got enough lift to move her left hand higher.

"Put in a screw!"

He wasn't sure if she heard him, but she left her axe in the wall and reached for the ice screw in her belt. Wow, the woman was strong, the way she screwed it into the ice, dangling from only her right hand, her feet barely nipping the bottom of the underhang.

He sat back in his harness to brace her if she fell.

"Slack!"

Shoot. "Slack!" He eased back with his brake hand and fished out the slack so she could move the rope into the anchor.

Her feet gave way. Her scream hit the walls, piercing and raw as she fell. Somehow, she hung on to her axe, self-arresting before her weight could pull him off his feet.

She dangled from her right-hand loop, spinning under the cornice. He braked, leaning back into the harness to give her some help.

She got both hands back on to the axe, still working to affix her feet.

"You got this!"

"I'm going to try and get better footing."

A fist had moved up to grab him around the throat as she put her left hand on the top of her axe and pulled herself up.

Her feet still bit nothing but air.

"A little higher!"

She unlooped her right hand from the axe handle to cap it over her left, to leverage herself up.

He couldn't breathe.

Her feet caught on the bottom lip of the cornice.

His chest eased.

"Stabilize yourself before you clip in, Jenny!"

Maybe she didn't hear him, because she reached down for her rope, grabbing it. Okay, well, she probably knew what she was doing. He frantically fished out slack.

She brought it up and lunged for the anchor.

Her axe slipped. "Falling!"

She toppled off the cornice, swinging into the mountain.

Her weight whipped him off his feet. No! He was so far out, he saw the crash against the wall coming and tried to brace himself. But he slammed into the ice with so much force it shucked the breath out of him.

He nearly let go—just his reflexes hanging on to the brake.

His leg, however. Oh—it took the brunt of the hit. His roar lifted through the chamber as pain shot through him, crippling him.

But he hung on, gritting his teeth, trembling.

Snow cascaded down onto the ledge—he heard at least one axe slamming behind him, tried to look for it, but it bounced away into the dark blue abyss.

Then, all went quiet, save his breaths rasping through his teeth.

"Jenny!"

Nothing. And, pinned against the wall, he couldn't see her. He tried to push out with his feet, get an angle, but the pain in his leg crumpled him.

He lay in the harness, his arms trembling, his jaw gritted, his brake hand straining to hold her, trying not to let out another shout, this one of frustration.

"Jen, please, answer me!"

Nothing.

He leaned his head back, praying for a glimpse of her. "Jacie. Honey, please! Answer me!" Just his own voice echoing against the icy blue walls, back to himself.

"C'mon!" More feral cry than word. He blew out a breath. Another. Willed his heartbeat to slow.

Think. Just . . . Don't. Panic.

Get her down.

Orion released his left hand and grabbed the brake rope under the figure eight with both hands, one farther down to give himself slack. Then he released the brake. His left hand slammed into the belay device, the rope slipping through his gloves. Grinding his teeth, he braked hard with his right hand.

The entire movement jarred his body, the pain embedding in his bones.

He didn't care. As long as she was alive.

Repeating the movement, he braked again, the rope jerking hard to arrest her fall. "Jen!"

Nothing.

He kept working, his gloves rubbed shiny with the raze of the rope, his arms burning as he lowered her.

She came into view and his heart nearly stopped in his chest. Her helmet was crushed, blood trickled down her face. Limp and dangling in the harness, she didn't rouse when he again called her name.

God, please don't let her be dead.

He didn't know why he was calling out to God. Certainly he'd learned the first time Orion had pinned all his hopes on him . . .

No. God couldn't abandon them now. But . . .

Orion didn't know what to think.

He lowered her all the way down, then let out enough slack to return himself to the ground.

He rolled over and crawled over to her. "Jenny."

She wasn't moving. He unclipped her helmet, fearing a crushed skull, but the blood came from a gash in her forehead, maybe where the helmet had been pushed back. She must have hit something—maybe another ice screw, maybe the sharp edge of the ice. Whatever it was, it tore into her head right above her eyebrow, at her forehead.

He pressed his glove over the wound. "Jenny, honey. Wake up. Please wake up."

For a second, he was sitting on the edge of the ice watching his father go out into the breach. *"Dad, come back!"*

"Just hold the rope, Ry! Don't let go!"

"Don't let go, Jace." He pulled her into his lap, bending over her. "Don't leave me again. Stay with me."

"Stay with me, Dad!"

"Rian, I think you're scared."

Jenny's voice caught him up, and he even lifted his head to see if she'd woken. No. She lay there, her face pale, her lips slightly open. Breathing, thank you, Jesus. But not awake.

And right then, yes, he was scared. The realization wound through him, around him, squeezing his breath from him.

Trapped. Broken. And very, very afraid.

Hope was a betrayer. Cruel with its blue skies and offers of peace.

Maybe it was better to stay in the darkness.

Orion lifted his eyes to the slice of blue, Jenny's body in his arms, and because he had nothing else, he screamed. He let out a roar that ripped through his body, tore out pieces of his soul, and let loose all the anger, all the grief . . .

The final fragment of hope.

The sound of it careened through the cavern, ripping through him and settling back into his body with the force of an avalanche.

It broke him with the violence, and he had nothing left when he leaned over Jenny, clutching her to himself.

For the first time since he woke in Germany, alone in the hospital, Orion wept.

Because clearly, they were all doomed after all.

CHAPTER THIRTEEN

S HE'D FALLEN.
Fallen.

And worse, she'd broken Orion Starr.

His bone-scarring scream had yanked Jenny from the darkness, a feral ripping through the layers to grab her, jerk her to consciousness.

She shouldn't have reached for that last clip. She knew it was a stretch, and she'd heard Orion yelling—but no, her brain said she could make it.

Her arrogance.

Her prideful belief that she could save Orion. Save both of them.

Right. The fire in her shoulder seared through her. Her head throbbed.

But worse than her broken parts was Orion's pain.

The man had his face buried into her shoulder, his shoulders trembling.

Oh no, he was weeping.

Weeping.

It was probably stress, and pain, and maybe fear, but seeing him torn asunder ripped apart any illusion that they might move on from this moment into freedom.

She'd broken him. And sure, she knew he was wounded, and still mending, but he hid his wounds well. She'd somehow betrayed herself into thinking that they might start over.

Made herself believe she could stop running. Which was exactly why she'd kissed him before ascending the wall, a touch that spoke of rescues and fresh starts. Apparently, she'd started to think that she could do something right.

What a fool.

Tears blurred her vision, and she looked away.

The movement alerted him. "Jenny?"

"I'm sorry, Ry. I shouldn't have reached for the last clip—my hold was too unstable."

"Please tell me you're okay." He leaned up, his gaze scanning over her, his glove over her throbbing temple.

The agony in his eyes could make her howl. Tears ran down his handsome face. His jaw was strung tight and he stared at her with such reddened eyes, she wanted to reach for him.

She moved her arm. And nearly screamed. She'd definitely broken something.

Orion swore, and his expression changed. Hardened. "Stop moving."

"I—"

"Your arm is hanging funny." He sounded almost angry.

She knew she wasn't helping with the moaning, but she suddenly couldn't seem to stop. He moved his hand over her arm and she bit back the wave of pain.

"Sorry!" By his breathing, he was clearly fraying as he examined her, his head shaking, his jaw so tight he might break molars.

"Breathe, Ry," she said. "I'm okay."

"You're not okay. You're bleeding from the forehead, and you definitely have a dislocated shoulder." He let out another dark word.

PTSD. She knew it well enough to see him in full-out unravel, starting with the scream and now in the fraying edges of panic around his eyes. He blew out another breath, almost starting to hyperventilate.

"We're going to be okay, Ry."

"In what world? The ice axe is still up there, and . . ." He shook his head. Covered his face with his hand, as if trying to hold back his emotions. "Sorry—I'll figure it out."

Oh, Orion. She should have expected him, really, with all his wadded frustration, to explode.

Yeah, she'd broken him because he just sat there, completely wrecked.

They would die here. Him, trapped in a cave. Because of her. Again. "I'm sorry I fell."

That, too, was the wrong thing to say. He looked at her with so much fury on his face she recoiled.

"Are you *serious*? I should have been the one going up that wall." He swallowed, his jaw tight.

"Rian, I'm a good climber—"

"You're a freakin' mountain goat! But I can't . . ." His mouth closed. He stared at her so hard it took the breath from her lungs. "But I can't watch someone I . . ." He swallowed. "Someone I care about die in front of my eyes. Not again."

Oh. Right.

No wonder the guy was panicking. And maybe it wasn't just Afghanistan but also watching his family be swept away that had fractured him. PTSD didn't always happen in war.

He looked away from her, and his eyes ringed red, his body trembling as if he might be trying not to let out another feral shout.

Keep him talking. "How did you get me down?"

"I lowered you." His voice was tight, as if trying to keep it from shaking.

"I'm sorry I scared you."

He looked away.

Closed his eyes.

Then he leaned over, and another crazy sound came out of his mouth, almost a moan, but deeper. As if torn from his soul.

"Ry?"

"I'm so sorry, Jen. I told you I'd rescue you, and—"

"You're blaming *yourself*? How is any of this your fault?" She wanted to sit up, to grab him, to make him look at her. Instead, she reached out for his jacket sleeve with her good hand. "This is *my* fault. I should have waited—"

"What?" He jerked away and stared at her as if she'd struck him. "You're amazing, Jenny. If you can't make it over that cornice— No, you didn't do anything wrong."

"Yeah, I did. First rule in climbing—calm down. Take your time. Don't crazily lunge for something." She shook her head. "Listen. Can you put my arm back in the socket? I can try again."

"Have you *lost your mind*?" His eyes were dark, unyielding. "There's no way you're going back on that wall. Sheesh. *Are you trying to kill me?*"

She recoiled. "Actually, no. I'm trying to save our lives."

His lips tightened into a bud of frustration and he pulled off his hat.

His dark hair was rucked up, snarled. He ran his arm across his sweaty brow.

His desperation shook her to her bones.

He refused to look at her. "I should have listened to you. Climbed up to High Camp. Instead, I thought I could get you down, and—"

"Stop." Her voice wavered, but she pushed through. "Just stop. This is *not* your fault. You're not the one who . . . who destroys people's lives with her stupid decisions."

He started to argue, but she couldn't stop. She'd broken this man in so many ways, and there he sat, blaming himself.

Not anymore. "I'm the reason you're stuck. I'm the reason you have a broken knee. I'm the reason you won't leave Alaska. I'm the reason your entire life blew apart."

His expression had morphed into a sort of confused horror, and aw shoot, they might die down here. And she couldn't bear to let it happen without him knowing the truth.

Answers. This poor man deserved answers.

He deserved peace.

"I wasn't a journalist in Afghanistan, Orion." Overhead, snow kicked down into the crevasse. She glanced up, hoping the cornice wasn't about to come down on them, even if it seemed the right finale to her epic mistakes. "I was a CIA profiler. And I'm the one who believed the Taliban informant."

His chest was rising and falling, but even as he stared at her, he was shaking his head.

"Yeah," she said, pushing herself up to a sitting position.

He let go of her.

"I was there to profile our informants, help root out the reliable ones . . . and the ones most likely to lie to us."

He swallowed, but he'd stopped shaking his head.

"I know I should have told you the truth—I . . . well, for security reasons . . ."

"I get it."

She wanted to wince at the cool rasp of his voice.

"So, you were . . . you knew the intel about the Taliban stronghold." His green eyes didn't leave hers.

SUSAN MAY WARREN

She nodded. "I knew Azzumi, the informant. He was working with one of our agents, and my job was to observe him, profile, and vet his information."

Orion didn't move. She fought a shiver, probably her body going into shock. She wanted to say something, but . . . well, what could he do? He was as hurt as she was, and her confession just might be sending *him* into shock.

They were both going to die down here. Now, at least he could die with the answers he longed for.

"He was ten years old, and he spoke English, and he seemed . . . well, he was well educated, liked Americans, and I just didn't believe a ten-year-old kid could have that much guile. My head said he was telling the truth."

But not her heart. Her heart had a check—but she feared her feelings for Orion—and her fear that he could get hurt—had compromised her thinking. Kept her from thinking clearly. So she prayed that she was right. That she hadn't sent the man she was falling in love with to his death.

Her throat thickened. "I went to Afghanistan because I wanted to save lives. I ended up killing two SEALS, two PJs, and . . . well, two good men were captured and tortured by the Taliban."

Orion said nothing. Just sat on the ice, his chest rising and falling.

She looked away, her body shaking.

Silence fell between them, and with it, the cascade of snow, dribbling down into the crevasse.

She didn't look up.

What did she expect? That he would forgive her? Sheesh, she didn't even forgive herself.

"Is that why you changed your name?"

She looked at him. His eyes had turned to ice, his tone brusque.

279

"I wanted to start over."

"Mmmhmm."

Nothing he could have said would have hurt her more than his quiet, deep-throated noise that told her the brutal truth.

Some people just didn't get to start over.

Her best hope was to keep running.

She closed her eyes. "I'm so sorry, Orion. Please, for—"

"Look out!"

Orion's body slammed over her, and in a second she was pinned down, his arms bracketing her, his face next to hers.

Snow cascaded down over them, slamming into their ledge. She screamed, grabbed his jacket. Closed her eyes. Buried her face in his chest.

And she was a fool because she simply stole the moment for herself, holding on to this man one last time. Giving over her heart to him, even if he didn't want it. Because this man—this wounded, loyal, courageous man couldn't help but rescue her, even when she didn't deserve it.

The snowfall ceased to a dribble, and Orion eased back. His eyes fell to hers, held there. His mouth opened—

"Orion!"

The voice from above jerked them both, and Orion's breath shuddered out as he looked up.

She too saw it, a man, dangling from a harness over the cornice, free rappelling down on a line. The end of the rope hit the ledge beside them.

"Ham!" Orion's voice ripped out of him, so much emotion in it, Jenny knew he'd been grieving.

"Get back! The top is pretty loose."

Orion hooked his arm around her and wrestled her back toward the wall to stay away from falling debris.

Ham landed next to them, and Jenny wanted to weep. He looked beat-up, exhausted, but his blue eyes shone. "Wow, you guys are hard to find. We were flying over the icefall and got a blip on our avalanche beacon. Just for a moment. Then, it vanished. And we weren't sure . . ." He unclipped from his line but stayed on belay and toggled his radio.

"Rescue one, they're here. Send down the litter, and some help."

Ham knelt next to Jenny, eyeing her gash. "We put down and were looking for you but we would have never found you if you hadn't screamed, Jenny. That was quite a . . . well, are you okay?"

She had screamed, maybe. But she looked at Orion, whose mouth tightened. So not her scream but his had brought Ham to their tomb.

"She has a dislocated shoulder, I think," Orion said, his eyes on her a long moment before he turned back to Ham. "How are you? We thought we lost you in the slide."

Another person was coming down the rope.

"It just missed me. I hunkered down behind a serac and watched as Jenny disappeared . . . and then, there was nothing. You must have fallen too far down for your beacons to reach the top. I hadn't a clue where you were." He had unzipped Jenny's jacket, was reaching inside to probe her shoulder.

He had warm hands, and she closed her eyes as he touched the loose socket. "We need to get that secured before we transport you."

"Orion's knee is busted, too."

"It's fine," Orion snapped.

Ham frowned as he got back on the radio. "Jake, send down a splint kit."

"Jake?" Orion said as the second person landed on the ledge. "He's with you?"

"We already got Sasha and Aria off the mountain."

"Sasha—is she—?" Jenny asked.

"She's on her way to the hospital in Anchorage," said a female voice.

Kit.

The woman's dark braids wound out of her wool hat, her face lined, probably with worry. She knelt next to Jenny. "As soon as we got her to Base Camp, her husband was there. She's in good hands."

Poor Lucas. He'd been through so much watching his wife suffer.

"Let's get you splinted up and into the chopper," Ham said.

"We have another telescoping pole in the pack," Orion said and gestured to their gear, still tied into the rope.

Ham made to get up, but Kit stopped him, her hand on his arm as she rose slowly. "Oh my . . . oh . . . ." Her face had paled and she looked at Jenny, then back to the pack. "Where did you get that?"

"It was frozen to some dead climber, in the ice," Orion said, but Jenny wanted to grab him, stop his words. Because she didn't have to be a doctor of psychology to see the shock, the grief rippling across Kit's face. She knelt next to the pack, rubbing her thumb over a patch sewn on to the top flap.

"He fell into the crevasse," she said quietly.

Orion looked at Kit, then drew in a breath. "Oh, Kit."

Kit's eyes closed.

Orion got up and limped over to her.

"Who is it?" Ham said.

"I think it's her missing husband," Jenny said quietly, watching as Orion, the rescuer, drew Kit close and wrapped his arms around her.

282

Her eyes filled and she looked away.

The litter came down, and with it the splint kit. Ham worked quietly, stabilizing her arm, then packaging her up into a sleeping bag, and finally lifting her into the litter.

Orion had brought Kit over to the ledge, pointing up to where her husband lay.

He never looked at Jenny.

Probably a good thing. Because she couldn't bear to look back and see all she'd lost. The could-have-beens.

The debris of her mistakes.

Ham clipped himself into the basket line and radioed up. In a moment, they were lifted off the ledge and into the cool blue of the crevasse, out into the open blue skies that blanketed the Denali massif.

Jake pulled them into the chopper. He and Ham lifted her out of the litter and secured her onto the platform.

She closed her eyes as a PJ took her vitals. He set up an IV line and gave her a shot of morphine.

Somewhere in there, Ham was lowered again with the litter, but he unhooked it and sent the line back up, empty.

"Ham says they're going to retrieve a body, and to come back for them. So, let's get you down to camp," Jake said, leaning over her, concern in his eyes.

She nodded. It didn't matter if she waited for Jake or not. Because she was already away, already running.

Already saying goodbye.

■ ■ ■

Rescue had come too late.

An hour earlier and he would have never known Jenny's secret. In truth, Orion wasn't sure he didn't want to rewind time and go back to that moment when he didn't know the broken woman in his arms had betrayed him.

Answers. He'd come onto the mountain seeking answers, and now his entire body was filled with poison.

He watched as Ham belayed Kit up the wall to retrieve her frozen husband. She'd been weeping as Ham had delivered Jenny to the chopper, but by the time he returned with the litter, Kit had pulled herself together.

Orion wished he could do the same.

"He must have fallen off the pass, just like Jenny and her team," Ham said. He fished out the belay rope as Kit mounted the bridge and anchored herself into the ice screws. She'd created a lowering system while Ham was splinting Orion's leg.

"Maybe he tried to hike down, like we did," Orion said, trying to pay attention, but really his thoughts kept cycling back to Jenny.

"I wanted to start over."

So, she'd run from the truth. Run from the people she'd hurt. Run from him.

Orion wrapped his arms around himself. Ham had given him a shot of morphine, so he might not be all himself, but the fact was, no one got away, not really.

He'd always be trapped, somehow, in the dark, cold crevasse of his anger.

God had brought him back to the mountain, all right. To connect him with hope. With a future. To restart his frozen heart.

Only to betray Orion again.

Kit had chipped her husband free and now pulled his frozen body into her arms. Bent her head down.

Ham looked away, giving her a moment.

Orion, too, looked away.

Pain followed you through life, and it was a miracle if you just got back up again after life knocked you down.

"I'm ready to lower him." She'd clipped the rope to a biner on his harness and then his rope into an anchor on the wall. Ham and Kit switched ropes, working with the pulley system she'd rigged.

She pushed the body over the edge of the wall and Ham lowered it to the ledge.

Then she rappelled down, leaving her tech in the wall.

Ham and she carried the body to a bag Ham had brought down. They zipped him up and loaded him into the stretcher.

Kit sat on the ledge, her hand on her husband's form.

"The chopper will be back soon," Ham said, unrigging the ropes to coil them back up.

Orion had nothing. Because what then? He got to spend more time in rehab, then maybe return to his homestead to finish his current novel?

Add another addition on the house?

The thought settled like a fist in his gut. Shoot, but Jenny had awakened something inside him, given him a taste for more.

He didn't want to return to the woods.

Ham hunkered down beside him. "Okay. I guess I would have thought you might be happy to get out of this crevasse. Sorta makes me wonder if you had planned to set up a vacation home down here, or if I found the bat cave. What gives?"

Orion looked at him.

"You were the one who shouted, weren't you?"

It really wasn't a question.

Orion blew out a breath. "She fell. It . . . rattled me."

"Sounded like more than that . . . but good thing because we hadn't a clue where you were. If I hadn't heard you, we would have kept walking. By the time you attempted to climb out again, we might have been long gone."

Orion looked at him.

"So, I guess God even uses our darkest moments for good," Ham said.

"Okay, whatever. I was mad. You can't take everything and turn it into a God-is-on-your-team moment, Ham."

"Why not? He is . . . and maybe he brought you up on this mountain—"

"To wreck my life. Again."

Ham recoiled.

"Guess what, Chief. The person I've been wanting to find, the one who had all the answers about the ambush that killed Nickles and Dirk, the informant who lied, and the CIA brass who didn't care and sent us in anyway—Jenny."

Ham just blinked at him.

"Mmmhmm. She was the CIA analyst who made the call—"

"She hardly had the power to make the call, Ry. The Taliban strike was confirmed by drones and on-the-ground Ranger intel—"

"The Taliban set us up, and she should have seen it coming."

Ham cocked his head. "Aw, dude, that's a little . . . I mean, nobody can read minds."

"She's a profiler. That was her job."

Ham's mouth tightened around the edges.

Orion looked away. "It doesn't matter. Like she said. It doesn't change anything. I'm still angry. Now I just know who to be angry at."

"You sure you want that?"

Orion looked at him. "Want what?"

"To carry all that anger around inside you. It's like . . . it's like you drank poison but you expect the other person to die. You're the one who suffers."

It did feel a little that way.

"You're right. God did bring you up here, but maybe to show you that the turmoil inside you has nothing to do with blame. Or even what happened to you. It's about the fact that you didn't deserve it. You were innocent, and it happened to you anyway."

Orion breathed that in. Maybe. "I went in to help people, and . . ." He shook his head. "I don't get it. Why?"

"That's the answer you really want. Why did this horrible thing happen to you, to Dirk and Nickles and my guys, when we're the *good* guys. We didn't do anything wrong. If we're going to go down, at least it should be because we deserve it, right?"

"Yes, actually. Because if it's not, then it's either random and grossly unfair or . . . God really isn't on our side."

"Or he is."

Orion gave him a look.

"Consider what we go through at BUD/S. We are tested. Pushed. Tried. And made into men through our suffering."

"So, God wants me to become a better person? That's why he punishes me?"

"Or, he chooses you because he has amazing plans for you, but you need to walk through that fire first. You need to contend with the darkness in your heart, learn to forgive, and realize that it's not about you. It's about who you could—*will*—be. Because of your suffering. And because you came through it."

The radio burst to life. The chopper, returning. Ham got up and walked over to Kit. "Ready to go?"

Kit found her feet as the chopper lowered the litter down to the ledge. Then she and Ham dragged over the body and loaded it in.

Kit grabbed the top strap of her husband's backpack, attached herself to the rig, and Ham radioed her up.

Leaving him and Orion on the ledge.

"Consider this, bro. Jesus hung on the cross. In front of him, he had betrayers and accusers, and beside him, a murderer and a thief. He, however, was innocent. And yet he hung there and suffered because he knew the future. He knew it would save us. He looked out at that rabble and he said, 'Father, forgive them. For they know not what they do.'"

The litter started coming back down.

"God brought you up on this mountain not to betray you, but because you matter very much to him, Ry. He does not want you to stay in your anger, does not want you to hide from your calling. And if getting you to face your fears is what it takes—making you helpless and letting you discover he's still with you—then that's what he'll do. Even if you have to suffer."

Ham caught the litter and brought it to the ground.

"Yes, life is unfair, and we will always have people who will hurt us. Who don't know what they do. But God wants you to let him handle the justice . . . you just give him your heart. Because that's what he's really fighting for. He wants to wash it free from the anger and fill it with his love. The question is, are you brave enough to let go and give him your heart?"

Ham picked up his pack of gear. "God is contending for your heart. And so am I. Because neither of us are done with you yet,"

Ham came over and hooked his hands under Orion's shoulders.

"I can walk." Orion growled as Ham lifted him to his feet.

"Yeah, I know." Ham gripped him around the waist, helping him to the litter. "But it doesn't hurt you to have a little help. That's what teammates are for."

He settled Orion in the litter and strapped him in. Then he

knelt next to Orion and clipped his harness to the rig. "Let's get off this mountain."

Jake was waiting on the deck of the chopper as they rose, and he pulled the both of them in. Kit was strapped in, her husband's body on the floor next to her. Ham shut the door.

Then they were descending. Orion watched the peak rise, fall away as they swooped into Muldrow Glacier, then around the mountain to the Denali Base Camp.

Snow kicked up into a whiteout as they settled on the icy surface of the Kahiltna Glacier. The door opened, and for a crazy moment, he hoped that Jenny might be there, waiting.

Of course not.

Maybe he shouldn't blame her quite so much for that, because she was hurt—*really* hurt—and they'd probably already flown her off to the hospital in Anchorage.

Wait. Amidst the roar of the dying rotor wash, the wind that seared the mountain, and the shouts of rescuers, he heard her quiet voice.

"I had a nervous breakdown."

"I wish I'd been there in Germany when you woke up. I was already in trouble, or I would have been there."

Already in trouble.

Already having an emotional breakdown?

"I went to Afghanistan because I wanted to save lives."

Oh, Jenny. No wonder she'd wept so hard when he told her his story.

Weeping for him. For his buddies. For her mistakes.

Maybe she had a little PTSD too.

Just like that, his anger snapped free. Just released, like a whoosh from his body. And compassion into the empty places flooded.

Or maybe he'd call it love.

Jake and Ham had carried him out of the chopper like he was some kind of invalid, and the moment they set him down and released him, he sat up and held out his hands.

"What?" Jake said.

"Help me up, dude. Is Jenny still here?"

Jake grabbed his hand. "No. We sent her on a flight to Anchorage."

Ham too had helped him up. "Then find me a ride, bros, because you're right. God isn't quite done with me yet."

Jake raised an eyebrow.

Ham just grinned. "Oh good. This is my favorite part of the rescue."

Orion looped his arm over Ham's shoulder, letting him help him off the tarmac while Jake ran to find a pilot. "What part?"

"The part where my buddy comes to his senses and goes after the girl he's been crazy about for three years."

Orion grinned. "Yes. Yes it is."

CHAPTER FOURTEEN

J ENNY SAT in the padded chair of the ICU waiting area in the Anchorage Regional Hospital, a blanket around her shoulders, five stitches in her forehead, her arm in a sling—not sure if she'd really ever be warm again.

Even with Aria's endless supply of coffee from the sludge machine in the corner.

"I keep telling them I'll make a new pot," Aria said. "There's nothing worse than burned hospital coffee." She sat down next to Jenny, propping her crutch against the sofa.

Her ankle was badly sprained, but not broken, and the descent from Denali to Anchorage had cleared her lungs of any pulmonary edema.

Aria and Sasha had arrived nearly six hours before she had, and Sasha had been admitted right into the ICU.

Jenny's entire body ached, right down to her bones. Especially with the news of Sasha's cerebral edema.

And her pre-trip miscarriage.

"I wish she'd told me about the baby. And her trip to Florida. I could have . . ." Jenny stared into her coffee. "I'm so sorry I talked you into this nightmare."

"What? She wanted to go on the trip," Aria said. "We all did."

Aria wore a sweatshirt she'd purchased at the gift shop with a moose embroidered on the front, a pair of scrub pants, and her polar booties. She'd showered, too, her dark hair clean and in waves down her back. With the fading tan on her face, she looked like a woman just back from vacation in Cancun. "You didn't talk us into anything, Jen. We wanted to go. We're stronger than we think we are, right?"

Jenny had nothing. Because no. She was tired of being strong.

Tired of everything, really. Tired of holding on to secrets, thinking she could run from them. Tired of trying to control everything. Trying to save people.

Just . . . tired.

Aria reached out her hand. "We're okay. And Sasha is going to be okay. Lucas is in there with her, and you know how tenacious he is."

It seemed she was surrounded by tenacious men.

"You should have seen him when we arrived off the mountain. He walked right over to Sasha, picked her up, and carried her to the plane, all the while tears streaking down his face. He really loves her."

Of course Aria's words stirred up the image of Orion, weeping, the sound of the scream that lifted through the crevasse.

"He really loves her."

Well, Orion certainly didn't love her—and not that she expected him to, but . . .

She turned away to stare out the window. Ironically, Denali soared, uncluttered by clouds, free from the caprices of weather. White-capped, the granite shoulders spreading out as if trying to call her back to its embrace.

If she closed her eyes, she could easily find herself back in Orion's embrace, waking to the smell of him, listening to his breathing, calm and steady.

Or, perhaps with him under the stars in Afghanistan. *"My parents named me after the constellation because it was the brightest one in the sky. But I like to think it was because Orion was a hunter."*

Yes. A hunter of the lost.

He'd saved her, and she'd broken him.

No, he wouldn't love her. But as she drew up her knees on the sofa, she couldn't deny the truth.

She'd loved Orion for years. Being with him only reignited the longing he'd first stirred in her.

Orion was safety. She loved the way he measured his words, the way he assured her everything would be okay. And sure, he'd had a moment of unchecked emotion, but that only told her that inside his cool exterior was a man whose feelings ran deep.

The way he'd kissed her only confirmed it.

Orion might be ice on the outside, but inside was a man of heat and passion.

With everything inside her, Jenny wanted to be loved by Orion Starr.

In fact, she wanted it so much, it frightened her.

Don't fall in love. Because that's exactly when it will turn on you.

But it wasn't Orion's fault . . . she wouldn't love her, either.

A hand squeezed her arm and she opened her eyes. Aria nodded toward the door, and she looked over to see Lucas McGuire heading toward them.

She sat up, a fist in her chest. "What?"

"The swelling is going down and Sasha woke up."

He stood over them, radiating the intensity that made him a sought-after ER doc. Now, it felt a little like he was trying not to unravel.

"Lucas?" Aria said and made to get up.

He shook his head. Sat down. Folded his hands behind his neck and leaned his head forward.

Said nothing.

Only after a moment of his rattled breaths did Jenny realize he was crying.

Oh. Uh.

Aria scooted beside him and put her arm around her colleague.

Jenny's eyes filled too. "Lucas, I'm so sorry I put you through this."

He looked up at her then, his eyes reddened. "This isn't your fault, Jenny. If anything, it's mine. I shouldn't have taken her to Florida right before your trip. I know about altitude sickness. That was just . . . stupid." He shook his head and leaned back, running his hands through his hair, rucking it up. "It's a miracle that she's alive. God was watching out for you."

Jenny didn't see it quite that way, and maybe her frown told him that.

"If Orion and Ham and Jake hadn't been here, climbing. If Orion didn't know the mountain so well, I'm not sure we would have ever found you."

Jenny's throat tightened. "Or, I could have not taken them up the mountain."

Lucas shook his head. "That's not the answer. We don't stop living life just because bad things can, or will, happen. We just keep going forward, trusting in God's plan for us, even if bad things happen. God is still there, still in control. Still saving us. Still protecting us."

"And what about a plan that . . ." She made a face. "The one that causes us to suffer? Puts my friend in intensive care?"

"God doesn't guarantee that we won't have trouble, Jenny. But he does say that he is with us in our suffering. And ultimately he has a plan that, despite the hurt, can be used for our good."

She looked away. "I don't believe that."

Silence.

She looked at Aria, Lucas. "Hello. God blew us off the mountain!"

"He also *rescued* you off the mountain. He proved to you that even when you're stuck in a crevasse, he can find you. He can pull you free. Don't assign truth to experiences, or your faith to your feelings. You have to base everything on who God is. Good. Loving. Our rescuer."

"Even if people die? What if his plan includes *that*?"

Lucas looked at her, a quick tightening to his jaw. "Then it includes death. I see it all the time. But even in that, God is there, and it doesn't mean he loves us any less."

"Love doesn't cause pain."

"Who told you that lie?"

She frowned at Lucas.

"Because love causes all sorts of pain. It requires us to believe, and forgive, and put aside our own justice and our own desires. Love is painful . . . especially when you think you might lose that love. Or cause hurt to someone you love. Or even be required to love someone who has hurt you." He swallowed, his gaze casting out the door, toward intensive care. "But it's worth it. Love changes you. Love makes you brave. Love can change the world."

She just stared at him, trying to sort through his words.

"Jenny, what if God brought you—all three of you—up on that mountain because of his great love for you?"

"So we could *suffer*?"

"So you could confront your wounds. Your fears. So he could break you free of the shame that holds us—*all of us*—hostage."

"We're going to escape this mountain, and then . . . What if I followed you out of the woods and back to Minnesota?"

Orion's words burned through her, and she couldn't breathe.

"What if God lets us suffer so we can reach out to him for comfort and in that moment receive everything he wants for us? Freedom. Hope. Love. The things we *wouldn't* have if we didn't have him. He is just that relentless in his pursuit of your hearts. Maybe it's time you let him catch you."

Out the window, a plane landed on the runway in the field behind the hospital.

"What if he doesn't?" Jenny's question emerged in a whisper. "What if . . ."

"What if your sins feel so great, you feel you haven't earned the right to be forgiven? To start over?" When she looked at Lucas, it seemed he'd spoken from his own wrecked spaces.

She nodded.

"I've heard Sasha say that your past—who you were, what you did—is not going to stop the promises of God in your future. Promises to protect you. Save you. Love you."

Her eyes burned, tears filming. "Then why do I feel so broken?" She hadn't realized she'd spoken that aloud until Aria's hand slipped over hers.

"You've always felt broken," Aria said. "But usually, you're running so fast to keep away from the pain . . . now, you've been forced to stop and feel it."

She wiped her hand across her wet cheek. "Yeah, maybe. I was in such a hurry to get out of the hospital before, to put it all behind me. But I didn't, did I?"

"Clearly not. And I know you're in pain. But that's what happens when God does surgery on your heart. It's painful." Aria smiled. "But you *do* get a new heart."

She'd like one that didn't always destroy people's lives.

"God never said that healing wouldn't be painful. But, he is about making you whole, Jenny," Lucas said. "The more you fill up your hollow spaces with other things, the less you'll see God. Sometimes we have to be desperate to finally figure out he is all we have left. And he's enough."

How she wanted to believe him.

Lucas got up. "I booked a room for you two at the Summit Hotel and Spa, just down the road. If you want, I can call you an Uber."

"What about Sash?" Aria asked.

"I'll be here. And she's improving by the hour." He said it with the smallest of tentative smiles, as if leaning into hope.

Maybe God *had* brought her to the mountain to make her slow down, confront her past. Tell Orion the truth, once and for all.

At least one of them could be set free. Start over.

"I could sleep for a year," Aria said, getting up.

Jenny didn't move. "Did Orion and Ham make it out?"

Aria's expression fell. "I don't know."

Jenny drew in a shaky breath. Of course they had to have made it. "They might have taken Orion to a different hospital." She eased herself off the sofa. "And it's not like he'd want to see me."

"Why not?" Lucas said.

Aria frowned.

Oh. Um. "I told him the truth about my involvement in the ambush in Afghanistan. I was the one who vetted, and approved, the information that cost . . . well, that cost him his knee. And the others their freedom, and their lives." There, she said it aloud. Twice, even, and coming out the second time didn't feel quite so—

Okay, it felt just as brutal, just as raw and ugly. But at least she said it. And maybe she could just start . . . well, taking a look at it. Facing it.

Stop running from it.

"That wasn't your fault, Jenny."

The voice came from behind them, and she turned as Ham stalked into the room. He was sunburned, his blond beard shaggy, and he hadn't changed, still wearing his thermal shirt and a pair of overpants held up with suspenders over those powerful shoulders.

His dark eyes met hers, almost fierce. "That wasn't your fault."

She stilled.

"Orion told me what you said to him, and here's the truth. Evil always seeks to betray. To destroy and separate and instill fear. And, on that day, evil won. But that doesn't mean we surrender the battle. We will not dishonor those who paid the ultimate price for freedom by giving up. Evil wants to shut you down. Shame you. Destroy your relationships. Keep you from being the person you can be. Don't let it."

"But—"

He held up his hand. "Orion is going into surgery. I think he'd like to talk to you."

"I don't think so." She headed toward the door.

"Jenny!" Ham's voice boomed across the room.

"Tell him . . . that . . ." *I'm sorry.* She blinked hard against her tears. "Tell him goodbye."

She was practically running by the time she entered the hallway.

She nearly flattened the man in the wheelchair. He sat with his leg out straight, a barrier to her escape, and she jerked back to avoid hitting him. Tripped, and nearly fell.

But her arm trapped in a sling kept her from bracing herself, and to her horror, she fell hard into the man's lap even as his hands caught her around the waist.

"I'm sorry—I'm—"

"Jacie, stop."

The voice was so calm, so bracing, that she just stilled.

Orion wore a hospital gown that looked downright ridiculous on him, thin and flimsy against his wide shoulders, his thick arms. He stared up at her, and for a moment, she couldn't breathe, caught in the depths of his gaze.

"Orion," she said in a voice she didn't quite recognize.

He was unshaven, his hair askew, his eyes cracked and tired. But he didn't move, just kept holding her as if afraid she might bolt.

She had the crazy urge instead to throw her arm around his neck. "You made it."

"Just in time to catch you." He ran his hand down her unhurt arm. "Don't run away again." He swallowed, and her heart nearly stopped when he added a tiny, "Please?"

She had no words. Because last time she saw him, he couldn't look at her—oh, wait. Morphine. He had to be on drugs.

"Orion, I—"

"Jenny, I forgive you."

She looked away, shaking her head.

His voice emerged husky. "I forgive so much that I hurt for you. I know you feel like you . . . you caused men to die, and yes, maybe you made a mistake, but that's what it was—a mistake. And it wasn't your fault. You were played."

"My job is to not be played."

"It's over. It's so over. Please, let it be over." He pressed his palm to her cheek, his voice achingly soft. "I need it to be over."

His gaze held hers with such intensity she felt it to her bones and it turned her weak.

"Dude!" Jake came running down the hallway. "What's with the getaway? I leave you for five minutes to hit the head, and you decide to go for a joyride in your hospital skivvies?" He looked over at Jenny, then beyond. "Sorry, Ham."

Only then did she feel Ham's presence behind her.

Jake's words jerked her right out of the moment with Orion, the one where she wanted to believe him, and Lucas, and even Aria.

The one where she finally walked in forgiveness. Truth. Freedom.

"*I need it to be over.*"

Yes. Of course he did. They both did. She disentangled herself from Orion's grip. "Get better," she said, stepping back.

Jake grabbed Orion's wheelchair. "You have a date with an orthopedic surgeon."

His mouth tightened into a thin line, his gaze never leaving hers as Jake wheeled him away.

"*I need it to be over.*"

Yes, he deserved that, regardless of what it cost her.

If it was the last thing she could do for him, she'd let it be over. She headed for the elevators.

▧ ▧ ▧

Three years of pining for Orion Starr—and why not? The guy had hero written all over him, even in his blue-patterned hospital jammies—and Jenny was *walking away*?

Aria might even call it a flat-out run, especially in comparison to her pitiful one-armed, crutch-aided limp. "Jen!"

Jenny stood at the elevator, her good arm wrapped around her slung arm. As if barely holding herself together.

Sheesh, the guy had even said *please*. In this soft, ripped-from-his-soul voice. Aria's own knees had gone weak.

Maybe she was still suffering from AMS, her mind addled with the reality of their rescue. And the sight of Jake running down the hall. He, too, looked fresh in from the mountain, wearing his black shirt, his black overpants, hiking boots. His hair was matted, his dark blond beard in a tangle, and he was a thief for the way his presence reached out, took hold of her heart, and stole it from her chest.

She'd thought coming off the mountain might have cleared him from her mind. Her heart.

Her longings.

Not. A. Chance.

But clearly she'd not made the same impact on him because he barely looked at her as he wheeled Orion away.

Not missing her at all. It wasn't like it had been days, or months since he'd last seen her. Still, a smile, a nod—

Get over him. He wasn't her true love—just a guy she'd spent a couple days surviving with.

But Jenny—she'd loved Orion for years, and . . . "Stop, Jen. *Stop!*"

Jenny looked at her, her eyes watery.

"See, I knew it. You've lost your mind."

"Did you not hear him? He wants it to be over." The elevator dinged and the door opened.

Jenny stepped inside. Aria followed her. "So the answer is yes, then. You have lost your mind."

Jenny's mouth tightened around the edges. She stared up at the numbers.

"For a psychologist, you're incredibly dense."

Jenny looked away.

"Orion doesn't want you to *leave*—he wants the pain to be over. The past to be over."

Jenny flashed her a look. "Yes, he does, including the people who *caused* his pain." She pressed her hand to her chest. "Me."

"He is about to have surgery and he ditched his buddy to find you. To chase you down. Hello. Wake up and pay attention."

The door dinged open and Jenny stalked out into the lobby.

"Slow down. I can only limp so fast."

Jenny glanced at her. Slowed. Through the glass window overhead, sunlight streamed down onto the gray carpet of the lobby. Aria cut her voice low, so as not to drag everyone milling around into their business, but she was ready to throw down here.

She didn't know why Jenny's walking away from Orion bothered her so much, but how many times did the past give you a second chance?

"Jenny. You want it to be over too. You know it. You've been trying to figure out a way to put it behind you, and it keeps finding you. Sheesh, we traversed an entire mountain—both sides of it—and you still ran right into your nightmares. Lucas is right. What if God brought us—all of us—onto that mountain because he really does want to set us free? Isn't that what this trip was all about? Rising above the traumas that try to hold us hostage? And maybe we're *not* stronger than we think. But . . . what if God is? What if he makes us brave?"

"When did you get religious?"

"You know when. Summer camp, when I was fifteen. And now it's all coming back to me." She offered a smile. Gentled her words. "Love makes us brave. Maybe it's God's love. Maybe it's the love we have for each other. But can you stop running from the past, letting it control your future, and start running toward the man who loves you?"

"Orion doesn't love me."

"Oh my—if chasing you down half-naked in a hallway doesn't prove it—okay, how about this, do you love *him*?"

Jenny drew in a breath.

"I should add, do you *still* love him. Because I'm your best friend and I know he's the one who got away."

Jenny ran her hand over her cheek. The elevator opened behind them, and Jenny looked up, then back to Aria.

"What if I . . . what if . . . I don't want to hurt him again?"

"No. *You* don't want to get hurt again. That's what this is about . . . believing in someone, giving away your heart for good. See, in Afghanistan, it was easy. Short-term. Someday you'd leave. Or he would. So you never had to end it. But now . . . now it could be real. And here you are, running."

Jenny drew in a shaky breath.

"Heart surgeon," Aria said. "We understand broken hearts."

Jenny offered a shaky smile.

"Be brave, Jen. Be the woman who just climbed Denali and survived. Be the woman who survived a nervous breakdown. Be the woman who helps people face their own brokenness every day. Orion needs you—"

"He doesn't need me. He's been alone for a long time—"

"The poor man climbed a mountain to find you!" Aria held up her hand, trying to school her voice.

"It's time for him to stop hiding, and he knows it."

She looked over and Ham strode up, right into their conflict. But maybe that's what he did, got involved in other people's crises.

"You should know that the one thing that kept Orion going in that cave back in Afghanistan was the thought of seeing you." Ham folded his arms over his chest, his legs apart, as if a wall of defense for his buddy. No wonder people looked to him for rescue. "He actually told me that his one regret was not kissing you."

"Really," Aria said and pinned Jenny with a look. "That sounds familiar."

Jenny's face reddened. She leaned close to Aria. "We kissed, okay?"

"When?"

Jenny glanced at Ham, who was clearly hearing their conversation. "In the crevasse."

"And?"

"What, are we thirteen?"

"Mmmhmm." Aria grinned.

"Yeah, it was worth the wait, but . . . we were stressed and scared and . . ."

"That dog," Ham said, smirking.

Jenny gave him a look.

"Listen," Ham said. "Orion didn't die that day in the cave. He woke up in the hospital in Germany—angry, alone, and hurting. Don't do that to him again. What if this time, you were there?"

Exactly what Aria had been trying to say, thank you. "Be brave, Jen. Love when it hurts. When it's scary. When you're not sure what the future might be. Love because you're definitely stronger than you think you are and it's a mountain still waiting to be climbed."

Aria could almost see Jenny's inner adventurer rising to the challenge.

Jenny looked at Ham.

"C'mon," he said. "I'll wait with you." He headed back to the elevator, and Jenny followed.

Aria was turning to join them when she spotted Jake leaning against the elevator wall, his arms akimbo, a smirk on his face. He reached down and pushed the button, his gaze never leaving hers.

The doors opened and Ham and Jenny got on. But Jake didn't move.

"Nice bedside speech, Hot Lips."

He looked amazing—the rake of his whiskers framing his renegade smile, those pale blue eyes pinned on hers, something unreadable in them.

"You made it off the mountain," she said, nearly a whisper. Except, inside she wanted more. *Did you miss me?*

"Caught an Uber," he said, still smiling.

Calm down, Aria. The guy was heartbreak waiting to happen. Jake was charm and fun and flirt, and Aria had a life back home that had no room for anything but work.

But here . . . in Alaska . . . She pushed aside Aria's warnings and found a Kia smile. "Are you stalking me? First, Denali, and now the hospital lobby. What's next? Are you going to turn up in my operating room?"

"Not unless I have a broken heart, right?" Then he winked.

She was the one liable to end up in surgery.

"Have you eaten anything?" her mouth asked while her brains berated her.

"Starved. I could eat a moose." His gaze flicked down to her sweatshirt. "I need a shower first."

"Lucas got us a room at the Summit. You can use my shower." *Hello? What are you doing?*

He raised an eyebrow.

She swallowed. Right. "I could order a pizza . . ."

Oh *my.*

"I left my pack upstairs. Let me grab it." He turned and pushed the elevator button.

Oh good. Maybe now she could come to her senses. Put the brakes on whatever might be happening here.

"Be back in a jiff. Don't get into any trouble while I'm gone."

She offered a thin laugh.

The doors closed behind him.

She'd turned into a person she didn't know, because suddenly she had a slew of crazy troublemaking ideas, the kind that had Aria running for the hills.

But Kia . . .

Love is brave.

Yes, but it didn't mean it was *stupid*. It didn't mean she threw away everything she believed in, had pledged to herself.

The elevator dinged open and she turned to see Jake walking out with his pack over his shoulders. He came over to her. He smelled good, despite his need for a shower. Husky, wild. Rough.

His smile was pure charm. "Ready to get out of here?"

She caught her lower lip in her mouth. His gaze tracked to it, then he touched her face with his hand. It sent a fire through her entire body, seared the thoughts from her brain. He caressed her face with his thumb. "You are so beautiful, Houlihan."

Oh.

Then he kissed her. Sweetly. Lightly, just a whisper over her lips, a hint of what might be waiting for them—

No—*no*—

He backed away, meeting her eyes. "You sure you . . . want . . . pizza?"

She let out a breath.

Nodded.

He smiled then, and it ignited everything but her common sense. Then, with one move, he picked her up into his arms, grabbed her crutch, and headed for the door.

She looped her arms around his neck, leaned into his embrace, and let him carry her away.

■ ■ ■

Jenny wasn't here.

Orion had been in and out for the better part of an hour, grappling toward consciousness, only for his grip to slip, for him to fall back into the dark pocket of slumber.

He'd finally clawed himself free, into the light of the day—or night—he hadn't a clue what time it might be. Just sunshine flooding into his room from the big picture window. Outside, Denali loomed, half-shrouded with an encroaching cloud.

Goodbye, Mountain. Because if he had a choice, he'd never climb it again.

Not even Ham or Jake had stuck around to see him out of surgery, and it stung.

Not that he needed anyone to hold his hand, for Pete's sake. But he'd settled into the idea of teamwork, cohorts on the mountain, and he . . . he longed for it.

Shoot, he wanted all of it. The new life Ham offered him on his team.

A fresh mission.

Jenny.

He lay back in his pillows. He really thought he'd see her at his bedside. Especially since he'd made a fool out of himself in the middle of the hallway. *"Don't run away again. Please?"*

He sounded pitiful and desperate.

Oxygen filled his nostrils from the cannula, and an IV ran into his arm, stretching out as he reached for a glass of water on his bedside stand.

"I need it to be over."

He'd thought his words had found her heart, dug in. Thought he saw the right answer in her eyes. He took another drink, then set the glass back on the table.

Well, just because she kept running didn't mean he had to keep hiding. As soon as he got on his feet again, he'd show up on Ham's doorstep. Because his friend was right. If God was contending for his heart—answering his prayers, setting him free—then Orion would do the same.

He wasn't done with himself yet, either.

Jenny, I'm coming for you.

The door to his room opened.

"Aw, you're awake. I just *knew* you'd wake up when I wasn't here." Jenny came into the room. She'd taken off her sling and wore a thermal shirt and a pair of yoga pants with University of Alaska down the side. Her hair was still wet, air drying in sleek blonde layers. No makeup, her lashes dark against her reverse-raccoon eyes, a sunburn on her nose, her mouth lifting up in a smile.

He might need resuscitation.

She came over and set a cup of coffee on his tray. "Decaf, but it's warm, and you were dreaming of coffee, so . . ." She lifted her good shoulder. "How do you feel?"

Like he'd left his body. "What—I thought—you're here."

Her smile fell. "I, uh . . ."

He reached out for her hand. "You're *here.*"

She made a funny noise, and nodded. Her eyes glistened as she sat on the bed. "I couldn't let you wake up alone."

He wove his fingers through hers. "I never want to wake up alone again."

Her eyes widened. And he didn't care that his words sounded like some crazy long-term commitment. Like he wanted her in his life forever.

Because, frankly, that wasn't long enough.

"Are you really here, or am I on drugs?"

"You're on drugs. And I'm really here." She laughed, and he let go of the last of his reserves and pulled her to himself, kissing that smile, that laughter. She tasted of coffee, of sunshine, of fresh starts.

Of wholeness.

She'd braced her hand on his pillow and her hair fell around him, a curtain of gold, as she kissed him back.

Jenny.

He wove his fingers into her silky wet hair.

It struck him that God hadn't only brought him to the mountain to set him free and make him whole, but . . . to show him his great love, just like Ham said. Because God had given him this moment.

And please, oh please, many, many more just like this.

Orion drank her in, letting go, love sweeping over him. So much that it caught him up, stole his breath.

She must have felt the rush inside him because she leaned back. "Are you okay?"

More okay than he'd been in . . . well, he couldn't remember when. "I love you, Jenny. I should have told you that before I left . . . before . . ." He shook his head. It didn't matter anymore.

"You should be wearing your sling."

"I'm fine, and stop being so bossy." She touched his face, her fingers in his beard, the other arm close to her body. Then she leaned forward and kissed him.

Okay, then. He wrapped his arms around her, pulled her tight against him, raking up the memory of holding her in his arms in the bivouac. She belonged with him, regardless of what name she called herself.

He wanted to call her his.

He knew it sounded like he might be some barbarian from the woods, but she'd rescued him as much as he'd rescued her, and he'd willingly hand over himself to belong to her too.

She eased back, caressing his lips with her thumb, meeting his eyes. "I love you too. And I'm so sorry I ran from you."

He touched his forehead to hers, fighting a rim of tears. "No more running."

"No more hiding."

"No more anger."

"Let it be over." She leaned back. "I want a future with you, Ry. And with everything inside me, I'm trying to be brave. To stop being afraid of the past."

Her words found his heart. "Yeah," he said. "I've lived with this anger so long, I'm not sure how to let it go."

She touched his chest. "I was thinking about something that Ham said."

Oh boy.

"He said that evil wants to shut us down. Keep us from being the person we are supposed to be." She drew in a breath. "I'm not strong. Or brave, really. When I had my nervous breakdown, it scared me. I never thought I was fragile, but suddenly, my life seemed to be shattering. The betrayal—and the cost—took me apart. I felt violated and ashamed and I had nothing to hold on to. Inside my head, I just kept screaming. But it didn't help. It just scared me more. And since then, I've been running hard away from the screaming."

She blew out a breath. "I've never told anyone that."

"Feels good, doesn't it?"

She nodded. "Big, actually. Healing."

Healing. He took her other hand. Met her eyes for a second, then closed his. "God, you did this thing. And we want to trust you for the rest. Forgive us for our anger and our fear. Take over our lives and contend for our hearts so they belong to you alone."

"And each other," Jenny whispered.

He drew in a full, free breath and opened his eyes. "And each other." Slipping his hand around her neck again, he pressed his mouth to hers.

Aw, she tasted like hope.

He let her go and met her eyes. "I promise to contend for your heart, Jenny."

She blinked at him, then nodded. "And I will contend for yours."

"That's an amen if I've ever heard one."

Orion let her go and looked over Jenny's shoulder. "Geez, Ham, knock much?"

"I told you I'd get you praying." Ham set a bag on his bedside table. "Good morning. I grabbed you a chocolate-covered donut. It's one of the team perks—fresh donuts at staff meetings."

Jenny grabbed the bag and peeked inside. "Two?"

"This offer is for you, too, Jenny." Ham crossed to the other side of the bed. "We need a profiler, someone who can assess the minds of the people we are working with, as well as the people we're trying to save."

She pulled out a donut, handed it to Orion. Licked her fingers. "I'll think about it."

"You'll get to work with Orion."

"I didn't agree to join your team yet," Orion said.

"Yeah, you did. You just didn't say it out loud." Ham walked over to the door. "I got someone out in the hall who needs to talk to you." His expression turned solemn, and his gaze flicked over to Jenny.

Huh?

Orion gave his head a tiny shake as Jenny dove into the bag for the next donut.

Ham lifted a shoulder and opened the door. "He's a little high, Senator, but glad to see you."

Senator?

Jenny got off his bed, maybe seeing Orion's reaction, the way he sat up, straightened his covers.

The silver-haired, former-SEAL, Clooney-lookalike Montana senator walked into the room. He was dressed down for the day in a leather jacket and a pair of jeans. "Orion Starr." He reached out his hand.

"Senator White. What are you . . ." Orion cast a look at Ham, back to the senator. "Doing here?"

"I have a rally later this morning, then I'm on my way to San Diego for the national conference. But your rescue made the morning's paper."

So, it was morning.

"And I wanted to catch up with you about . . ." He glanced at Jenny.

"She knows about Royal. She was . . . she was there. Senator, this is Jenny Calhoun. Former CIA profiler. She worked with us in Afghanistan." He looked at her. "In fact, she was instrumental in the planning of our mission." He said it without indictment and she offered him a small smile, then turned to the senator.

Jenny shook his hand. "Nice to meet you, sir. What is this about Royal?"

"I did some digging. After Petty Officer Benjamin was liberated, he was invited to . . . join another team."

Orion read between the lines. Black ops, wet work. Something the CIA didn't want known. "And what better than a guy who is already listed as dead."

"But as you know, neither Logan Thorne or Royal Benjamin were dead. You already know Thorne's story—"

"He said the CIA was trying to force him into working for them, so they set him up to take the fall for a Pakistani diplomat," Orion said. "And I have to believe him. The CIA tends to play games with our lives. Which means maybe Royal was forced into covert ops."

Jenny wrapped her arms around herself, her mouth tight around the edges.

"My office is looking into those allegations, but for now Thorne is safe."

Behind him, Ham let out a long breath. So he'd been worried too.

SUSAN MAY WARREN

"As for Royal, my office is following a lead about a rogue group who are behind the bombing a couple months ago in Texas and are apparently trying to affect the presidential election. One of our CIA informants relayed to me information through a contact in Eastern Europe who heard about a possible assassination attempt on a Russian leader. He was thinking that contact might be your guy."

"Why?"

"His code name is Roy."

Orion shook his head.

"As in Royal?"

Huh.

"I just wanted to let you know I hadn't forgotten you." Senator White held out his hand again. Orion shook it, then he turned to Jenny. "Nice to meet you too, Jenny."

Ham opened the door. "Sir, did you ever track down that bomber from New York City?"

The senator shook his head. "But we have good security, Ham." He clamped him on the shoulder. "However, I'm having a little soiree at the Summit Hotel after the rally today, if you and your team want to show up. We can always use extra eyes. You know what they say—if you see something, say something."

"Yes, sir."

He glanced at Jenny, then Orion. "And, I'd appreciate your votes, if I'm chosen to represent the party this weekend."

"You got it, sir," Ham said as the senator left.

"You know Senator White?" Jenny asked as the door closed behind him.

"Ham does."

"I served with him for a very short time over a decade ago." Ham leaned against the wall. "I don't like that they never found the guy."

"What guy?" Jenny asked.

"A couple months ago, I was in New York City and we happened to run across a guy who we think might have been a bomber," Orion said. "He showed up at a rally and left a backpack bomb behind. It never went off."

"Thankfully," Ham said. "Who would want to kill White? He was a patriot. Served his country. Was shot—he's the kind of guy I'd want in charge."

"I'd like to go to the reception," Jenny said. "Hear what he has to say. I'm all for a safer, smarter, stronger America. Maybe he's the future."

Orion tugged her back to his bedside. He didn't care where his future was going, as long as she was in it. "Take a hike, Ham. Staff meeting is over."

Ham grinned. "Welcome to the team, Starr."

Orion drew Jenny down against him. And, for the first time in weeks—no, maybe years—he was no longer cold.

CHAPTER FIFTEEN

HE JUST MIGHT BE in love.

Okay, maybe he was fast-forwarding, but Jake could very easily fall in love with Aria Sinclair.

The thought wasn't quite as terrifying as he thought it might be. Love. Commitment. Knowing someone, and letting her know him, too.

At least the guy he was trying very, *very* hard to be.

Jake lay back against the edge of the sofa, propped against a king pillow in the double executive suite of the Summit Hotel overlooking downtown Anchorage. Light spilled into the room, over the gold carpet, and across the makeshift camp he'd made on the floor of the living room area with the duvet and pillows from the king bed. The room service tray of their pizza ordered last night sat near the door.

A rerun of *M*A*S*H* that he'd found on the cable TV lineup played on the flat screen, but he really only heard the shower going in the next room, his heartbeat on overdrive.

What was he *doing*?

He'd made it all the way to morning without being stupid. All the way to morning, even with Doc Sinclair in his arms, before he'd let his mind go to . . .

No, *return* to the thoughts he'd had when she'd let him into her room last night.

In truth, panic had him around the throat. Panic and desire and the fear that he was about to do something he'd regret.

Last night, pizza had saved him. That and his brilliant idea to take the blanket off the bed, grab the pillows, and set up base camp in the area in front of the television.

He should have expected that she'd drop off, still clothed, exhaustion taking her down. He'd watched her in the dim light until he found himself waking next to her, the television still playing.

She rolled over onto her side, smiling at him, those beautiful doe-brown eyes in his. "Mornin', Hawkeye."

Really, he shouldn't panic. Because a woman like Doc Sinclair wouldn't actually . . .

"I'm taking a shower, if you want to stick around. You can use it after me."

Then she'd smiled, something in her eyes that looked very much like . . .

Yikes.

He should probably leave.

But her words and the way she hadn't locked the bathroom door had paralyzed him and all he could think about was . . .

Don't go in there.

Of course, don't go in there.

But, she'd sounded like . . .

No. No, it didn't matter what she made it sound like. Or that he'd lost his mind a little when she looked at him with those eyes, almost hero worship in them.

Oh boy. He ran his hand through his sleep-tousled hair.

The door opened.

And his world stopped. Aria stood there in a bathrobe, her dark hair down and glistening, looking so pretty, so amazingly tempting he couldn't think. She came out and hooked her hand on the doorway to the room.

"It's your turn," she said quietly.

He really didn't want to read what he thought he saw in her eyes. Because suddenly his body was working again and he was on his feet, walking over to her.

"My turn," he said softly, almost a groan.

"For the shower."

And he heard a voice in his head. *No. I'll get my own room, my own shower, thanks.*

Except that wasn't the voice that emerged. In fact, nothing emerged except the deep breath that made him draw in her fragrance, the fact that her skin was still wet, and almost without thinking, he reached up and traced a droplet of water trickling down her beautiful face.

Then, he kissed her.

Oh *no*, he kissed her.

He heard the sirens, felt the crashing around him of everything he'd told himself he wouldn't do, and he might have been able to walk away if she hadn't made that little sound in the back of her throat and wound her arms up around his neck.

He was too aware of the flimsy material between them, too aware of his feeble efforts to slow them down, to *not* wrap his arms around her waist and pull her to himself, to not inhale her as if she might be the first real nourishment he'd had in . . .

No. She was nothing like anything he'd experienced before and—

And he was going to destroy it.

317

He leaned away, his breath ragged, his heart a hammer in his chest. "Um, I—"

It wasn't her fault. But once she started kissing him, it was a little like trying to hold back the sunrise. The more he kissed her, the more his body would turn molten, the more he would ignore the voices in his head.

She ran her fingers through his beard, her mouth tipping up. "Skipping the shower, then?"

He nodded. Because maybe, just maybe, what they'd started on the mountain they might continue here on earth.

Continue, not end.

Still, "Are you . . . sure?" he asked softly.

No. *No.* What he really wanted to say was, *Aria, I'm a little bit crazy about you, and I don't want to blow it. Please . . . help me back up . . . help me—* Because he couldn't be the guy who took the wrong shot again.

But she nodded, offered a tentative smile. "Are you?"

"Oh, honey."

She grinned, and the tight hold of panic around his heart loosed. See, this didn't have to be a bad thing. It wasn't like this was the last time he would see her. She lived in Minneapolis.

This could be easy.

Could be something real.

He braced his hand on the door frame and lowered his mouth to hers again. Silenced the voices in his head and listened to desires.

Listened to the way she relaxed in his arms.

Aria— He reached for the belt of her robe.

The click of the door opening registered in the back of his mind, somewhere, but he was already unhinging his heart, stepping into a place of no return when—

"What is going on?"

Aria pushed him away so fast he nearly tripped over the sofa.

Jenny stood at the entrance to the room, her mouth open. Blinking at him.

And of course, that's when he realized that he was shirtless, wearing only his thermal underwear.

Barefoot.

Okay, that probably didn't matter, not the way Jenny was staring at him, her eyes widening by the second as she took him in, then looked at Aria.

Who paled right before his eyes.

She looked at Jenny. Then at Jake. Back to Jenny.

Then in a move that took out his soul, Aria clutched her robe around her, turned, and practically sprinted back to the bathroom.

The lock turned.

Silence dropped into the room with the weight of a sledgehammer. His heart thundered against his ribs and he didn't know whether to run to the bathroom and pound on the door, or . . .

"Jake—" Jenny started.

"Nothing happened." He glanced at the campout in the living room and suddenly wished he'd cleaned it up.

"Oh. *Really*. Funny but it looked completely opposite to *nothing* just a second ago." She walked into the bedroom, near the bathroom door. "Aria, are you okay?"

It was the way she asked, as if Aria might have a reason *not* to be okay, that made him feel like a jerk. No, *more* of a jerk.

"Why wouldn't she be?" he said, nearly snapping at her. But he noticed that the door to the bathroom didn't open.

Aria didn't answer her.

What—?

Jenny's mouth tightened into a bud that looked very much like anger.

What on earth? Okay, he got it. Girlfriends were protective of each other. But Aria was a grown woman. A doctor, for Pete's sake.

Still, Jenny was staring at him, her gaze running from his chest, down to his feet, and back up, her eyes pinning him with something that looked like accusation.

And in his gut, he knew he'd screwed up, and bad.

Yes, regardless of Aria's behavior, he should have put on the brakes.

Jake pressed his hand on his bare chest, feeling his heartbeat, the tender cracks that had started to open.

"I think you should leave," Jenny said quietly.

"I . . ." But what could he say? That Aria invited him in? That she was all yes a few moments ago? That he'd asked . . .

It didn't matter. It wasn't about what had or hadn't happened, but what was *about* to happen.

And what had been *already* happening, in vivid color, in his head.

He hadn't a hope of being the kind of guy that Aria really deserved.

Now a terrible dark heat filled his chest, thickened his throat. "I . . . care for—"

"Get out."

He recoiled at Jenny's tone.

She schooled her voice. "Sorry. But . . . you need to leave, Jake."

He wasn't sure what was going on here, but he knew without a doubt that he'd somehow destroyed whatever it was he'd wanted to start.

"Sorry," he said quietly and strode over to pick up his overpants, to shuck them on, slide his bare feet into his boots. He grabbed his socks and his pack, slipping it over one shoulder.

He picked up his jacket. Paused. "Aria—"

"Just go, Jake," Jenny said softly.

He drew in a breath, paused, then shook his head and strode for the door.

Jenny closed it behind him.

Locked it.

He felt like a felon. Or an abuser. Or . . .

Just a shallow jerk who'd traded something good and real for . . .

For something that wasn't in his heart at all.

Wow, what was his problem that he always screwed up the good things in his life?

He wanted to throw his pack down the hall, let out the curse filling his chest. Instead, he stalked to the elevator and punched the button.

Fishing through the pack's side pocket, he pulled out his cell phone. He hadn't turned it on for nearly three weeks, but the battery was still full.

He speed-dialed Ham.

To his shock, Ham picked up. "Where are you?"

"At the Summit Hotel."

Ham didn't even ask why. "Great. We are too."

The elevator doors opened. "We?"

"Orion checked himself out of the hospital."

"Is that safe?"

"You've met him, right? He's fine. We're cleaning up. Senator White is in town. We're going to a reception at the hotel."

Huh. Small world. Jake punched the ground-floor button.

"Clean up and meet us."

He didn't want to ask if Jenny might be joining them. That would be a fun conversation. "Aye aye, Chief." He hung up.

The doors opened and he walked out into the lobby and immediately felt like a hobo in his grimy pants and shirt.

He should have picked up a clean pair of jeans, a shirt, but he'd been in a hurry to . . .

Shoot. His only clean clothes were in Ham's truck back in the town of Copper Mountain.

His dark mood must have bled through because the woman at the front desk shot him a couple extra smiles, maybe to nudge the growl from his face. Or perhaps to ease his pain when she told him they were running behind on clean rooms. "You're welcome to wait in the bar and lounge," she said. "We can call you when a room opens up."

Perfect.

He hauled his pack up to the second-floor lounge and propped it against the bar. Climbed onto a high-top stool. A baseball game played on the flat screen. The bar overlooked the open lobby, and from where he sat, he could see the stairs that wound up to the second floor.

He may or may not catch up with Ham and Orion when he saw them.

"What'll you have?" the bartender, an old sourdough with lines in his face, asked.

And for the first time in years, Jake skipped right over *I don't drink* and ordered a whiskey.

If he was going to be the guy everybody hated, he might as well live up to his reputation.

■ ■ ■

Well, she hadn't seen that coming. Jenny sat on the bed in Aria's room, her arms folded, staring at the locked bathroom door, trying to find words.

Okay, so she hadn't spent much time with Jake. She didn't exactly know what kind of man he was, but . . . but an honorable guy didn't take advantage of a tired, injured woman who may or may not be under the influence of painkillers.

Aria didn't exactly have a history of taking men home.

Ever.

"Aria? You okay in there?"

Silence.

"Ari, he's gone. Come out, let's talk." Jenny drew in a breath. "Did he . . . was . . . he didn't . . ." For Pete's sake. She was a trained psychologist. She knew how to talk to women who'd felt pressured into . . . well, whatever had happened here.

"Honey, you're safe here. And no judgment. Just come out. I need to know if you're okay."

"I'm okay." The voice emerged stronger than Jenny would have thought given Aria's reaction to her sudden arrival.

Maybe she didn't know Aria as well as she thought.

No, that didn't make sense. She'd known Aria since they'd roomed together at the University of Minnesota.

"Sweetie, I know this isn't normal behavior for you, and I just need to know . . . um . . . just . . ."

"I'm okay!" The door opened, and Aria stood in the frame, fully dressed, her hair up in a ponytail. No makeup, her expression a little fierce. "I knew exactly what I was doing when I invited Jake back here, so in case you're wondering if I've taken leave of my senses, no."

"Then why did you—"

"Hide in the bathroom?" She came out and brushed past Jenny, yanking up the duvet from the floor and dragging it to the bed. "I don't know. Reflexes, I guess. So many years telling myself to wait—" She shook her head. "I was just tired of waiting."

Jenny stepped back as Aria arranged the duvet on the bed. "Okay."

"I've spent my entire life waiting. First for a heart, and then love. And I don't know what to call the spark between me and Jake, it just feels like maybe I shouldn't listen to my head and let my heart have a little fun."

"Fun? That's what you're calling this? Really?"

Aria picked up a king pillow and chucked it onto the bed. "Yep. That's what I'm calling it."

Okay, no, she didn't know *this* woman. "Aria, you're the one who always told me that you are worth waiting for—"

"It's no big deal. Like you said, this isn't church camp. We're all grown-ups here."

That shut Jenny down for a full moment. That and the sheen of moisture in Aria's eyes. "It would have been a big deal—"

"What happens in Alaska stays in Alaska."

A knock came at the door and Aria stalked past her to open it.

For a moment, Jenny feared it might be Jake. But he looked so stricken when he fled she doubted she'd see him again.

Feared that Aria wouldn't either.

"Do you want maid service?" asked a uniformed housekeeper in the hallway.

"Later," Aria said. "Thank you." She closed the door. Stood with her hand pressed to the door.

"You know that's not true, right?" Jenny said.

Aria turned and frowned at her.

"That saying. What you do *does* follow you."

"It doesn't have to." Aria shook her head and walked over to the coffeemaker. "I've been saying that to you for years."

Jenny drew a breath, not sure how to respond.

Aria filled the pot with water. "Want some coffee?"

Jenny shook her head, mute.

"Fine." Aria filled the machine and set the coffee to drip.

Silence fell as the coffeemaker gurgled.

Finally, "Okay, fine. Of course it's a big deal, but for the record, I was the one who invited him back here. And he . . . well, I promise he wasn't the instigator. I was the one who walked out in a robe. He even asked me if I was sure."

"And were you?"

Aria lifted a shoulder. "Yes." She paused. "Maybe. I don't know."

Jenny said nothing.

"I . . . I think I could be in love with Jake. Which I know sounds crazy, but he's charming and brave and sacrificial and . . ." She looked up at Jenny. "I wanted him to want me. Aria. But I always think too much. I get in my own way. So, I thought maybe if I could do what Kia would do, maybe that would be better. She was brave."

Oh, Aria. "Honey. You don't need Kia to be brave. And, you are perfect the way you are." Jenny walked over to her. "Listen. I get it. It was a traumatic week, and Jake . . . he saved you . . ."

"I totally embarrassed myself." She grabbed a mug and filled it with coffee. "It was probably good you came in when you did. Imagine what a guy like Jake would have thought when he found out it was my first time." She turned, offered a half-smile. "You saved me, roomie." She took a sip of the coffee. "I need to leave Alaska and get back to my real life."

"Okay, listen. Jake . . . he lives in Minnesota, right? So maybe—"

"I don't want to see Jake again."

"Why?"

A pause. "I'm so embarrassed." She set her cup down. "I'm not that woman, except now Jake probably thinks I am and . . ." She looked away, her eyes filling. "What was I thinking?"

Jenny had no words.

Aria shook her head, swiped her hand across her cheek. "Listen, really. I'm okay. But . . . no. I don't want to see Jake ever again. I just want to go home."

"Um, okay. Book us flights. I need to talk to Orion—he's going to this political reception. Then I'll be back up."

"No. I need to be alone. Go to the party. I'll book my own flight." She offered a smile. "Just because I was stupid doesn't mean you are. Orion is a great guy. What you see is what you get with him. You can trust him with your heart, Jen."

"I promise to contend for your heart, Jenny."

Yes, yes she could.

She drew Aria into an embrace, then got up, retrieved her bag of clothes, and went to her suite.

Ham had bought her a little black dress, leggings, and flats. It felt a little weird to be standing in the department store with him. To let him purchase something for her.

But she'd left her wallet back in storage in Copper Mountain.

Besides, he also bought Orion a pair of pants and a clean shirt.

Ham had called it a work expense. Whatever. But the idea sank inside her as she brushed out her hair. Join Ham's search and rescue team? He'd told her about it as they left the hospital.

An international team that answered the call of the desperate and lost.

She couldn't deny the nudge inside her to say yes. Work with Orion.

Help the world.

She pulled on the leggings, slid on the dress, and slipped her feet into the flats. Nothing fancy, but it would do. She didn't know why Ham and Orion had jumped so fast on her suggestion of going to the reception, but she didn't hate hearing what

Isaac White had to say. She wasn't invested in politics, but she did want a safer world.

Aria's door was closed as she exited her room and left the suite.

She took the elevator down onto the second floor, where the mezzanine overlooked the lobby. A small crowd spilled out of open doors to a reception room. Waiters wandered in and around the crowd, carrying champagne and hors d'oeuvres. Her stomach growled.

She spied Ham standing by the door, talking with Senator White. Ham had cleaned up well in a white oxford, the sleeves rolled up over his strong forearms. A climber's tan seasoned his face, but he'd shaved and looked every inch the former Navy SEAL in his bearing. Not unlike the senator. But maybe that kind of stress and combat made for wider shoulders. A cool head. The impression that he wouldn't let people down.

Good qualities for a president.

Then Orion appeared. He wore a blue button down and a pair of black trousers and leaned on his crutches. The fact that he'd checked himself out AMA had sent a thread of panic through her, but he'd been down this road before.

Trust me, he'd said as Ham had retrieved his clothes, those green eyes in hers.

Fine. Okay. Yes.

He had shaved, too, and now smiled as White said something to him. It lit up his entire face.

Oh, he was a handsome man. The memory of being in his arms, of kissing him, spilled through her, lit a fire in her bones.

She understood Aria too well.

Then Orion glanced over and spotted her. And if she thought he was smiling before, his entire countenance changed.

She did that to this man. It took her breath away.

So maybe they had a real chance at that happy ending.

A waiter bumped into her, walking past her as if he didn't see her, and nearly knocked her over.

"Oh!" She tripped and he turned, catching her before she fell. Her hand fell on his chest as she righted herself. White, midtwenties, clean cut, his hair nearly military short, and he bore a hint of an accent, something East Coast—when he said, "Sorry, ma'am. Are you okay?"

"Yeah."

He offered a quick smile, and she noticed a line of sweat along his brow.

She stepped back, straightened her dress. "Thank you."

"Sorry again." He strode away.

When she turned again toward Orion, he was already halfway to her. "You okay?"

"He just bumped into me. I'm fine."

Orion came right up to her, leaned on his crutches, and took her hands. "You clean up well."

"You're not so bad yourself, PJ." She touched his chest.

Wait. Something about his chest . . .

She searched and found the waiter and spotted him just disappearing into the room.

"What's the matter?"

"Nothing. Just . . . I don't know. It sorta felt like that waiter had a bulletproof vest on."

"He might be undercover security."

"Mmmhmm." She lifted her face and leaned into Orion. "You smell good."

"Just soap, honey. You've been stuck with me too long in the ice." He leaned down and kissed her, sweetly, just barely lingering.

"But I'm thawing fast," she said.

He laughed. "I gotta hit the head. Save me a spot in there." He kissed her forehead and walked away.

She let herself watch the way he handled himself, even with the crutches. Yes, there was the man she knew in Afghanistan. Confident. Charming. Capable.

Hers.

The senator had entered the room, but Ham was waiting by the door. "Hey." He looked past her. "Is Aria coming?"

Jenny shook her head, hoping for a benign face.

"I should probably be in the sack, snatching some z's, but I love listening to Isaac. Even when he was on the teams, he'd give us some rousing pre-mission speeches."

He turned and gestured for her to enter. Nothing but cocktail tables inside the room, standing room only, and country music played on the overhead speakers. No dais, so apparently the senator was going to keep this casual. He was glad-handing his way around the room.

"Something to drink?"

"Water. And one of those yummy-looking cream puffs."

Her gaze cast around the crowd as Ham went to retrieve her order.

The waiter from earlier was carrying a tray of champagne glasses, but he'd stopped, his gaze on . . . Ham?

Yes. The man's eyes tracked Ham all the way to the buffet table, something unreadable on his face.

Then he set down the tray, turning to put his back to her. But he was breathing funny. As if seeing Ham had rattled him.

Weird.

It kicked up all her instincts, because as the man's shoulders rose and fell, his body language seemed very much like he was trying to sort himself.

Or maybe talk himself into something.

The vest . . .

Her mind tracked back to the short conversation with the senator in the hospital room. *"We happened to run across a guy who we think might have been a bomber. He showed up at a rally and left a backpack bomb behind."*

She glanced around, but Orion hadn't returned. And Ham was across the room.

The waiter was making his way to the door.

To close it? Trap them?

Her PTSD training was working overtime, imagining scenarios. But . . .

You know what they say, if you see something, say something.

She glanced at Ham, but his back was to her.

Call it crazy, but she wasn't going to stay quiet and let someone hurt people again.

She headed toward the waiter. "Sir?"

He didn't turn.

"Sir—"

He glanced over his shoulder, and his gaze landed on her. Then past her.

Just like that, she knew. Maybe it was the twist of his face, or the way his mouth hardened. Even the look in his eyes, cold, remote—

She was *right*.

"Stop!"

He grabbed her wrist. "Shut up."

It was too late, because a hush had descended over the room.

Before her eyes, the waiter morphed into a terrorist. He whipped Jenny around and pulled her hard against him, wrapping his arm around her neck.

"No one move!" He held up his hand, a trigger in his grip, his thumb over a switch.

What—?

Her breath spiraled out and her gaze connected with Ham, who'd dropped the plate of food, the drink, and had sprinted through the crowd toward her.

"Stop!"

Jenny, too, held out her hand. "Ham, stop. Just . . ." *Breathe.* Okay. Think.

You're a psychologist—*talk.*

"Listen. No one needs to get hurt here," she said, letting the waiter walk her backward, out into the hotel mezzanine. He was breathing hard, sweating, his arm shaking against her neck.

"Just take a breath. My name is Jenny, what's yours?"

He'd walked her out to the railing. The glass ceiling of the hotel soared above them. A bomb would take down the ceiling. Rain down glass on everyone in the lobby, not to mention injure everyone in the blast radius.

She didn't search for Orion, didn't want the bomber to know she had someone to worry about.

"Are you from the East Coast? I thought I heard an accent—"

"Akif."

"That's your name? Akif?"

No answer. "So, Akif, why are you doing this?" She glued her gaze to Ham, holding him back with her eyes.

He swallowed, stricken.

"White and his people are warmongers. They just want to kill and destroy. No more wars."

And the irony . . . "Okay. I get that. So . . . do you have a family, Akif?"

Out of the corner of her eye, she saw Orion. She didn't dare

331

turn her head. The way Akif was holding her, his head next to hers, she was probably blocking his view of Orion. But she didn't want to give him bait.

"Because I do. I have friends who love me and . . . people I love . . . Do you have people you love?"

He shook his head.

"Really? No one? Not even your mother?"

Trust me. Orion's mouth moved and maybe he didn't really say that, but she wanted to believe he did. Then he moved out of her periphery, and she was alone.

"My mother's dead."

"I get that, Akif. My mother died, too. She was murdered by someone she trusted. That's a terrible way to die—to be betrayed, right?"

"America betrays its people," he snapped. His hand was trembling.

And she didn't know how hard it might be to hold his thumb over that trigger, just right, without accidentally depressing it, so . . .

"America isn't just the government. It's the people too. Good people who want to just go home and love their family and live safe lives. People who don't betray each other. People who believe in good—and do good. Can't we do that—go home to the people we love? Do good to each other?"

He hesitated, and a tiny whimper emitted out of him.

"Akif, is someone making you do this terrible thing?"

Nothing.

Ham had edged away, disappeared.

"Akif, you can trust me. And my friends. We can help you."

"No one can help me," he whispered. His arm tightened around her neck, started to cut off her air. "And now no one can help you, either."

Her hand went to his arm, pulling at it. "Akif, this is not the way to change the world—"

"Shut up." He cursed, and the vile sound of it went to her bones.

Maybe it's time to let God fight our battles, too.

Yes, God, please—

Then she spotted Ham. His gaze drilled into hers and he gave her a tiny nod.

She closed her eyes.

Then, her world exploded.

■ ■ ■

Orion's old instincts, worn, tried, hardened—like his boots—simply kicked in.

He'd taken too long to put himself back together, splashing water on his face, telling himself that he wasn't an idiot for checking himself out of the hospital after surgery. He hated hospitals with everything inside him. And he hadn't wanted to spend one single moment away from Jenny.

Clearly for good reason, because he'd exited the bathroom to find her in the grip of the jerk waiter who'd bumped into her.

His heartbeat had gone into overdrive.

But it didn't take long for Orion to do the math. For him to not only recognize the danger, but also the woman he saw on the mountain, the determined champion climber who looked at him with steel in her eyes before she tried to ascend the wall to rescue them.

Yeah, she was a warrior—even a rescuer—and he must have been blind not to see that part of her heart in Afghanistan. He'd been so wrapped up in himself and the fact that he was Something Special.

Right. His injury had kicked that right out of him. Maybe that's what had him the angriest.

He wasn't the man he thought he was.

But maybe that guy dying made room for him to be the man he was supposed to be.

He had to admit that his timing emerging from the bathroom was exactly right, because after he'd gotten over the sheer terror at seeing Jenny in the grip of that man, he realized . . .

The man couldn't see him.

That's when Orion tucked away the panic and found the place he hadn't really forgotten. The place where he saw it all like a math problem, where emotions couldn't have their sway. The place he'd fled to when a missile had shot Nickles and Dirk out of the sky. The place he'd tenaciously guarded when the pain tried to find him.

The place he'd hid when his anger wanted to dismantle him. *"It is not the mountain we conquer but ourselves."* His fear. His hurt. His panic. His helplessness.

Thanks, Dad.

Now, *think*, son.

A security guard had hustled up. Lanky, early twenties, the man looked fresh out of rent-a-cop school. Orion stopped him, grabbed his radio. "Sorry. I'll give it back."

"Hey—we need that."

Orion ignored him. "Ham, tell me you're listening."

He stayed back, and from this angle couldn't see well into the room, but yes, there, in the back—Ham had moved away from the crowd. He turned and backed a security guard into the wall, took his radio from him.

Mmmhmm. No one argued with Ham. "I gotcha, Ry. Where are you?"

"South of Jenny, by thirty feet or so, by the bathrooms. They can't see me."

"Isaac's people are all in the room with us," Ham said. "It looks like this guy is serious. Jenny is trying to talk him down."

Of course she was.

"The Anchorage SWAT team has been called, but—"

"They're never going to get here in time." Jake's voice cut into Ham's words.

Orion looked up, searching. He spotted Jake waving from across the open lobby, in the lounge on the opposite side. He lowered his hand.

"One of the local security guys loaned me his weapon. A .45 XDM. It'll do the job."

Loaned? Orion noticed that Ham didn't ask.

"It's only thirty feet. I can take the shot, but . . ."

"What about the bomb? And Jenny?" Orion said.

"You get the shot, Jake," Ham said. "Orion, you get Jenny. I'll cover the bomb. If we can separate him from that trigger—maybe I can push him over the edge, away from the crowd."

Orion didn't like the sound of any of that.

Neither, apparently, did Jake. He cast Orion a look across the expanse. But really, what choice did they have?

"Let's give Jenny a chance to talk him down," Orion said. "I'm going to get closer."

Tucking the radio into his belt, he eased toward the now-empty mezzanine. Just Jenny and the bomber edged up next to the balcony.

He stopped just inside her periphery. *Jenny, look at me.*

She might have heard his internal pleading because she moved her eyes in his direction. She was speaking in low tones to the man. "I have friends who love me and . . . people I love . . ."

Her words threatened to release the latch on his emotions. But maybe . . . maybe that wasn't such a terrible thing.

His gaze didn't waver off Jenny, and he moved his mouth. *I love you, Jenny. Trust me.*

He prayed she'd seen him as he edged away.

"SWAT is twenty minutes out," Ham said.

Orion kept his voice low. "He's sweating and trembling, and I don't think we have twenty minutes."

"They're already clearing the building," Jake said.

Indeed, the lobby was empty, and even the room behind Ham was being cleared, minus the senator's security guys.

Wait. Something about the bomber . . . "Ham . . . look at this guy. Isn't he the guy from the rally in New York City? The skinny kid on the subway?" Orion studied him, tried to imagine him in a sweatshirt and a NYU backpack.

"I think it is," Ham said. "Maybe that's why he freaked out— maybe he recognized me."

"If it's him, then this is his second attempt. Which means he's serious. So serious, he's going to be here to see it through."

"Give me the shot, Chief," Jake said.

No, they weren't in the military anymore, but Jake still wouldn't do anything without Ham's say.

And Jake had been a sniper. A sharpshooter.

But Jenny's head was . . . right there. Right against NYU's and . . . "Wait," Orion said, his voice shaking. "Count to three, pull on four. Please."

"And I got five," Ham said.

"On your count, guys," Jake said.

Orion didn't glance at Jake, but he knew he was bracing himself on the wall, breathing out, centering his shot.

Just for a second, Ham's words thundered into his head. *"Make our steps safe, and go before us. Finish the task you've pressed us to."*

Yes.

336

"One," Ham said and Orion took off, limping, half-running.

And yeah, he'd just had surgery, so he used his crutches for leverage. But he felt no pain as he threw himself at Jenny.

Two. He shouted, just enough to jerk NYU's hold on Jenny.

Then she was in his arms as he tackled her away from NYU's grip.

Three. They hit the ground.

Four. The shot was crisp, and Orion prayed it hit the target.

Five. Ham erupted in a shout as he launched himself at NYU, flinging his body over the side of the balcony.

Orion covered Jenny's body, bracing himself for the worst.

Nothing.

No explosion.

They'd stopped him from depressing the trigger. Or maybe, miraculously, it was a dud. Either way—no terrorist win.

"Ham!" Jake's voice boomed across the lobby, and Orion rolled over, untangling himself. Jenny scrambled to her feet and grabbed his hand.

Ham was dangling over the forty-foot drop, one arm on the bottom rail of the overhang. Akif must have gotten a grip on him and pulled him over with him.

However he got there, hanging like that made Ham look like a freakin' superhero.

Orion grabbed his abandoned crutch off the floor. Lowered it to Ham. "I always gotta rescue you."

Ham grabbed the crutch, and in a moment Jake had joined them, helping Orion pull him up.

They grabbed Ham's belt, working him over the side. He dropped on the floor, breathing hard. "Yeah, well, that's your job, PJ."

Orion grinned. Then he caught the look on Jenny's face. She

was double-gripping the railing, staring down at the bomber. He glanced down.

That was a mess. SWAT had started to pour into the building, with shouts and warnings and Jake put his gun down and raised his hands, got to his knees.

"No need for that, Silver." Isaac White came out of a nearby room. "I saw the whole thing, as did my staff. Brave work, all three of you." He helped Ham off the ground. He looked at Jenny. "Four of you."

Orion cared nothing for White's words. He pulled Jenny into his arms. "You okay?"

"Now I am." She wrapped hers around his back, holding on. And holding on.

Clearly not going anywhere.

Except, back to Minnesota.

With him.

He backed away and lifted her chin. "Jenny?"

She smiled then, a shine to her eyes that invaded every quiet, compartmentalized pocket of his heart, busting it open, filling it with sunshine and hope and happy endings.

"Yeah, PJ?"

"I think I deserve a kiss."

She grinned. "Yes. Yes, you do."

So she kissed him.

What Happens Next . . .

HAMILTON JONES wasn't the kind to second-guess his team, but Jake had him holding his breath.

Fighting a roil in his gut.

Praying hard.

Because he'd seen Jake at the bar as he'd come up the stairs from the lobby. And what he was holding in his grip didn't look like lemonade.

But Jake was his best guy, and if he said he could make the shot—

Ham still felt a little like losing it even after SWAT had swept the reception room for any other threats. Which, in his gut, Ham knew weren't there.

Right now.

But someone was after Isaac White—he had no doubt. Ham very much wanted to hop on White's plane with him and head down to San Diego. But White's team was top-notch, and Ham couldn't be everywhere, all the time.

In fact, he didn't have to save the world.

Really.

Maybe it was enough to check on Jake, see what was eating at his former teammate as he sat at the bar, watching the baseball game on the flat screen, working his way through a basket of wings.

Jake, the guy who could take down a terrorist, then slough it off with an order of hot wings and blue cheese dip.

Except Ham knew better. Much better.

He did notice that Jake had switched to a bottle of root beer as he sat down next to him at the lounge bar.

"Good shot," Ham said. The bartender came up to them, an old rail-thin sourdough who had Alaska in his demeanor. Ham gestured to Jake's fixin's and pointed to himself.

"Thanks," Jake said, not looking at him.

"What's going on?"

Jake picked up another wing. "I gave my statement to an investigator."

"I'm not here to harass you, Silver. But, I saw . . . please tell me you were dry when you took that shot."

Jake glanced at him then, something dark and hard in his eyes. "I sat with that drink for a while, but . . . yes. I was stone sober. I didn't even have a sip. And besides, I know better. I wouldn't have risked Jenny's life."

Ham held up his hand. "Okay. Good. I thought so. It's just— you haven't had a drink since—"

"I'm not drinking." Jake held up his root beer bottle. "So take a step back, Chief."

Well, something was eating at him. And, "So, it was just lucky that you were in the bar."

"Yep. Luck." Jake threw down the bones of his wings. "Stupid, dumb luck."

Ho-kay.

"How's Orion?"

"EMTs checked him out. He didn't rip open any stitches, but he's pretty sore."

Jake took a drink of his root beer. Kept his eyes on the game playing on the flat screen.

The bartender served Ham the long-necked root beer. "We're headed up to Copper Mountain in the morning to pick up the gear. And take Orion back to his place."

"I thought he was coming back to Minnesota." Jake wiped his hands.

"He is. Just, well, he *is* in a cast. And he has to pack up. Jenny's going to stick around to help him."

Jake made a sound, something Ham couldn't decipher.

"Okay, Silver. What's eating you?"

Jake ignored him.

"Something happen with you and Aria?"

Jake looked at him, a tiny narrowing of his eyes. "Why?"

Ham recoiled. "No reason, just . . . I guess I would have thought . . . well, maybe that you two would be hanging out. She's staying here too."

"I know." Jake took another drink. "I think my room's ready." He pulled out some cash, dropped it on the bar, and turned to Ham. "That's why I was in the bar—because they were still cleaning my room."

He slid off the high-top chair.

"Jake—"

"Leave it, Ham." He rounded on him. "Listen, just . . . I'm fine."

"Is it the shooting? Because I know that's never easy, and maybe it's dragging up demons—"

"It's not the shooting! Sheesh—give it a rest, will ya?"

Ham shut his mouth. Right.

341

Jake shook his head, wrapped his hand around his neck. Blew out a breath. "It's not the shooting. It's what I do. I hurt people. Sometimes even destroy lives. I'm very, very good at that. You of all people should know that."

Ham ran his hand down the cold neck of his bottle. Said nothing. But something had spooked Jake. Really rattled him.

Silence fell between them.

"By the way, you should tell Orion that his dad is famous." Jake gestured to a mural on the outer wall of the bar.

Ham turned to look. Newspaper clippings, a drawn picture of a climber who looked vaguely like Orion on the cover of a *National Geographic* magazine.

"There's a whole display of famous rangers and Denali guides. Apparently, when his father died, he also managed to save the life of this famous photographer. The guy had fallen off Denali Pass and couldn't get back up, and Dirk Starr got him to the top. The whole story is in the paper. The photographer went on to scale Everest, K2, and even Annapurna. He credits Orion's dad for giving him the courage to keep climbing."

"My guess is that Orion already knows, but I'll tell him."

"Tell me what?" Orion had limped up, Jenny beside him. The guy was a champ, because even Ham could see his pain meds were wearing off. But Ham suspected he was holding off letting Jenny out of his sight.

The guy had nothing to worry about. The way she was looking at him, the feelings were mutual.

He liked it when he was right about something. Especially these two.

Jake nodded toward the wall. "Your dad. The hero."

Orion turned. Huh. Maybe he *didn't* know because he just stared at the mural.

Then he moved over to it. Jenny joined him. Put her hand on his back.

It occurred to Ham that Orion was just like his dad. Inspiring others to keep climbing the mountain he'd loved.

"He's agreed to join the team, right?" Jake said.

"Yeah," Ham said. Orion had confirmed it, finally, while Jenny was giving her statement. Ham was no fool. "It helps that Jenny is going to jump aboard too."

Jake stared at him, looking a little undone, almost panicked. "What?"

"I just . . . are you sure, Chief? I mean, she's—"

"Aria's friend?"

He'd hit it on the nose because Jake's mouth closed, and his lips tightened to a thin line.

"What happened between you two?" Ham asked quietly.

Jake's jaw hardened. "I . . . I don't know. Listen, I gotta check in and get some z's. I'll see you in the morning."

Jake picked up his pack, shouldered it, and Ham had the uncanny sense that he was watching his number one man take a slow walk into darkness.

Lord, whatever it is, help him.

Orion was still reading the mural.

Funny, that's how life seemed to work. Just when you thought you were in the clear, it rounded on you.

Sometimes for the good.

But often it took you out at the knees. His gaze followed Jake as he took the stairs down to the lobby.

It didn't change Ham's belief that God was in charge, however.

"Here're your wings," said the bartender and set the basket on the counter.

Ham's phone buzzed in his pocket. He pulled it out but didn't

343

recognize the number. Almost didn't answer it. But sometimes he got random calls from people in need of help.

"Ham here." He reached for a couple napkins.

"Is this Senior Chief Hamilton Jones?"

The voice on the other end was brusque, military, and Ham answered in kind. "Former Senior Chief Jones, sir. How can I help you?"

"Hold for Lieutenant Hollybrook."

Ham got up from the stool, a knot forming in his gut.

A woman's voice came on the line. "Senior Chief, this is Lt. Marilyn Hollybrook calling from the Naval Air Station in Sigonella, Italy."

Huh. "How can I help you, ma'am?"

"We have a patient here who has claimed that you are her next of kin. She was thrown overboard in a yachting accident and when they rescued her, she identified herself as an American, so they brought her to us."

Ham had nothing.

"Sir?"

"I'm sorry—did you say next of kin? I don't have any—" Except, he hadn't heard from his half sister, Kelsey, recently. She played in some country band. They weren't touring Italy, were they? "Who is she? Did she identify herself?"

"Her name is Agatha."

More silence.

"Sir?"

"I don't know anyone named Agatha."

"Agatha Jones?"

"No."

"She's ten years old. And she says you're her father."

He stilled, his throat tightening. His hand went out to grab the railing overlooking the lobby. "What's her mother's name?" He didn't recognize his own voice.

"Just a moment, let me double-check."

A pause, maybe as she was covering the phone to ask, but in that blink of time, Ham tracked back to the one time he'd found himself in over his head. The one mission he hadn't completed.

The rescue of the only woman he'd ever loved.

His wife.

"The report says her name is Signe. But she was lost at sea when the yacht sank."

His chest was imploding, his breaths running over open shards, gutting him.

Right then Orion chose to come up, stand beside him, concern growing on his face. "Ham, you okay?"

Ham looked at him but didn't see him.

Saw, really, only Signe. Her green eyes, her blonde hair. That smile that made him feel like . . . well, like a hero, maybe. *"There's never been anyone else, Ham. I knew you'd find me . . ."*

He shook his head. Swallowed. Then, somehow, he spoke into the phone.

"Tell my daughter to stay put. I'm on my way."

Susan May Warren is the *USA Today* bestselling author of over seventy-five novels with more than one million books sold, including *Wild Montana Skies*, *Rescue Me*, *A Matter of Trust*, *Troubled Waters*, *Storm Front*, and *Wait for Me*. Winner of a RITA Award and multiple Christy and Carol Awards, as well as the HOLT Medallion and numerous Readers' Choice Awards, Susan has written contemporary and historical romances, romantic suspense, thrillers, romantic comedy, and novellas. She makes her home in Minnesota. Find her online at www.susanmaywarren.com, on Facebook at Susan May Warren Fiction, and on Twitter @susanmaywarren.

Loved this book?
More action awaits in the MONTANA RESCUE Series!

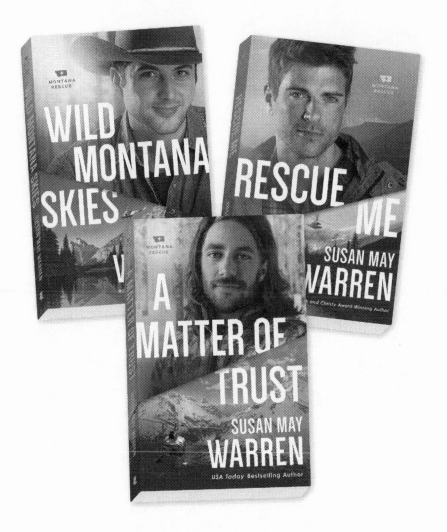

"Warren's stalwart characters and engaging story lines make her **Montana Rescue series** a must-read."

—Booklist

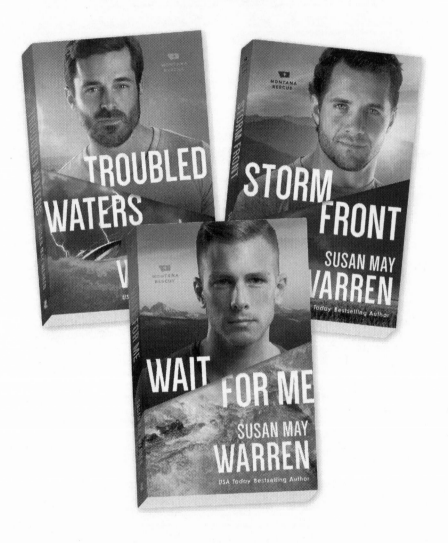

Connect with
Susan May Warren

Visit her website and sign up for her newsletter to get a free novella, hot news, contests, sales, and sneak peeks!

www.susanmaywarren.com